THE WOMEN OF SATURN

~~~~~~~~~~~~~~~~~~~~

Copyright © 2017 Connie Guzzo-McParland

Except for the use of short passages for review purposes, no part of this book may be reproduced, in part or in whole, or transmitted in any form or by any means, electronically or mechanically, including photocopying, recording, or any information or storage retrieval system, without prior permission in writing from the publisher or a licence from the Canadian Copyright Collective Agency (Access Copyright).

We gratefully acknowledge the support of the Canada Council for the Arts and the Ontario Arts Council for our publishing program. We also acknowledge the financial support of the Government of Canada through the Canada Book Fund..

Cover design: Val Fullard
Cover artwork: Enzo De Giorgi, "Il girotondo," 2006, oil on canvas, 120 x 100 cm. Artist website: www.enzodegiorgi.it.

The Women of Saturn is a work of fiction. All the characters and situations portrayed in this book are fictitious and any resemblance to persons living or dead is purely coincidental.

Library and Archives Canada Cataloguing in Publication

Guzzo-McParland, Connie, 1947–, author
    The women of Saturn / a novel by Connie Guzzo-McParland.

(Inanna poetry & fiction series)
Sequel to: *The girls of Piazza d'Amore*.
Issued in print and electronic formats.
ISBN 978-1-77133-357-3 (softcover). — ISBN 978-1-77133-358-0 (epub).
— ISBN 978-1-77133-359-7 (kindle). — ISBN 978-1-77133-360-3 (pdf).

    I. Title. II. Series: Inanna poetry and fiction series

PS8613.U99W64 2017   C813'.6   C2017-900303-8
                                                                                     C2017-900304-6

Printed and bound in Canada

Inanna Publications and Education Inc.
210 Founders College, York University
4700 Keele Street, Toronto, Ontario, Canada M3J 1P3
Telephone: (416) 736-5356 Fax: (416) 736-5765
Email: inanna.publications@inanna.ca   Website: www.inanna.ca

THE WOMEN OF SATURN

~~~~~~~~~ A NOVEL ~~~~~~~~~

Connie Guzzo-McParland

inanna poetry & fiction series

**INANNA PUBLICATIONS AND EDUCATION INC.
TORONTO, CANADA**

ALSO BY CONNIE GUZZO-MCPARLAND:

The Girls of Piazza d'Amore

For my brother, Vincenzo, who loved telling stories, and for all those who have dared cross rough seas toward unknown shores.

For last year's words belong to last year's language.
And next year's words await another voice. And
to make an end is to make a beginning.
—T.S. Eliot

importante é imparare
che l'immaggine vera é nel profondo –
contentarsi di sembrare
(di essere)
incoerenti incompleti –
ricominciare ogni giorno
sereni
il percorso della vita
—Elettra Bedon

CONTENTS

PROLOGUE: ROME, JUNE 2016   1

PART I: OCTOBER 3, 1980
1. How's Your Bird?   7
2. WLHS   13
3. Angie Was Here   22

PART II: THE VOYAGE, 1957
4. Days One and Two   29
5. Day Three   37
6. Day Four   45
7. Day Five   49
8. Day Six   53
9. Day Seven   58
10. Day Eight   67
11. Days Nine and Ten   70
12. Day Eleven   75
13. Day Twelve   79

PART III: OCTOBER 4-5, 1980

14. Sean and J.P.	85
15. Lucia and Angie	90
16. *Fare l'Amore*	94
17. The Journalist	102
18. Sean and I	106
19. Sunday Lunch	115

PART IV: OCTOBER 6-7, 1980

20. The Finger-Waving Lesson	125
21. The Ultimatum	132
22. Reading Glasses	136
23. Bad Air	139
24. The Perm Lesson	142
25. Stink Bomb	144
26. Miss Park Ex	147
27. Alfonso	153
28. The Proposal	161

PART V: THE LANDING, 1957-1961

29. A New Home	171
30. First Winter, 1957	173
31. Sundays on Tenth Avenue, 1959	177
32. Ville Verte, 1960	184
33. The Wedding Dance, Spring 1961	187
34. Heat Wave, Summer 1961	190

35. Back to School, Fall 1961	200
36. November 1961	205

PART VI: OCTOBER 13-17, 1980

37. Thanksgiving	217
38. The Hair Straightening Lesson	222
39. Bar à Go-Go	232
40. Bruce	238
41. Modern Furniture	243

PART VII: OCTOBER 18-24, 1980

42. The Ethnic Wife	249
43. The Canadian Brigand	258
44. Supervision Duty	265
45. Règlement de Comptes	267

PART VIII: TOTU, 1964-1967

46. The Italian Tour, 1964	275
47. Of Men and His Worlds	282
48. The Roller Coaster Ride	288

PART IX: OCTOBER 24-27, 1980

49. A Settling of Accounts	295
50. The Hairdressing Lesson	303
51. Pasquale and Micu	309
52. Venetian Masks	315

53. The Missing Pieces — 323

PART X: OCTOBER 31, 1980
54. Costume Day — 329
55. Deceptions and Floating Devices — 337
56. Looking for Angie — 347
57. The Office — 357

PART XI: NOVEMBER 1, 1980
58. The Fall Out — 369
59. Angie's Halloween Party — 377
60. Girotondo — 384
61. The Lullabye — 385

PART XII: NOVEMBER 2, 1980
62. A New Beginning — 392

EPILOGUE: ROME, JUNE 2016 — 398

ACKNOWLEDGEMENTS — 401

PROLOGUE: ROME, JUNE 2016

IN MY CHILDHOOD IMAGINATION, life—my own and those of friends and people around me—was to be lived like the black-and-white cinematic images of the post-war Italian films that the village parish priest projected onto an open-air screen on religious holidays. That perspective would soon be altered by a momentous, though woozy, trip across the Atlantic that promised new vistas and experiences.

The journey began in the deep of winter of 1957, at a train station in Santa Eufemia, and ended at Windsor Station in Montreal, twelve days later. I had planned to keep a diary of the sea voyage, so that I could write about it to my friends back home. No one else I knew had done this before. It was as if people left for another world, and once they were there, the passage itself was forgotten, like a bad dream. We heard about the seasickness and about passing customs, but nothing about what it was really like to live on a ship for ten days, and then slog for another full day on a train to get to our final destination.

The idea of writing came to me when, a week before leaving, I received a perfect ten on my last composition assignment. There was also a note from my fifth grade teacher, Signor Gavano, telling me to keep up the good work in the new country. I had decided to pack a notebook along with a book of prayers and a copy of a novel that Signor Gavano had given me to read on the boat.

To savour my perfect mark, I doodled with the zero of the ten, sketching rays around it like a sun. Then I drew a larger sun next to it and numbered it like a clock from one to twelve, for each day of the journey. I would circle a number at the end of each day, as I wrote about it. That the total duration of the trip fit inside a perfect circle, like a clock, was the happy coincidence that made the voyage and writing about it feel like a game.

For a few days afterwards, I kept on playing with the drawing of twelve small suns inside a larger one, dividing each day into hours and another twelve smaller zeros. If a twelve-day trip required so many suns to recount, I wondered how many circles inside other circles it would take to write about all the hours of one's life. One would need a sphere as large as the planet to contain all the stories on earth.

The voyage left its indelible mark on an impressionable young girl, and, for years afterward, in my new home, I replayed in my mind the hazy images and scenes I had recorded so fervently in scribbled notes.

It was in 1967, in the euphoria of Montreal's Expo 67, and in an effort to impress a journalist friend of mine, that I divulged my secret ambition to write and "preserve my memories." He answered, "The only thing worth preserving is *giardiniera,* and even then...." " Still, I offered him a story based on the crossing, which I had titled, "The Voyage." I sought his advice, but I mostly craved his approval. He offered neither. With a bruised ego, I stopped writing altogether, but buried my face deeper and deeper into books.

In the autumn of 1980, some unfortunate happenings to common friends of ours brought the journalist and me together again. In spite, or maybe because of, the turmoil around me, my creative juices kicked in again, and in a four-week period, I managed to reconstruct my old manuscript, as well as write drafts of several new stories while keeping an extensive journal of present events.

I resolved to use the material to write a novel. But for reasons too complicated to explain in this brief note, it would take many more years, to reconcile the voyage with the landing, the past with the present, the written with the unwritten...
—Cathy Anastasia

PART I
OCTOBER 3, 1980

1. HOW'S YOUR BIRD?

I AM STONEWALLED BY A full-length mirror, unable to go on with my day. None of the clothes on my bed fit me properly this morning. Everything hugs and pulls—my petite body proportions thrown out of sync by a mere five-pound gain. It's Friday, and I wish I could be more relaxed about my clothes, like everyone else at school. But I'm the beauty care teacher, trained and conditioned to make the pursuit of esthetic perfection the ultimate objective of each of my lessons. I want to look the part, especially this morning. I have a meeting with my school principal and an old friend of mine, Lucia Abiusi *in* Tonnelli, whom I haven't seen in years.

I pause to listen to the radio news when I hear "epic journey towards Saturn." Actual photographs of Saturn's rings are to be transmitted to earth by Voyager 1. The mention of Saturn reawakens an old childhood fascination with the planet, named after the Roman god of harvest and reaping who fled to Rome from Greece and established the Golden Age—a time of perfect peace and harmony.

But it's the sleek free-standing mirror I brought home from the Danish House yesterday afternoon that is stalling my movements the most. I'm as unnerved by its teak frame as by my reflection within it. In the morning light I notice with disappointment how badly its beige colour jars with the yellowed wood of the bedroom furniture that belonged to my parents. Convincing Sean to buy a new mirror was one thing, but getting him to invest in a brand new bedroom suite will prove a bigger challenge. It's the eternal question of commitment!

"How's your bird?" the DJ, Ralph, booms from the clock radio on the nightstand. Echoing bird screeches jump-start the groggy brains of those who must be out of the house and in rush-hour traffic before eight. After the weather and traffic reports, newsflashes repeat the headlines I've already read in this morning's *Montreal Star*: momentous discoveries in outer space; in the Middle East, Iranian planes strike a nuclear power plant; south of the border, Ronald Reagan appeals to religious fundamentalists as the election race with Jimmy Carter heats up; teachers' unions across Quebec threaten the government with massive school disruptions; a former chairman of Montreal's executive committee is accused of fraud in connection with the 1976 Montreal Olympics; another Italian café in St. Leonard is torched; an unnamed woman is found unconscious on her kitchen floor, a victim of domestic violence.

I know the street where the marital dispute occurred. The victim's name isn't released. The only pertinent information given is the link between the family and Jack Russo, a well-known underworld figure, followed by the allegation that there might be a possible connection between the café torching, the domestic violence story, and the Montreal underworld. The suggestion that a woman's beating is related to these events sounds unlikely to me.

"Are you ready to go, old chap?" a voice calls out from the kitchen.

It's Jean-Pierre, a close friend of Sean's who likes to stay with us on his frequent visits to the city. J.P. is *pure laine* Québécois, born and bred in southeast Montreal. His annoying British accent and vocabulary are the result of a year's stay at Oxford.

"We're on our way," Sean yells from the kitchen. "Bye, Cat."

Over breakfast I had a little tiff with Sean and J.P., and I'm still mildly irritated by Sean's attitude.

"They must have a set of stock stories they rehash on slow news days..." I said.

"Such as?" J.P. has a habit of putting me on the spot whenever I try to make an original point in a conversation. Sean looked up from reading the paper.

"Conflict in the Middle East ... the Quebec government's disputes with public employees ... corruption in the construction industry," I stammered. "Urban crime in the city, and now domestic violence in the home. The news has not only become predictable, but ... categorizable."

"Maybe 'generic' might be a better term," Sean interrupted, folding the paper, "urban and city mean the same thing, and domestic and home are also synonyms."

"Whatever. You know what I mean," I said, getting up to go get dressed.

I become completely inarticulate whenever I get nervous, especially if J.P. is around. The way Sean corrects my choice of words in front of J.P. makes me wonder if he's trying to apologize to his intellectual friend for my poor command of the English language. I should have retorted that, unlike J.P.'s, at least my accent is genuine and not a put-on.

The mirror reflects fleeting slivers of life outside my apartment building. It's a flawless Indian-summer day, jewel-bright and clear. A briefcase hanging from his right hand, J.P. strides confidently toward his car, followed by Sean, who carries a heavy knapsack on his shoulders and a thick binder under his arm. J.P. works for the Liberal Party of Canada. He's a party strategist and a weathered politician; Sean, his assistant, tries earnestly to follow in his footsteps.

The evening before, the two men had talked through the night, preparing for an important meeting with some key party members. I had been grateful to be left alone, preoccupied as I was with my own problems at work. Today I must argue the case for Lucia's daughter, Angie, who has been placed in my class on a trial basis. At the urging of the assistant principal,

I have invited her parents to a meeting to discuss her progress (or lack thereof, as he would view it).

I had long ago lost contact with Lucia. Only since her daughter's inclusion in my class have we spoken again and, every time, images of the past sneak into my consciousness.

Angie's behaviour in class has been disruptive, though not unexpected. Even my mother discouraged me from getting involved with the girl.

"What did you expect from Lucia's daughter?" she said. In her Calabrian village mind, character, and destiny are predetermined by the family into which one is born.

My destiny seems defined by mismatched furniture and ill-fitting clothes, I muse as I stare at the unmade double bed, piled like a bargain table of used clothing with the skirts, blouses, pants, and dresses I've taken from my packed closet, tried on, and found unsuitable. Scattered next to my pillow, underneath the clothes, are some fashion magazines and a book, *The Betrothed*, my bedtime reading from the previous night. It's a translation of the Italian novel I had read in the lounge and on the deck of the ship that brought me to Canada, the *Saturnia*, while a Roman steward, who claimed to be a descendent of the god Saturn, hovered around Lucia. By sheer coincidence I came across the book at the Concordia University library during the summer, after I heard from Lucia, and I brought it home.

But last night the book didn't help me fall asleep. I felt agitated by the stilted and forced English translation. I stood out on my balcony for a while to admire the new moon before returning to bed. I fell asleep half-dreaming of floating in outer space and reaching for Saturn's rings.

Nearly eight already! By now I should be out of the house, but after all the outfit changes I still look frumpy and pudgy in the beige linen dress. It's not how I want Lucia to see me. She was a slim eighteen-year-old with teasing eyes and a perky bosom when we travelled together, and I was barely out of childhood. Had she become as matronly as some of the other forty-year-old women from the village whom I now see at weddings and funerals?

"Five minutes to the hour," the DJ reminds me. Still facing the mirror, I lift the two shoulder seams with my hands and find the solution. I grab a blouse from the heap on the bed, snip off its shoulder pads with nail clippers, fit them under my dress' shoulder seams, and secure them with a straight pin. The larger pads lift and square the shoulder line, making my hips look less prominent. It's enough of an improvement to give me the confidence I need to face Frank, the assistant principal, though the pins make me feel like a prickly pear and I hope no one will squeeze my shoulders.

I collect the magazines from the bed, head down the hall, and note how neat the kitchen is compared to the mess in the bedroom. Sean tidied up before leaving. He always does, and he has become as predictable as the news. Just as I grab my purse and car keys from the table to leave, the telephone jolts me.

"Did you hear about Comare Rosaria's daughter?" It's my mother. I'm annoyed. Why is she calling me to gossip about a *paesana* this early in the morning?

Before I can reply, she goes on, "*Madonna mia*, could it be? Tina called me to tell me that a woman was found beaten on Chabot Street. Maybe it's Lucia."

"Why does Tina think it's Lucia?"

"Her husband read the story in the French paper," my mother says. "It says that a woman was found beaten up in her mother's home, in a duplex on Chabot Street, facing a park. Tina is afraid that it might be Lucia, and wants to know if you've heard anything."

Suddenly I realize why the street name sounds familiar. Comare Rosaria lives on that street, not far from my apartment. Her address is on Angie's registration form. I had looked it up the day before to find Lucia's phone number so I could call her.

"If it's really her, I'll hear about it when I get to school," I say. "She's supposed to come to a meeting this morning with Pasquale."

"Oh, *Madonna mia*. I hope they didn't fight about school. What did I tell you? Do not get mixed up with Lucia again!" I can almost see the panic in my mother's eyes.

"I'll call you if I hear anything. I'm late already. I have to run."

"Don't say that you know anything," my mother says. "Who knows what that husband of hers is mixed up in. Pretend you don't know anything."

I hang up, rush to my car, throwing my purse and magazines onto the passenger seat. Suddenly, my head is swirling with images of characters I had known and written about some time ago, people I haven't seen in years. I drive off, feeling as if I'm in one of those wind-up toy cars that leap from one's hands the instant they touch the floor and run wildly around the room, smashing against walls and spinning in circles.

It seems to be the story of my life.

2. WLHS

JEAN-TALON STREET CUTS THROUGH every area I have lived or worked in since immigrating to Montreal. The area around the school—Park Extension, or Park Ex, as everyone calls it—has now been appropriated by Greeks and immigrants from Arabic-speaking countries. An abrupt, unexpected stop stalls me as I reach Wilfrid Laurier High School. The automatic, metal-paneled door to the parking garage, usually wide open, is closed. This side entrance of the massive cement-and-brick building, which sprawls over half a block, is at the end of a low incline. I have to get out of the car to open the door. I fumble nervously in my purse for the key. I can't remember when I last had to use it. I had never even noticed the black graffiti marks that look like Alice Cooper scratched into the paint of the garage door.

Bruce McLaughlin, the tall, lanky, and good-looking Special Ed department head, pulls up behind me and gets out of his car. He inserts his key into a small metal box next to the door, looks my way and waves. Like a magic cave, the huge, dark lot opens up for me, Bruce, and the string of cars that have collected behind him.

Bruce is the guy I turned to when Lucia asked me to help her with her daughter, a troubled special education student who had been expelled from the French school she attended.

I'm already late, and don't want to get into a long conversation, but Bruce catches up with me. Bruce is dressed casually, in cords and a plaid shirt, his thick brown hair touching his shoulders. I can smell sweet pipe tobacco on his clothes. "What's with the closed door?" I ask. I follow my mother's advice and say nothing about what I've heard.

"New directives from the captain ... vandalism ... fear of mutiny..."

I find Bruce's slightly sarcastic sense of humour appealing.

"Vandalism in the morning's rush hours? Do you have any idea why Frank called a meeting with Angie's parents this morning?"

"The little Napoleon shit hasn't advised me of any meeting. Why am I the last shmuck to hear about it? New problems with Angie?"

"I have no problems, but Frank insists on creating some," I say. "He wants Angie out of my class. Why else would he call a meeting? He won't give her a chance."

"It can't be that serious, or I'd have heard about it. Just stick to your guns, Cathy." Bruce sounds cheerful.

"Ah, no matter what I do, Bruce, things always get twisted around with those guys."

"Everyone's trying to protect their asses. I've told you before, there's a lot of politicking going on."

"You'd think they were running the FBI, for Christ's sake. It's only a high school, Bruce."

"Yeah, but look at the fucking size of it!"

Wilfrid Laurier High School, or WLHS as it's commonly called, spreads out over a city block, rises to five levels, and houses over two thousand students. Conceived as a new breed of polyvalent high school, it offers technical-vocational workshops as well as business and general academic education. It's modern Quebec's bold version of the quintessential little red schoolhouse that teaches everything to everyone under the same roof.

Other teachers are breezing by. Bruce and I walk into the school's receiving area. The large space looks more like a warehouse or manufacturing company. Our voices are drowned out by the sound of another garage door, which is opening up for a supply truck. The truck will drive down into this below-ground level, which also leads to the automotive classes. The area, used to store donated, rusty old cars to be serviced by the apprentice mechanics, resembles a junkyard. Bruce takes my elbow to help me climb a low loading dock to reach the school's basement level, but I brush him off, afraid he might touch my shoulders and the pins.

Sensing that he might be offended by my brusque movement, I say, "Bruce, I'm okay."

On the dock, Frank Masters stands on supervision duty and hands us the daily bulletin. He's smiling too brightly today. I've learned to read his smiles. The upper lip is raised too high, and the jaw is immobile. Morphology is part of the hairdressing curriculum; I know all about facial muscles, and how some of them cannot be made to lie. The amount of false radiance that is forced out of a smile has a direct correlation with the degree of deception behind it.

This morning's smile tells me to keep my guard up. I don't even trust the small, thoughtful gesture on his part of handing me the bulletin. It could be construed as a statement that, technically, I'm late since I didn't have time to pick up my own mail before class.

"Did the parents confirm?" he asks with the same disconcerting smile. I feel relieved: nothing must have happened to Lucia, or he would have heard by now.

"The mother hopes the father will be able to make the meeting," I say.

"Should I attend?" Bruce asks.

"We'll take care of it," Frank answers.

A group of male students makes chirping bird sounds as they pass by.

"What a circus!" Frank mutters, shaking his head, and walks away.

Bruce whispers, "He's right. Too many fucking clowns in this place, and I don't mean the students."

I open the door to Room 105, the professional hairdressing class, just as the first homeroom bell rings.

A poster on the door, hand-drawn by last year's students, reads: *Studio 105 – The Amazing Beginners*. The heavy cardboard has become unstuck on one corner and tilts precariously to one side. Two students, Franca and Fotini, who are always on time, greet me at the door. The others trickle in slowly before the second bell.

"Oh, new dress! Do we have something special today, Miss?" asks Franca, alert as usual.

I'm used to students commenting on my clothes and speculating about my private life. I smile at Franca, and place my things on the desk. I ask the two girls to set up a comb, spray bottle, and mannequin for a demonstration. I station myself in front of the door, but not before checking my reflection in one of the many mirrors on the walls. My face looks strained and dull. Beige is not my colour. I watch the procession of vocational students scurrying to classes. My other students—Mary, Voula, Olga, and Christina—make it on time. Linda, Gina, and Angie are not in yet. I leave the door open. Students are considered late only after the teacher closes the door. To gain more time, I take a roll of masking tape from my desk drawer and re-tape the poster on the door, but the corners are curled up and refuse to stick.

The hairdressing classroom has the same unfinished look as most of the school basement. Counters running along three walls hold rows of mannequin heads. These are used to practice basic hairdressing skills until students are ready to work on live clients. Four shampoo sinks are installed along the fourth wall. Over the counters and shampoo sinks hangs a row of round mirrors, like portholes. Through them I can see the students' movements reflected no matter where I stand. The students have decorated the unpainted cement walls between mirrors with a collage of hairstyle photos that keep falling off. A reception desk, located in the centre of the room, is meant to give the classroom the appearance of a professional hair salon. A special perk, much appreciated by both the students and by me, is a working telephone on the desk to receive hairstyling appointments.

Students file in and sit on the heavy, hydraulic hairstyling chairs facing the teacher's desk and a movable chalkboard.

Time to close the door. Frank peeks into the classroom, "Angie's not in yet?" Then flings his arms in the air, "God, what's with these special-ed students! If they're not absent, they're late."

Despite his English name, Frank is of mixed heritage. When I first met him he told me his family's name was Mastropietro, but his grandfather changed it to Masters after emigrating from Italy in the 1920s and marrying an Irish woman. He only knows a few swear words in Italian. He has never been to Europe, but he's endowed with Mediterranean good looks—dark, wavy hair that he keeps short and away from his face, a suntanned complexion, and a brilliant smile that he flashes when it's least expected. His brown eyes are small and inquisitive.

When Frank first came to WLHS, I found him attractive. He had a certain self-assurance and charisma about him. Though he's part of the administration, he spends more time in the teacher's staff room than at his office. A clique of teachers congregates there in the mornings, at recess, and at lunch, for coffee and small talk. Frank pontificates about the issues of the day, both political and school-related, and the gossip is constant.

Little by little, I've noticed how Frank's form of gossiping is different from the idle but harmless talk of the others. I've detected a subtle but consistent pattern in his modus operandi. When he slips innuendoes or unconfirmed rumours into a seemingly innocent, joking manner, I don't laugh and sometimes I even question his comments. My initial attraction has turned to antipathy.

I shuffle the papers on my desk and take attendance.

The hairdressing group, now in their last year, is made up of nine students, all girls. Gina, Linda, Voula, and Christina seem to be cut from the same cloth: tight jeans; knit tops barely covering their midriffs; long, below-the-shoulder hair with a centre part; heavily made-up eyes; and pouty, glossy lips. Linda is rumoured to be an aspiring exotic dancer; Gina to have had an affair with a married teacher. Based on their appearance, if not on their ability, they will probably find employment in the stylish, trendy downtown salons. The four other girls—Franca, Mary, Josie, and Fotini—are more modestly dressed. They aspire to work in the prosaic neighbourhood beauty salons along Park Avenue, and maybe eventually own one.

When Angie first came in, wearing grungy black pants and sweater, she stood out from the rest of the class, and she still makes little effort to fit in. What I find most surprising is that Angie has befriended Linda and Gina, the two most fashion-conscious of the group.

I can't stall closing the door much longer. I look at the daily bulletin, read the first part meant for teachers. Teachers are to lock the garage door as soon as they enter the garage. Some problem students have been spotted there. I then read aloud the section for students: "Because of recent vandalism in students' bathrooms, a teacher supervisor will be assigned to each of the student bathrooms during recess and lunch breaks. Toilet paper dispensers will be installed outside the bathroom doors."

The students squawk: "No way!" "I can't believe this!" "Are they for real?"

I quiet them down, and continue reading: "If this measure doesn't stop the abusive use of toilet paper, we will be forced to ask students to bring their own paper from home. We also want to remind the Tech-Voc students that they are not permitted to use the teachers' bathrooms on the basement level."

There's a teachers' bathroom facing my classroom. This directive will be difficult to monitor.

I say, "Don't expect me to unlock the teacher's bathroom anymore."

"They're treating us like kids."

"You're lucky to have bathrooms. When I went to school, we had a hole in the floor for a bathroom."

"What century was that, Miss?"

In fact, the first elementary schoolhouse I attended in Mulirena did belong to a different century. The school had been converted from a large home in the centre of town. An ancient, thick, weather-beaten door, which had turned black over the years, led into an open courtyard with empty stalls that, at one time, had housed the donkeys, pigs, and chickens of the household. I can still recall the lingering smell of damp earth and manure. From the courtyard, the children would go up a flight of stone stairs. The classrooms had large balconies that let the sunlight in and the scent of oleanders from the adjacent houses, as well as the incessant chattering of the housewives. It was the robust voice of the village crier who announced the arrival of the fishmonger or other travelling merchants that signaled the end of the school day.

I take a last look down the corridor before closing the door. Linda and Gina are running toward the class, both in high heels, their breasts wobbling in their tight knit tops. I motion for them to hurry up.

"Miss, did you hear the news about Angie's mother?" Linda yells as she reaches the door.

"What about Angie's mother? Lower your voice, please," I pull Linda by the arm towards the corridor. Gina follows. The two girls talk simultaneously:

"She's in the hospital."

"She was found almost dead on the kitchen floor."

"How did you hear?" I ask

"Angie called me this morning," says Linda.

I let go of Linda's arm and stand motionless while the two girls join the class.

The students have overheard and they huddle around Linda and Gina, all asking questions at the same time.

"Quiet!" I shout as I return to class and close the door.

I ask them to open their *Standard Textbook of Cosmetology* to chapter eleven, on "Finger Waving," and to start reading it quietly. Now that I know for sure that something has happened to Lucia, I look up Rosaria's number again and call her on the class phone.

An uncertain, elderly voice answers, "*Allo.*"

"Comare Rosaria?"

"Who are you?" the woman asks.

"I'm Caterina, Teresa's daughter," I say in dialect.

"Ah, Catarinella? *Bella mia,*" the old woman says, almost wailing. "What has happened to us? What has happened to all of us?"

In a screechy voice, Comare Rosaria explains that she was visiting her son Pietro, when she got a call from her other son, Alfonso, that Lucia had been found unconscious on the kitchen floor, her head bleeding. Angie had been out at the park, and she had walked into the scene after Alfonso had called the police. Lucia has fallen into a coma. Her husband, Pasquale, blamed for the assault, has disappeared.

I stand immobile by the desk, not knowing what to do next. Should I be the one informing the principal?

The class can't settle down, despite my chiding them to work quietly. I take the thick hairdressing book from my desk, leaf through it, and ask the students to open the accompanying workbook to the fill-in-the-blank exercises on finger waving, and copy the answers directly from the textbook, a mindless exercise that will keep them occupied.

Why do I still feel guilty about responsible for Lucia's fate, even though I have no idea of what has happened? I had spoken to her at around eight-thirty the evening before. Maybe that call, or a call I made to her husband a week earlier, sparked an argument between them.

The workbook exercise can't sustain the students' attention until recess, yet I can't force myself to give the demonstration on finger waving, as planned. I walk around the classroom, as in a daze. The students chatter, speculate, and build their own script about what might have happened to Lucia. I think back to our time in the village, the summer evenings spent sitting by our doorsteps, telling stories, and then the long sea voyage. Were the seeds of this tragedy sowed early on, without any of us realizing it?

3. ANGIE WAS HERE

FRANK HEARD ABOUT LUCIA from Linda and Gina during recess, and is discussing it with the principal, Marc Champagne, as I arrive at the meeting.

"It seems the family is ... well-connected, Cathy," Frank smiles.

"Angie's father and uncle are in business, and they have contacts with all types of people," I answer.

"What kind of business?" the principal asks.

"Construction and real estate."

"Aren't they also in the importing business?" Frank asks. "Calabria Foods belongs to them, I believe."

"Oh, yes, that's the younger uncle who looks after it."

"I hear that the Calabrians and Sicilians are in a power struggle. It's going to be getting ugly," Frank says.

I'm puzzled by the remark. "What's the reason for the meeting?" I ask.

"Okay. I'll get to the point," Frank says and goes on to explain that a report sent by Angie's previous school board had clearly labelled her a "school phobic," a condition that requires special help not available at WLHS.

I want to answer that half of the school's population—students as well as teachers—could be labelled "school phobics," but I turn to the principal. "Mr. Champagne, you had agreed on this special project in June."

"Yes, Cathy, you're right, but we didn't have all the documentation on this student then, and it was clear we'd accept her on a trial basis. Frank has done thorough research on her file and there are just too many irregularities," he concludes.

Frank continues, "Not only has Angie been admitted without proper assessment, but she comes from a French school board, without the proper Quebec eligibility certificate."

The new language laws in Quebec make Angie ineligible for English-language schooling, since neither of her parents had attended school in the province. Some Italian parents in the suburb of Saint-Leonard had challenged the law earlier by setting up clandestine English classes in church basements. In June, Mr. Champagne had told me he wasn't bothered by Angie's ineligibility for English schooling, since the "illegal" students had been pardoned. If necessary, he would request a special exemption for a special needs student. I remind him of this promise.

"Unfortunately things have changed since then. We're in tough contract negotiations with the government," Mr. Champagne says.

Frank adds, "I'll have you know that, yesterday, Angie vandalized the teachers' bathroom across from your classroom. That's the last straw."

"Are you sure about the vandalism?" I remember that I had opened the bathroom door for Angie, but other students had used those facilities throughout the day.

"We're sure. Go and check for yourself," Frank says.

The principal sums up: "Since the school has not been officially informed of the latest happening, and no names are given in the news, we will proceed as if nothing has happened. Angie will be sent back to her own school board."

I try to argue, "I don't understand why we can't give her another chance, especially given the circumstances."

"Cathy," Mr. Champagne says forcefully. "The circumstances and timing make it even more pressing to act. Her parents are rumoured to be involved in organized crime. Have you not read the papers? Cafés are being torched, people are getting killed. The sooner we take action, the better."

"But ... those are only rumours..."

Frank cuts me off. "The family hasn't seen fit to contact us yet. Obviously, they want to keep the whole thing quiet. The longer we wait, the harder it will be to get rid of her, especially if Social Services gets involved. Let's hope they haven't heard about the beating yet."

I don't know what else to say. Frank seems pleased with the new developments, as if he has been proven right.

Mr. Champagne continues, "I'm sending the parents a report that Angie should be sent to a special program at St. Justine's Hospital," he says. Then adds: "Cathy, this is not a formal reprimand, but it would be appreciated if you'd try to set a more professional example for students and arrive a few minutes before them. And do try to stick to the rules about the teachers' bathroom."

As I leave the office, one of my shoulder pads comes loose, and seems ready to slide down my back.

Frank walks besides me. "Angie's school was just an excuse for her mother to leave her husband."

"How do you know?"

"Cathy, you're so naïve. Imagine, after twenty years of marriage, she decides to leave him, now that he's getting old. She must have found a younger sweetheart. Can you blame him for the whack on the head?"

I walk away. Life without Angie in my class will be a lot easier, so why am I so upset about losing her?

Since she's been in my class, I can't help thinking of her mother and our ocean crossing. Lucia was a married woman, yet she was hardly older than her daughter is now. The defining moments of that trip all had to do with Lucia; the rest is a hazy memory.

I walk into the teachers' bathroom to fix the errant shoulder pad, and to check on the vandalism Angie is accused of having committed. I break into a broad smile when I see ANGIE WAS HERE written in bright red marker, the large scrawl unmistakably the girl's handwriting.

I go straight to class and call the Social Services Agency.

PART II
THE VOYAGE, 1957

4. DAYS ONE AND TWO

ON THE FIRST DAY OF the trip we travelled from Calabria to Naples by train. That day blurred into Day Two because we had travelled by night and arrived in the early morning hours on the day of the boat departure. It was after midnight when my mother's brother, Zio Pietro, came into our train compartment and pulled the suitcases down from the racks above our heads. He yelled, "We're in Naples!" as if he were warning us as much as waking us up.

"Naples is full of *scugnizzi*," Zio said. "Don't trust anyone to touch the suitcases."

Zio shooed off the porters that circled around us like flies, but then he negotiated with an older man, who took the heaviest suitcases and walked us to the nearest hotel. I felt as if I was sleepwalking, but had to keep up with their brisk pace.

The hotel, which was only a few metres from the train station, looked dark and dirty. Three women with bright red lipstick were huddled together at the entrance, trying to keep warm. They were arguing, their hands and cigarette smoke moving nervously up and down to the rhythm of their loud voices.

"We're in good company," said Zio.

Mother and Lucia looked at each other in disbelief. "What are they doing out in the cold at this time of night?" Mother whispered.

"We all have to make a living," the porter said, as Zio paid him.

"We're only here for a few hours," Zio said apologetically. I slept soundly, sharing a room and a bed with Mother and Lucia, while Zio and my brother, Luigi, slept in the room next to us. At the first hint of daylight, we dragged ourselves out of bed and took turns using the smelly bathroom in the corridor. From a rusty nail on the wall hung strips of cut-up newspaper that were to be used as toilet paper. We pulled on a chain to flush the toilet, but it didn't work. Mother splashed some cold water, which trickled from the faucet of a stained sink, over my face, but stopped short of using a towel to wipe it dry.

"Don't touch it," she said fiercely. We lugged our own suitcases back to the station, hungry and shivering with cold.

Groggy, I still peered out the bus window, wanting to see Naples. But the city, too, was still half-asleep, as were the street sweepers who moved lethargically, pushing garbage from one side of the curb to another. The shops were closed, but the street vendors were setting up their stands. Some were ready for business, sitting next to small lit-up furnaces, bundled in heavy coats and shawls, offering cigarettes, magazines, small toys. They called out loudly to passers-by in the Neapolitan dialect. They sounded as if they were singing. The bus sped directly to the port and parked in the shadow of an immense ship.

I had seen pictures of the *Saturnia*, and of its twin, the *Vulcania*, on a poster tacked up on Zio's wall in Mulirena. He processed all the paperwork for people who emigrated, and handled their travel reservations with the shipping company, Italian Line. The two ships took turns sailing between Naples and Halifax. Third class, in winter, was the cheapest way to travel. The poster showed the whole fleet of ships, including the brand new *Cristoforo Colombo* and its sister ship, the *Andrea Doria*, two luxurious liners that did the Naples-to-New-York route. During the summer before our departure, the *Andrea Doria* sank. Zio went into mourning for a few days, as if a family member had died.

On the poster, the *Saturnia*, photographed from a distance and surrounded by an expanse of ocean, looked like a boat made of folded paper. It was long and slim, its hull painted black, the railings and outside upper decks white. As we approached it, so close to the pier, we could hardly see the water behind it. We faced an enormous black wall with tiny portholes that looked like small, mysterious eyes. I had to close my own eyes in fear of the massive shape before me. Mother made the sign of the cross.

"There are as many people in that boat as there are people in all of Mulirena," Zio said.

The departure was scheduled for later. Once the luggage was checked in, we went to get something to eat nearby. We passed by a cart selling oranges, and I nudged my mother to get me one. Zio went up to the cart, and with hands in his pockets, asked the price.

"*Cento lire*," answered the woman.

Mother hit her brother's arm from his pocket. "Are you crazy?" she said. "Paying a hundred *lire* for an orange? What is it made of? Gold?"

"*Ebbé*," replied Zio. "We can all share it."

"Pay a hundred lire for a slice of orange that won't even reach our throats?" Mother snorted and then yanked me away.

Zio wanted to show us the Galleria and some of the other sights in the area. He walked us briskly past a castle, the Castel Nuovo, and the Royal Palace. Both imposing buildings had been residences to the French and then Spanish rulers of Southern Italy. Don Carlo's ancestors, the founders of our home town, Mulirena, must have lived here once, I thought. We then stopped at a bar across from the palace and had *caffè e latte*, and a *sfogliatella*.

"These are a specialty here in Napoli," Zio said.

I had never eaten one. When I bit into the flaky, crusty pastry filled with sweet custard and candied fruit, I forgot all about the orange.

Zio had spent time in the navy and loved talking about ships. He took us on a tour of the pier, pointing out to Luigi the different types of sea vessels with foreign names and flags. We followed them, I holding Mother's hand, and Lucia, walking behind, uninterested and mute. Then before we headed back, Zio stopped at a stand, and before Mother had a chance to protest, he bought Luigi a harmonica.

A procession of people was already boarding the *Saturnia*, dragging bulging cardboard suitcases and parcels held together with string. There were only a few couples travelling together. Mostly, it was either men alone or women with children. Zio had special permission to come aboard and help us settle into our cabins. As we set foot onto the gangplank, the sound of hard metal underneath our feet made us walk cautiously down narrow steel stairs, clutching the railings. The ship resonated with the sound of footsteps, of luggage thumping against metal stairs, of children crying, mothers shouting, and cabin doors opening and shutting in the hidden corridors below us. Luigi ran excitedly in front of us, rattling his metal harmonica against the railings.

"Slow down. Isn't there enough noise on this ship that you have to make more of your own?" Mother yelled. "I'm already getting a headache." The further we climbed down into the ship, the narrower and more congested the corridors and stairs became. Luigi finally found our cabin with our suitcases already inside it.

I was surprised to find a thin, older woman with a brown furrowed face and grey hair knotted into a bun, sitting with two toddlers on the lower berth of a bunk bed against a dark corner of the cabin. There were two other bunk beds besides the one occupied by the woman. She introduced herself as Giuseppina, from Frosinone. The children were her two granddaughters. The woman's daughter had left the girls behind when she emigrated two years earlier so she could work unencumbered and make enough money to send for them. Now there was a third child on the way. Giuseppina would go live with her in a place called Windsor and babysit all the children. Luigi was allowed to stay in the same cabin as us. Zio went to check that Margherita, a woman from Amato, who was travelling to Winnipeg with her child, was also settled into her cabin, not far from ours.

A steward dressed in a white jacket arrived. He was a tall man of about thirty, broad shouldered and husky, with dark straight hair brilliantined in place behind his ears. He turned on a switch near the door and a faint light came on. "There's electricity on this ship," he said with a smile. "I'm Armando, your steward. I am from Rome." He kept smiling as he checked everyone over from head to toe. In his white uniform and white gloves, he looked like he might be the ship's captain. He marked off our names on a list and then examined the tags on each suitcase on the floor. He placed the bags next to the beds.

Pointing to Mother and Giuseppina, he said, "The two *signore* should sleep on the lower beds. The two children can sleep with Grandma or on the top berth. If they fall, they won't make as much noise. The boy can climb up too." Then he bowed to Lucia. "The *bella signorina* will decide whether to sleep on the top or on the bottom, as she pleases." I wasn't given any choice, or any attention.

Giuseppina, who in a few short minutes had not only told us all about herself and her daughter, but had inquired about all of us, answered sternly. "There are three *signore* in the room. The *bella signorina* has a husband waiting for her in Halifax."

Armando answered quickly, his eyes on Lucia. "*Ammazza!* They married you off before giving you first communion?" Lucia, for the first time in recent memory, chanced a small smile.

Zio had just come back and shot back at him: "What kind of questions are these? Show some respect, or I'll report you."

"Report me for what? You people are so hotheaded. It was only a question," he said, then explained how to get to the dining room and lounge for lunch, and left.

"He was just trying to be friendly. He didn't mean anything by it," Lucia said, sounding annoyed.

Zio quickly retorted: "*Ma*, what business is it of his when you got married?"

"Don't trust these *chiaccheroni* from Rome," Giuseppina added.

Zio, satisfied that everything was in order, said he'd have to leave. We all followed him up to the ship's deck, while Giuseppina and the girls stayed in the cabin. Zio hugged all of us and left quickly before we had a chance to cry. "I'll stay on the pier until the ship departs," he said, walking away. Then, before descending the gangplank, he turned and added. "Luigi, I beg you, eh. Take care of your mother and your sister."

From the deck, we watched the group of people assembled below, looking up at us, waving their handkerchiefs and blowing kisses. They formed an island of raised arms, surrounded by a swarm of people in motion, pushing baggage-loaded carts in all directions, like ants around an anthill. The whistles of ships, and the screeches of white seagulls hovering over us, deafened our ears. We spotted Zio, waving his handkerchief with the others.

The *Saturnia* finally blew its foghorn and started moving away slowly, as if still held back by heavy weights. The waving became frenzied for a while, and then calmed down, until only a few diehard kept it up. We looked until we could no longer distinguish the white handkerchiefs from the flapping wings of the restless seagulls following the ship or scavenging for food around the pier.

After accompanying Mother and Lucia back to the cabin, Luigi and I followed Armando's directions and explored the ship. In the dining room, we admired the chandeliers and the rows of tables, all dressed in starched white tablecloths, and topped by hundreds of shiny glasses and dinnerware.

"If this is third class," Luigi said, "imagine the luxury in first class!" We sank into the sofas in the large lounge, the first and only hint of softness in that huge palace of steel. The beds had felt hard, and the cabin had been dim even with the light on. I decided that this is where I'd come to read.

Back on deck, we watched the waves get higher as the boat moved deeper into the sea, until Castel Nuovo and the Gulf of Naples receded completely from our vision.

We spotted a fish jumping over the waves; Luigi was sure it was a swordfish. "This is nothing," he added. "Wait till we see sharks and whales!"

We lost track of time, and when we went down to our cabin, the others were waiting for us to go up for lunch. Mother was upset that we had stayed away so long. It was nearly two o'clock when we sat at a table and were served pasta and thin cutlets by a waiter from Naples, who kept offering us seconds.

"What service!" Giuseppina said.

After lunch, I wanted to stay in the lounge with the prayer book I had brought with me, but Mother said we should all go back for a rest, and we returned to the cabin. Lucia had chosen the lower berth next to the wall on the opposite side of Giuseppina, but I didn't mind climbing the small ladder to the top. It was more private and I could see all the others, except Lucia below me. I arranged my purse, my book, and my notebook against the wall. My mother and brother took the beds in the centre of the room, in between us and Giuseppina.

I knew most of the prayers in my prayer book by heart, and they didn't mean anything anymore—just words we had repeated so many times before. I asked Luigi if he wanted to look at the thick novel, *I Promessi Sposi,* which we would have studied in high school had we stayed in Italy. He was practicing on his harmonica, cupping it in his hand to muffle the sound.

"I'm trying to compose a tune. I'm not spending my time here reading a book. Anyway, I know the story already."

Everyone knew the story of Lucia and Renzo, betrothed to each other but prevented from marrying by a powerful man. I started reading; the print was so small, I could hardly see it in the dim light of the cabin. "*Quel ramo del lago di Como che volge a mezzogiorno tra due catene non interrotte di monti, tutto a seni e a golfi, a seconda dello sporgere e del rientrare....*" The first sentence seemed never to end, and I fell asleep before finishing it.

5. DAY THREE

WE DIDN'T GO TO DINNER that first evening on the ship. I fell asleep after the heavy, late lunch and slept right through the night. When Armando woke us all up the following morning, I was confused as to what day it was.

"*Buon giorno, signore e signorine*," he said cheerfully. "You slept very well. But don't think of spending all of your time in bed. My advice to you is to stay up as much as you can, even when the weather gets rough."

"How much rougher than this will it get?" asked Mother timidly.

"Eh, what do you expect? It's February. Wait until we cross the Big Rock, then the dancing will begin."

"*O Dio mio*," said Giuseppina and made the sign of the cross as if to pray for salvation.

"Don't blame God. Blame your dear husbands for sending you out in the ocean in the middle of winter ... but if I had beautiful wives like you, I'd want you with me, too, to keep me warm in frozen Canada. But just think, in less than twelve days, you'll be with your husbands. When you feel like throwing yourselves off the deck of this ship, just think of the joy of being in their arms." He smiled.

"What a *chiaccherone!*" Giuseppina answered. "But remember, we're serious women here ... with children."

"And I'm the most serious waiter on the Italian Line. At eleven, after breakfast, you all must come on deck for a safety drill. And after lunch, we will be approaching Gibraltar, and you'll see the Big Rock."

"If we look at the water, we'll get sicker. I'm staying in bed," Giuseppina said.

"After what I just told you? That, Signora Giuseppina, is the worst thing you can do. There's only one way to survive the crossing: dance with the waves. When you feel a wave coming, instead of saying, 'O Dio mio,' and making the sign of the cross, say, 'What a beautiful wave, let me jump on it … the higher the better.' I tell this to all my beautiful ladies. Some believe me, but some don't."

"Eh, it's easy for you to joke. You're used to this," Giuseppina replied.

"Try doing it all year long in this *casino,* and then you'll see how easy it is! Believe me, Signora Giuseppina, listen to my advice, learn to dance with the waves. It's the only way to survive! Now I have to go. *Ciao,* and remember to come up and see the Rock."

"But why did we have to get someone like him?" said Giuseppina after he left.

"I think he just likes to joke around with everyone. It's his character," said Mother.

"*Si, si,* that's what you think, but that one is hungry. Who knows how long it's been since he's eaten?"

Breakfast was coffee with warm milk and some sweet breads, and we all ate well. Then all the passengers met on deck. Luigi and I kept trying to guess what kind of fish we saw jumping out of the sea. Lucia chatted with Margherita, the woman from Amato. The ship's crew members came on deck with lifejackets on their arms. Armando went straight to Lucia and Margherita, and helped them put on lifejackets. Giuseppina nodded at my mother as if to say, "See? What did I tell you?"

The captain of the ship welcomed us, told us to pay attention to the safety instructions, and left. The attendant pointed to the small boats roped on the side of the ship and told us that they would slide off the sides and into the ocean in case of an emergency. Women and children would be the first to go down.

"What will these little things do for us if the boat sinks?" Mother asked, removing her lifejacket.

"They're not called *salvagenti* for nothing. They'll hold us up in the water until help comes," said Luigi. "Unless the whales come first. Geppetto was saved by a whale."

"Sure, believe in Geppetto!" said Mother.

I had visions of the *Andrea Doria* being gashed on its side by an iceberg, then tilting sideways before collapsing completely, like a soldier shot in the heart. Fifty-two people died in that shipwreck. And it had only happened that past July. Zio had given us all the details and shown us pictures from the newspaper. Half the rescue boats had tipped over before people could get into them. I knew that Mother must have been thinking the same thing, judging from her white, drawn-out face, while everyone else trying on the lifejackets laughed.

As soon as the drill was over, the two older ladies went back down to the cabin, and asked us to bring them some bread for lunch. Mother was afraid that she'd feel sick quicker if she walked up and down.

We could already see a difference in the height of the waves, and I tried to practice lifting myself up with their movements. I had never been on a boat before and had never swum in the sea. The only time I had passed by the beach in Catanzaro Lido with my family, Mother had held me so tightly that my wrist hurt.

The two younger kids stayed with us for lunch, but didn't eat anything. I tried playing with them, but they sucked their thumbs and cried for their grandmother. We went back down with Lucia and brought some bread and cheese for the others.

Lucia and I decided to go back on deck and join Luigi to see the Rock of Gibraltar. As soon as we left the cabin, Mother called me back in. She said in a soft voice, "Stay close to Lucia," as though I was supposed to look after the older girl.

The deck was full of people, and the sky, hazy, threatening rain. It was hard to tell where the waves finished and the clouds began. Luigi was the first to notice the shape that looked like a huge whale in the distance. "The Rock," he yelled.

The Rock, in size and shape like a mountain, seemed like a shadow that appeared and disappeared in the mist. Armando showed up behind us, and suggested that we go up to the first-class deck, because the view from there would be clearer. We followed him up happily, as both Luigi and I had wanted to see what first class looked like. Besides being higher, the view, as far as I was concerned, was the same—except that there were fewer people around us.

As we got closer to shore, black-skinned men in small boats rowed toward us. They were Moroccans, Armando said. They sold colourful scarves with pictures of the Rock of Gibraltar and other souvenirs. They pushed up a small basket on a long stick with the purchased item, after people had put their money in. They made a couple of sales, mostly to the men.

Looking toward the Rock, I was overcome with the same feeling of fear as the day before when I had stood next to the ship. I turned my head and watched the people's faces in first class. They stared in awe at the sight and I forced myself to look again.

After a while, I became accustomed to the shape of the Rock of Gibraltar before me. The small boats returned to shore and the people on deck slowly dispersed. Armando stayed with us and started a conversation with Lucia. Luigi had made friends with a couple of boys who took turns playing his harmonica.

"I'm going to check out the lounge in first class," he told me excitedly before he sped off with them.

I sat on a bench with the book I had brought with me. All through the train ride, Lucia had hardly said anything, immersed in her own sorrow. I figured that she was very sad to be travelling alone without her family, and I wondered if she still thought about Totu, the boyfriend she had left behind. She never once mentioned his name—yet they had been sweethearts for as long as I could remember. Now, I noticed how animated she looked, listening to Armando. She still didn't speak much. She mostly laughed at Armando's jokes or nodded at him. I heard him say, "But tell me, you never answered my question yesterday."

"What question?"

"How long have you been married?"

Lucia mumbled that it had only been a few months.

"Then why didn't your husband wait for you?"

Lucia just shrugged and looked into the water.

It took Armando a couple of instants to blurt out, "I think I understand! You must be one of those proxy brides. Then I was right yesterday. I'm never wrong about these things. You've never met your husband and you're still a *signorina*."

Lucia nodded.

He answered. "I've seen it before—many times. You're not the first one. But you're by far the prettiest. Your husband has won the lottery. He will be a very happy man when he sees you."

She remained silent; he changed the subject. "Look at that piece of rock. It looks close, yet we can't see it clearly. I've seen it I don't know how many times in the last five years, but whether the weather is clear or hazy, it always looks the same to me. I've never been able to see its colour or to see if anything grows on it. I ask myself, *ma*, what purpose does it have? Is it a mountain? Do people live on it, or is it just this mass of rock stuck in the water?"

He paused for a few instants and then continued. "A couple of times, on clearer days than today, it looked as though I would be able to see more of it. But just when I think it's becoming clearer, the ship starts backing off and the Rock becomes a blur again. It's as if the captain does it on purpose to tease me. Who knows? Maybe one of these days, I'll get on a boat with the Moroccans and I'll get to see it up close."

Realizing he was carrying on a conversation with himself, he turned toward Lucia and said, "Open your mouth."

Lucia seemed puzzled, but opened her mouth anyway. "I just wanted to see if you have a tongue. You Calabrese are the quietest women I have ever met. *Ebbé*, I better go down to the dining room and get things ready for dinner. Come back here tomorrow morning, between ten and eleven, and maybe we'll have a chat—now that I know you have a tongue. If you shut yourself up in that room, this boat will seem like a tomb. You passed the Rock. We're now in open water. Gibraltar was once considered the edge of the world. *Si salva chi può*."

She smiled and nodded. He turned and seemed to have noticed me for the first time. "You, *Calabrisella,* don't listen to the old ladies. Their heads are filled with nonsense ... but it's not their fault. You two, now, must learn to think for yourselves." Then he stared at the book I was holding on my chest. "*Ammazza*, you're reading that book at your age?"

I hadn't read much yet, but I tried again after he left, while Lucia stood leaning against the railing, looking toward the Rock. I skipped the first few pages, which were full of descriptions of the countryside around Lake Como. I decided to use the reading method that Signor Gavano had taught me in third grade. I read the first sentence of each paragraph. If it sounded interesting, I read the rest; if not, I went on to the next one.

The first character to draw my attention was Don Abbondio, the parish priest of the area, taking a stroll in the countryside and reading his breviary. The priest trembles at the sight of two *bravi*— henchmen for the most powerful landlord of the area, Don Rodrigo. They stop him and ask, "You're intending to marry Renzo Tramaglino and Lucia Mondella tomorrow?"

"We're just servants of the public," Don Abbondio answers in a quavering voice.

"There's not going to be any marriage, not tomorrow or any other day," says the *bravo*.

Just then Lucia shook me by the shoulder and said we should go down. As I moved to follow her, I noticed a man with thick black hair leaning on the railing and staring at both of us. I had watched him earlier as he bought something from the Moroccans.

"Why are you staring at me like that?" Lucia said. I thought she was talking to the man, but she looked at me. I was confused for a few instants.

"Don't say anything about the waiter talking to us," Lucia said. I had already figured that out by myself. If she noticed the man listening to us, she didn't show it, but my eyes met his as we left and his intense stare scared me. His dark, coarse hair stuck out on his head, and grew low on his forehead, making him look like a menacing bird, or like one of the *bravi* shadowing Don Abbondio.

At supper, the dining room was full. Margherita shared our table. I looked around for the man-bird but he wasn't in the dining room. We had pasta and meat again but nobody touched the meat except Luigi, who ate everything on his plate and then mopped it clean with a piece of bread. The elderly Neapolitan waiter made us laugh. "You saved me from having to wash this plate," he told Luigi, then advised us to follow his example and eat as much as possible in the first three days, to build up a reserve for the rest of the trip, when we wouldn't want to look at food. At the end of the meal, Armando came by our table with a napkin full of bread rolls, cheese, and fruit.

Mother said, "He's very thoughtful."

To which Giuseppina replied, "A little too thoughtful, if you ask me."

"What are you laughing at?" my mother asked me. I hadn't realized I was laughing to myself—not because of what Giuseppina had said, but at poor Don Abbondio in the book.

When the groom visits him, insisting he perform the wedding as planned, the priest panics and falls sick. I laughed remembering the author's comment: "…Don Abbondio did not have to search around for this expedient, as it came up of its own accord."

6. DAY FOUR

MOTHER AND GIUSEPPINA FORCED THEMSELVES to walk up once during the day for lunch and some fresh air, then went straight back to bed. The two little girls never left their grandmother's side, their thumbs always in their mouths. On our fourth day on the boat, Margherita had sought out Lucia, but Lucia brushed her off quickly. She wanted to go to the first-class deck, but didn't feel right, she told me, bringing others along. Luigi spent time playing ping-pong and cards with his friends in first class, carrying his harmonica everywhere he went. Sometimes people would congregate to listen to him play on deck, and he revelled in their applause. I was stuck to Lucia, who met Armando regularly at ten. I wished that they would meet to talk in the lounge so that I could sit comfortably on a sofa and read my book, but they spoke standing up, leaning against the railings as if meeting there by accident.

The man-bird hovered around the first-class deck, very silent at first and then greeting us as we passed by him. He spoke in a Calabrian dialect. I had become so engrossed in the story of Lucia and Renzo that all I wanted was a place to sit and read. I was captivated when I read about "a necklace of garnets alternating with filigree gold beads" that Lucia wore over "a fine bodice of flowered brocade, with the cuffs open and laced with gaily-coloured ribbons." Getting dressed on her wedding day, the Lucia of the book reminded me very much of a young *pacchiana* in her wedding costume. Both my mother and grandmother owned a garnet necklace choker. I found other similarities in the book.

This story took place in Lombardy at the same time that Mulirena was being founded by people from the north. Signor Gavano had given us a history lesson on the village and the Spaniards who ruled the Kingdom of Naples at the time. The name Mulirena stood for "best sand," much desired by the village founders for making stones. When I read about a "Most Illustrious and Most Excellent Don Carlo D'Aragon," I wondered if it was the same Prince Carlo after which Piazza Don Carlo, where I had lived, had been named.

Don Rodrigo of the book and his strongman, Il Griso, were also Spanish. Maybe the landlords who had controlled the lives of the poor in Lombardy, like Lucia and her mother, were the same that sent teams of peasants down the Appenines looking for sand, and then had them cultivate olives and chestnuts for them. The landlords had all probably lived in the Castel Nuovo and the Royal Palace we had just seen in Naples.

Except for the parts that reminded me of Mulirena, I skipped most of the long historical and descriptive passages, as I was only interested in the story, which I imagined happening in Mulirena and in the countryside around it. It could have happened to my own mother. In our village, before the war, Don Stefano and his gang used to go into people's houses at night and force castor oil down the throats of men who refused to get a membership card for the Fascist party—something that Don Rodrigo's *bravi* would be capable of doing. Don Abbondio I imagined as part Don Raffaele, the priest, but also Ntonarello, the town's drunk and buffoon, who sang on his way home every night.

When a plan by Renzo to bamboozle and force the priest into performing the wedding ceremony against his will backfires, the couple and Agnese have no choice but to flee, for fear of Don Rodrigo and his men.

Lucia seeks safety in a convent. She has never left her village, and when she gets on a boat on the banks of the Adda River in the middle of the night, she looks around her at the familiar landscape she is forced to leave and weeps quietly:

Farewell home, where sitting among her secret thoughts, she had learned to pick out from all others the sound of a footstep awaiting with a mysterious awe.... Farewell, church ... where the secret longing of her heart was to be solemnly blessed, and love ordained and called holy: farewell!

The two little girls kept us awake most of the night with their sniffling and crying. They were sick with fever, and Giuseppina tried singing them to sleep, then cajoling them. Then, she started talking to God out loud. "Dear God, do me this grace, don't let anything happen to them on this boat. If you want them, please take them after I've brought them to their mother."

After the girls finally fell asleep, I dozed for a while but woke up again in the middle of the night, feeling nauseous. I had started having one of my recurring nightmares—being alone in the forest and running for dear life, afraid of a howling wolf—but the nausea woke me up and it took me a few instants to realize where I was. As children, we had been lulled to sleep by a lullabye about a wolf eating a sheep, but it had only been in the last months before leaving the village that the nightmares had started. I heard the other beds in the dark cabin creaking from the rocking of the waves. I could hear Mother tossing in her bed, the old woman coughing and making strange sounds, as if she was trying to spit. I couldn't believe that only four days earlier, I had been with my friends and family in Mulirena. Here I was in this hard bed that bobbed up and down like a wooden raft, sleeping in the same room with people I had just met, as if they were supposed to be part of my family. At about this time in Mulirena, we would have been awakened by the old drunkard, Ntonarello, who walked home late every night from the *osteria*, and who rattled his cane on the cobblestones, and sang over and over the refrain from a song he had made up: "*Ntonarello nu more mai; Ntonarello nu more mai.*"

"Ntonarello will never die," he sang every night, and because I had heard his song so often, I believed it to be true. How I wished that I could still be sleeping on the lumpy, corn-husk mattress I had shared with my mother that was all hollowed out to the shape of our bodies, and had held us snugly, like a cocoon.

7. DAY FIVE

THE WAVES ROSE HIGHER AND higher as the weather grew rainier and windier. Mother and Giuseppina had stopped going to the dining room altogether, as they vomited up whatever went into their mouths. Large tin pails, which Armando emptied whenever he came, were kept next to each bed. We brought them dry bread to eat, but they only wet their lips with water, and only got out of bed to go to the toilet. As my mother walked to the bathroom, steadying herself on the walls, and wearing the thin slip that she slept in, she looked like a fragile ghost of her former self.

We had all tried to find out what worked best to prevent us from throwing up. Luigi and Lucia were the only two who never complained about feeling sick. Though nauseous and suffering stomach pains, I had not yet vomited. We thought it was because we spent so much time in first class. But at night we were stuck in the room below with everyone else vomiting, and with Giuseppina and the crying girls, who were constantly sick with fever.

The advantage of sleeping on the higher berth was that, while I heard the sounds of retching into buckets, at least I didn't have it raining down on me while I slept. The top was also better lit for reading and writing. At times, reading in bed made me more nauseous, so I reserved my journal writing for the evenings, and read mostly in the first-class lounge. When I couldn't fall asleep, I tried to imagine what my new home would be like. But I had so little to go by that I couldn't really picture it. Mostly I tried to think of all the things about my life in Mulirena that I would miss the most. I hoped that by writing about them, I could somehow retain those memories. When I remembered picnics I had taken in the countryside with my girlfriends, the picture that swept through my mind was of tall red poppies swaying in the breeze against the yellow wheat fields. That image was all light and softness. I relived the processions on the holiday of Corpus Christi, when I had been chosen to dress up as a crusader. I had walked next to the priest, scattering rose petals at his feet as he shook incense at the onlookers, who kneeled, with their heads bowed in prayer. Would I be doing any of those things anymore? What would I write back to my girlfriends when I got there?

I remembered walking on air the day that I was chosen to play the role of St. Bernadette in the church play. My neighbour Aurora was to play the Virgin Mother. In reconstructing those scenes in my head, it occurred to me that that was the beginning of the end of my joyful memories with my friends. Gossip and insinuations about Aurora flirting with Totu intensified until I watched her being brought down from Don Cesare's house like a rag doll after she ingested a bottle of pills. It was a very public spectacle and yet no one spoke openly about the details of what had really happened, only in whispered conversations, so the children couldn't hear.

These memories distracted me from the seasickness, as I frantically jotted them down in my notebook.

Lucia, Luigi, and I spent as little time in the cabin as possible. Luigi was always the first out of bed in the mornings. "Can't you stay still and rest for a while?" Mother kept yelling at him.

"I can't rest in bed when there's so much to do outside of this cabin," he'd reply and run out to meet his friends.

I often got stomach pains, but I still accompanied Lucia to the dining room and to the first-class lounge, where she and

Armando met every day for a few minutes during his breaks. We took to using the lounge even when Armando wasn't there, and people spoke to us as if we were first-class passengers.

Another traveller who sat with us frequently at the lounge was the man with dark, spiky hair that had frightened me the day we crossed the Strait of Gibraltar. His name was Nicodemo. Lucia readily accepted his offer of a drink from the bar after he told her that he came from the same village as her husband Pasquale. He spoke in Calabrian dialect with her. He was also headed for Montreal, and had many acquaintances there. He knew all about Pasquale's construction business.

"Good person, Pasquale Tonnelli," Nicodemo said, and he ordered an aperitif for her and an orange soda for me.

Nicodemo seemed to coordinate his presence with that of Armando, and left the lounge a few minutes before the steward arrived from his work shifts. One day, when Armando noticed the man move away just as he was arriving, he said, "Watch out for the Calabrian ... he's shifty."

It's precisely what I had thought on first seeing Nicodemo. Watching his figure leaning on the bar as we entered the lounge and then disappear on cue always left me with a subtle sense of fright. Lucia huddled and spoke freely with him, but in whispers. With Armando, she smiled and giggled at what he said, but he did most of the talking. I preferred our time with Armando who spoke loudly and often included me in the conversation. I often thought of afternoons in our village when Totu spent hours leaning against the wall facing Lucia's window and the two of them exchanged glances and gestures. At the time, I never thought their story would end. Lucia and Totu had seemed destined to be together forever. As Lucia would often say later, Totu was never the same after the Aurora incident and after his uncle sent him away to Rome to study.

Of her whisperings with Nicodemo and visits with Armando, Lucia would insist, "There's nothing bad between us, we're just friends." In Mulinera, a woman could only be friends with another woman. I tried to sit as far away from Nicodemo as as I could.

Our absence on the third-class deck raised some suspicions. Margherita came to our cabin a few times, and asked us where we spent our time since she never saw us up on deck. Lucia answered that we had become accustomed to going to the first-class lounge, to avoid getting seasick. Margherita answered, "I'm fine where I am. Armando asked me up once too, but I told him no. That one tries to make it with every young married woman he sees. Who knows how many he's had. He thinks that we're all whores, just because we've been away from our husbands."

8. DAY SIX

THE OCEAN HAD BEEN VERY stormy, and all of us in the cabin had been awake most of the night. My mother and Giuseppina moaned the loudest. They hadn't eaten for days. They kept on making vomiting sounds, but had nothing to throw up.

I fell asleep reading about the other Lucia who is safe in the monastery, and poor Renzo who encounters one complication after another as he travels through Milano, a city looted by a famished population. I liked Renzo best of all. He is bitter about his helplessness in the hands of the powerful Don Rodrigo, but he's all heart, sincere and kind, and means to do no harm. Totu, on the other hand, never even left a word for Lucia when he ran away to Rome.

In the morning, the three of us, Lucia, Luigi, and me, still managed to get up to go for breakfast.

"Where are you going?" Mother asked weakly.

"Upstairs. I can't take it in this cabin anymore," answered Lucia.

"How can you even think of eating?" Mother asked.

Armando, as usual, came to check on us and to empty the buckets. He brought dry bread, and tried to cheer us up. He had wanted to bring Mother to see the doctor, but she said the thought of walking up all those stairs made her feel sicker.

"This trip has to end soon. So many other people have made it. How many days are left?" she asked.

"You have five-and-a-half days left," Armando said in his cheerful tone. "You've made it past the midway point—the point of no return."

"Has anyone ever died of seasickness?" Giuseppina asked.

"No, no one I know has died of seasickness," he answered, "but a few people have wanted to throw themselves overboard. I assure you that the treatment doesn't work."

"What are you saying?" she asked.

"I'm saying that different people will try different things and some would rather throw themselves to the sharks than live in misery. To each his own medicine. And who can stop them? Sometimes it's the only way to survive." Armando spoke so seriously that he confused even me for a while.

He continued, "I say to everyone: if you want to throw yourself into the ocean, that's your business. I only help those who stay on board. '*Si salva chi puó,*' as we say in Rome. Just remember, if you fall in, hold on to whatever you can that will keep you afloat—a shred of wood, a plate, a fork ... anything. Grab anything you can."

"But who is talking about falling into the ocean?" Giuseppina said. "Now you really want to scare us."

"You have already fallen in, *signore e signorine*. Remember, *si salva chi puó*," he said as he left. He returned a few seconds later and added: "A bit of laughter helps too, eh? But you southern women are too serious. Always ready to cry, but never to laugh."

"Did you understand anything? The more he talks, the less sense he makes," Giuseppina grumbled after he left a second time.

Mother asked Lucia again, "How can you even think of eating after the night we've had?"

Lucia was piqued by the question, "I eat just to eat. I have to go up for air."

"Too much air is no good either," Giuseppina answered as she walked to the toilet.

Mother then called Lucia to her bed and whispered something to her.

"I've done nothing wrong," Lucia blurted out loudly. Mother tried to shush her.

"Maybe there's nothing wrong to you, but things can happen. After all, he's a man," Mother said weakly.

Giuseppina came out of the bathroom and Lucia stormed out of the cabin with tears in her eyes, saying, "Even on this boat I have to meet malicious people."

"But who is malicious?" asked Giuseppina.

"*Madonna mia*," answered Mother. "I thought I knew her well, like a daughter. When will this voyage end?"

"We'll be on land in five days. The worst is over, Teresa. Then your husband will be meeting you in Montreal and you'll all be together."

"When we land in Halifax, I'll make the sign of the cross, and no matter what I find in Montreal, I will never make this voyage back again. I swear it on my dead father."

I had never heard my mother swear on anyone before, but it was like her to swear not to do something ever again. But, how could she sound so final about never going back to Mulirena?

Mother said, "You go and stay with Lucia. All I need now is for something to happen on the last days."

I screamed at her, "Why don't you get up from bed and stay with her yourself, if you don't believe her? Do you think that the ocean will swallow you up just by looking at it? You're always afraid of everything and now you say we'll never go back! Look at you ... you look like a ghost! You're worse than Don Abbondio!"

"That's the way I'm made, I can't change that," she said.

"Who's Don Abbondio?" I heard Giuseppina say as I also stormed out of the room.

At the dining table, I couldn't touch my breakfast. I had to hold my stomach; the cramps hurt me so much.

"What's the matter?" my brother asked me. "You're white like a ghost."

"I'm in pain," I said.

"You read too much. You should come play with my friends. You should run to the bathroom, or you'll vomit all over us," he said.

As I ran towards the bathroom, holding my tummy, I felt a warm, slimy flow drip down my legs. When I sat on the toilet, my thighs were all bloody. I screamed and then fainted on the floor. When I regained consciousness, I walked to the sink and splashed cold water on my forehead. I had fainted once before, when I fell on cement steps and saw blood run down my chin. After that whenever I saw blood, I knew to lie down and splash cold water on my face. This time I was really taken by surprise. I hadn't fallen or cut myself in any way. Then I did what I could to clean myself up with one of the white hand towels on the ledge of the sink. I looked for signs of a cut on my legs, but couldn't find any and saw the blood trickle down from inside me.

I stared at the bloody towels and I remembered the red rags that the women of Mulirena kept hidden at the bottom of their baskets and beat on the cement slabs of the *funtanella* on wash days. Once I asked one woman if she had cut herself. She laughed at me and said I was too young to know, but that in time I'd find out. I figured now that this had something to do with that part of the body that the women whispered about amongst themselves. I remembered Lucia, Aurora, and Tina often complaining of stomach cramps, but always in hushed tones, as if there was something shameful about it. I didn't want Mother to know what had happened. She hardly had enough strength to raise her head from the pillow, and I didn't want her to be worried, especially if what I had was some kind of disease that women got down there.

I took another towel and put it inside my panty like a diaper, and returned to the dining room as if nothing had happened.

After breakfast I sneaked a couple of napkins inside my satchel, in case I needed them.

The napkins also made me remember the time my mother had sent me with a gift of eggs to visit Aurora after she had returned from the hospital. Before I left, the girl asked me to hold her arm as she got up from bed to go to the bathroom. Her nightgown was spotted with blood and she picked up a white napkin from the dresser. When I helped her get back to bed, she placed a folded up soiled rag into a basket.

When I was alone with Lucia, I wanted to ask her about what had happened to Aurora and what was happening to me. They had said she had been pregnant. Was I pregnant too? The question was too shameful and Lucia didn't seem to be in a state of mind to care about me. I changed my mind and waited to see if whatever I had would pass on its own.

9. DAY SEVEN

THE DINING ROOM WAS ALMOST empty the next day for lunch. When Armando saw us he came by and hugged us both. "*Brave, ragazze,*" he said and sat with us. "Get ready for action. The *Saturnia* is beginning to dance. Can you feel it?"

I had felt the ship's movements during the night, but I was more concerned about the blood that kept on dripping. In the morning, before breakfast, I had again used the dining room bathroom and walked away with all their hand towels. I was more frightened than ever. This time I'd have to tell Lucia, but she'd have to promise not to tell Mother until we landed.

"I couldn't wait to get out of that cabin, and away from that old witch," Lucia said to Armando.

"You're in the worst part of the ship, but you're welcome to use my cabin in second class anytime you want. I've told you before," said Armando.

Then he turned to me. "Do you know what this boat is named after, Caterina?"

I shook my head, but then took a guess. "Saturn?"

"Of course Saturn, but which Saturn? There's the planet— the one with the ring around it— and there's the god, my ancestor. I'm from Rome, you know. They say that Saturnia was the name of the village where the god Saturn lived before it became Rome."

Armando was very animated talking to me. Lucia sat there and looked bored, but I was smitten. "Saturn, the god, ran away from his kingdom in Greece and flew to Rome ... like everyone does ... Roma, Roma, *captut mundi*! How I miss her."

At the mention of Rome, Lucia got up as if upset and wanting to leave. I also missed Rome and the fun I had had when going there to get our visa to come to Canada. Totu had taken time off to bring us sightseeing. Was she also thinking of him? "Rome ruined many men," I remembered her saying more than once after Totu broke up with her.

Armando caught Lucia by the arm. "Where are you going? If you're not feeling well, you can sleep in my cabin tonight. I'll sleep at the top and you can sleep at the bottom. It's simple, you know."

"You're crazy," she said.

"We Romans are all crazy. We like to live, that's why. It's in our blood. Now the ancient Romans, they really knew how to live it up. They had a festival every year called Saturnalia. Eh, *capito?* Sa-tur-na-li-a. They drank and ate like pigs. Imagine what *baccanale*! Everything was turned upside down."

He lifted Lucia's chin to better look at her face. "You don't look well, *signorina*. I'm concerned. Let's take a little walk, it will distract you."

Before she could answer, he turned back to me. "Saturn was the god of the vine, but also the god of the underworld, the night. The *Vulcania*, the sister ship, is named after Vulcano, the god of fire and light. Eh, we Romans know all about these gods. I'll tell you about it at another time. Now Lucia and I will be back in a few minutes. You can wait for us in the lounge. I want to distract her from feeling sick."

Lucia just walked away with him, without saying anything, and left me there by myself.

I heard Armando say, "I still can't believe how a kid like her wants to read all the time. She should have made friends with girls her own age."

I was really annoyed at both him and Lucia for treating me like a child. Just because my spoken Italian was not as perfect as his, because I spoke with a Calabrian accent, he probably expected me to be a dummy. It wasn't my fault I wasn't born in Rome with all of his gods and goddesses. He probably thought of himself as a god too, or a pope with all of his preaching. Lucia could have said something. She knew about my perfect tens in school, but if she could forget Totu so easily and overlook the fact that she was married, I couldn't expect her to speak up for me. I had done all I could to help her in the village.

When Totu returned from Rome and he started courting Lucia again secretly, she used me as her messenger. Now on the ship, I was relegated to the task of chaperoning Lucia, while Armando made fun of me. She never once said a nice word to me.

After another trip to the bathroom, I went to the lounge by myself and sat curled up on the sofa. I felt queasy but the flow was not as heavy as the day before. There were only a few spots on the towel. Armando had managed to distract me from my worries. Despite his dismissive attitude, I liked what he told me about the origin of the name *Saturnia*, and I hoped he would pick up on it another time. I thought of the planet Saturn and I couldn't imagine how big a circle it had around it. To my drawings of circles, I added one with a loop around it. I pretended to ride the waves, as Armando had told us, but even in first class that morning, the boat lifted me up and then threw me down. My stomach didn't seem to have time to adjust to the movements, and when the boat came down, my stomach was still up. I didn't want to embarrass myself by vomiting in the lounge, but I couldn't leave without Lucia, so I read a few pages, and then closed my eyes for a while. I reopened them again to read a few more pages, but felt more and more nauseous.

In my book, the innocent Lucia is tricked, sent out on an errand, then kidnapped and brought to the castle of l'Innominato—the Unnamed—a man so powerful and evil that the author could not even name him.

I felt weak, and really wanted to go to our room and lie down. I decided to go look for Lucia. She wasn't on deck, or in the dining room, or in the first-class or third-class lounges. What was I supposed to do, run around the ship looking for her, bleeding as I was? And Armando wondered why I didn't make friends. After a while, I was so frustrated that, not knowing what else to do, I went to the dining room and looked for the Neapolitan waiter, and asked him if he knew where Armando could be. He pointed and I turned to see Armando busy setting a table. He seemed surprised to see me.

"You're alone? Where's Lucia?" he asked.

"I'm looking for her. I thought she was still with you."

"That one is a mystery to me."

"I have to find her. I need to go back to the cabin."

"Have you checked with the hawk?"

"Who's the hawk?"

"The Calabrian who follows her like one, who else?"

I wasn't the only one who had noticed that Nicodemo had the appearance of a menacing bird.

Armando jotted a number on a piece of paper. "Check this cabin. It's on this floor."

When I got there, I could hear noises inside, but I didn't have the courage to knock. I was sure that Lucia was in the cabin, so I sat in the corridor and forced myself to read my book. At least I knew where she was.

I skimmed through long passages about the life of the l'Innominato. The book had so many stories to keep up with that I skipped whole chapters. All I cared about was finding out what would happen to Lucia in the hands of the evil man. She pleads with him, "God forgives so much for one deed of mercy!" In her prison, Lucia prays continuously for help, and then, to my surprise, she makes a vow of chastity in exchange for safety: "I make a vow to you to remain a virgin. I renounce my poor Renzo forever in order to be henceforth yours and yours alone."

I was utterly disappointed at this turn of events. Even if Lucia was saved, she would not be reunited with Renzo. What kind of ending was that? I felt bad enough that Lucia's and Totu's story had ended as it did!

I leafed through the book to see what Renzo was up to. Each time I spotted his name, he was in a different place, looking desperately for Lucia, even as he observes the misery of the outbreak of a plague around him:

> *Ceased everywhere were all sounds from shops, all noises of carriages, all cries of street vendors, all chatter of passersby; only rarely was that deadly silence broken by anything but the rumble of funeral carts, the lamentations of the poor, the moaning of the sick, the shrieks of the delirious....*

Vandals called *untatori* are rumoured to purposely spread infection with plague-tainted objects. Renzo ends up in the *lazzaretto*, a place set up to contain the thousands who are infected with the black skin blotches of the plague, often to die of hunger, but, most often, from thirst. But Renzo never gave up on his search for his love—not like Totu who had let Rome get to his head.

After I had been reading for about forty minutes, I knocked lightly at the door. Nicodemo came out and looked surprised.

"Ah! *A picciotta*," he said, "Come in."

He took me by the hand and closed the door. Lucia was lying on a cot, hair dishevelled, straightening her clothes. She walked to the bathroom, saying, "I better go, before they have the whole ship after me." Then Nicodemo sat on the bed and stroked my face as I stood facing him. It wasn't the usual friendly tap on the cheek, but a slow caress. He took my hand and moved it over his chest towards his waist. I felt a strange sense of fright in being two women alone with a man, but also of pleasure at Nicodemo's unexpected gesture of affection. No one had ever done that to me before.

"*Stai cca*," Nicodemo spoke to me in dialect, asking me to stay. In a strange mixed feeling of both fright and curiosity I felt like staying, and moved to sit on the cot, just as Lucia came out of the bathroom.

She looked flustered and angry, rushed towards the cot, took my hand and pulled me away before I could say anything.

"Let's get out of here," she said.

Once on deck, she let go of my hand, pushing me against the railings.

"Why are you mad at me?" I screamed at her. "You're jealous because Nicodemo wanted me to stay?"

"You're so stupid," Lucia said, as she leaned against the railing, looking into the water.

"You're stupid, not me. I'm tired of watching over you like a baby." She kept staring at the water with a glazed look in her eyes.

"I'm a woman, you're a baby," she whispered. "You shouldn't have come into that room. You should be playing with girls your age."

"How can I, when I have to follow you all the time?" I screamed at her. "Stop running around with other men. Don't you care about your husband?"

"How can I care about someone that I don't know?"

"So whom do you love now, Nicodemo or Armando?"

"Who is talking about love, you stupid thing? And what do you know about life? You're still a baby. You think you're smart just because you're good in school?"

"I'm not a baby, and I'm smart enough to know that both Armando and Nicodemo are only fooling around with you,"

"What do you know about what I know? You make me laugh, with your face in that book all the time. All you know is what's in that book."

"At least in the book Lucia and Renzo love each other and they won't go with anyone else."

"That's a book. It's not real, stupid. They can write anything they want in a book."

"Stop calling me stupid. If you were smarter, maybe Totu wouldn't have run to Rome to get away from you, and you wouldn't have married someone else so fast."

She turned and slapped me on the face. The slap took me by surprise, and I regretted what I had said to her, until she yelled at me, "If you hadn't forgotten your stupid jug, maybe Totu and I would still be together."

If she had hit my head against the railing, it wouldn't have hurt as much as those last words. Lucia and Totu, too, had tried to elope one night in late summer and I was to be their accomplice, and prevent them from getting caught. If I had played my part well, their scheme wouldn't have been botched up and revealed.

I broke down in sobs, but she didn't try to console me. Instead she yelled, "I don't ever want you to mention his name to me again." She returned to the railing, looking down into the water, and mumbled something I didn't understand.

Finally, I yelled, "I'm sick and you don't care. I'm sick of you. I'm sick of this ship." She didn't respond. I yelled louder, "I'm feeling sick. I'm bleeding, do you understand? I'm bleeding." She didn't seem to have heard me. "I want to go to bed. What am I supposed to tell the others when I go back to the cabin without you?"

She kept staring into the ocean, mumbling to herself. Was she really thinking of doing something crazy? I went closer to her and said softly, "Sorry, I'll never mention him again. Come to the cabin, so the others won't talk."

She ignored me and kept on mumbling in a low monotone voice. I moved even closer to her and pulled on her sleeve. I heard her talking to herself as if in a wail, the way older women moaned at funerals to show their sorrow.

"I was already dead when I set foot on this boat. I embarked as a walking corpse ... feels neither joy nor pain. I eat just to eat ... can't tell the difference between a pear and a potato. I can't even vomit ... my body is numb ... stuffed in a suitcase ... it belongs to someone else ... someone will claim it and I don't care where it's taken. I walked to my own funeral ... dressed in white. My heart was torn from my body when I said yes to a ghost. I didn't even cry when I left my mother, my father, my brothers, the home where I was born, the home I wanted to live in. How can a body cry without a heart? The only person that can re-join my body to my heart stopped listening ... what point is there in crying? Who will hear me?"

I knew that nothing I'd say would make her feel better. But at least, I understood why she had paid so little attention to me. She didn't care about herself, how could she care about me? I left her to her mumbling, leaning on the railing. It was only five in the afternoon but the sky was already dark and the mist was so thick that I wondered if we would ever see land again.

I didn't know what to think anymore. I had told Lucia off for being with Nicodemo. I also felt dirty and shameful for the strange desire to stay in his room after he had caressed my face. The other Lucia would never have done anything like that. This Lucia was also being delivered to a man against her wishes, even if she had gotten married in a white dress she had designed herself and with the longest veil I'd ever seen. She hadn't been kidnapped, but I couldn't blame her for acting like a prisoner held against her wishes.

As I walked toward the cabin, I had to hold onto the railing. I felt dizzy and weak. I couldn't wait for this trip to be over and to walk on solid ground again.

When I returned to the room, I found Luigi, Giuseppina, and the two kids in their beds as usual, but my mother's bed was empty.

"I finally convinced her to go to the infirmary," Luigi said. "They'll keep her there for the night. She's too weak."

Why had I not been here to take my mother to the infirmary

with my brother? "I want to go see her," I said.

"No," replied Luigi. "They're all sleeping. She's better off there than here."

When Armando came down, he saw me crying. "Don't worry," he said. "There's a doctor and a nurse watching over her. They'll give her something to regain her strength."

"I want to go see her." I felt so guilty for having stayed up on the deck for so long and for having blasted her about Lucia.

"First thing tomorrow morning, I'll bring you there myself. You have my word," Armando promised.

I went back to my book, but I couldn't read anything. Finally, I dozed off, crying.

10. DAY EIGHT

IN THE MIDDLE OF THE NIGHT, I heard a man come to my bed. He whispered, "Come with me."
 I didn't want to make him wait, so I got up in my slip. I took his hand, and went with him quietly, trying not to wake the others. We went down a staircase. Funny, I thought, I didn't think the ship had a deck lower than ours.
 "The hospital is way, way up," he said. "But we need to go down before we go up. We still have a long way to go." I should have taken my shoes, my coat, before leaving. I didn't even have underwear on. I touched my bum and it was naked. I walked along a long corridor. Some of the cabins were open, but so dark I couldn't see any people inside them or even any walls—only emptiness. I screamed when, inside one, I saw huge columns rising, like in a church. "*Untatore, untatore,*" people screamed, while a priest all dressed in gold held up a gold ostensorium that sparkled like a sun. It must be the feast of Corpus Christi. I looked for my basket of rose petals to take to the procession, but the man pulled me by the hand.
 "Let's run out of here," he said, alarmed. A mother kissed a baby girl on the forehead, then laid her down as if putting her to bed. "Goodbye, Cecilia! Rest in peace."
 "Where are we going?" I asked.
 "Finally, we're in Milano." It was Armando.
 "Good," I said. "I'll see my father here. Where's my mother? I stayed out too long. I want to see her before she dies."

"Sure, sure," he answered. "Come with me and you'll find your mother and your father."

"You're tricking me," I screamed at Armando. "*Chiaccherone, chiaccherone.*" A wave as high as the boat raised me up to the ceiling. The boat bobbed up and down and I felt very sick, but I kept myself from vomiting. I was too embarrassed. All around me I saw litter—bloody rags, rotting bandages, infected straw.

I tried running up a hill but I kept slipping backward on the brown vomit that flowed down like mud. I heard a bunch of kids playing ring around the rosie, running round and round, covered in vomit and shit, while an old woman threw a pot with yellow piss at us. Here and there lay corpses ... and I can hear the lamentations of the poor. Men in brown sackcloths, their heads bent and covered with brown hoods, carried stretchers on which naked bodies were dumped one on top of the other. Shrieks of the delirious....

A surge of warm vomit made me reach for the bucket, but it was at the foot of the bed and I threw up all over the blanket. "Ma," I tried yelling, but no sound came out. I folded the slimy wet cover away from me. I lay back again, but it was so cold without the cover. I scrunched myself up into a ball, and pulled my slip down to cover my bum and bloody rag.

"When will I see my mother?" I cried. I started running away in a labyrinth of narrow streets and alleys, but no matter how hard I tried, I was going nowhere. My slip rode up above my hips and I was completely naked, cold and ashamed, and with nowhere to hide.

I heard muffled voices. I opened my eyes and saw Armando walking slowly toward my bed, holding Mother by the arms.

"Caterina," he said. "Wake up. I have a surprise for you." I tried to pull the cover over myself, but it felt sticky and damp. Mother was smiling.

As she came to kiss me, she felt the folded-up blanket. "You're throwing up now? I finish and you start?"

"I had a bad, bad dream," I mumbled groggily.

Then mother must have noticed spots of blood on the sheet. She lifted my slip up and felt my bum.

"That's all I needed, now," she said, smiling, and pulled my slip down.

"See, Caterina," Armando said, "I always keep my word. I went to see her this morning and she insisted on coming back down here. I tried to convince her to stay up, but you Calabrese women are all the same—hard-headed!"

"You look better today," Giuseppina told my mother.

"You're joking," she replied. "*Paru na morta.*" Then she went over to kiss Luigi, who was just waking up. She acted as though she had been away for a long time. Then she asked, "Where's Lucia?"

I looked around and saw that Lucia's bed was empty. I didn't remember hearing her come in after I had gone to bed. My heart leaped into my throat in a rush of panic.

I remembered her staring into the water. I jumped out of bed.

"I'll go look for her," I said.

"When you find her, come back right away. I want to talk to you," Mother said with a sigh.

"She must have felt really hungry to get up this early," Armando said, not sounding at all alarmed. "That one gets hungrier and hungrier the stormier it gets."

I washed, and went looking for Lucia. I felt better now that I had finally thrown up and relieved that my mother had seen the blood and had not been frightened. I had been so happy to see Mother back, but now I had to worry about Lucia, again. Had she stayed out all night, or had she come to bed and then gone out again? Had I dreamed that a man came into the room? Or had it been Armando looking for Lucia? "Come with me," he had whispered. Had he called to me, or to her?

I passed by the deck and went to the dining room, but there was no sign of Lucia. Then I ran to the first-class deck and lounge, but still no Lucia. I contemplated going to Nicodemo's room, but as I walked down the stairs, I heard her call me from the top deck.

"Where were you all night?" I asked her when she came down.

"I slept on the sofa in the lounge. I couldn't take it in the cabin with those two little pests, crying and sniffling, and everyone vomiting all over. I got up in the middle of the night and went to the lounge." She sounded normal as if nothing had happened between us the day before.

"It scared me when I didn't see you in the room."

"What could have happened to me?" she asked.

"I was afraid you had really jumped into the water."

"If I had the courage to jump into the water, I wouldn't be on this ship."

"I heard someone come into the room during the night. Did Armando come to get you?"

"No, I haven't seen him since yesterday afternoon. You must have been dreaming."

"I had a nightmare. Why did you go to Nicodemo's room?"

"Caterina, I didn't do anything wrong. When you're older you'll understand. You can be with a man and not do anything really wrong. In Mulirena we were really stupid. They made us believe that just being alone with a man was a sin, that everything we did for ourselves was a sin. It's too late for me, but you're still very young. Don't let anybody tell you what's good for you."

"But why would you go with someone like Nicodemo and not Armando, who is so much smarter?"

"Armando talks and talks, but he lives in the clouds all the time.... I don't trust people like him anymore."

I would have chosen Armando over Nicodemo anytime, but I held my tongue and said instead, "I need to go back to the cabin, to tell Mother you're okay. She wants to talk with me."

Mother took me aside in her bed and explained to me in a low voice what the blood meant. She seemed uncomfortable speaking about it, but she assured me that it was all normal, that I wasn't sick, but that I would have to be very careful about what I did with boys from now on, that I wasn't a little girl anymore.

Later that evening, I decided not to ask Luigi or Giuseppina if they had seen Lucia come to bed the previous night. If they had noticed her absence, they would have mentioned it. I didn't care anymore if she had spent the night with Nicodemo. It was her words from the day before that hurt me most. In her eyes, my mistake had cost her her freedom. But I had failed her in another way. On my return from the trip to Rome with my family to get our visa, I never told Lucia that we had spent time with Totu, and that he confessed the reason why he drove away from the elopement. It was not out of fear as many thought, but from the humiliation of the act itself. He told us that he was committed to the Communist Party that would bring Italy into the future. He loved Lucia, but she would always remind him of the medieval ways of life in Mulirena and he wanted no part of it. It would be less hurtful for Lucia to believe that her elopement had failed because of me, than to know that Totu left her because he loved Rome and his Party more than he loved her.

From my berth, I looked around the cabin as everyone prepared for another night of troubled, queasy sleep in our rumpled up sheets that smelled of vomit and blood. If only, I thought, I'd wake up in Mulirena the morning after. Armando, Nicodemo, Giuseppina, the two whining brats, the Rock, the plague, and the seasickness would have been nothing but a bad, jumbled-up nightmare.

11. DAYS NINE AND TEN

IT WAS AS IF MY ARGUMENT with Lucia the day before had never happened. When Lucia and Armando went for their usual walk, I didn't follow them. Even though the weather had turned colder, the sun was strong enough in the middle of the day for me to sit on deck and read. Armando had promised to give me a prize if I could prove to him I had read the whole book. I wanted to impress him. With about two hundred pages left unread, I cheated and went straight to the end. Not only are Lucia and Renzo reunited, but, "Before the first year of marriage was over a fine baby saw the light..."

Renzo spends many a night recounting his adventures to his brood and the lessons that he learned from his misfortunes. He and Lucia come to the conclusion that "when trouble comes, whether by one's own fault or not, confidence in God can lighten them and turn them to our own improvement."

Having read the ending, I felt satisfied. I spent the rest of the day skimming the boring parts I had skipped previously.

The next day, the sea was calmer, the air sharper and clearer. I spent most of the morning on the first-class deck going back and forth in the book, preparing for Armando's quiz. I went straight to the top of the stairs where I knew he would pass, and waited for him.

"I came to tell you I finished the book," I said.

"Good," he said," If you wait for me here, I have something for you."

After a few minutes he came back with a card in his hands. "I won't have to test you. I believe that you finished the book. It's impossible to find a medal on this ship, though, but take this as a souvenir." It was a postcard of the Rock of Gibraltar.

"I didn't write anything on it, because I want you to remember the place and not me when you look at the card."

"Thank you," I said.

"This card makes you officially a woman of Saturn," he said with pomp and a flourish

I looked at him with expectation. I wanted him to speak to me about Saturn again.

"Let me explain what being a woman of Saturn really means. Because you've crossed the ocean on this ship, your life will never be the same. I don't mean your life will be better or worse, only that you have been transformed by the voyage. Remember that the *Saturnia* is inspired by Saturn, but, Caterina, only you can choose what type of woman you want to be. Saturn, the planet, can make you gloomy, *saturnina,* as we say in Rome, but Saturn the god can make you strong." He pinched my cheek, and he was off. "I have to run. Everyone is beginning to eat like wolves again, and the dining room looks like a zoo."

The colour postcard of the Rock was beautiful. A bright ray of sunlight shone on one side and was reflected in the water. White seagulls perched on its edges and the waves around it were white and foamy like clouds. But that was not how I remembered the Rock. The place in the postcard was clear and sharp-coloured, a place one could easily see and touch. What I remembered seeing was a blurry and mysterious mountain that, no matter how hard you reached for it, would always recede beyond your grasp. Even Armando had doubted he'd ever get to that place.

I put the postcard in my book. They'd both be a reminder of the voyage. I couldn't really tell if there was any truth in what he had said about Saturn, the planet, and Saturn, the god. In time I hoped to learn more about them. With Armando it was difficult to tell what was real and what was not, but he had been the first besides my mother to call me a woman.

12. DAY ELEVEN

DURING THE LAST TWO DAYS of our crossing, I hadn't followed Lucia around anymore. I sat in the lounge by a window looking at the ocean, anticipating the joy of the arrival, while she went for long walks on her own. When she was with Armando, they laughed at one another like two playful friends, each making jokes at the other's expense. She had shown Armando a picture of her husband—a smiling man of small stature, with dark, curly hair, sitting on the hood of a big car. Armando joked about her learning how to drive the car, and about spending time in her big, new home, like a *signora Americana*, while he would have to keep on crossing the ocean, cleaning up after seasick passengers. Nicodemo was never far from the group, though he didn't participate in the bantering. I saw Lucia give Armando her address written on a small piece of paper. Armando put it in his uniform pocket and I wondered how easily he'd lose it.

Father would not be meeting us at the port, but Lucia's husband was expected to be there. Lucia showed up for lunch dressed in the new brown wool suit that she had reserved for meeting him. Around her neck, she wore a scarf that I had never seen before, blue and bright yellow, with a picture of the Rock of Gibraltar.

"What a beautiful scarf," Margherita commented. "I'm sorry I didn't buy one from the Moroccans. I'll never get the chance again."

"That's why I bought it," Lucia said, touching the silk scarf with satisfaction. She glanced at me, smiling as she said it, still in the habit of censoring me from revealing her lies. I knew she had not bought it herself, and she knew that I knew. The way she caressed her scarf and the look on her face made me think that receiving it had made her feel special too. So I smiled back at her to assure her that she could trust me with the small deception. I never told her or anyone else that Armando had given me a gift.

When land became visible, we joined the other passengers on the third-class deck. I kept my hands inside my coat pockets. Though we could see our breath rise up in the air, and though the cold was sharp and icy, it was not as impossible to endure as we had thought. As the ship neared the port, I looked for signs that this was Canada, especially for snow. I saw patches of white in the fields beyond the port, but the ground on the pier was clear and cement grey. The trees and bushes were thin, bare, and also grey. Our first view of the harbour was of a place different from any I had ever seen before. But nothing about it stood out or made Luigi exclaim in awe.

"These buildings are not that high. They look like boxes made of cardboard," he said.

Halifax seemed flat and empty compared to the noisy chaos of Naples. It was what was missing that made it look so different—no mountains, no castles, no colour, little noise, few people. Some men were working around the pier in heavy jackets, wearing hats that covered their ears, but there were no large crowds of onlookers waiting for us. The people on the deck were just as quiet as we were, as if they didn't know whether to be happy or sad.

The ship moved slowly towards a large building. It had a number, 21, above its wide entrance, and I smiled at the coincidence of the inverted 12, for our twelve-day trip that would end in Montreal the next day.

I watched in awe as the ship aligned itself with a bridge that opened directly into the large hall of the pier. I was surprised that we would not be setting foot on the dock. I felt like a Geppetto being swallowed by a whale. I went down with Luigi to get Mother.

Mother's slow walk kept us behind everyone else. I watched the sea of people move toward the open mouth of Pier 21. From here, we would all be going in different directions, Montreal, Winnipeg, Toronto, Saskatoon, Windsor, and other places we had never heard of before. None of us really knew what our new lives would be like, but we all held the same hope that a bright future awaited us.

I looked at the women stepping down nervously from the movable, shaky ramp into the cemented ground of the huge receiving hall, helped by Armando and the other stewards: Giuseppina, who could have enjoyed her late years in her familiar surroundings, but had selflessly made the trip for her daughter's sake; Margherita, with her small child connected to her hip, looking around the hall to find her bearings, smiling as she had when I first saw her. There were so many other women like her, holding on to older parents or children of all ages. These women had all been strangers to me when we boarded, but now I felt a deep tie to them. The pained look they had carried on the boat had magically disappeared. Most knew that they'd be expected to work in the factories of large cities, in farms, or at other menial occupations alongside their men; they looked forward to it with courage and with joy.

I turned my gaze to Mother and she smiled at me. The day before, she could hardly stand up by herself. She still had to hold on to us, but by the look on her beaming face, I knew she had already put the suffering of the crossing behind her.

I saw a short man, wearing a heavy winter jacket and ear muffs, walk toward Lucia. He must have recognized her from her photo, since he came straight to her and shook her hand. Lucia wore her non-smiling look. He took her arm and moved on, ahead of us. I could tell by Lucia's stiff walk that she was not very happy. Her husband was even shorter than he had seemed on the photo, and his legs looked really funny and skinny under the jacket that seemed inflated like a balloon.

Everyone seemed to be in a real hurry to move ahead. A line of attendants directed us toward a row of benches. We couldn't keep up with the others in our party, and we inched our way slowly forward. A smiling woman in a uniform stopped us and gave us kids a brown paper bag each. We stopped to look inside the bag and found an apple, some crayons, a colouring book, and a pair of woollen mittens, which we put on right away. "*Grazie*," Mother said weakly. She crossed herself as we took hold of her arms again. She still wobbled and looked around her, maybe disoriented at being still indoors.

"When will we land?" she asked.

Luigi and I looked at one other and laughed. We answered at the same time. "Ma, we're here already."

13. DAY 12

Passing customs turned out to be the easiest part of our journey. None of our luggage was opened or searched. A customs officer with a red, freckled face and white eyelashes stared at us for a while, and then, without even asking any questions, stamped our passports with "landed immigrant" and gestured to us to go on.

Pasquale had slipped through the gates to meet us at the pier. He tried to explain to the customs official that he had come to translate for us, but he seemed to have problems being understood, and had to show his identification papers.

"No one speaks French here. In Montreal, they all speak French," he said irately before being told to wait for us to clear customs.

While waiting to board the train in the cavernous immigration office, Pasquale offered to buy us something to eat. "There's nothing good to eat on the train and it's a long ride," he said.

Mother took out some dollars that Zio had given her in Naples, and she asked Luigi to go with Pasquale to buy some bread. The two came back with a loaf of sliced bread, and three bottles of Coke. Mother squeezed the bread, which was the whitest and softest bread we had ever seen, and said: "But it's not cooked."

"That's the way bread is here," Pasquale said. "But in Montreal, we finally have some good Italian bakeries."

Lucia had resumed her silent demeanour and said nothing as Mother cut up the red apples from our lunch bags with my brother's penknife.

When we finally boarded the train, it had started to snow softly. It was only five in the afternoon, but it was already dark, and once inside, we could not see out the windows. The moist, thick glass reflected only our tired faces. We still had a long way to go—many of us were going to Montreal; others were headed even further, for Windsor, Toronto, Thunder Bay, Winnipeg, Vancouver.

The train slogged along slowly, stopping suddenly every few miles amid open fields. People wondered whether there was some malfunction, since it took as long as an hour at a time before the train would start up again.

"At this rate, we'll get there for Easter," Mother said.

We all felt hungry. Mother took out the small *sopressata* that Paola, Aurora's mother, had given me on the last day in Mulirena, and cut it into thick slices. She offered it to Pasquale and Nicodemo who sat next to each other. Nicodemo had introduced himself and the two men had started a conversation in a thick dialect about Pasquale's family and friends back home. They discovered they had many common friends in Montreal as well. Pasquale wrapped the spongy white bread around each slice as he spoke and ate it heartily. We all did the same.

"*Mangiamu all'americana*," Luigi said. We all laughed as we sipped our Cokes and ate our *sopressata* in a sandwich, American style.

"This you won't find in Montreal," Pasquale said of the salami.

The stop-and-go pace of the soot-covered train lasted all night long.

"I'm surprised. We have better trains in Italy," Luigi said.

"That's because in Italy we had Mussolini," Pasquale said.

Tired as we were, we slept most of the night. In the early morning, my brother and I were transfixed by the snowy winter landscape—nothing but fields, farmhouses, and barns that seemed covered in white cotton sheets, like furniture in deserted mansions, but in the deep freeze of February.

"Where are all the people?" Luigi asked. "No wonder they want immigrants. Look at all this empty land." I feared the home that awaited us in Montreal would also be a ghostly barn buried in snow.

When we finally arrived at Windsor Station, there was no one waiting on the platform. Like the pier in Halifax, this train station led us indoors with no crowds jostling to see loved ones arrive. Meanwhile, the rest of the passengers cleared and disappeared, and we even lost sight of Pasquale and Lucia. We were looking around and feeling lost, until I spotted Father running down from a staircase toward us. He had pushed his way past guards at the arrival's gate when he didn't see us come up with the rest of the passengers.

"What happened to you?" Father asked Mother. "You're all bones."

"It's a miracle I'm still alive," Mother said, and crossed herself.

We went up the stairs and were met by a horde of people, waving, calling out our names, while a guard kept pushing them back. Everyone was there: my aunt, uncle, Tina, and cousins. We all hugged, kissed, and cried.

When we finally walked out into the street to wait for our ride, I watched car after car move smoothly and quietly with lights flashing in the sleek wet pavement. All the tiredness left my body as I raised my face to the night sky and closed my eyes to feel snowflakes falling lightly on my face.

PART III
OCTOBER 4-5, 1980

14. SEAN AND J.P.

SEAN AND J.P. HAVE SPENT the morning, sitting in the living room, poring over newspaper clippings, drinking coffee. The kitchen is spotless; the bedroom still in a state of total disorder. Yesterday morning, I had dumped garments on my bed, oblivious to the tragedy that had developed at Rosaria's home. Then, too distressed to tidy up the room in the evening, I simply piled all the clothes onto a chair. My fixation with appearance is a frivolity I can never rise above, a personality flaw that niggles at me as I return the clothes to my overstuffed closet.

I keep thinking about Lucia and worrying about Angie. Reconstructing the voyage here from a distance of time and place has been easy; it is the present that is a mystery to me. That long ago day, when her new husband reached out for her on the dock in Halifax, Lucia took on the same stony disposition she had adopted after the night that she and Totu had tried unsuccessfully to elope. On the ship, I saw glimpses of her old, spirited self while Armando and Nicodemo flirted with her, then watched her turn stiff again when she met her husband. I wonder if she has lived in a self-imposed coma from the day she met her husband for the first time to the evening of the blow-to-the head incident. Have there been any tender moments between them?

I walk into the den and notice that J.P. has also put the den in order. The re-arranged books on the shelves lining the room are a tell-tale sign of his presence. J.P. may have skimmed through some of the books while trying to fall asleep. He's jealous of my library, he often tells me. One of the reasons he likes staying over at our place is the chance to leaf through the unusual selection of old books.

Whenever J.P. comes to town, I'm on edge, making sure everything is up to par. I prepare for his visits, buying the best cuts of meat, the best cheeses to go with the wines that Sean researches and chooses. Yet my efforts always feel inadequate.

"He's discriminating. He's always lived well," Sean says about J.P.'s tendency to criticize breezily the quality of foods and wines. Sean keeps reminding me that J.P. can afford the best hotels in Montreal on his expense account, but he chooses to stay with us out of friendship.

"He's cheap," I reply. "He's been in politics too long."

J.P. was an aide to the federal Member of Parliament, Alex Di Principe. When the Liberals lost to the Conservatives the previous fall, J.P. was promoted to party strategist to help reorganize the troops and passed on his old job to Sean. J.P.'s efforts paid off when Joe Clark's minority government was defeated last February.

"Some interesting and major changes may be brewing for me, Cat," Sean says, gravely, as I join them in the living room.

"Oh, I'd like to hear about them," I reply. There have been too many changes lately both in Federal and Provincial governments that have kept the two huddled together for hours.

The night before, I had filled them in on what I'd heard about Lucia and my relationship with her. J.P., ever sensitive to the nuances of news reporting, only comments on the coverage the domestic violence story received on the radio and Saturday paper. "I find it unusual that they should report a domestic quarrel when there are no confirmed deaths," he says. "Maybe there is a link with the café torchings. Still, connected families don't take it out on their women and children. They settle their private affairs differently, wouldn't you say, Catterrina?"

"How would I know?" I say, not bothering to correct his mispronunciation of my Italian name. "But I can't believe them tying such a story to the Mafia."

"It's a bloody ethnic slur!" Sean says. He gets more easily upset by media stereotyping of Italians than I do.

"What do you think?" J.P. asks me. "I'm only asking because I want to understand how an 'ethnic' would perceive the innuendo."

"It's not an innuendo when they report a family squabble and make it sound as if it's a mob hit, just because the family involved is Italian," I reply.

"Are you two thinking of getting married?" J.P. suddenly asks.

Neither Sean nor I react to the unexpected question, as if each waiting for the other to answer. This is a delicate subject between us, one we have not broached in a while, and it surprises me that J.P. would bring it up so casually. The telephone rings. It's my mother.

"Poor Comare Rosaria ... she's at the Jean-Talon Hospital. You'll take me, won't you?"

It's a very Calabrian thing to do, to rush to the hospital as soon as we hear about a close friend's sudden illness. These visits have become a point of contention between my mother and me. I feel uncomfortable rushing to someone's bedside. I try in vain to explain to my mother that, if the illness is serious, most people want to be left alone. But, among Southern Italians, the desire to show concern by making themselves physically available is stronger than common sense. By their presence, visitors like my mother want to express, "We will leave everything behind: the cooking, the dishes, and even work if necessary, to be here with you." Offering assistance by telephone doesn't mean a thing.

This time, I want to go to the hospital, to get more news from the family. I also hope to see Angie, and warn her to expect a call from the Social Services worker to whom I spoke earlier.

During lunch, Sean discloses what had been discussed at the party meeting and what has been speculated for a while: Di Principe or "The Prince," as he's jokingly nicknamed by friends, is expected to be appointed a Senator. Di Principe's appointment is seen as a reward for the financial support his fundraising efforts have contributed to the party and also to win more favours in the Italian community of Montreal that helped elect the Liberals.

J.P. is trying to convince Sean that he should grab the opportunity to run for office in a by-election for his boss's vacant seat, and has set up a lunch meeting with key party supporters to discuss just that possibility.

Sean is especially pensive. He doesn't seem ready to jump at the idea, though he complains continually to me and J.P. about the instability of his position once Di Principe moves on.

"I don't know if I could stomach the stress of another campaign, so soon after the last one, and the referendum. Politics in Quebec is getting too dirty for my liking. They're still rehashing the October Crisis," Sean says. Pierre Trudeau's draconian measures to subdue the Separatist movement in Quebec in 1970 have been receiving a lot of media attention.

"C'mon Sean! Get out of that sixties haze, and wake up to the realities of the eighties," J.P. interjects. "The people of Quebec spoke out in May, remember. With a fifty-nine percent vote of confidence for federalism, the PQ and separatism in Quebec will soon be ancient history."

Sean remains quiet, and J.P. insists: "I'd switch your major to Political Science, though. It will look better on the ads."

Sean is enrolled at Concordia University, still pursuing a Master's degree in Philosophy, which he started while working in education. He resumed his studies this past fall after a three-year break. J.P. has already questioned the practicality of such a degree now that Sean works in politics.

"Stick to politics. You're still young enough to start at the grassroots level," J.P. continues. "And your tie to an ethnic community is an asset." Then he turns to me: "Imagine one day being invited to a dinner at 24 Sussex Drive as a special guest of the Senator."

While serving a platter of veal *scaloppini* with mushrooms and cream, I, nonetheless, take notice of how J.P., polite and suave as ever toward me, only manages to include me in the conversation when he brings up my "ethnic tie" to Sean.

"Would Sean be working mostly out of Ottawa?" I ask.

"Once the election is called, he'd be working the Italian constituents in the riding, so it would be best to establish his home address here," J.P. answers, and then turns again to Sean. "By the way, Sean, how's your Italian shaping up?"

"Sean's idea of speaking Italian is to add vowels to French words: *la tabla, la chaisa, la porta*.... Sometimes it works," I say, laughing. But Sean is too immersed in thought to find the comment funny, and J.P., while he's a silver-tongued speaker, doesn't have much of a sense of humour.

"I'd have to brush up on it," Sean answers pensively.

Sean would surely be running against a Conservative candidate of Italian origin. J.P. asks for permission to use a photograph of Sean and himself taken with me and my family at one of our Sunday lunches, to use on a potential promotional brochure.

15. LUCIA AND ANGIE

AT THE END OF THE SCHOOL YEAR, I had been surprised to get a phone call from Lucia. "I don't know what to do with Angelina. Maybe you can speak to someone in your school?" my old friend begged.

An only child, Lucia's daughter had spent most of her high-school life in special-education classes. In her fourth year of high school, the guidance counsellors informed her parents that the girl had exhausted their resources.

"They want us to go to St. Justine hospital and meet there every week with a psychologist," Lucia had explained. "Her father doesn't want to have anything to do with it. He thinks all she needs is a good spanking."

According to Lucia, the main problem with Angie is that she'd never taken to the French school. When she started, she spoke Calabrian dialect and some English she had learned from watching American cartoons on television.

"The minute she went to school, she became a *babba*," Lucia said. "She didn't want to do anything. They put her in the special classes, but *babba* she was and *babba* she remained. When it suits her, she can be very smart, and she won't let a fly pass by her nose. Her father says it's the fault of this bastard country we live in. I think that the country has nothing to do with it. It's destiny that has to go this way.... Maybe if she learns a trade like you did..."

"I'll see what I can do," I replied.

"Do me this favour. Don't you remember our *ruga*? I can still see you with that big pink bow in your hair. You were like my little sister."

The mention of the large pink bow had the power to transport me to another life. Sometimes a scent, a song or a picture could also spark an image out of nowhere. Lucia still spoke as if she had just stepped off the balcony in Mulirena and called me at her house to give me some figs or cherries that her mother had picked from their fruit orchard. Never once, however, did Lucia mention our crossing in 1957, as if it had never happened. This is the Lucia I had known before the summer of 1956, before our voyage. How could I refuse her a favour?

I asked Bruce to intercede. He convinced the school guidance counsellor and the principal, Mr. Champagne, that admitting Angie would provide the perfect opportunity for a trial project between the Vocational and Special Education departments. Other vocational teachers had refused to accept special-ed students in their classes before, fearing that it would deter regular students from taking their courses.

With Angie starting school in September, Lucia had moved into her mother's apartment in the city, leaving her husband alone in Sainte-Rose, Laval. She had lived in an upper-scale housing development that Lucia's brother's construction company had built. Since Lucia and her family had moved there, years before, they had isolated themselves from the rest of the *paesani*, so I had seen even less of her than of the others. Whenever I see other *paesani*, at weddings, funerals, first communions, I no longer associate them with their village life. In their solidly built, all-stone, ceramic-tiled duplexes in Saint-Léonard, Lasalle, and Rivière-des-Prairies, they have constructed an existence that is far removed from their past and yet not quite in-step with the present. They work and function in broken English, broken French, and even broken Italian. They've become the "ethnics," an entity unto themselves, and a useful demographic group courted by politicians during election periods.

To me, these older, first-generation immigrants seem to have become quite smug in their newly-forged identity. I find that the younger generation I teach at WLHS seems just as comfortable with the label. It's my age group, the eager beavers, who try to straddle both sides of the cultural fence, that feel the most unease in this predicament.

When Angie walked into my class for the first time, dressed completely in black, I was taken aback by her scruffy appearance. She wore ill-fitting polyester pants and a turtleneck sweater, rather than stylish brand name jeans and a T-shirt as most of the other students. Her wiry, dishevelled hair and thick unshapely eyebrows gave her a somewhat sinister look. Her thick lips pouted, not in the self-conscious sexy fashion of the other girls, but in a perpetual sneer.

What lay behind that sneer? Her mother's temper had been easily provoked from what I remembered, though she could be coy when it suited her. Angie's uncle and Lucia's brother, Alfonso, was known to short-circuit easily. I don't know Angie's father well since he isn't from my village. He hasn't socialized much with the rest of the *paesani*. He's a small contractor compared to his brother-in-law Alfonso, whose construction company has built and sold many residential developments in Laval and is now involved in major city projects,

I wondered whether anyone would ever be able to break through Angie's façade. Her first interaction with the class hadn't been promising. Considering the trouble that I had gone through to have her placed in my class, Angie showed little sign of appreciation. When I asked her to throw out her chewing gum, I saw her mouth the word "bitch" as she reluctantly pitched the gum in the wastepaper basket.

I gave her the usual talk about class rules and regulations—the dos and don'ts—personal cleanliness, punctuality, dress code, no gum chewing, no swearing, no loud talk or gossiping among students. "Always pretend there are clients present, even when you are just working on the mannequins," I told

Angie as I handed her the short uniform smock that was part of the dress code.

"Why should I wear that ugly thing?" Angie asked.

"Everyone in the class has to wear it. It's more professional."

"Nobody sees us down here in the basement. This is not a professional saloon."

"You mean salon."

"Salon, saloon. What's the fuckin' difference?"

"Watch your language," I replied sternly. "Using the right language is very important when dealing with the public. People will judge you by the way you speak. This business is all about impressions and image. There is a difference. A saloon is a bar. A hairdresser works in a hairdressing salon in English, and a *salon de coiffure* in French."

"You teach languages too?" asked Angie with a smirk.

The rest of the class laughed, and judging from the look on her face, Angie had enjoyed the attention.

I thought the exchange had gone far enough. "Angie, you have two choices. Wear the uniform and stay in this class, or don't wear the uniform and go back home."

Angie wasn't ready to give in. "It's bullshit! This is a pretend place with pretend clients," she said loudly, pointing to the mannequins on the counter. "Pretend I'm wearing it."

Maybe this kid is much smarter than she looks, I had thought, and then wondered whether Angie also saw me as a pretend teacher in a pretend school.

16. FARE L'AMORE

SEAN AND J.P. LEAVE FOR the afternoon and will be out for dinner for an official party event, after which J.P. will drive back to Ottawa. I tidy up the kitchen and get ready to pick up Mother in Notre Dame de Grace.

Since I've known Sean, I've seen less and less of my friends from the village. It's not a surprise to me that Lucia's brother, Alfonso, is said to be associated with some shady characters through his business and in-laws. But I'm sure that the mafia association is highly overestimated and if there's any connection at all, it stops with him. The media suggestion that Lucia's immediate family is also directly involved with organized crime is hard to swallow. I can't picture Comare Rosaria in the company of such people, any more than I can imagine my own mother cooking for known criminals.

That the private problems between Lucia and her husband are receiving some attention is a result of the media's penchant for sensationalizing anything remotely associated with Jack Russo, a good-looking gangster in his fifties. He's reputed to be the head of the Montreal Mafia. Still, Russo, of Calabrian origin, has been immune to prosecution, despite the questionable dealings attributed to him.

Mother lives with my older brother Luigi, his wife Rita, and their baby Teresa, named after my mother. It's the accepted norm in Calabrian families for a widowed mother to live with a married son. Mother looks after the baby, and runs the household. My brother had been attracted by the older established neighborhood of Notre Dame de Grace, or NDG as it is popularly known, after another *paesano* from our village Gaetano, and his wife, Tina, bought a duplex there. Luckily, there's no traffic on the Decarie Expressway, and the drive is quick. The day has been sunny but cool, the days getting shorter. Mother is waiting for me at the door of my brother's modest bungalow on Trenholme Street, wearing the sombre face she reserves for funerals and hospital visits. She's bundled up in her fall, navy-blue coat, and in the paisley blue scarf that I have matched for her.

Before getting into the car, Mother asks, "*Mangiasti?*" as if to suggest that we'd go inside in case I haven't yet eaten.

I drive a block from my brother's home to pick up Tina too.

In the car, driving east toward the hospital, Mother keeps going on and on about her friend, Comare Rosaria. I remind her that it's Rosaria's daughter, Lucia, who has been beaten unconscious.

Rosaria and my mother call one other *comare* because sometime in their shared village past, someone in each family had served as godmother to the other. I never could keep track of all the *comare* relationships; they could go back a generation or two. The two women are not related by blood, but the fact that they had shared part of the house in Piazza Don Carlo is a kind of unspoken tie. Both their husbands were musicians in the village band. I often heard about how the two men used to gather with their friends in the evenings and take turns serenading the girls. This tradition of serenading disappeared after the war. Maybe it was because most of the young men were away so much of the time. As I drive the long stretch of Jean-Talon Street, I listen to Mother and Tina recount how the fortunes of Rosaria's family changed after the war.

"Comare Rosaria was never fortunate," is how Mother puts it.

Rosaria's family had lost favour with her wealthier cousin Don Cesare, heir to Don Carlo's title, the richest and most influential man in our village, because her husband, Don Mario, had been a Fascist, while Don Cesare was a staunch Christian Democrat. During the Fascist heydays, Don Mario had worked at City Hall and had supervised his wife's olive groves, which provided them with an income, but political fortunes changed after the war. He suffered a wound that left the right side of his body paralyzed. He could still move around the town but was unable to trek to the countryside by the river to oversee the harvesting of olives. Every year, groups of women from the countryside and from the village were hired to pick the olives off the tree, one by one. It was back-breaking work. In payment, they received their yearly provision of the emerald-coloured olive oil.

"After Compare Mario returned from the war, all he could do was walk with a cane and talk politics," Mother says. "Poor Comare Rosaria. She couldn't keep up, and her children were not much help."

The children had been spoiled, Mother claimed. After Don Mario's incapacitation, Alfonso had tried to take over the family farms, but he wasn't cut out for the task. Apart from the difficulty of handling so much land, times were changing. Getting women to pick olives had become increasingly difficult. The peasants were emigrating to the U.S., Canada, Argentina, and Australia. Those who couldn't emigrate left to find work in the northern Italian cities. Most of those who stayed behind had relatives who sent money orders in each letter—not huge amounts, but enough for them to buy their own olive oil in the grocery stores. The younger girls stopped going to the country altogether. Like most of the other young men, Comare Rosaria's youngest son, Pietro, had tried going to Milan to work, but he came back after only two weeks and became a joke around town. He seemed at a loss to explain why he hadn't been able to get used to the life of a labourer in the big city. He simply said: "Come lunch, who would cook my *pastasciutta*?"

In the early 1950s, when most other families were hoping to find a way out of the village, Lucia's family had no relatives overseas to sponsor them. Comare Rosaria faced a despondent husband, two ineffective and unemployed sons, and Lucia, who spent her days on her balcony embroidering her trousseau and making eyes with Don Cesare's nephew, Totu.

"Once girls started wearing high heels and nylon stockings," Mother says, "who would pick olives? It still hurts me to think of those beautiful olives rotting on the ground."

Outside the hospital, we run into Filomena, a distant cousin of Lucia's husband, Pasquale. She confides that Pasquale, ten years older than Lucia, has been very jealous. Filomena criticizes Lucia's move to the city to be with her daughter against her husband's wishes.

"Surely she should have known her husband by now," Filomena says in the elevator. "Could she not have made other arrangements?"

The corridor near Lucia's room is packed with family and close friends. Her older brother, Alfonso, is there, greeting people, repeating the story that everyone has already heard. He had met his sister and her husband at their mother's home to help them make peace. Everything seemed to be going well. He left the kitchen to make a phone call. When he returned, Lucia was unconscious on the floor, Pasquale gone.

The hospital staff at the Jean-Talon Hospital is used to Italians filling up patients' rooms during visiting hours. They allow only two visitors at a time. When our turn comes, Mother and I walk into the room timidly. Lucia lies unconscious on the bed, connected to tubes and a catheter, her face half-covered by a respirator mask, visibly swollen. Short wisps of tinted hair with grown-out roots spread out on the white pillow, between the head bandages, like reddish brown spiders with grey dots. I didn't expect to see a stranger, even though I hadn't seen Lucia in years. What had happened to the spirited woman with long, dark curly hair? I looked for the beauty mark below her lip, half hidden by a plastic tube.

Her mother sits next to her bed, oblivious of the people coming and going. She moves her head back and forth, grieving for her daughter, in the old Calabrian custom, wailing in a singsong trance. *Oh Lucia, Lucia mia ... cchi te capitau a ttie ... Oh Lucia, Lucia mia....*

It would be considered impolite to pay our respects and leave. We make our way to a small waiting area at the end of the corridor. Only the women sit there. The men walk around the corridors or look for a place to smoke. If they sit with the women, they might have to talk about what brought them here.

The women smile warmly at Mother; she is well-liked and respected by all of our *paesani*. She's especially admired for having raised two children by herself, her husband having died young. In their eyes, our family has done very well for itself, except maybe for the fact that I am still unmarried. My living arrangement with Sean has never been made very clear to them.

The women are Lucia's age, maybe only a decade or so older than me, but they look and carry themselves like middle-aged matrons. These are the women who scamper out of buses on their way home from factories around Chabanel Street. In drab clothes, and with no hint of make-up, nondescript, invisible, they rush home concerned about the evening meal, the washing, the ironing, the preparing of lunches for the next day. This routine is rarely broken for the sake of a leisurely outing intended solely for their own enjoyment.

These were once the young women in Mulirena I used to meet in the evenings when I went out for a stroll with the girls in my neighbourhood: Lucia, Tina, and Aurora. With the pretense of getting fresh water at the communal fountain, the Funtanella, they also exchanged glances and love notes with their sweethearts. They were as preoccupied by their appearances and boyfriends as young women everywhere.

Sitting across from me is Rosalba. Her family had lived next to the church. Rosalba had looked after the kindergarten kids, and had been my Catholic Action group leader. She had also played the mother in a play about Saint Bernadette; I had been the saint; Aurora, the Virgin Mary.

I remember these women sitting on their balconies, embroidering sheets and pillowcases with delicate little flowers, hearts, and butterflies. They once daydreamed of sharing those worked linens with a soulmate. How many have found one? Lucia certainly hasn't. Now in their early forties, they have become efficient, selfless, almost asexual housekeepers, whose personal aspirations and desires are never worth talking about—silly, insignificant nonsense next to the needs of their families.

Usually talkative and jovial, Tina comes to sit next to me, her eyes moist. A whispered conversation begins.

"She might be in a coma for a long time, if ever she'll come out of it," Tina says, wiping her eyes with a tissue.

"*Madonna mia*! Who would have believed it?"

"When she was young, in Mulirena, she could have made love to anyone she wanted," says Tina. "Making love for us didn't mean what it means for us here, Cathy."

The women all laugh. "In Mulirena, we made love without touching each other," says Rosalba.

I remembered well the hours that young men spent beneath a girl's window, speaking to each other in facial gestures. When messages had to be sent, they pitched notes to each other. This was how couples "made love," or what in North America is called "courting." No wonder that living together before marriage is still an unthinkable concept for these women.

A lull falls over the waiting room, until Rosalba asks, "I hear the girl has given her mother a lot of trouble. She takes after her father's race." Then she asks Tina, "Did she ever tell you anything bad about him?"

"What could she say? We all know what our men are like," Tina answers.

"One has to find a way with them," Filomena says, and then goes to join her husband in the corridor.

"Did she get offended?" Tina asks. "Look at what Lucia got compared to what she could have had, all because of the malicious tongues in the village."

No one has mentioned Totu's name, but we all know what Tina refers to.

"I saw the journalist at the travel agency this summer," Tina says. "The woman he had been living with left him, he told me."

I shiver, involuntarily. I remember the day on the ship when Lucia demanded I never mention Totu's name again. By flippantly nicknamimg him "the journalist" since his arrival to Montreal, my *paesani* have unintentionally bestowed on Totu a new identity that has somehow erased his old one from my mind.

"He hasn't lasted long with anyone," Rosalba adds. "He and Lucia made love for a long time,"

"He practically wore out my door, leaning against it for so long," Tina says. "When I looked out from my window, I was able to know what time it was by his long shadow on the pavement. Piazza Don Carlo was never the same after they broke up."

"But did he leave her or was it the other way around?" Rosalba asks. "I never really understood what happened."

"Things got tangled up," Mother says. "She had no choice but to leave. They just weren't destined."

"And Aurora," Rosalba says. "The poor girl. All the things they said about her. She had to run away to Argentina to get away from all the talk. We haven't heard much about her."

"It's as if people disappear after they go to Argentina," Tina says. "We were all in such a rush to leave. What did we think we would find?"

"We found the Superstyle factory," Rosalba says laughing. "Remember the factory, Cathy? You worked there too, one summer."

"How can I forget?" I reply. "I cut threads at the finishing table with a bunch of Syrian ladies ... for fifty cents an hour."

"They didn't pay much, but the work was light."

"Those were other times," Mother sighs. "We had no choice."

"*Grazie a Dio*, things have changed now," says Rosalba. "I'm going to be quitting soon too. There aren't as many Italians left in the factories anymore, you know. They're full of black people now. They come from Haiti, from ... from ... I don't know where they're all coming from, but they're coming in herds."

Mother replies, "The world is a wheel, *gira e rigira*."

"*Se, se,* Teré, you're right.... They have to eat too." The women laugh and then resume their whispering. The sound of Comare Rosaria's wailing can be heard coming from the patient's room. I close my eyes and remember Lucia as a young woman, exchanging furtive glances with Totu from her balcony. He always tapped me on the cheek as he passed by my doorstep where I use to sit, play, and watch.

We remain silent in the waiting room, each absorbed by our own thoughts, until Mother suggests it's time to leave. Outside the hospital, I'm in a daze, confused as I try to remember where I have parked the car. We walk a block on Jean Talon Street toward the Italian church—the hub of the Italian community in this part of town. Next to the bakery, florist, and travel agency there's a café where a group of men, some of whom were at the hospital, are sitting, smoking and gesticulating animatedly.

"Eh, look who's here," Tina says.

A tall slim man with a slight limp gets up from his chair. I haven't spoken to him in ages.

"Let's cross the street. I don't feel like talking," I say. From the corner of my eye, I get a glimpse of his silhouette looking our way, waving a hand at us. Mother and Tina wave back. I pretend not to see him and start the car.

17. THE JOURNALIST

Lucia's call at the end of June and then Angie's appearance in my class in September had already disturbed the still waters of memory held back by years of willful forgetfulness. The visit to the hospital and then the wave of the hand brought up undercurrents of bitterness that unresolved resentment often breeds.

When I get home from the hospital, Sean is still out and I eat alone. I have no one to talk to about the day's events. But what would Sean understand about centuries-old courtship rituals, codes of conduct, sense of family obligations that resurfaced for me at the sight of Lucia in her comatose state? He would probably make some sarcastic remark about love and marriage, Calabrian style.

I mindlessly watch the late evening news until a picture of Lucia's husband appears on the screen and a reporter gives an account of the police investigation on his disappearance. Pictures of the café torched on the same day as Lucia's beating appear soon after. A writer of a book on Montreal crime offers his views on the battle of control between Mafia families. He predicts that more action is to be expected in the next weeks. Then a long report follows on the investigation of the cost overruns in the construction of the Olympic Stadium. The PQ government has promised that it will open a commission to investigate the bidding process in the awarding of public contracts, and further discredit the Liberals who had been plagued by scandals in the years leading to their defeat by the separatists.

These stories, placed one after the other, give the impression that they are somehow connected. I prepare for bed and look for something to read in the den.

The stash of old books I brought from Italy still hold the faint smell of Mulirena and that other world that refuses to be relegated to a folkoric village past to be recounted in amusing anecdotes, but has claimed a presence to be reckoned with. Seeing Lucia has left me with the disconcerting feeling that her life, having taken such an ugly turn, had continued, after the landing, thornier and more complex than we had anticipated.

The boat journey itself had been very confusing for me, a young girl barely out of childhood, immersed as I was in the story of one chaste Lucia while following another one, a flirt, around the ship. I tried recreating that trip once to show to my so-called friend from Mulirena, "the journalist," when he first arrived in Montreal.

He was an academic, highly educated in Italian literary criticism. He had studied and worked in Rome for years as a journalist before his move to Montreal, so it was not surprising when he found similar work in this city. Looking back, I smile as I realize how brash and naïve I had been to bring him my juvenile writing. He claimed to have lost my story before even reading it, and thus never commented on it.

The lady he married, Chantale, was a Quebec poet and a staunch sovereignist, and he quickly prescribed to the same ideology. For a while, he wrote for a local Italian paper, and contributed a column in the French paper *La Presse* under the name Antoine, French for his real name, Antonio. He still uses that name. Neither his marriage to Chantale nor his collaboration with the Italian paper lasted long. After only a couple of years, he separated from both to work independently. He started his own community magazine, *Arte&Cultura*, in which he criticizes and lampoons Italian Canadian community leaders, and now and then still contributes articles to the mainstream French papers on diversity, ethnicity, identity politics, and the new buzz concept, multiculturalism. He shares an office with a travel agency near the Italian church, and he supplements his income by moonlighting for the agency.

I don't subscribe to his magazine, but I usually read it at my mother's. His column on art and culture in the city is mainly focused on literary criticism of Italian and Quebecois writers. He's especially harsh on the mainstream Canadian literary establishment as well as local Italian Canadian writers, often ridiculing them. In an article on minority writing he wrote a year or so ago, he pontificated, "The immigrant experience story has been done *ad nauseum*. It's time we transcend the voyage and move on to other themes."

I was incensed by this dismissal. I had always hoped to someday resume writing, but have I waited too long to write my story? On impulse, I decided to start a conversation with the journalist under my own pseudonym:

Dear Antoine,

What are we supposed to do, hide our writing just because others have written about the same topic before us? And why does everything we write have to be labelled immigrant writing? Many other peoples' stories I've read deal with some form of voyage or passage, and every story is different even if the theme is the same. I've lived in this country three times longer than in Italy. I don't feel like an immigrant anymore.
Rina

Dear Rina,

It's because we live in multicultural heaven. If your name is Italian and your writing has a departure, a voyage, and a landing, it's going to be labelled an immigrant story, whether you like it or not. The industry, especially academia, thrives on classifications. They classify us in order to keep us in our places.

As representatives of cultural communities, we jumped onto the multiculturalism bandwagon too readily, I believe. Multiculturalism started off as a political ploy to defuse separatism in Quebec while appeasing us "others." We have become pawns in the tug-of-war between the two founding nations, and by willingly playing their games, and fitting into the peg they have created for us, we're unwittingly creating a no man's land, a third solitude for our artists.

That answer flustered me. Why does he have to politicize everything? I thought. No wonder he had so little concern for my writing. But how could I possibly write about Lucia and my own experiences without focusing on *our* departure, *our* crossing, and *our* landing?

Whenever I've thought of the lost manuscript, I've felt nauseous, as though something that might still be alive is buried somewhere. Yet, until now, I never gave Lucia's new life any thought, as if her story had ended rather than started in Halifax.

"They just weren't destined," my mother said at the hospital.

I wonder if Lucia's blow to the head was a consequence of having resisted the force of her destiny, or of having succumbed to it in resignation. Is one's destiny worth fighting?

18. SEAN AND I

TIRED, I FINALLY GO TO BED, and still don't fall asleep. I've often felt a sense of strangeness in lying in my parents' bed, next to Sean. This evening I try to understand the feeling. What forces of destiny conspired to bring us together? I, a village girl from the mountains of Calabria; Sean, blond, three years my junior, a man of small stature, who had been raised in Winnipeg. What an unlikely couple we make!

I would never have thought of Sean as a possible husband or even as a casual date if I had met him outside of WLHS. Physically, Sean is not my type. Throughout my adolescence, I had daydreamed about the tall, dark, and enigmatic men who were the staple of the Italian *fotoromanzi* I collected. When I first read *Wuthering Heights* in high school, I felt captivated by the presence of the shadowy Heathcliff, and I fantasized about love affairs that swept me up, above the trivial cares of life. Images of the windswept English moors, echoing with the calls of the tormented lovers, merged with remembered stories about ruthless brigands hiding in the Calabrian hills, and about the women who followed them, leaving everything behind for the love of their lives. What would it be like to feel the kind of passion that outweighed the comfort of home, the security of family?

When Sean and I first became friendly, he seemed surprised that I was not seeing anyone. "A nice Italian girl like you! I'd think you'd be hooked up by now."

"What makes you think that all Italian girls are just looking to get hooked up?"

"I must admit that I haven't known many Italian girls. I apologize for the cliché," he said, looking contrite and uncomfortable.

In truth, since I had turned twenty, there hadn't been very many knocks on my door or calls for dates. And yet I had been at my prime. I had lost the extra weight that had plagued me in my early teens. I was at my slimmest when I first met Sean—a perfect size eight—what the fashion industry labels as petite, in height, that is. My hips and thighs could use a taller frame, but I can camouflage them with the proper clothes. Thanks to my hairdressing training, I know how to minimize my defects by maximizing my good points. I never wear jeans or flat-heeled shoes. I keep my hair shining and my face well made-up, with the hope that my less than perfect features won't be too noticeable.

From the age of fifteen until my early twenties, my *paesani* had considered me a good catch; I had been courted by a string of young men. I had turned them all down. "You never get attached to anyone," my mother complained.

She had no other way of explaining my refusal to have anything to do with the succession of serious young men with yearning eyes and tender hearts who wanted to do things properly, with the respect due such a well-regarded family. They followed customs, and sent relatives to our house as go-betweens, making it clear that marriage was their only goal.

"They put the cart before the horse," I complained to Mother, who didn't understand what the problem was.

"Isn't it better to deal with someone who is serious about marriage, and not only thinking of joking around?" she'd say.

"What if I don't like him? How can I pull back after the whole family has been involved?" I refused every offer. I especially spurned men who seemed to have all the right qualities for good potential husbands: I could see my future too perfectly mapped out in their eyes. What would they make of my quirks and whims? I might as well have taken my childhood dreams, sealed them in the green trunk we had brought with us, and dropped it into the ocean.

Word got around that I was difficult, and after a while no one approached the family.

There is no corresponding word in Italian for dating, a North American institution I missed out on as a teen. In high school, I hadn't been allowed to go to school dances, let alone be picked up at home by a boy to go out for the evening.

At twenty-five, I felt awkward around men, especially those to whom I felt most attracted. I often asked myself what a girl in a large city needed to do to meet an interesting man, short of advertising oneself in the classifieds or, worse still, parading one's wares in the meat markets of discos and bars. Diane Keaton in *Looking for Mr. Goodbar* confirmed my distaste for the smoky nightclub scene.

Sean's courtship turned out to be anything but conventional. We were both swept up by the enthusiasm of our first teaching job at WLHS. Ours was a young staff and the school offered such a variety of activities for teachers as well as students that I felt like the high school teen I had never had the chance to be. After the first month, Sean and a group of senior students recruited me to help out in the production of the musical, *My Fair Lady*. It didn't take much effort to convince me to coordinate it, especially since I saw it as a project tailor-made for my hairdressing class to practice elaborate period hairstyles.

Because I had a car and Sean didn't, I found myself doing most of the tedious work of driving around the city, finding and then carting furniture for props for the stage sets. After the Christmas holidays, the two of us spent more and more time together after school, and Sean often ended up having dinner at my house. He lived with two roommates in a basement apartment in the McGill ghetto, and ate out most evenings.

I lived with my mother in the same apartment I live in now.
Mother tried hard to get used to the idea of me bringing home a male friend. "He's just a friend," she would tell her relatives with a shrug, "Do you understand anything?"

One Sunday, Sean and I spent the afternoon at his place, finalizing the odds and ends of the show that would be taking place the following Saturday. His two roommates were out, and, for once, his apartment was quiet. It was a warm day. I wore a summer T-shirt and a long, loose gauze skirt. We had snacked on cheese and bread, and drank a bottle of red wine, which made me feel sleepy. I wasn't accustomed to drinking more than half a glass. I lay down on Sean's bed to rest before going home.

Sean put on a Leonard Cohen album, and lay next to me. I kept my eyes closed. The whispery monotone of the poet's voice and melancholic tone of the song about Suzanne taking him down to the river had me practically dozing, when Sean turned around and put his face on my chest. I felt a sudden rush to embrace him, but all I could do was stroke his hair. He caressed my breasts, and I was overwhelmed by the desire to offer them to him. I waited for him to lift the T-shirt, remove one breast from the bra cup and kiss it greedily. His other hand moved up my bare legs. I hadn't expected anything to happen, but it felt natural, and I didn't object. There was no piercing pain, no outbursts of joy, only a mellow, drowsy sensation of pleasure. It was as if I had fallen asleep on the beach at the end of a sun-drenched day, lulled by the repetitive sounds of the rise and fall of the ocean, then jolted slightly by the soft shifting of the wet sand.

"You're soft and cuddly," Sean said, snuggling against my back. Maybe it was the warmth from the red wine; my cheeks felt flushed, as if caressed by the setting sun.

During the next week, the details of the last-minute preparation for the production took over all our energies and conversations. The show was a great success. Sean welcomed all the special guests, including J.P., who because of his friendship with Sean, had come as a representative of the local MP, Alex Di Principe.

In June, Sean and I attended the school's first graduation dance as a couple. I, who had never attended a prom dance before, was as excited about it as my sixteen-year-old students. By the end of summer the two of us were spending our free time together, our relationship smoothly and effortlessly slipping from being colleagues to friends to lovers. The differences in our upbringing and lifestyle didn't seem to matter. When I was with Sean, I was so engrossed with the present that, for once, my past was forgotten. When I asked Sean how he felt about being with someone of a different culture, he quoted John Lennon. We should imagine ourselves to be people "with no country and no religion too ... living for today."

Sean never spoke much about his family, except to tell me that his mother had left home when he was three. He was raised by his father, who remarried soon after his mother's departure. While in high school, Sean was shifted to his paternal grandparents' home because he didn't get along with his stepmother. After high school, he left Winnipeg for Saskatoon, and moved east. He lived in Toronto, then Ottawa. There, he met J.P., obtained a degree in English Literature, and started a Master's Program in Philosophy. He moved to Montreal and, through J.P.'s connections, got a teaching job at WLHS. His birth mother had reconnected with him; he spoke to her on the phone from time to time. He seemed to hold no rancour toward her. I especially liked that Sean's mood was always even. No heavy, dark clouds rested over his head. Around him, I felt weightless.

By the start of the new school year, Sean and I had started talking about getting married the following summer. Sean didn't believe in the conventional rites of engagement and marriage, especially as practised by my Italian friends. We spoke of a possible marriage as one of the many things we would do together, much like travelling to Europe on a Eurail pass, staying in youth hostels, or backpacking and camping our way across Canada.

The summer passed. Our marriage and travelling plans were put on hold. Sean became preoccupied with his dwindling career prospects in education. At J.P.'s insistence, he joined the youth wing of the Liberal party. I registered at Concordia University to continue my studies in Italian literature that I had started years before. Sean often accompanied me to family gatherings, but the topic of marriage was only raised by my relatives.

"They're in no rush," Mother said to them. "They want to finish their studies."

My relatives have pampered Sean. He has enjoyed their attention, their sharing of traditional foods, and especially watching my uncles make wine in the fall and sausages in the winter. But he's not as keen to fulfill all the *doveri*—the family obligations—that are part and parcel of belonging to a close-knit Italian family. My family excuses Sean for his flightiness with the usual, "He's English."

Another summer came and went. Sean spent more and more time volunteering for Di Principe's riding associations. When J.P. was promoted to work in Ottawa as a party strategist, Sean had been eased into J.P.'s position as Principe's aide, and left WLHS.

That year, one day in late October, Tina's husband, Gaetano, offered me some books. Gaetano lived on the lower floor of a duplex on Trenholme Street in NDG. The top floor had been occupied by a professor from Loyola College, who disappeared without notice, and with three months' rent unpaid. He left behind his worn-out furniture and, in his living room, wall-to-wall shelves of books on theology, philosophy, literature, history, psychology, and other scholarly subjects that Sean found impressive. Sean and I fell in love with the homey place and with the street, which, at that time of year, was resplendent with fall foliage.

"Take whatever you want," Gaetano told me. "What you don't want, I'll put into the garbage. The whole place smells, and I'll have to fumigate it before putting it up for rent."

"Don't throw anything out," I said. "I'll take all the books." That evening we talked about the value of the books and of the semi-antique furniture.

"I'd love to live in that duplex," Sean said. "Maybe we can rent it and just move in, as is."

"We move in?" I asked, incredulous that he still hadn't understood the impossibility for an Italian girl like me of living with a man without being married.

"Why not? It's too good an opportunity to let slip. I'm spending less and less time in my apartment anyway. Why pay the extra rent?"

"Because I don't think it would go over well with my mother," I said, and then added, as an afterthought: "What happened to our marriage plans?"

"How will a church ceremony and a piece of paper change how we feel about each other? Living together is commitment enough."

I regretted having asked the question. I felt as if I was proposing to him. If it weren't for my family, I would have liked living with him for a while.

As I had expected, both Mother and Luigi thought I had lost my mind to even consider it. "Are you crazy?" Mother said. "We're not English. Maybe it's okay for him, but not for us. If he doesn't want to get married, tell him to find someone else to live with him."

"He's afraid of the commitment. It's understandable. Look at his family history," Luigi said, and tried to convince me to, at least, compromise with a civil wedding. "Just for the sake of the family and the *paesani*. You know how they'll talk."

"I don't care about the *paesani*," I insisted.

"Don't be so hardheaded and selfish," Luigi told me. "Think of Mother and what it will do to her."

Mother had already accepted the fact that Sean and I wouldn't marry in a Catholic church. Sean is a non-practicing Anglican, and I'm a Catholic, who only attends Mass at Christmas and Easter. In practical and philosophical terms, our different religions didn't pose a problem. Sean agreed that, on principle, a civil wedding would be fair ... when the time was right.

Once the topic of moving in before marriage was brought to the table, it didn't seem like such a taboo subject anymore. I had grown to passionately dislike the elaborate and tacky Italian weddings that I was forced to attend with my family. For once I took a firm stand with Mother. I went to Gaetano with a month's rent and offered to rent the upper duplex.

He seemed embarrassed by the proposition and said he had already offered the unit to a friend from work and couldn't break his word. He offered me the furniture and the books. I suspected that my mother had warned Gaetano of my intentions. Upset at both Gaetano and Mother, I started looking for other available apartments in NDG.

Meanwhile Mother was spending more and more time at Luigi's home. She took care of the baby born the previous spring, so that my sister-in-law could return to her job. Luigi convinced our mother to move in with them. By the end of October, I found myself living on my own without actually having to move out. Mother took my single bed and left her bedroom set behind since it was too large for her new room. After that, Sean started spending some evenings at the apartment and little by little moved in his few possessions. But he also spent time in Ottawa, and with his old friends at the McGill ghetto, so that it still wasn't clear where he actually lived.

My apartment in the east end of the city doesn't have the same appeal to Sean as the duplex in NDG, but he pays half the rent and uses it whenever it's convenient. The only furniture we bought together is a set of bookshelves, with which we lined the room that had been my bedroom, and a sofa-bed for visitors, mostly for J.P., turning that room into a study/den.

"I've never liked cheesy Italian weddings," I explain to my friends at school. "The hall, the photographers, the bridesmaids, I never wanted all of that. Eventually we'll have a simple civil ceremony with a few close friends."

"We'll get married when Sean is more settled in his new job," I told my mother.

As far as the *paesani* are concerned, I pretend I'm living alone, and that Sean is only a frequent visitor. The chances of any of them visiting me late at night are slim. Though this duplicity about our living situation had, at first, seemed humourous to Sean and me, it makes me stumble whenever I'm asked about my marital status. With my friends and family, I act as if the marriage date is unimportant to me, but I do want to marry Sean and have a family of my own before it's too late. I'm grateful, though, that, at least, I didn't have to move my things out of the house against my mother's wishes, and my reputation with the *paesani,* at least on the surface, remains intact.

Sean and I joked about this outcome. "In the logic of the Calabrian love story," he said, "this is the most romantic scenario you could have wished for."

19. SUNDAY LUNCH

I CAN HARDLY MOVE, sitting in bed with Sean, the thick weekend paper on my lap, and his papers and books strewn all over the bedspread. On his side, Sean has propped his philosophy textbook, from which he's taking notes, against my thigh. Now and then, he refers to other books piled between us. On the bed are a number of books on Jung he uses to research his topic, "*Synchronicity-Integration, Wholeness and the Self.*"

I have taken to reading the book reviews every week. Sometimes I'll even go out and buy one of the featured books.

"You're taking up all the space," I say, as I try to fold a section of the newspaper.

Sean is immersed in thought and says nothing. He spent Saturday afternoon until late evening at his party headquarters, planning for the next course of action. He fears he'll have to suspend work on his thesis once a by-election is called.

I put the paper down and leaf through *The Secret of the Golden Flower: A Chinese Book of Life,* and become particularly intrigued by drawings of a mandala painting by Jung with his own words under the picture: "Only gradually did I discover what the mandala really is: 'Formation, Transformation, Eternal Mind's eternal recreation.' And that is the self, the wholeness of the personality, which if all goes well, is harmonious, but which cannot tolerate self-deceptions." I'm hypnotized by the bursts of shapes and motifs and the seemingly infinite variety of possibilities within the frame.

As I shift my body, his philosophy textbook closes. "Sorry," I say. "We either get a queen-size bed, or you do your studying from a desk."

"Aren't you going to your mother's for lunch?" he asks.

"I guess I better get going," I say. Then, as I walk toward the dresser, I add: "Can we reconsider the furniture we saw at the Danish House? This mirror really doesn't go with this set."

"I thought the set had sentimental value to you. Just return the mirror."

"I like the mirror."

"Then maybe all you need is a re-staining to salvage the furniture."

I had never considered that option. For years, Mother had cleaned and rubbed the furniture every Saturday morning with a lemon-scented polish. The original color may have suffered from this over-diligent use of furniture wax. The set still looks modern with its play of basic rectangles in birch veneer. Short, slanted, spindly legs, painted black, give the utilitarian dressers a dainty and precarious appearance. What an odd choice, I think, for a man of my father's temperament to make. I imagine my stockily-built father, wearing his bricklayer clothes, with specks of white cement in his hair and on his hands, alone at Meubles Legaré on St. Hubert Street, selecting beds, tables, and frilly curtains for over the kitchen sink.

"Are you coming for lunch?"

"What's the story about your friend's husband and her brother Alfonso being connected to the mob?" he asks.

"How would I know?" I reply. "It's a domestic matter. Why can't people just focus on that?"

"J.P. is concerned. It seems that both her husband and brother have ties to some underworld figures ... including Jack Russo."

Jack Russo's name has come up a number of times in regard to rumours of collusion in the awarding of important construction contracts.

"And why J.P.'s sudden concern about my family's friends?"

"It's not official, yet, so you can't talk about it, but Di Principe's old riding is definitely open for grabs."

"Does that mean you'll run?" I ask.

"I have to prepare myself for the eventuality of running ... and rounding up some supporters," he says. "I'm planning on entering the race in the very riding this incident happened. I'll be scrutinized like crazy. It doesn't take much for the media to make connections."

"Connections with whom?"

"Well, in politics we have to be very cautious. I wouldn't want you and your family to be associated with this woman's family and their problems. They're deeply involved in the construction business, and in Laval, of all places, where City Hall is known to be a den of corruption. J.P. plans on ordering ten thousand brochures with your family's picture on them."

I put my hands up in exasperation. "J.P. should wait until I speak to my family about the picture."

"I thought you already had."

"Well, I haven't. I just can't believe what you're saying after all the years you've known my family. What does *my* family have to do with what happened? We're not even related to that family, and even if we were, would we be automatically held responsible for the actions of Alfonso's wife's family? I don't even know who they are, for Christ's sake ... never even met them.... Okay, I saw them at Alfonso's wedding, but never even spoke to them. Are we suspects simply because we're from the same village or because we're Italian? Tell J.P. he's watched *The Godfather* too many times."

"No need to get worked up, Cat."

"I only get worked up because we are dealing with a family tragedy here, and you only see these people as stock mob characters. You're doing what you've always objected to, judging people without knowing anything about them ... only by their affiliations or their nationality. You've always disapproved of stereotyping. Anyway, if J.P. isn't comfortable being seen in this house, he'll do me a favour by staying away."

"J.P. is going out of his way to get me nominated. It could be something good for me ... for us. I'm just repeating what I heard. And, actually, he's only reacting to all the coverage on *Allô Police*."

"Well, if you believe *Allô Police*, Italians are always settling accounts. We're either the best or the worst accountants around. As if other people's murders are not about settling of accounts," I conclude.

Sean doesn't respond. I start getting dressed and change subject, "It's funny how stories continue in real life without us noticing," I say.

"What stories?" Sean asks.

"I'm thinking of my *paesana*, Lucia, and what has happened to her. Twenty years ago, she was a young girl married to a man she had never met. Because of gossip and politics, she left her boyfriend of many years to come here. I thought that was a story in and of itself."

"Well ... wasn't it?"

"Yes, but what I'm trying to say is that, once a story is written, you'd think that would be it ... the end of the story, right? I never gave the characters another thought, as if their lives after the crossing didn't matter. But for twenty years, these people have continued living that story. Now these people make the local news, and it all sounds so banal when we read about it—no hint of how or why it started ... then."

"I really don't know where you're going with this, Cat. Stories are happening all the time."

"I'm thinking of the beginning of this story ... the past ... the village ... the voyage, and how real-life stories never quite end, and until they're written down, it's as if they don't count. They only become stories if they get written down."

"I'm having a hard time following you. You're going around

in circles ... as usual. First of all, stories don't always have to be written. They can also be told orally, or sung, as in ballads. Your story sounds like an Italian opera—husband is jealous, accuses wife of cuckolding him, kills wife, cries, and sometimes kills himself too. Leoncavallo did it in *I Pagliacci*; Shakespeare before him in *Othello*. Here, it's material for a Calabrese soap opera."

"How come it's called a tragedy when Shakespeare does it?"

"Well ... Shakespeare was a genius, that's why. It's not so much the story that's important, but how it's told. One's tragedy can be someone else's melodrama. In any case, Cat, just so you know, this story is not that interesting for the general reader. It's been done a few times before, and the ending is predictable."

"There is no ending yet."

"If you insist."

"And everything's been done before. *Gira e rigira,* we say."

While Sean and most of the city lazes in bed, I force myself to get dressed and drive to my brother's house in NDG for Sunday lunch. When we first started going out together, Sean had been only too happy to join in the tradition, and to eat platefuls of pasta, but he broke the practice when he started spending weekends in Ottawa.

Mother accepts Sean's need to stay home on Sundays in the same manner that she accepts his other reasons for not complying with family customs. "He's English," she explains to herself and to her friends. But Mother would only consider a major snowstorm or an illness to be acceptable reasons for me to stay away from Sunday lunch. She always packs plates of leftover food for me to bring to Sean.

I call my mother by phone every day, but I prefer to talk about anything of importance during these relaxed Sunday lunches, when the topic can be bounced off all the family. I mention the news about Sean running in a by-election and the family picture J.P. wants to use for publicity, but the conversation centres on Angie and Lucia.

"You shouldn't have taken the responsibility of taking someone like her daughter in your class," Mother says

"What do you mean, *like her daughter*? You haven't even met the girl."

"I don't have to meet her. From what I've heard, her own parents have been having problems with her."

"Maybe her parents haven't been much help," my brother says.

"Especially her father," I say.

"Let's not always blame the father.... Maybe we shouldn't talk before we know all the facts," Luigi replies.

"Don't you remember Lucia?" Mother adds. "Her brother had to pull her by the hair more than once before she got married. And remember the voyage? It seemed to last a hundred years because of her."

"Ah, 'the voyage,'" my brother says. "What took you so long to bring it up? We always end up talking about 'the voyage.'"

Mother still speaks about the ocean crossing in terms of both dread and awe.

"If we have to talk about it..." I add, turning toward Mother. "You never got out of bed the whole time. I was the one stuck looking after Lucia, while Luigi played with his friends."

"And I was the one to worry about her," Mother says. "You were too young." Then, she adds, "Have you forgotten how her husband treated your father? And now I have to worry about her daughter?"

"Ma, let bygones be bygones. You worry too much," Luigi says.

"Yes, let me do the worrying this time," I say.

"If her daughter is anything like Lucia, you have reason to worry," she says. "Don't think that Lucia has been a saint."

I look at my brother, exasperated. I want to answer, "And why should she have had to be a saint?" but I say nothing. It would not serve any purpose to try to argue with my mother, or my brother, about these things anymore.

My brother says, "Ma, we were not in the same room with her and her husband when this thing happened, so we can't talk"

She says. "*Il buon giorno si vede dal mattino*—you can tell from the beginning how a story is going to end up."

"Tell me—since you're so good at storytelling—how is this one going to end?" I ask, somewhat amused.

Mother tastes the pasta, brings the pot of boiling water to the sink, and throws it in the strainer before responding: "It's already ended. Her husband was a difficult man ... maybe he was even the devil. But a bad and a good never make something bad happen. It takes two bad people for that. A good wife should know how to keep the peace in a home and talk sense into her husband."

I simply shake my head. A family photograph we took on the last Palm Sunday my father spent in Mulirena has a prominent place on the dining room buffet. Mother points to it. "Your father was as good as a piece of bread, but even he had his moments. He would not have forgiven what they did to him."

"If he hadn't died so soon, he would have had his day. He would have shown them all," Luigi says.

We eat quietly. I think of my father and of his absences from our life. In Italy, he left regularly to work in Milan as a stone mason and only spent a few days with us in the village on special holidays. His returns from Milan were always filled with joy, as he brought candies and small toys to all the children in the neighbourhood. I remembered his jolly face and how his cheeks puffed up as he played the trumpet in the village band.

The photograph was taken on the last summer he spent with us. His usual happy disposition changed whenever he spoke of his impending trip to Canada, as if he was somehow betraying his own country by leaving it. He left because everyone else was doing so, and he had had big dreams.

After lunch, Tina arrives and joins us for coffee. The conversation again turns to Lucia and the village.

"The summer your father left was the last good summer we had," she reminds us.

PART IV
OCTOBER 6-7, 1980

20. THE FINGER-WAVING LESSON

NEWS OF ANGIE'S MOTHER'S BEATING has spread through the school. Suddenly her husband's violent temperament, his disappearance, Lucia's reclusive character, and especially their connection to Jack Russo have become public knowledge. In class, I try to discourage the gossip; theories of what may have happened are too easily thrown about. As usual, Linda and Franca have different views.

"The poor woman looked spaced out when I saw her a month ago," Linda tells the class. "She was shopping with Angie on St. Hubert. Maybe she was really unhappy and just wanted out."

"She's been married for twenty years. Why hasn't she tried to leave him before? I think her husband and brother are mixed up in the Mafia," Franca answers.

Then Maria, one of the shyest students, offers a scoop of her own. Her neighbour, who knows the family, had been at a function at the Casa D'Italia just a week before the beating, and had seen Lucia there, all dressed up like a twenty-year-old, but without her husband.

"My neighbour said it was the first time she'd seen Lucia look so friendly. She always looked lost in her own world, but that time, she was smiling at everyone," Maria says

"See?" Linda responds. "She was probably flirting and having an affair and he found out."

"And he put a contract on her because she knew too much.

You don't fuck around with these people," Franca replied.

Oh, Lucia could be a flirt all right! I remember her black eyes, piercing and direct when she was upset, but coy when she smiled. And smile she did at both Nicodemo and Armando on the ship. Was that her last hurrah before she met her older husband in Montreal, or did she continue betraying him, and with whom?

A few weeks before the assault Lucia had been seen smiling. Now I wish I knew what had made her come out of her "spaced-out" state before she was forced back into sleep.

Her sudden appearance on the community banquet circuit baffles me. Lucia's brother, Alfonso, and his wife, have many connections in the community, and they attend many social functions, but Lucia and her husband have been known as recluses in their Laval home. Why the sudden change in Lucia since moving out of her home, and what made her attend the function? Maria doesn't know what the event was all about. I should try to find out. Was Lucia experiencing an awakening of sorts, the euphoria of a new beginning?

I listen to all the talk with the uneasy feeling that I have been a silent witness to whatever in Lucia's past conspired toward the blow that put her in a coma. As a child, I recorded the events in my life and Lucia's life as quaint customs of village life, as reminders of bygone days, but I had never really stopped to think about how the woman's mind and soul may have been affected by it all.

I prepare a mannequin to give the demonstration on finger waving. I approach the demonstration with apprehension. The hairdressing technique has gone the way of flappers and prohibition, and to justify the tedium of the manual exercises, I have to first persuade students of their purpose and usefulness. Finger waving is the most basic of hairdressing skills, I tell the class, and the first that needs to be mastered before moving on to the newer techniques. To myself, I reflect: untangling the past with a fine-toothed comb can be, in hairstyling as well as in life, a useful exercise when attempting to understand the present.

As for every practical hairdressing lesson, I ask the students to form a semicircle around me. First, I show the photo plates from a *Vanity Fair* magazine I had bought at a flea market. I lecture on how the clothes and short hairstyles of the Roaring Twenties reflected the spirit of merriment and abandon that overtook America during the era of jazz and prohibition. Pictures of speakeasies and women dancing the Charleston in bobbed hair make me remember the stories that my grandfather had told me in Mulirena.

He, like thousands of other southern Italians in the early twentieth century, emigrated to North America to earn some money before returning to the *paese*. He never took to the New World and ran away from it, unable to tolerate the harsh life of the early immigrants, exploited by their own kind, and treated like pariahs by the rest of society. It disgusts me now how the *Godfather's* infamous Don Corleone is mythologized as a hero, especially by young people, even though his empire was built on murder and modelled after the Black Hand, the vicious organization that preyed on the early immigrants and was the precursor of the Mafia in the U.S.

Grandfather had told mother and me more than once, "Good thing you're going to Montreal. New York is a bordello of a place." Judging by the news, it looks as if Montreal is catching up to New York on that count.

The finger-waving technique itself is simple enough to describe to the class. I draw a zigzag pattern on the board, and then shape a semicircle on the mannequin, then another semicircle in the opposite direction creating a ridge in between two valleys. In slow motion I repeat a few times each hand movement necessary to shape another ridge, another valley.

"It looks easy," one student says.

"It is easy. One hand follows the other. Each hand must complement the other."

I then instruct the students to practice on their own mannequin. I walk around and repeat my instructions to each student as I guide their hand and comb movements. Some students pick it up almost instinctively; others are all thumbs, and can't coordinate their two hands to work as one.

I wonder what it is that makes some people find the perfect balance of give and take, pull and push. Looking at the drawing on the board, I wish I had a better trick to help my struggling students—the rows of triangles are too pointy to illustrate the rounded movements of a wave. The zigzag drawing is too simplistic and all wrong. It makes me think of uncertainty, a going forward and retreating without a clear destination ... an impasse, while a wave is all fluidity. My drawing skills are as limited as my verbal ones, and I wish I had a better teaching device to express the beauty of the undulating line, flowing freely into peaks and valleys, harmonious, unbroken, endless.

Some students have difficulty with the exercise and quickly lose patience and become restless. "It's so old fashioned, Miss," they complain. They compare each other's efforts and laugh at the zigzagged clumps of sticky hair on some of the mannequins.

Mr. Champagne walks into the class with the guidance counsellor, Julie. He looks disapprovingly at me while some of the girls, preparing for the lunch break, are putting on their makeup, their combs and wet towels still scattered all over the counter. I try to attract the students' attention and call them to order but with little success. They are unconcerned by the presence of these superiors.

The principal speaks in a strained voice to tell me that Social Services called him. Given the fact that Angie's mother is still hospitalized, they have advised him to keep Angie in school until they can sort things out with the family.

"But," he adds, "We'll have to set some strict ground rules for her, if she is to return."

Then Julie, using the slow, soft voice of those who work in the caring professions, tells me I should work with the support of the Special Ed department in handling Angie.

"Bruce has already offered his help," I say.

Julie then explains not to expect Angie in yet. There's a problem with her living accommodations. She says. "Angie's uncle informed us that his mother and niece would be moving to his house in Laval. The older woman refuses to stay alone in the city after what has happened." At the suggestion of Social Services, Julie is considering finding a foster home to place Angie in, from Monday to Friday, closer to school to make it easier for her to attend classes.

"Oh, I doubt that her family would allow her to stay in a stranger's home," I say.

"Well," says Mr. Champagne, "Attendance is compulsory and lateness will no longer be tolerated."

Julie says she finds it hard communicating with the family. The uncle's English is very weak, and the grandmother doesn't speak it at all. "Cathy, could I ask you to translate for me next time I speak to them?"

"Absolutely. Anytime. Look, this is only a thought..." I add instinctively. "I could probably have Angie stay with me while her mother is at the hospital. I have an apartment not far from the school. I'd drive her to school in the morning."

Both Julie and Mr. Champagne seem startled by my suggestion.

"I have a spare room. My apartment is not far from where Angie lived with her grandmother," I add.

"It's something to consider, but I'll have to clear it with a few people—especially the family," Julie says.

"Oh, I'm sure that the family won't have any problem with it. They know me well."

The principal turns his stare on me, but doesn't say anything as they leave.

Angie's move to Laval comes as a surprise. Angie has never confided in me; our relationship so far has been very formal.

I instruct the students to tidy up before leaving for lunch and call Linda to my desk. I ask her if Angie has spoken to her about her family's situation.

"She's told me that her mother is not all there. I met her once and she looked out of it ... and her Dad's a dick, always out working. Angie is really alone."

"Have you seen her much after school?"

"Not after school, but she likes to hang around with us at recess and lunch. At first we didn't like it, but she's a scream to be with. She's very different outside of class. When she comes back to class, we'll take her to the club to cheer her up."

"What club?"

"You know the club we go to—Bar à Go-Go—on the corner of Bleury and St. Catherine."

"Why there of all places? Isn't that a strip club?" I ask, alarmed.

"Yeah, but it's not what you think. In the afternoons, they give dancing lessons."

"Is that where you've been taking your jazz dancing lessons?"

"Yeah, me and Gina. They give us lessons for free."

"Why would they give you free lessons?"

"They might hire us ... as dancers ... after we graduate."

"Do your parents know you go there?"

"Not really. But it's not a big deal, Miss. In the afternoons, it's a regular bar. Once we even saw Frank Masters there. He knows they give us dancing lessons there."

"Who are 'they'? Who owns that place?"

"Jocelyn is the dance teacher; Charlie is the bouncer and Nico, I think, is the owner."

The name Nico raises my suspicion.

"You mean the wrestler?"

"Yeah, Nico Demon, the wrestler."

My suspicions were correct.

I become more worried as I speak to Linda. The club in question is known to be a hangout for some underworld figures—Jack Russo's hangers on, no doubt—and Nick Demon is the same Nicodemo, who travelled on the Saturnia with us. He developed a wrestling career and a long criminal record after he landed in Halifax.

His picture has appeared more than once in local papers in connection to organized crime in Montreal. I still shudder whenever I see his face. I'll need to keep Angie away from him.

21. THE ULTIMATUM

I SIT IN THE DEN, staring vacuously at the bookshelves. I'm reflecting on my rash offer. Sean won't approve, and how will I explain his presence in the apartment to Angie? With Angie occupying the den, J.P. won't be able to stay overnight on his visits to Montreal. But I want very badly to do something for Lucia—to make up for the times I let her down in the past.

The bookshelves line three walls and contain hundreds of books, which I've arranged by topic: Sean's books on education, literature, and philosophy, my hairdressing textbooks, and other Italian and English books on various subjects. Mostly, though, the shelves are stocked with the old books I inherited from Gaetano. I believe that it's those books that Sean is so fond of that have settled our relationship like nothing else before—or after. But Sean has shown no interest in sharing his knowledge with me, as I had hoped would happen naturally. Since his involvement in politics, the distance between us seems to be widening exponentially.

"Are you meditating?' Sean asks. I hadn't heard him come in.

"Actually, maybe ... we may be having a guest," I answer.

"Is it actually or maybe? What do you mean, Cat?"

I explain to him about the possibility of Angie staying with us for a while.

"You offered her the den without discussing it with me?"

"It will only be for a couple of weeks, until her mother is

out of the hospital. I was wondering if you could stay with one of your friends when she comes."

"Her mother is in a coma, and you have no idea how long it will be. I could stay at a friend's for a day or two, but not for a couple of weeks. You know how I feel about getting involved with this family. I should have been consulted on this."

"You never consult me when J.P. comes over."

"J.P. is like family to me."

"Angie is like family to me."

"You never saw her before this September and she's family? Anyway, J.P. is expecting to stay here after the Thanksgiving weekend, so I hope the den is free by then."

"Thanks for the advance notice. If Angie is still here by then, J.P. will have to go to a hotel. He can afford it."

"And your Mafia-connected student can't?"

"She's a sixteen-year-old girl, and her mother is in a coma and she has no one to talk to ... to take care of her, for crying out loud and..."

"You can't even talk straight, let alone think logically."

"I can't think logically? It's your inconsiderate ... you're so *menefreghista*...." As I try to find the right words in English, I kick the sofa-bed in frustration.

"I'm a what? That's a new one." Sean shakes his head. He walks into the bedroom and, before slamming the door behind him, says, "Remember I pay half the rent for this lousy apartment. I'm entitled to use half the space as I wish."

I pitch one of his books at the door, throw myself on the sofa-bed, and have one of my muffled crying fits before I sit up and try to figure out what is happening between Sean and me.

We started out as colleagues, became friends, and enjoyed a short stint as lovers before assuming the role of playmates. But he quickly lost interest in playing house. We now eat at different times and he's often out of town. Our sex life has diminished to the point that I feel that our relationship has entered a new phase: that of roommates, with very dissimilar housekeeping habits. Tonight we have become two estranged property owners fighting for turf.

"A bad and a good never make something bad happen," my mother would say. I'll never be able to trade subjugation for the sake of keeping peace in the family as Mother's words would suggest, but I must at least try to communicate intelligently to Sean not only my sense of obligation towards Angie, but above all, our obligation to each other. I'll speak to him in the morning when we've both cooled off our anger.

Our spat still lingers in the air as Sean and I sit quietly having breakfast, each of us perusing a section of the *Montreal Star*.

Sean must leave for Ottawa and be there till Sunday to meet with J.P. and his election committee. They must finalize his candidacy for the by-election.

"Did you come up with some names?" Sean asks.

"What names?" I ask puzzled, and then I remember. J.P. has given Sean the responsibility of updating a list of Italian-Canadian community leaders and media personalities, and Sean had asked for my input. "Sorry, but I can't be of much help. I've been away from the community for a while now."

"Don't you have a journalist friend who publishes that left-leaning paper? I heard he's endorsing the conservative candidate," he asks.

"Oh, Antoine? Yes, he sided with the PQ in the referendum."

"Precisely. His PQ cronies are also backing Martillo, that TV announcer. He has the support of the community's literati. Maybe we can work at getting him on our side, being your *paesano*. We should invite him for dinner one evening when J.P. is here."

"Don't count on me for that," I say, "and I wouldn't bet on him helping you out of friendship for me. He doesn't do anything for anyone."

"Sorry I asked for your help," Sean says.

"Sean," I say, "we need to talk about something very important ... about our relationship ... where it's headed."

He flings the paper off the table and gets up, "Right now? Be reasonable. I have a battle on my hands as it is in my campaign against this Martillo. You're asking me to surround myself with the most negative of ethnic images ... whether real or not, and you want to talk about relationships?"

I keep my voice as calm as possible, "I know, it's never a good time to talk about us, but I want to make this very clear before you leave: If my offer to Angie is accepted, I won't go back on my word. We'll simply have to work around it. But most importantly, when you come back on Sunday, I want a clear indication on your part on whether you're ready to commit to me before the craziness of the campaign starts."

"Are you talking marriage? Is this an ultimatum?"

"Call it what you want, but I want a real home, a real companion, and yes, a real marriage, in the true sense of the word. If you're not ready for it, I'll understand and we'll simply part ways." I walk away to go get ready for work. He leaves the apartment without saying goodbye.

22. READING GLASSES

ANGIE WILL BE PLACED IN my care. Julie pops into the classroom before the first period bell to tell me Social Services has approved my proposal and give me Angie's new contact information.

"Who gives a shit?" Angie answers, sounding indifferent and far away, when I call to tell her of the school's decision.

"It's important that you come back to school as soon as possible," I tell her.

The only bit of information that Angie volunteers is that her uncle, Alfonso, has informed the Canadian authorities that Pasquale is not a Canadian citizen. If they find him, they could extradite him back to Italy.

"He's lived here for fifty years, and he never bothered to become a citizen. What does that make me?" Angie asks.

"You were born here," I say, "You're automatically a Canadian citizen."

"Big fucking deal," she snorts. "My mother's in a coma; my father disappeared, and if they find him, they'll send him back to Italy. That makes me a fucking orphan, that's what."

I don't know what to respond. I ask about her mother's condition.

"Her usual happy self ... dead to the world."

People that know Pasquale have said that Angie is her father's daughter. From the few times I saw Pasquale before Angie was born, I don't see any physical resemblance between them except for their wiry, unruly hair. I remember a short man with a bony face, thin lips, and a recessed chin, while Angie's chin line is strong and well-defined, her lips plump and defiant. They do share the same lack of social graces. I remember the telephone conversation I had with Pasquale two weeks ago that left me unsettled for several hours.

After having Angie in my class for a month, it had become obvious to me that the girl was practically illiterate. She couldn't read from the English textbook, nor from the French one that I brought in for her. I felt exasperated, thinking she was being uncooperative.

"I need glasses. I can't see," Angie repeated touching her eyes with her hands.

"The old man doesn't want me to get them. You know how they are, Miss. He thinks I won't find a husband if I wear glasses."

She told me how every effort made by her other school to get her eyes checked had gone unheeded by both her parents. I made arrangements with the school nurse to have Angie's eyes tested.

"You can have them tested, but it doesn't mean I'll get glasses. You don't know my father, *testa dura Calabrese*," Angie said, knocking on her head. Those were the first Italian words I had heard her say.

I had called Lucia, who knew about the problem but somehow didn't seem overly concerned. "I have never seen her open a book, with or without glasses," she said. Then she gave the receiver to her husband

"The problem with Angelina ... it's not the glasses," the father said, talking to me laboriously in Italian rather than in dialect. "Angelina has always been pigheaded and lazy. The glasses are just an excuse."

"But if she can't see, she can't read."

"Can you guarantee me that if she gets glasses she'll start studying?" he asked.

"No, that I cannot guarantee. But I can guarantee that if she doesn't get them, she will never be able to read. Signor Mancuso, Angelina is illiterate!" I was beginning to raise my voice. I felt my face flush with anger. Pasquale half-heartedly agreed to have her eyes tested. To make sure he'd get her glasses, I got Julie, the guidance counselor, involved, who in turn contacted Social Services. At the time, I had been mostly upset at Angie's father, but as I think about it now, Lucia's behaviour was also inexcusable. Where has she been all this time? None of it makes any sense to me. If anything, these people—my people and Angie's people—have the major fault of smothering their children with love. Even when they fail you, you somehow feel obligated toward them and love them back. "What has happened to this family?"

Angie, almost "orphaned," as she herself pointed out, will now, more than ever, need someone to care for her. I think of the irony of labelling someone like Angie "special" and then making her feel like a misfit. Imagine the distortion in the child's mind! Any hint of difference, any little spark that might make her stand out from the bland and the uniform, has been snuffed out of her before it had any chance of shining. Small fires can burn undetected for a long time. Maybe, in Angie's case, it is this spark, repressed for so long, that has turned into a sneer.

I end the telephone conversation with Angie. "Come back to school, Angie, as soon as possible. We miss you."

23. BAD AIR

STEVE, THE UNION REPRESENTATIVE, calls an impromptu staff meeting. Teachers across the province are gearing up for a strike to protest the school boards' plans to set up systems of accountability and teacher evaluation. Instead of a general strike, the different unions are proposing surprise sporadic walkouts in different schools each day. This will create more confusion for the school boards than a one-day protest strike, and will get more frequent news coverage for the teachers.

At the meeting, I sit next to Bruce. He sought me out as he came into the auditorium to ask me about Angie. Bruce has a soft, relaxed manner of speaking. He looks me straight in the eyes with a curious expression when I mention my visit to the hospital.

Steve's voice booms across the room, "Be ready to walk out at any time!" and goes on to explain the system for advising teachers when to walk out. Bruce glances at me sideways, nudges my arm, and reminds me that the deadline for applying for department head is the end of the day. He's heard there's only one other applicant, the electro-technology teacher, Mike, who is very close to Frank.

"Go for it, Cathy. Let's not let these clowns get the upper hand," he says. I nod and feel myself blushing.

"Something else needs to be discussed in the presence of the union representative," Steve goes on, "The b-a-a-a-d air in the school!"

For the last couple of years, many teachers have complained of persistent headaches and dizziness. Some blame it on the poor quality of the air circulating through the ventilation system. A heated discussion ensues between the more militant teachers and the more ethically-minded ones about what protest measures we should take.

With Bruce sitting next to me, I listen to this debate with only half an ear, grinning as he pulls a face. Susan, one of the secretaries, has had her eye on Bruce for some time. She once remarked that Bruce has a tendency to undress the ladies with his eyes. "I fear he may be a womanizer," she said, but she still pins her hopes on him.

Bruce unsettles me. It has been a while since I have felt anyone looking at me the way he does. I wouldn't mind feeling undressed by someone as gentle-mannered as Bruce. Sitting next to him, I wish I didn't have to talk at all. Words can be both a burden and a barrier. I have a hunch that Bruce might be the type of man who would know you just by being next to you. I wonder why the touch of my arm brushing against his makes me feel as if we could easily melt into each other without saying much.

The union representative ends the meeting by promising to bring the matter of the bad air to the attention of the union executives.

Everyone applauds and Bruce turns towards me, "When Angie comes back, we'll have to meet more regularly. We'll make sure she gets the help she needs."

I smile broadly and mumble, "I'd like that."

After the meeting, I walk down to class with the French department head, Cecile Campeau. She's to be the live model for the perm lesson, since she was the first to come forward when I advertised for volunteers in the daily bulletin. She has a very resolute manner of walking and talking, and as we head downstairs we listen to Mike and the other vocational teachers disagree loudly about the walkouts, but only because the plan would penalize teachers where it hurts the most: our pocketbooks.

"We have no bargaining power," Mike says. "We need the janitors on our side. With their help, we'll close down all the schools in Quebec."

Mike and his friends keep talking as they enter the Tech.-Voc. staff room and we continue on to the hairdressing class. Cecile can't contain her disgust at the behaviour of the teachers. She can't believe that the same teachers who have complained about the principal's easy-going attitude are now ganging up against him because of his stricter policies. I know the men will be huddling in the room, concocting schemes for how to get WLHS on the six o'clock news.

24. THE PERM LESSON

I SETTLE CECILE ON A hairstyling chair and ask the students to form a semi-circle around me. I tell them that the challenge of giving a good permanent is not in just getting hair to curl, but in getting it to look more natural than the natural.

"The trick is to change the natural shape of the hair gently, without force." Cecile sits and listens, absorbed by what I have to say. She will be getting a free perm and a hairdressing lesson in the bargain.

I ask the students to analyze Cecile's hair, and decide on the proper selection of lotion and rod size. The students move quickly and seem keen. They touch Cecile's hair and write down their observations on a client record card. I don't disagree with any of their observations. That Cecile has fine, limp hair is visible to anyone a block away. But as I handle the hair, my own fingertips tell me another story.

I feel a slight coarseness in the texture of her fine hair that has the potential to frizz. I suspect that if I use the small size of rods suggested, Cecile wouldn't really be happy with the results. I visualize tight curls springing up around Cecile's large forehead, leaving it exposed and hard.

It's only a hunch and I can't decide if it deserves an explanation.

"Girls, I think that the grey rods you suggest are too small for her hair," I tell the class hesitantly. "I'm afraid her hair might frizz."

"I think the whites are too big," Franca says.

"I agree, so we need to improvise along the way," I say.

I decide to use the grey rods but take thicker sections of hair than usual, and roll the hair loosely, almost messily. As I reach the hairline, I also leave out a few loose strands, uncurled. I decide to go with my hunch. How do you explain a hunch? I wonder. How do you teach students what you feel with your fingertips?

I want to tell them that textbooks don't contain all the answers. Life is not always played out in black or white, and grey offers many options. But all I say is, "Think of all the variables. Your success in hairstyling depends on understanding the client's individual needs."

The students look at me blankly. I can't tell whether my explanation makes any sense, but Cecile nods in agreement. She keeps her eyes closed as the students and I move around her to complete the perm.

After the rods are removed and the hair is rinsed, the students ooh and aah at how softly and naturally the curls fall. Cecile's fine and now wavy hair is quickly dried into shape and she seems genuinely pleased with her new look. She gives Franca a tip and thanks me profusely.

"You should wear it like that all the time; it makes you look younger," Franca says, already displaying the qualities of a successful hairstylist.

Cecile leaves, patting her hair and smiling.

"For once she doesn't look like a dork," Gina snorts, and the class bursts out laughing.

I'm also relieved by the result. Yet as Cecile closes the door behind her, a sense of tiredness at the futility of the two-hour procedure overtakes me. I know all too well the ephemeral quality of our work. *Some art!* After all that deliberation, within days, the hair will grow out of shape, the curls will drop, colours will fade, and there will be nothing left but the tenuous hope of the hunch—the brush of the arm that seems to awaken you from slumber and that carries you off in a new dream.

25. STINK BOMB

I FINALLY DECIDE TO FOLLOW Bruce's advice and apply for department head, and I feel more resolved than ever to keep Angie in my class. It feels good to stand up to Frank and his gang, but another motive seems to be slowly taking shape.

I've completed my degree in Italian literature, and after eight years of teaching the art and science of hairdressing in the "pretend *saloon*," and with Sean moving on in politics, I feel restless to embark on a project of my own. Quite unintentionally, Angie has reconnected me to Lucia and my past, and, in a roundabout way, has spurred me to turn my thoughts to writing again.

Susan, the secretary, has just seen Cecile's hair and wants to know if I could use another model. After taking my application form, we're working out an appointment, when everyone in the office raises their heads from their desks. A sickening smell has suddenly permeated the air. Office doors open. Mr. Champagne comes out of his office, sniffing. The principal moves quickly toward the students' lockers. I follow him. Students are scurrying, getting their lunch bags or putting away their books. They all seem to be in a frenzy. Holding their noses, they squirm and talk excitedly, as if they have been both the butt of, and the perpetrators of, a huge practical joke.

"A stink bomb! A stink bomb!" they repeat. The stink, though, wafts through the ventilation system, so it's clearly not just a student's silly prank. The principal returns to his office. After a couple of minutes, an intercom message comes on: "All classes are dismissed and everyone is asked to leave the building immediately. The building will be thoroughly inspected."

A loud roar of approval rises from the locker areas. Everyone flows out of the hallways with big smiles at the unexpected afternoon off.

A traffic jam forms inside the garage as everyone tries to drive out of their spaces at the same time. I'm stuck in my spot while a line of cars drives slowly past me. Someone honks. It's Bruce. He rolls his eyes at the craziness of it all. I shrug my shoulders and raise my hands in helplessness at being unable to move. It's hot, so I roll down my window. He stops his car, gets out, and motions to the others to back up so I have enough space to slip out. I wave to thank him.

My car moves sluggishly, with a grating noise. Bruce motions me to stop, and comes next to the car window.

"You've got a flat tire," he tells me, "wait for me."

He moves his own car to let the others pass, and then returns. Luckily I have a spare and he changes it expertly.

"Someone slashed your tire," he tells me when finished. "Let's go in and report it."

The clanging of doors opening and closing, the sound of engines and the blaring of car horns bounce off the cement walls, floors, and ceiling of the garage. The smelly fumes and the thought of someone purposely slashing my tire makes me nauseous.

"Not right now. I'll do it on Monday. I need to get out of here," I say.

I finally drive out into the open, but my eyes, accustomed to the dim garage, are blinded by the sudden, brilliant sunlight hitting my car window. I squint, and for an instant, feel disoriented.

In Mulirena, in my last year of school there, I used to walk home with my teacher, Signor Gavano, who came all the way from Piemonte and boarded at Don Cesare's house. Out of nowhere, images of people from the past pop into my mind, as though hiding around the corner I just turned.

26. MISS PARK EX

THE SCENE OUTSIDE THE SCHOOL is chaotic. Over two thousand jeans-clad teenagers, with shiny skin and stringy hair, have poured out of the school entrance and into the residential street, already narrowed by cars parked on both sides. Usually the junior students are let out half an hour earlier to avoid this congestion.

The crowd disperses by the time I reach Jean-Talon, but I still drive slowly and absent-mindedly. Was the tire slashing a random act of vandalism by students or a more sinister act to threaten me for defying the department? Mike had fumed at me for having accepted a special-ed student in my class.

On the way to the garage, I had entertained the thought of going shopping for winter clothes at the posh Rockland Shopping Centre in the Town of Mount Royal, but in my new state of mind, I decide to head for home. The afternoon is bright and sunny and I drive slowly in cruising mode

The shopping centre separates wealthy TMR from poorer Park Ex. Since working at WLHS, I sometimes drive through the bucolic streets of this "Town" within a city, with streets named Roselawn Crescent, Walpole Road, Sunset Circle, and dream of having a home with Sean there. The maple trees are so old and tall that in some streets their branches and foliage meet to form a protective canopy. From what I hear, the cost of homes in this part of town is prohibitive, but I like the tranquility provided by greenery. Living here would be the closest thing to living in a village all over again, but I wonder whether Sean and I will remain together long enough to ever even consider affording a house in this area. One thing is sure, though. If we do marry, I don't want to move northeast to the new developments, with rows of monotonous duplexes and triplexes, and no green spaces, built by Italian contractors who have made a bundle of money in the cement and asphalt business, some of whose names are beginning to pop up in the news in connection to the investigations.

In contrast to the fashion boutiques at Rockland Centre, the windows of the little shops along Jean-Talon Street are cluttered with merchandise. One store in particular catches my attention with its sign, *Nouveau Acropolis: Vêtements Pour Toute la Famille*, in blue and white ceridic letters—the colours of the Greek flag. The household goods on display—the embroidered tablecloths, brocade bedspreads, first communion white dresses—would be right at home in a remote Mediterranean or Greek mountain village.

What made the owners of *Nouveau Acropolis* choose such a grandiose-sounding name for a dry goods store? I muse. Are they hoping to establish their own new Acropolis on the corner of Wiseman and Jean-Talon, or is it a futile attempt to hold onto their past?

I impulsively stop my car and park it in front of a Greek restaurant, Miss Park Ex. I feel like eating something to relieve the gnawing in my stomach. On entering the restaurant, I'm hit by a surge of hot air, permeated with a mixture of smells that I can't identify. Miss Park Ex is really a greasy spoon, as well known for its all-dressed pizza as for its Greek fare. I know the owner, Costa. In his twenties now, he's a graduate of WLHS and runs the restaurant for his father. The short-order cook looks familiar too. I could swear that he's the night janitor I saw coming out of the Tech-Voc staff room with Frank and the others earlier, but he doesn't seem to recognize me. I order a souvlaki. "Go easy on the *tzatziki*," I tell Costa.

He replies, "Got you, Miss," as if he were still in school.

"You're expecting a busy night," I say, pointing to the empty pizza boxes, stacked on the counter, ready to be filled and delivered.

"E-e-v-e-e-r-y night is a busy night here," Costa replies, dragging himself around, as he gives the order to the cook who, unlike Costa, moves nervously from the pizza oven, to the hot plates, to the toaster.

On the menu above the counter are plastic-laminated pictures of a jumbo hot dog, a hamburger, and a club sandwich, each on a plate garnished with heaps of French fries and coleslaw. The restaurant is long and narrow. It's stuffy, and smells of cheese melting over pepperoni, and of Costa's sweat. The wall-to-wall carpet, judging by its stains, looks as if it hasn't been cleaned in years.

"I can imagine the stink," Costa says. Noticing my puzzled expression, he explains. "I heard they stink-bombed the whole school, Miss. I freaked when I heard it. It was bound to happen, sooner or later."

"You've heard already?" I ask.

"Here, I hear everything, Miss. If parents only knew what goes on at that school, they'd freak out, but ... say the truth, Miss. We were never that bad. We talked about doing things like that, but we just talked, but today.... It's bad in there, Miss, say the truth." Costa becomes animated, and he spreads his arms as he talks.

"Oh, it's not as bad as it looks, Costa," I say. "Most of the kids are okay. You know how it is. It only takes a handful..."

"Then it's the pushers. I think there's too many dope heads in there. It's bad. A whole generation of kids, and families too, are being ruined, not just the school, Miss, believe me."

The cook stops fidgeting and, with a spatula in his hands, comes closer to the counter, trying to cut into Costa's ranting, "I hear they want to lock all the doors. Pretty soon they'll be hiring guards," he says and returns to the grill.

Costa looks back at him and replies, spreading his arms, "Well it's about time, George. They gotta do something about those pushers. They're pushing dope on the first year kids these days. What do you expect the school to do, open the doors to them?"

"Yeah, Costa, and you think that's going to stop the kids from getting the dope? It's supposed to be a school, for Cris' sake, not a jail." George seems angry. He stuffs the meat into the pita bread, wraps it in wax paper, and throws it on the counter, while Costa rings the cash register.

Costa whispers, "George is pissed off at all the changes the principal is trying to make."

"Do you work as night janitor? Weren't you in the Tech-Voc staff room just a little while ago?" I ask.

"Yeah, I just returned from my night shift," George replies morosely.

"You can tell how hard he works at night. He comes straight here, nice and rested. Eh, George?" Costa says, laughing. "Have a seat, Miss. I'll bring you a drink. What do you want? A coffee? A Coke? It's on me," Costa offers cheerfully.

"Nothing, Costa, thanks anyway. I feel like eating outside." I pay for the *souvlaki* and walk out, unfolding the wax paper so I can take a bite.

I walk slowly as I eat, dawdling in front of each store window, but there's not much to look at in that stretch of street. The *souvlaki* is tasty but too greasy for my liking, and I throw it in a wastebasket and return to the car.

I cross Park Avenue, drive under a rail underpass, and enter Little Italy. I live east of here, past the open-air Jean-Talon Market where, as a pre-teen, I used to go with my mother every Saturday to buy fresh vegetables and fruits, and even live chickens. I pass Jean-Talon Hospital, where Lucia is still in a coma. I should visit her again one evening, maybe with Angie.

At the next stop sign, I make a jerky U-turn and get back on Jean-Talon. For a moment, I think of stopping at the journalist's office, with the excuse of wanting to buy his latest book of essays, *Multiculturalism: The Institutionalization of Ethnicity*, whose launch had been advertised in his magazine about a month ago. On Papineau Street, I panic, and drive back in a circle to my apartment.

The apartment is flooded with sunlight and every speck of dust on the furniture and windowpanes seems magnified, but I'm in no mood for cleaning.

I really want to talk about everything that has happened, but to whom? Will I have the courage to ask Sean to move out if he won't commit to marriage? Most of the furniture is mine and I can't be the one to move now that Angie will be living with me. Bruce would probably make a good listener. But I can't just go up to him and say, "I'd like to talk." I'd feel silly. In any case, it's not like me to open up to just anyone like that.

I browse through the stories I had written about my life in Mulirena, before the sea voyage, and reread one about my third grade teacher, Signor Gavano. It was the need to recapture those very moments, places, and people that had formed my childhood that had made me want to write in the first place. How do I go beyond that? I would like to connect the past to the present that is unfolding and changing in ways I had never imagined. The task feels overwhelming. Maybe I should leave things alone, let the past be, and just concentrate on my own personal issues with Sean.

Yet, memories arrive unannounced. The store *Nouveau Acropolis* brought back an image of the only shop in Mulirena that sold men's shirts, white muslin cottons, and the floss used by girls to embroider their trousseaux. My neighbours often sent me there with colour samples to buy embroidery floss for them. The small store was dark and cool and had its own particular smell from the bolts of new cotton and the smooth silk threads that begged to be transformed into borders of delicate flowers and multicoloured butterflies for the marriage-bed sheets and pillowcases.

Signor Gavano also smelled of clean cotton. I haven't heard a single word about him in the twenty-odd years since I left Mulirena, yet he makes an appearance in my thoughts from time to time in his beige-and-brown tweed jacket and limpid clear blue eyes. Of Canada, he only taught me about the immense expanse of land and water, but what could he know at the time of polyvalent high schools, Park Ex, and jumbo hot dogs?

27. ALFONSO

IN THE MORNING, I PUT a new notebooks in my briefcase. I'm determined to keep a close journal of what is happening now and tie it to my previous writing. How coincidental to have become reconnected to Lucia through her daughter at this turning point in her life. And at what point is it exactly? Is this its ending? It can't be. What if this is not an ending yet, but another beginning, both for Lucia and me?

On Sunday afternoon, after the family lunch, Tina, Mother, and I sat on the balcony and chatted for over three hours. Tina had also been jilted by her village sweetheart, Michele, after he left for Rome, even though they had been engaged. I wonder if, after all the years, the hurt of having been abandoned by Michele had lessened for her. She now has two husky sons and a very docile husband who depend fully on her to run the household. I see her frequently and yet I know very little about how her past life has impacted her present.

And what about Aurora? No one has seen her or heard much from her since she immigrated to Argentina after she married in her Sunday best, but without a white dress and veil. All I remember about her are her grey eyes and light-coloured hair, and the blue satin sash that she was going to wear in the play as Our Lady of Lourdes.

The past is far removed. How reliable is my understanding of what happened? I had seen things through the eyes of a child and I only know the women's side of the story.

If only the journalist had been more forthcoming with me when I first had asked for his help. I'm sure he'll still discourage me from investigating the past. I wrote to him a second time:

Dear Antoine,
   Why do you ridicule the efforts made by young Italian Canadian writers to write about their past?
Rina

Dear Rina,
   First, let us put the ethnic label to rest. It smells of ethnic cleansing to me. The compulsion to write is typical and normal for the children of immigrants who have come of age, to either record their experiences for posterity, to purge themselves of guilt, or of perceived hurts, or to pay tribute to aging parents. But they often do so under the glow of nostalgia because they don't really remember; they can only imagine the idyllic pastoral life of their nonnos. *Well, reading about nostalgia gives me gas pains, because I remember a time back home when people tore at each other's throats for a bucket of water and some sold their souls for a visa to America. The diarrheic confessional memoirs of the first generations may be of therapeutic value to the writers but they contribute nothing to the community's body of literary works. My concern is to enlarge our own reality, to rise above the personal, and aim for literary truths that will lead to universal truths.*

Should I bother to go and see him? I think. He raises the bar so high for first-time writers like me. I simply want to tell a story—my story and that of the people I know that may be similar to others, without having to worry about his academic ramblings.

"Wow, it's quite the mansion!" Julie exclaims as we drive into Alfonso's driveway. We're there to discuss Angie's move. "He's in the construction business, and he's done very well." The home is more grandiose than I had imagined, a luxurious, sprawling, two-storey house, facing the Lake of Two Mountains, in the residential Laval-sur-le-Lac. The house is surrounded by empty lots still covered in underbrush, and his front yard looks newly landscaped. The bare rock garden and the rolls of turf piled in front of the garage reveal that work is still in progress. A short distance away, other homes under construction bear a large sign, Habitations A&V Construction: "A" for Abiusi and "V" for Vaccaro, the name of his partners and of his wife's family.

By all accounts, since Alfonso arrived in Montreal a couple of years after Lucia, he has been very successful, both in business and in personal life. The Vaccaro family into which he married is well established in the city's Italian community. One of his brothers-in-law is a notary, and another, a lawyer. The patriarch of the family, Joe Vaccaro, took Alfonso under his wing when the young man befriended his daughter and eventually made him a partner in his business.

Alfonso has gravitated toward his wife's side of the family and rarely socializes with *paesani*. He speaks more French than English, like the Vaccaros who had immigrated to Montreal before the forties and had married French-Canadian women.

When his wife, Dominique, answers the door, it looks as if she has been expecting us. She's polite but cool and leads us through the large marble-tiled foyer into the carpeted living room, with a mirrored wall, a marble fireplace, and modern all-white furniture. She then walks stiffly up a circular staircase and calls, "*Alfonso, vos amis sont ici,*" and disappears to the top floor.

Alfonso comes down the stairs and shakes hands with both of us. He speaks in accented English. "What's going on at that school? I hear they had a bomb scare?"

"No, No. It was just stink bombs ... nothing serious," I say, laughing.

Comare Rosaria walks up a staircase that must lead from the basement and asks, alarmed, "There were bombs in the school?"

She kisses me. I try to explain as best as I can about the stink bombs placed in the ventilation system, but can't find the word for stink bomb in my halting dialect.

"*Madonna mia*, the things these kids come up with," Rosaria says.

"That's not the work of kids," Alfonso says. "It must be an inside job."

"They're investigating it," I say. "Is Angie home?"

"I'll call her," Comare Rosaria says, and walks slowly toward the open door from which she has just come. "Angelina, come upstairs," she calls.

Meanwhile, Julie explains to Alfonso the reason for our visit: my guardianship of Angie on weekdays so she can attend school. She mentions that my boyfriend sometimes stays over. If the news surprises him, he doesn't show it. He looks at me and says, "I understand that your fiancée is a close friend of Jean-Pierre Menard. I know Menard quite well."

"Oh, J.P. and Sean have been friends for years," I answer. I don't correct his use of fiancé. The corresponding *fidanzato* in Italian simply means boyfriend.

"Jean-Pierre is a good party man ... heard the news about your fiancé running in the by-election. The Conservatives are pushing Martillo. You know him, don't you?"

I shake my head.

"He has a big reputation in the community and the Italian papers are backing him. It's going to be a tough race," Alfonso says.

Sean's candidature is already public knowledge, it seems, and Alfonso is more interested in discussing it than talking about Angie. I know that Alfonso has been active within the Liberal

Party, especially in fundraising events for Alex Di Principe during election periods. I'm uncomfortable with the exchange. Julie is shuffling papers from her briefcase. "I don't get involved in any of this political stuff," I say. "Julie has some papers that need to be signed."

Alfonso agrees to let Angie stay with me, but if the process is too problematic for me, he'll find a school closer to home, he says.

"Not all schools offer the type of program offered at Western Horizon," Julie says, "and not all programs are open to special students."

"Special, special ... what's so special! I'm sure the girl can try learning something else besides hairdressing if she wants to, but I leave it up to her," he says.

Julie then discusses Angie's expenses and the forms that must be filled out if Alfonso wants Social Services to cover them. He dismisses her. "I don't have time for that. I'll cover all her expenses. I don't need government assistance. Angie is not on *bien-être sociale*. She has us."

"No need to worry about expenses for me," I say. "We'll settle it between ourselves."

"But we must sign the guardianship papers. Those are a must." Julie pulls out a long form, which she has already filled out. Just then, Comare Rosaria comes back with a tray fragrant with espresso and almond cookies "It smells good," Julie says, and puts the form back into her briefcase.

While we drink our coffee, Comare Rosaria gets up again to call Angie. "Maybe she fell asleep watching TV," she says.

Angie walks up from the basement, dressed in the same black pants and top that she wore at school. Her eyes are red and swollen, as if she has been crying.

Julie holds out her hand to Angie, which she accepts hesitantly. "Angie, do you really want to return to the hairdressing program, or would you rather do something else, maybe in a school close to your home?" Julie asks.

"There's nothing close to here ... except the river," Angie says, pointing toward the window.

"That's not true. Her aunt could drive her anywhere she wants," Alfonso says, "but I leave it up to her."

"I wanna go to Montreal," Angie answers loudly, crossing her arms over her chest.

"We must tell you that, if you go back, you'll have to follow all the school rules," Julie says.

"Any rules for stink bombs?" Angie says with a smirk. "I wasn't there for that one."

"I'm sure they'll find the people responsible for that," Julie says. She pulls out some papers from her briefcase.

"You'll have to sign a contract with the principal. It's school policy after a suspension. If you break any rule, you'll be expelled for good."

Angie shrugs her shoulders.

"I have to sign for your good conduct, too," Alfonso says, pointing at the documents in Julie's hands. "Do you know what that means?"

"It means they go after you if I don't behave. I guess what goes around, comes around."

Julie looks at me, then at Alfonso.

Alfonso answers. "You'll notice that my niece has a strange sense of humour when upset. It's understandable. A lot has happened in the last few days."

"Yes, of course," Julie says and looks at Angie. "Angie, I'd like to finish with your uncle first. We'll speak to you again before we leave."

"Sure," Angie says, "make sure you ask him about the boogey men hiding in the mountains." She waves her hand, then slips back down to the basement.

"What was that all about?" Julie asks. "Your niece seems distraught."

"This has been hard for all of us," Alfonso says, "but it must be extremely hard for Angie to accept what her own father did to her mother. We've just received the news that my brother-in-law has finally been located in Italy."

"Really?" I ask.

"He went to hide in Italy, in his hometown, of all places, as if we can't go after him there."

I look at Comare Rosaria and ask in dialect, "So, they found Pasquale?"

She shakes her head and sighs, "I don't understand anything anymore."

"I'm trying to talk to the Italian police. He's not a Canadian citizen. But you know how slowly things get done in Italy."

"Is that why Angie is upset?" Julie asks.

"She's been crying all day, since she heard the news. I can't understand why, but she doesn't want me to go after her father. But I have no choice, he nearly killed my sister."

"We understand," Julie says, and she goes over Angie's travel arrangements with Alfonso. I chat with Comare Rosaria and explain that she has no reason to worry about Angie, that I will take good care of her.

"I trust her with you ... with someone else, maybe not. But with you, yes," Rosaria says smiling. "*Bella mia*, it seems like just yesterday you were a little girl yourself, playing in Piazza Don Carlo." The old woman wipes her eyes with a tissue.

On our way out, we ask to see Angie.

"I'm watching *As the World Turns*," she yells from the basement. We smile at each other and leave.

In the car, Julie asks me if I feel comfortable not having clarified the paying of expenses. I explain how hard it is for Southern Italians to talk about money among family and close friends. We firmly believe in the give and take, and even if things are not always clear, it usually all comes out in the wash.

"Oh shoot," Julie says. "I never got the guardianship papers signed. I feel so stupid. I'll have to come back on my own."

I laugh. I remember Alfonso negotiating his sister's marriage to Pasquale, at the fair of Santa Lucia, as if he were negotiating the sale of a donkey. I'm sure there were no written contracts drawn, but the unspoken understanding was that Alfonso and his family would gain much from that union. The visit to his home proved that he had certainly achieved his goal. He had become wealthy by exploiting two of the most basic needs of immigrants: their craving for authentic foods, and their dream of owning a piece of land and a home worthy of an ocean crossing.

28. THE PROPOSAL

MY ANNOUNCEMENT AT SUNDAY LUNCH to my mother about Angie moving in with me provokes as big an argument as when I told the family I wanted to move in with Sean. This latest disagreement is somewhat connected to the first, because, with Angie staying with me, my ambiguous living arrangement with Sean will become public knowledge. As long as it has been kept hush-hush from the *paesani*, our living in sin hasn't seemed real. How will Mother explain that she has allowed the shameful situation?

"I've already told Sean that if he doesn't make up his mind, I'm leaving him," I announce.

"After you've lived with him?" she asks, dumbfounded.

I understand that, in my mother's eyes, the only acceptable option at this point is marriage. I'm a marked woman for living with him; I'll be more so if I leave him. "You know I don't care about what the *paesani* think," I argue.

"Because you're hardheaded. You only care about yourself," Mother replies.

I leave the kitchen and run to the back balcony to cool down, rather than raise my voice to my mother. I never make any sense when I'm upset. I understand my mother's concerns, but it infuriates me to be accused of selfishness when I try so hard to please.

"You're in good company with that girl," I hear my mother saying from the kitchen. "She's probably just as hardheaded—

like her mother. You're all one and the same." When I don't respond, Mother continues, "Don't you remember anything about what Lucia did?"

I still don't answer. I remember the cloud of shame that hung over Lucia during our last summer in Mulirena, and, as a child, I never questioned it. Then, on the ship, I learned to accept her errant secretive behaviour and my complicity in it, not so much as normal, but as necessary. For someone whose life choices had been imposed on her, secrecy and deception seemed like the only possible way out. "Hold on to anything," Armando had told us.

I sit on the balcony, silent and sad, until Luigi walks up from the basement where he has been practicing his trumpet. "You've heard what they're saying in the papers about Alfonso and Jack Russo," he says. "There must be something there that we don't know about."

When neither Mother nor I respond, he says, "What's with the long faces?"

Mother blurts out about my crazy decision to take Angie in and the argument between Sean and me.

"She can't go back on her word to Comare Rosaria and Alfonso," he says, ever the pacifier between Mother and me, "but I'm sure we can work things out reasonably with Sean. I'm not working tomorrow. I'll come and talk to him if necessary. Maybe he'll agree to a simple civil wedding."

I had already planned on inviting everyone over for Thanksgiving.

"Okay," I say relieved that some of the pressure has been diffused. Luigi then resumes talking about the news.

"The papers always exaggerate," I reply.

"There must be something," Mother repeats. "I always said that he became rich a little too fast and too easily—for someone who knew nothing about construction."

"Hey, you don't need to be a genius to do well here," Luigi interrupts. "Look at some of the people who have made it big.

Most of them are illiterate. Alfonso is a shrewd businessman, and we can't take that away from him."

"He only became a businessman here," Mother says. "In the *paese*, he couldn't do anything right, and he used people, including your father."

"We were too young then to understand what was going on. Today we wouldn't let that happen," Luigi says.

"In any case," I answer, "he told me not to worry about any expenses."

"For that, he won't remain behind ... now that he's rich," Mother says. More than anything else, our *paesani* hate feeling indebted to others, and will always find a way of repaying a favour. By the same token, they remember when one isn't paid back.

When Rita comes into the room with the baby, we all sit down to lunch and the conversation lightens up. We chat about the baby's progress and then my brother regales us with his latest jokes, until Mother changes topic again and lets me know that there are certain things she won't forget. "We were left indebted once because of Alfonso and his friends. Your father died of heartache because of it."

That was a painful period for all of us that we rarely speak about. Again we all remain quiet with our own thoughts.

I spend Sunday afternoon preparing the den for Angie's stay. I remove some of my clothes from the closet to make room for hers. I pick out the books from the shelves that I'm likely to use the most. Besides the thick *I Promessi Sposi* and its translation, I choose three other books to keep on my night table to reread: *Il Gattopardo* by Giuseppe Tomasi di Lampedusa, *Light in August* by William Faulkner, and a book of short stories, *Lives of Girls and Women* by Alice Munro. I had read these books before and had been captivated by them, especially by how well—though written in different periods and in different countries—they had managed to capture the sense of their time and place while speaking to all. Despite the journalist's highfalutin pronouncements, I must agree with him on this one writing principle. I think about removing my stack of notebooks from the bottom shelf, with the rough drafts of the story I've just rewritten. But, it's unlikely that Angie will bother to read through them, and even if she tries, the handwriting is indecipherable, so I decide to leave them where they are.

I cram the clothes from the den into my already packed bedroom closet.

"You hoard things," Sean has often complained.

"And you throw everything away," I say.

I find it especially difficult to throw away my old clothes. They remind me of the changes in my life, the ups and downs, the weight gains and the losses. Some pieces of clothing have never even been worn and still have a price tag on them. They were mistakes in judgment. I either had been carried away by a sale price, or had purchased the item in a panic before a special event, fearing that I had nothing else appropriate to wear. These clothes make me realize how, at times, I compromise too easily, accept what is available for fear of being without. Once the clothes make it home, I rarely return them. There is always something I like about them, and think that, maybe at a different time in my life, I might find a use for them. It must be my immigrant background, this squirrel-like compulsion to hoard things for a rainy day. It seems to me that I'm always shuffling books and clothes from one place to another.

I'm restless waiting for Sean. I haven't been able to get rid of the nervous feeling in my stomach I've had since the slashed tire on Friday afternoon and then my argument with Sean. Lucia's condition is neither improving nor deteriorating, so I can expect Angie to be with me for a longer period than I had originally thought. If Sean and I patch things up, I'll have to worry about her sharing space with J.P. when he comes into the city.

J.P. always acts as if he owns Sean. Sean described him as a kind of mentor, someone who helped him straighten out his head, while he was aimless and living in Ottawa. The first time he visited us, after Sean and I had started seeing each other, I had prepared a special meal for him at Sean's place. When J.P. walked into the kitchen to greet me, I was flushed from cooking. He looked me over and said, "So this is the Italian *mamma*." In spite of the jovial tone of voice, I sensed a disapproving look in his eyes, and I disliked him immediately.

As J.P. visits frequently, I have become aware that Sean changes his manners when his friend is around. I worry that with a by-election in the planning stages, J.P.'s visits will be non-stop. Angie's presence in the small apartment will make things even more awkward between us.

Late in the evening Sean enters the apartment and drops his heavy knapsack on the kitchen floor, looks around and smells the air. "It smells of lemons," he says.

"It must be the furniture polish I used."

"This place hasn't been this clean in months. You must be expecting *paesani*," he says wryly.

He's smiling and seems in a good mood and I tell him I've invited my family for Thanksgiving dinner. Then I ask if he has given some thought to what we discussed before he left.

Sean brightens up. "Yes, but first let me tell you that Di Principe's appointment will be announced officially this week and so will my nomination to run." He bends his waist as in a bow.

"Congratulations," I say. "Are you excited?"

"Not yet. I'm too preoccupied about the work involved. The election will be called for after the holidays. It's going to be intense from now on."

I uncover the plate of pasta and meat Mother gave me at lunch, put it in the microwave, and set the table.

Sean takes a beer and, holding his chin, he says pensively, "I did some thinking while I was on the bus. You were right the other day. I think it may be time for us to make some important decisions."

I wait for him to go on.

"I think we should start thinking about getting married before all the brouhaha of the election. If we don't do it now, we may never do it," he says, looking at the floor and nodding his head, as though agreeing with his own decision. "Yeah, I think it's about time."

I open my eyes wide and move my head back, as if I were doing a second take. "Gee, is this proposal for real?"

"It sure is," Sean says smiling broadly. He keeps looking at the floor and pinches his chin as he usually does when he's nervous. "I've been thinking of how little stability I've had in my life. It's time I plant some solid roots." He sits down.

"It's quite a sudden change in your thinking, I mean ... are you sure it's what you want?" I sit down facing him, and try to read his pensive expression, but his eyes are still focused on the floor.

"We grow. We change, and I feel I'm entering a new phase in life," he says and then looks up. "Aren't you happy?"

"Yes, of course," I say, "and it will make my mother very, very happy." I smile, just thinking of my mother's reaction.

He gets up. "Then it's a deal!"

I get up too, and hug him. "When are you thinking ... can I announce it to my family?"

"Of course ... announce it to everyone. I guess we can set a date for just after the holidays. The by-election will be held sometime in February, so it would be good to do it just after Christmas, before the circus of the campaign starts."

I put my hands to my face. "Wow, so soon! I can't believe all this is happening now."

"On that note, I'm going to eat my pasta, and then go to bed," Sean says. "I'm beat."

I kiss him and sit next to him. I feel elated. "I hadn't expected this," I say.

"Your mother will be especially happy when she hears that we're getting married in a Catholic Church."

"Are you serious?"

"We might as well go all the way."

I watch Sean gulp down his pasta and then he gets up, and removes his tie and shirt to go to bed. "I'll come to bed in a few minutes," I say. "I'll just have to put the turkey to defrost for tomorrow evening."

"Don't let me stop you," Sean says. "I'm going to bed. I'm pretty tired."

I kiss him again. Then I quietly call my mother to let her know the good news, but ask her to act as if they don't know until Sean and I announce it at Thanksgiving dinner.

After filling the sink with cold water and placing the frozen turkey into it, I undress and slide into bed next to Sean. He's already asleep, rolled over on his side. I lie still, facing the ceiling, savouring the elation of the proposal and anticipation of finally planning a wedding. I want it to be a low key but elegant reception with only the closest of friends and relatives, but still there is planning involved. Will I buy a ready-made white dress or have one sewed? Sean would certainly want J.P. to be his best man. Who would I ask as my maid of honour? I'm too agitated to fall asleep. There are other questions I should have asked Sean: Won't he have to convert to Catholicism to get married in a Catholic church? Would he want children right away?

I get up to make myself a cup of tea. Even with the apartment vacuumed and the furniture polished, the place still looks like a third-rate hotel lobby. Will we buy a house? Alfonso will most certainly think of my place as a beggar's home, compared to his semi-mansion. Homes are considered the most obvious symbol of success for someone like Alfonso and most of my *paesani*.

I tell myself that whatever we decide, I'll be happy. Things are finally falling into place. I can finally make good on my promise that Sean and I would eventually get married, and his stay in my apartment can be justified to Angie's family. The timing of Angie's stay may be inconvenient, but I must keep my pledge to Lucia to help her daughter.

These thoughts keep me awake and too excited to go to bed, so I lie on the sofa and leaf through the old notebooks, until I fall asleep with the happy thought that my own story is unfolding as it should.

PART V
THE LANDING, 1957-1961

29. A NEW HOME

OUR NEW HOME WAS A basement apartment on Tenth Avenue in the east end of Montreal. When Uncle Peppe stopped in front of that red-brick apartment building and told us we were "home," Luigi and I sighed with relief that our house was not one of the desolate shacks we saw along the stretch of country between Halifax and Montreal. I felt thrilled to have made it to the big city.

Tina had convinced Lucia and Pasquale to stop at our house for something to eat before being driven home by Pasquale's friend, Joe Vaccaro. Nicodemo's family was also at the train station and they shook hands as if they all knew each other. They declined our invitation, but the others followed us to the house and together we made a noisy and excited entrance.

My aunt Rosina, Father's older sister, had prepared a feast for us: chicken soup, pasta, meat, and all kinds of pastries. After coffee was served in the largest cups we had ever seen, Lucia and Pasquale left with their friend.

"I had expected someone different for Lucia," Father said. "He's a bit of a *cafone*, but he's a good man. Here, the less educated you are, the more money you make."

Pasquale, with his Neapolitan friend, Joe Vaccaro, a real-estate agent turned contractor, had spoken of the land he had bought for development in Laval. Father had agreed to think about buying a lot, too. "Land is the surest investment," he said. "It never loses value."

After everyone left, Father gave us a tour of the apartment, which he had furnished himself. A large, brown furnace had a prominent place in the centre of the hallway. Father told us not to touch it or we'd get burned. We could hear and smell the fire blazing inside its belly. Father explained how it was fed by an oil tank in a shed at the back of the house. A pipe ran from the furnace to the ceiling, and snaked its way along the long corridor and into the kitchen. The living room was still bare, with only a folding bed in a corner for my brother. My bedroom too was furnished with only a bed. The kitchen was half furnished, with an electric stove but no fridge yet. Father was especially proud of the master bedroom, with the cream-coloured birch set, with its black, lacquered legs set on a slant. "It's elegant and modern. We're young too, no?" he said, winking at Mother. "After the summer, I'll get a fridge, a TV, and a chesterfield, and then we're complete."

"We have plenty of time for that," Mother answered. "Let's be happy for what we have."

30. FIRST WINTER, 1957

FATHER DECIDED THAT, BECAUSE THE English school was a long walk from our house, it would be best to wait out the rest of the school year. I spent most of the winter watching our neighbours' legs as they passed by our windows, with large Kik bottles and silver-foil pouches hanging from their hands. After I asked Father what the pouches contained, he bought me a bag of potato chips to taste. The saltiness jolted me at first, but when I had finished eating the bag, I craved more. From our kitchen window, which looked into our backyard, I watched children tumbling like balls on the snow banks, all bundled up in brightly-coloured snow pants, scarves, and mittens.

After our first week in Montreal, on a mild day, Father took us to St. Hubert Street to buy galoshes that we could slip over our shoes, so we could walk to Aunt Rosina's house. Hers was a full house, with her four sons and with Uncle Peppe's two brothers who also boarded with them. Father had also lived there before we came. Every Saturday night, we all sat in front of their TV set to watch *Hockey Night in Canada*, *The Juliette Show*, and then wrestling. An Italian, a Maestro D'Agostino, not only led Juliette's musical band, but was married to the bubbly, blonde singer, Father proudly informed us.

Tina, accompanied by her brother, Francesco, often joined us. A friend of Francesco, Gaetano, joined the company after he became officially engaged to Tina. Francesco and Father spoke continually of music and the orchestra they had put together.

The other major weekly outing with Father was a long walk to an Italian grocery store on Belair Street. It was run by a large Sicilian family. The parents had just bought a farm, where they made the fresh ricotta and Italian cheeses that they sold at the store, while the sons and daughters ran the city business.

"You'll see, this family is going to make a fortune because they work together," Father said.

Mother stayed home for only one month, and then insisted she go to work in the factory with Tina. It was light work, making ladies' lingerie, and Father didn't object. He was still unemployed for the winter, but he went out every day to meet his friends at the Casa D'Italia, and he brought back an Italian newspaper, *Il Progresso Italo-Americano*. In the evening, we all listened to the Italian program on the radio and political commentaries of Camillo Carli. The news was rife with stories of the Hungarian revolution, and of children and women dying in the streets of Budapest.

Luigi stayed home too, but after school, one of our cousins would come by and they'd go out together. Luigi befriended Francine, a French girl who lived in our building, and my cousin, who went to French school, would translate for them. With no TV in the house and everyone out, I had lots of free time. I read the day-old Italian newspapers with news of social events happening in New York and Brooklyn. The paper also featured a serial story about outlaws hiding in some hills, and I cut out each installment to paste in a notebook. I wrote letters to my friends back home, telling them that the best time of day was the evening when the family was together and we listened to Italian songs on the radio.

I also liked it when Francesco, who played the guitar, came to the apartment accompanied by an accordion player and a saxophonist. With my father on trumpet, they practiced Latin American tunes in the living room.

Also, in the evenings, a parade of travelling salesmen found their way into our apartment, offering products and services that we had never heard of before. One man spread stainless steel pots and pans all over the kitchen floor. "Just like gypsies," Mother said. Another vacuumed the mattresses with a tissue over the vacuum nozzle to show how well it sucked, and asked us to imagine how well it would clean our floors. An impeccably dressed insurance agent born in Venice, Alex Di Principe, came to offer advice about investing in life insurance.

One evening, Di Principe returned with Pasquale, accompanied by Joe Vaccaro, and a well-known personality in the community, Jack Russo, whose name was mentioned regularly in the local Italian newspaper. He organized feasts with local entertainers and fundraising balls. To my surprise Nicodemo accompanied the three men. He was dressed in a dark suit, his hair tamed into a brush cut. He had found work with Jack Russo. They had photographs of the development project in Laval, and sold lots for next to nothing, promising that in a few years they'd be developed into a model city called Citta Verde, or Ville Verte. They convinced my father to arrange for my uncle and his brothers to attend a meeting the following week. I was hoping to see Lucia again, but she stayed home. "She doesn't like to go out," Pasquale said. Lucia had already started the paperwork to sponsor her brothers' emigration to Montreal.

"*Qui tutto fa brodo*," my father used to joke. "Here everything makes soup," he said about the mishmash of dialects and improvised occupations of the immigrants whose badly-spoken Italian betrayed their peasant background—with the exception of the insurance agent. My father and my uncle and his two brothers all bought land without needing to see the actual location, and Father even bought a life insurance policy from the Venetian. But my mother couldn't be sold on the magic power of stainless steel, or on the vacuum's ability to make her a better housewife. She served these people drinks, coffee, cookies, and even the special homemade Calabrese sausages that we had smuggled from Italy. After they left, Father always found something funny to say about each one, and that had us laughing for days.

During the day, to pass the time, I tried to take up drawing as a hobby, but all I managed to draw were geometric shapes. I spent hours fitting circles into squares. It was lonely not to see or speak to anyone for hours on end, and I found solace in the serial story of the fantasy world of the brigands, and of their lovers who left all behind to follow them. Mother left prepared lunches for me to eat. For snacks, I discovered the pleasure of Oreo cookies, and developed a special liking for peanut butter sandwiches. The brown wool dress I had brought from Italy got tighter and tighter, until I couldn't button it anymore.

News of the misery of the people in Hungary who had to flee from their homes made me relive the frightful images of the plague-infested streets that Renzo had walked through in his search for Lucia, in the novel that had so occupied my time on the ship to this country. Lucia and Renzo had found each other in the end, but their time and place pulled further and further away from me.

31. SUNDAYS ON TENTH AVENUE, 1959

It was always on Sundays that I felt the most restless. Anticipation kept me edgy for the better part of the afternoons. When the day ended much like any other, disappointment set in, week after week, with the realization that my enthusiasm and my Sunday clothes had been for nothing.

Shifted and dislodged from another place, the queasiness that had overtaken my whole family while crossing the Atlantic had become for me a constant companion. I felt as if we had disembarked, but never arrived. We had landed on a shaky, movable dock—a no-man's-land—safe from storms but neither here nor there. I wanted badly to go to shore, go somewhere less confining, run free and do things. But I was stuck in transit, and the gap between where I was and where I wanted to be was as wide as the ocean.

We had been living on Tenth Avenue for a little over two years. A predictable Sunday routine had been established, and I was helpless in changing it. With my mother, I would walk to the French church, Sainte-Bernadette, on Seventeenth Avenue, to fulfill our Sunday obligations, while my father and brother stayed home. They only came to church on special occasions when we all walked to a basement Italian parish on Papineau Street. The Mass at Sainte-Bernadette was a formality—in and out in under forty-five minutes.

"It still counts," Mother would say, even though she only understood a few words of the sermon.

The ragù for the pasta simmered slowly all morning while we were at Mass. My father kept it stirred, tasting it frequently, dunking chunks of bread into it, and seasoning it with the spices and herbs—nutmeg, cloves, rosemary—that he had learned to use when working in Milan. After lunch, my father and brother might practice their scales on the trumpet. Later, my brother, who was as fidgety as I was, would go off with his friends to flirt with Francine and her friends. I would be left alone with my mother to tidy up and mope around, sulking at having nothing interesting to do. At the very most, my aunts and uncles might drop by for a visit. My cousins, all males, were not much company since they were only interested in hockey and wrestling.

I often wondered why we had left Italy just as things were beginning to look up there. Unlike Jewish immigrants or Hungarian refugees, we had not escaped persecution or even dire poverty. Yet having been sponsored by relatives to come across had felt like winning a lottery prize. It was as if a millionaire uncle or aunt had opened up their mansion, with a bountiful buffet all set out for us from which to pick and choose. How could our parents have refused their invitation? We left in hordes, looking for better feeding grounds. When I watched the graceful formations of geese flying south every fall, only to come back home in the spring, I thought how much rougher and less elegant our own transatlantic passage had been. Ill-informed, inadequately dressed, and retching all the way from the Rock of Gibraltar to Halifax.

After the first winter spent shut in at home, I ventured out and made friends with the French kids who lived in our building and I eventually learned French from them. I emerged chubby and round like an inflated soccer ball, and felt clumsy and shy.

Tenth Avenue was at its best in the spring when, coming out of its winter hibernation, it blossomed with crocuses, tulips, and daffodils. The scent of lilacs permeated the length of the street. From our building to the other end of the block, on Jean-Talon

Street, stood rows of similar small, white, clapboard homes that, we later learned, were built by the Canadian government for war veterans. They seemed reproduced from a child's simple crayon picture: triangle roof, square box body and windows, white picket fences, trellised arbors on the side for climbing clematis. Once the spring bulbs had run their brief course, the homeowners, mostly English-speaking, seemed to spend most of their leisure time cutting lawns, trimming hedges, and grooming and decorating their little rock gardens with petunias, begonias, wooden figurines, and plastic pink flamingoes.

By the beginning of our first summer, the owner of the building, a tall, broad Polish man who liked our family—or so he said—offered us the third-floor apartment, which had a balcony. Sometimes in the evenings, I would sit on the balcony with my parents, who watched the homeowners fuss around their little playhouses. My mother admired how meticulously the men worked, while my father thought they were fools.

"*Il polacco*—the Polish man—now he is smart," my father kept saying about the landlord. "He has lived here maybe less than twenty years, and he owns an apartment building. These people have lived here all their lives, have gone to war, and all they have is a wooden box. They can play all they want with their little flowers but they still live in a box. Their flowers don't even have an aroma."

I wanted to speak up for the lilacs, but with Father there was no point, since I could guess his response. "The lilacs, you smell them once and they are finished, not like the oleanders that grow everywhere and last all summer long." He was always comparing. Whether he spoke about the weather, houses, food, or flowers, Father always weighed Montreal versus Milan.

My father, whom relatives and friends now called Joe for short, had also gained weight. Working as a bricklayer, he had the ruddy complexion that comes from exposure to the sun in the summer, frost and wind in the winter. In the summer, he played with a musical band at all the religious feasts on Dante

Street, and when we went to a family gathering, he brought his trumpet with him just in case someone asked him to play.

"Joe, give us a Carnival of Venice," someone would inevitably ask.

With his large, sweaty forehead and his puffy, red cheeks, he looked like a white Louis Armstrong, blowing his horn to the applause of his friends. Now he practiced his scales more out of habit than necessity. The band he had formed with Francesco had played at only a few Italian weddings. They played the Latin American tunes that were popular then. They wore silk shirts with puffy sleeves and took turns playing the maracas. When practicing in our living room, my father always seemed self-conscious and unenthusiastic about shaking those brightly painted wooden balls to the rhythm of "Tico-Tico" and "Besame Mucho." He argued with Francesco and refused to move in unison with the others in choreographed fashion.

"We look ridiculous, all jumping up at the same time, like grasshoppers," my father complained. But the demand for their type of music slowly dwindled.

"We should be playing more rock-and-roll," Francesco argued with father, who wouldn't hear of it.

When we first came over, Father still surprised me with little presents when I least expected them. Once he bought me a watch from a travelling salesman. Another time, on the first warm day after the first long winter, he came home with a Bat-a-Ball.

But, as time went on, he became sullen and easily upset, especially when he had no work. Then he stayed home, ashamed to be seen by his friends. The more time passed, the more he seemed to lose the sense of humour he was known for, and even when he tried to be funny, he sounded angry. So I learned not to argue with him and I spoke to him less and less. My mother was my go-between when I needed to ask him anything important.

Of our English neighbours on Tenth Avenue, he'd say, "They think they live in a palace. These people haven't seen real palaces!"

My mother's spin on palaces was that she never wanted to live in one. "People who live in palaces have bigger problems than we do. I'd rather be healthy and happy in a small home."

We didn't associate much with our neighbours, except for an Italian family who lived on the second floor, and then later, with two other families who arrived the summer after us and who lived on the other side of Belanger Street, above a movie theatre, The Montrose. To me, the English people who lived in the little houses were like the American families I saw on TV: not totally real. I imagined their daughters attending proms and school dances in crinoline dresses with flower corsages wrapped around their wrists, which their fathers placed on them with a proud smile and a "Have a good time, Betty."

But neither did I feel close to the Italians I saw on Dante Street on religious holidays. The street was festooned with little Italian flags and people ate cold tomato pizzas and *granita*, while the band played "Faccetta Nera" and other Italian marches. The dignitaries and community leaders that surrounded Councillor Di Principe and spoke on stage were mostly second- or third-generation immigrants. Their parents, who mostly lived around Mile End, had come to this country long before us, and some of them had been interned during the war for their fascist leanings. They spoke Italian with a mixture of French and English. The more recent arrivals, like us, lived mostly around the newer Italian church, Notre Dame de la Consolata, or north and east towards Saint Michel and Saint Leonard, and attended English school.

My father had insisted that unless we went to English school, we would never learn the language. French, he told us, we could learn on the streets of east-end Montreal. In September, after our arrival, he walked us to Saint Brendan's School on Fourteenth Avenue. I was put back two grades into grade three, and my brother, who should have been in high school, was put in grade four. We teased him for looking as old as the teacher. Some of the other Italian boys were even older than my brother. They smoked and shaved. Mr. Foster, the fourth-grade teacher, fresh out of teacher's college, had probably less experience than they did.

"Maybe you can teach him a thing or two," my father joked with the boys.

As for me, school was no struggle. My first English reader had lots of pictures with a few words in large print: "ANN RAN, DAVID RAN, ANN AND DAVID RAN." I ran as fast as I could to catch up to them, while my brother was too impatient to even try. He said he didn't like school at all. He asked Father to give him trumpet lessons and I had to listen to both of them practice every night. At the end of the first school year, my teacher recommended I skip fourth grade, and then, once in high school, I would skip one more grade, and graduate with my age group.

I spent most of my Sundays watching hordes of teenagers lining up in front of the Montrose Theatre, with Elvis staring at me in life-sized movie posters from across the street. I used to beg my mother to let me go to the movies, but she never once gave in. It's not as if I was fanatical about Elvis, like Heather, my friend at school, who wore an Elvis button on her coat and carried a small picture of him in her mittens. My father felt, in no uncertain terms, that Elvis and his success stood for everything stupid and incomprehensible about this side of the world, which was disappointing him more and more. But I still wanted to see what the excitement was all about.

After the Sicilian grocers on Belair Street sold their store to expand their cheese factory, my father stopped going there, and Mother started shopping at the A&P on Belanger Street. My imagination was fueled by *True Confessions* and *Photoplay*, magazines I read as I followed Mother with a cart around the aisles of the store, and then slipped back onto the shelves at the checkout counter. I also kept up with the Italian counterparts to *Photoplay*: the *fotoromanzi* and *Sorrisi e Canzoni*, in which I followed the antics of the European jetsetters on the French Riviera, in Monaco, and San Remo. At school, my Italian friends who had arrived most recently argued constantly that Elvis and company could not hold a candle to Claudio Villa and Luciano Taioli. Since I liked to keep a foot in both camps, I wasn't always sure which side had the most merit. Without a doubt, the Italians had it on the voice, but Elvis and Pat Boone were easier to look at

At school I made a best friend, Antoinette, who lived in Saint-Michel, which was a bus ride away. I wasn't allowed to travel there by myself, so I spent most Sunday afternoons listening to the endless trumpet exercises, watching my mother perform her household chores in her church clothes, and reading or talking on the telephone with Antoinette. My brother insisted I also take music lessons, maybe the accordion, so we could form a duo. Father taught me solfège for a few weeks, but I wasn't as committed as Luigi and he gave up on me.

Instead, for the first year or so, I wrote diligently to my girlfriends from Mulirena, but eventually the writing dwindled until it stopped completely. I often dreamed of Mulirena. And when I wrote about it, I wondered whether things had really happened as I remembered them, or whether I was confusing memories and dreams.

Tenth Avenue was real, though.

Nothing much ever happened there on Sundays, but I still slept in hair rollers every Saturday night and wore my best clothes to church—in eager expectation. Wishes and dreams were tender crocuses that dared, bravely, to spurt out of the ground in spite of the frost and trampling feet. While I lived there, the multicoloured neon lights of the Montrose Theatre marquee blinked on and on with endless possibilities.

32. VILLE VERTE, 1960

MOTHER WARNED FATHER NOT TO get his hopes up too high. After buying a lot from Lucia's husband, Pasquale, Father often met with him to discuss job opportunities for when the development project in Laval went through.

"He talks too big," Mother said.

But Father said there was no harm in trying. Pasquale and Lucia paid us a few visits, usually on Sundays. She had started working in the same factory as Mother and Tina. Her husband, she confessed to Tina, was jealous of the men who worked there, and had ordered her to stay home. But she wanted to work, if only to get away from the whiny renters at the duplex her husband had bought in St. Michel.

Lucia lost no time sponsoring her brothers and by early 1960 both had settled in Lucia's duplex basement unit. With Pasquale's financial backing, they set up Calabria Foods, importing salami, cheeses, and olive oil from Calabria. It was also through Pasquale that the brothers befriended Nicodemo, Jack Russo, and their circle of friends, which included the contractor Joe Vaccaro and the smooth-talking Venetian Alex Di Principe, who dabbled in municipal politics.

The well-dressed and suave Alfonso, and the strapping Nicodemo, frequented bars and nightclubs together with the French girls that flocked around them. The food business took off well, thanks, in part, it was rumoured, to Nicodemo's strong-armed tactics in convincing restaurants to buy Alfonso's food products. But Alfonso had set his sights elsewhere. He delegated the food business to his younger brother, Pietro, and spent less and less time in clubs, especially after he started courting Joe Vaccaro's daughter, Dominique. Vaccaro helped fund Di Principe's political campaign until he was elected city councillor in Laval. Alfonso quickly moved in very different circles than my family and we didn't see much of him.

"How did they get rich so fast?" my mother asked of the people around Alfonso and connected to the Laval project.

Nicodemo's star was connected to Jack Russo and his contacts in the entertainment business. He spent his days in body building gyms and his evenings in nightclubs, and he was quickly groomed as Russo's bodyguard. Through Russo's connections, he became a professional wrestler and changed his name to Nico Demon. He set up a café in St. Michel under that name that soon became a hangout for Russo's cronies. Nico would often be seen driving his large Chevrolet Impala with its sweeping tailfins along Jean-Talon, close to the factory where Lucia and Mother worked. Pasquale sent him to spy on Lucia, Tina had surmised, but Mother had a more suspicious streak.

"He's circling the factory too often, at all times of day. Doesn't he ever work to pay for that boat?" Mother said once.

Father wanted to keep up his friendship with Pasquale because of his work. He showed him the papers that proved he had studied masonry in Milan and even brought out the thick books from which he had studied. But whenever he asked Pasquale about the Laval project, he was told that they had to wait until all the lots were sold before they could plan for construction. Then one evening Pasquale and Alex Di Principe showed up with a briefcase and some official-looking documents and offered Father shares in the construction company if he had at least five thousand dollars to invest. Father was at first cold to the idea, since he didn't have the money, but after Di Principe showed architect's plans for the Ville Verte, with colour drawings of the homes, parks, a piazza, and even a bocce court, he became obsessed, against my mother's warnings, with somehow securing the money to become connected to the project.

He pestered my uncles to go in with him, but they all declined. "If you don't risk you never get anywhere in this country," he kept repeating. After much arguing with Mother, he and Di Principe met with a bank manager and Father beamed with delight when he returned home with a ten thousand dollar loan and documents that made him a partner in Aménagement Ville Verte.

33. THE WEDDING DANCE, SPRING 1961

OUR FIRST WEDDING INVITATION IN Montreal arrived on one of those slushy spring days when sewers can't keep up with the flow of dirty, melted snow forming little streams down city streets. It was to attend Alfonso and Dominique Vaccaro's wedding in a new reception hall in St. Michel. I remember opening the pearly white, embossed card gingerly on my return home from school. My clothes had been drenched in muddy water by a speeding car on Belanger Street. I was excited about attending the wedding that had been the talk of all my *paesani* for months, but I dreaded Father's reaction to the invitation. His mood turned foul anytime Lucia's family was mentioned.

The Ville Verte project was not advancing as planned. Pasquale's partner, Joe Vaccaro, had problems having the zoning bylaw changed from agricultural to residential, Pasquale kept telling Father. Yet Di Principe had reassured Father that the zoning change was only a technicality, and that, being part of the civic administration in Laval, he would make sure the deal would go through. Nevertheless, Pasquale seemed really distressed by the slow pace of developments, and Father didn't know whom to believe. According to Pasquale, Di Principe was meeting stronger resistance to the proposed plans from the non-Italian city councillors than they had anticipated.

"They're jealous of us Italians buying so much land," Pasquale complained.

"Bunch of ignorants," Father said of Pasquale and his friends. "In Italy, they only knew how to feed pigs. Here they've all become *mastri* and big businessmen, but can't convince a bunch of farmers to turn a useless parcel of dirt into a model city."

"No need to panic," was Di Principe's response to Father's demands for an explanation. Meanwhile, a friend informed Father that Vaccaro had bought lots of other underdeveloped land in Laval and together with Alfonso started A&V Construction.

Father seethed at the news and called Pasquale. "How come they had no problems with those lots?"

"It's a smaller project in a different municipality," Pasquale told him. "Let's be patient."

Father threw the opened wedding invitation in the garbage, but I retrieved it to show Mother when she returned home from the factory.

"Don't lose your head and health over this," she told Father. "We go to the wedding, and then if nothing happens after that, you tell them you want your money back. Let them hustle like gypsies and let them keep their big houses and cars."

A scurry of shopping on St. Hubert Street followed for me and my mother. We had to look for the right dresses and particularly for the hats, which my aunts told us we had to wear in the French church where the wedding would be held.

A week before the occasion, I had my long hair cut short and curled into a bob. In my new dress and my first pair of high heels, I looked ten years older than my age.

At the reception, I sat bored at my family's table watching everyone dance while father berated the excesses of the lavish party. We watched as Lucia danced with the best man, Nicodemo, and anyone who asked while her husband sat alone drinking wine.

"Poor Pasquale, he never even got to dance at his own wedding," Mother said.

"He's a lackey for Alfonso and Vaccaro and a bigger *cornuto* than I thought," Father bristled.

On my way to the washroom, I stopped at Lucia's table. She commented on how grown up I looked and invited me to sit with her, and we chatted for a while. Just as Nicodemo came toward our table, another man pulled Lucia from her chair to the dance floor. Nicodemo took me by the arms and twirled me around in a fast dance. I was taken by surprise and couldn't keep in step with the music and tripped on his toes, but he asked me to dance a second and a third time after which I excused myself. I felt uncomfortable with the way he stared into my eyes as we danced. I could see my father looking at me sternly. When I returned to my table, my father snapped, "If you don't know how to dance, just sit and stop making a fool of yourself."

"How can I know how to dance when this is the first time I've ever gone to a party?" I snapped back.

"Well, well, you should send her to dancing school, so she can go out dancing on Saturday nights," one of my aunts said laughing.

I sat out for the rest of the evening.

As soon as we got home, my father slapped me hard across the face. "Today you showed me what you're really like. You behaved like a *puttana,* hand in hand with your friend, Lucia." It was the first time, my father had laid hands on me and the slap left me numb. My mother remained silent. From then on, I hated attending Italian weddings.

34. HEAT WAVE, SUMMER 1961

THE SUMMER OF 1961 TURNED out to be especially oppressive—the most humid in years, the weatherman said. Walking along the city sidewalks on my way to work, I could feel the sun's power hitting me twice: first, as it dropped its heat down to the pavement; then, as it radiated it right back up, smothering my body with sticky wetness.

At the beginning of summer I had managed to get a job at the Superstyle Lingerie Company where my mother worked. I was especially keen on working so I could spend money on clothes and books as I pleased.

My mother was impressed at how easily I had talked myself into a summer job at the factory. Mother had been told I should get a social insurance card before applying. But when I called for information, I was told I was not old enough to be issued one. I took matters into my own hands, and called the factory owner and asked him if he could make an exception since I only wanted a summer job.

"You called the Syrian boss?" Mother was stupefied.

"Who else would I have called if I wanted the job?" I told her.

The boss seemed cheerful on the phone, or amused, and told me to report for work the next day. Two days later, though, he stopped my mother on the stairs and told her, in slow French, that I had to work faster because, by law, he couldn't give me less than fifty cents an hour, even though I was underage.

The factory was on a side street off Jean-Talon Street, two blocks away from St. Hubert Street where I liked to go shopping. The owner and the office staff were all Syrian or maybe Lebanese, but the workers called them the Syrian bosses; the forelady in charge of the operators was French Canadian. But most of the workers were Italian, with the exception of two very wide, obese, elderly Syrian or Lebanese sisters who worked at the "finish" table, which is where I was placed. Lifting their feet seemed to require more effort than they could muster, so they moved around the large table by shuffling their heavy bodies along. They only spoke Arabic to each other and looked at me suspiciously. Our role in the manufacturing of white and pastel-coloured nylon ladies' panties was to cut the threads left by the over-lock machines on the seams and cro tch.

After the boss' reprimand, I watched the two ladies attentively. After years at this job, they had developed a rhythm to their movements as they got up from their seats, lifted dozens of packaged panties off one bin, carried them to their posts, untied the bundles, cut three threads off each pair, re-stacked them, and finally threw them back into another bin.

By the afternoon, even with all the windows open, the air in the factory became as heavy and condensed as a Turkish steam bath. The women's movements around the table became more laboured, their fleshy underarms dangling from their sleeveless dresses, and flapping against their bodies as they dragged the heavy packs of underwear. They sat at opposite sides of the table, and looked like two massive Buddhas guarding and controlling with nimble hands the movement of the bundled panties from the overlock machines to the finishing table to packing.

I didn't exchange many words with them. Outwardly I felt as sticky and uncomfortable as they looked, but it didn't bother me. I knew that by the end of summer my stint at the factory would be over. By the third day, I was going to the bins as frequently as the other ladies, and the boss never complained about me again.

Since I'd gotten the summer job, I played less and less with the French kids, who suddenly seemed so much younger than me. But I spent hours on the phone with my friend Antoinette, though I still wasn't allowed to go by bus to her house on Saint-Michel. During her last visit to my house, one Sunday afternoon, she had showed up wearing lipstick. My father said he didn't trust her parents, who came from Campobasso, and were too liberal and lenient with their three daughters. After that Sunday, whenever the phone rang, he always ran to answer it. Once, five minutes into my conversation with Antoinette, my father pulled the phone out of my hands and listened.

"I know the tricks used by some boys," he said later. "They have their sisters call for them. But you won't fool me."

With Antoinette, I mostly talked about the new high school, Saint Pius X, which we would both be attending in the fall. At the end of June, our seventh-grade teacher had taken the whole class to visit. The long corridors with rows of lockers next to each classroom, the large cafeteria, and the gym all still smelled of fresh plaster and paint, and seemed ready to contain all the fun teenage activities that my reading of *Archie* comics promised.

Together we had selected a pattern for a new school uniform tunic that her mother would sew for us. The pleated ones sold at the store we thought were too boxy and babyish, but every time I asked to go to her house to get measured my father would give me some reason why I couldn't go.

I was afraid to push him on the issue, knowing how preoccupied he was over the Ville Verte project. At the last council meeting at the end of summer the project was rejected, and he couldn't get a straight answer from anyone as to when or whether he would get his investment back.

"What do we do with the five lots we bought?" Uncle Tony asked.

"We can grow lots of tomatoes in the summer," Father joked bitterly.

"We'll try again when a new administration is elected in the fall," Principe reassured him. "These things take time."

That summer Father's back had given out, and he often worked in pain, but he didn't want anyone to know, for fear that contractors wouldn't call him during the busiest time of the year. In the evenings, he'd sit on the balcony, the breeziest part of the house, sweating and cursing the humidity and making fun of the English homeowners gardening in the heat.

I often watched him peruse the thick book with the onion-skin pages containing illustrations of columns, friezes, and mouldings, which he had brought from Milan. Now he laid bricks, row upon row of red or white bricks. And sometimes he had to carry his own loads up the scaffolds because the contractors couldn't afford *manovali* to assist the *mastri*, as in Italy.

"We look like Christs, carrying crosses," he said, about the V-shaped wooden box with a long handle that they used to cart bricks on their shoulders.

"*Che bella scoperta!*" he'd say, referring to Christopher Columbus, when he was upset at something. "Couldn't he have discovered a better country? Here you can't work in the winter for the cold, and then you die of humidity in the summer."

Each evening, Mother would rub Heet on his back, and he'd put a leather vest lined with sheepskin over his bare torso to help the product penetrate better. In the impossibly hot air of the apartment, the combination of smells from the medicinal cream, the wool, and his sweat was overpowering. He insisted that the sheepskin vest also helped absorb the humidity. How could my father and my whole world have changed so much in one summer?

On a particularly hot and muggy day, Father had returned from work in a cheerful mood. A contractor friend of his was close to getting a big contract in the city's west end, and he'd asked Father to go with him to help give an estimate.

"Teré," he told my mother. "You should see the house I saw today, in Westmonte. Now that's a house! All stone! It belongs to a big Jewish doctor. We went inside to look at the ceilings, and we had to take off our shoes; the carpet was this thick! But you wouldn't believe how cool it was inside."

"They have a *ventilatore* to make it cool?" asked my mother.

"What *ventilatore*? The plasterer told me that they use the same furnace that heats it in the winter to remove the humidity. I'm going to try it with our furnace."

"Are you crazy, in this heat? How can heating the house make it cool? You believe everything they tell you."

"You women don't understand anything about these things. It's the humidity that kills us here, not the heat."

My brother was still out at the park with his friends, and I was on the phone in the hallway just outside the kitchen. My mother was busy preparing supper, spreading freshly cut homemade pasta on the kitchen table, which was covered with the white sheet she reserved for this purpose. In the centre of the hallway, Father fidgeted around the oil furnace, which had been idle since the spring. He checked the on-off lever, then shook the pipe going up along the length of the corridor wall into the kitchen.

Mother looked at me and gestured with her eyes, as if to say: "This is a good time to talk to your father."

I cupped the phone and asked out loud. "What should I tell Antoinette about this Sunday? Can I go to her house for the measurements?"

"We'll talk about it on Sunday," Father answered, seeming overly preoccupied with the furnace. He proceeded to light it up. As its belly burst into flames, it started spewing smoke, black soot, and unbearable heat all over the house. I hung up the phone and ran into the kitchen.

"Turn that thing off before we all die," screamed my mother. "The heat has really made you go mad!" The smoke engulfed the kitchen almost instantly.

We could hear the thumps of my father kicking the stove, yelling over and over, "*Che bella scoperta! Che bella scoperta!*" "Have you gone crazy?" my mother yelled. She became frantic, pacing back and forth in the kitchen. She picked a dishtowel and moved toward the hallway, tried to fan the smoke away. I did the same. She bumped into my father, who pulled the towel away from her. In the skirmish, she tripped, lost her balance and fell right in front of the blasting furnace. I rushed to help her up, but father pushed and kicked me to get me out of the way, so he could move toward the side of the furnace to turn off the hot lever with the towel. Then he helped Mother get up, ran to the kitchen and opened the back door, fanning the smoke out with the towel. After the air cleared, he threw the towel at mother's face and went to sit on the balcony.

Crying, Mother checked the cut-up pasta, but it was covered with blackened soot. I tried to wipe the strands of soft dough, one piece at a time, but she pulled them from my hands angrily and threw handfuls of it in the wastebasket. Then she started pulling at her hair and shaking uncontrollably. "I'm going to pull the last hairs left on my head if he keeps on talking this nonsense" she screamed, directing her words toward the balcony. "He's acting like a *pazzo*." I tried to hold her still.

"What is the matter with you?" I yelled at the top of my voice at both of them.

From the balcony, father shouted, "Who is *pazzo* here, eh? You and your daughter, that's who! Things will change around here from now on. And forget about Saint-Michel on Sunday. And I'll tell you one more thing; she's staying at the factory with you instead of going around with that *puttanella* from Campobasso."

"You're crazy if you think I'm staying at the factory," I yelled back. "I'm going back to school with my friends."

"Don't you scream at me or I'll give you another one of these," he said, walking toward me and showing me the back of his thick hand. He didn't need to shout to make his point.

"Stop it now," Mother said. "Let's worry about cleaning up this mess."

By the time my brother returned, everyone had calmed down, though the walls in the hallway were blackened, and the place smelled like a chimney. Then, Mother prepared some store-bought macaroni with chickpeas, and we all ate silently. I figured Father had spoken out of anger, and couldn't possibly be serious about school.

"If only this humidity would stop," Mother said at one point, wiping her forehead with her dirty apron. Without realizing it, she streaked her face with black soot.

"Ma, you look like an Indian," my brother said, and we all had to laugh. To me she looked more like a sad chimney sweep.

"If we stay in this country, we'll all become Indians," Father added.

The following Sunday morning, before lunch, one of Alex Prinicipe's insurance agents came to the house. Father decided that though he couldn't do anything about getting his investment money back, he could do something about the life insurance policy he had bought from Principe. The agent noticed the black smoke streaks on the ceilings, even though Mother had spent all of Saturday washing the walls. Father told him that our furnace was defective but didn't go into details. The heat had not relented and Father had, at last, discarded the sheepskin vest, and took to splashing cold water on his torso every hour or so. The agent spoke in a curt tone, even though Mother served him coffee and anisette cookies as usual.

"You're making a big mistake," he told Father. "In this country, you need as much insurance as possible. What about fire insurance? Anything can happen." He pointed to the ceiling.

"Insurance is nonsense, an American invention," Father said. "Why should I kill myself working to pay for something that will pay me only if I die? What kind of investment is that?"

"You still have two school-aged children. If something happens to you, they won't be left in the street."

"They're able to work," he said. "My daughter has a job already, and Luigi wants to learn a trade. They won't starve."

Nothing had been said about school since the last outburst, and I was afraid to bring up the subject. My mother, busy serving refreshments and preparing lunch, didn't object when Father went ahead with the cancellation of his life insurance policy. After the agent left, Father organized the papers scattered all over the table. "Nice investments he sold me. They should call it death insurance policy. If he thinks I'm dying in this country, he's crazy."

"Will you stop talking about dying?" Mother said, raising her voice.

"Well, I'm telling you, whether you want to hear it or not," he answered loudly. "I'm not dying in this country! I'm going back to Italy, dead or alive. I'm going back."

"You're talking nonsense," Mother added. "Where do you think you're going with two children growing up here? Are we going to go back and forth like *zingari*?"

"I should never have come here; I should have stayed in Milano," he screamed.

"Milano! Milano!" my mother mocked. "That's all I hear. What did Milano ever give us after all the years you struggled there?" Their voices were getting louder and louder.

"You don't read the papers. I do," Father yelled. "Things are booming in Italy today. Have you heard about *il miracolo italiano*? Have you? Even in the *paese*, they're buying cars, while here I have to beg for work from these crooks."

"Who is making all these miracles, when in Italy they've thrown all the saints off the altars? We're not even supposed to believe in them anymore."

My father laughed. "See? I'm talking about the economy; you talk about saints. Ehh!" He gathered his papers and left the kitchen.

Mother kept on talking above the sound of running water coming from the bathroom. "All I know is that, at least, here, we're all together. We work, we eat, we have a nice apartment, even if that deal doesn't come through. What else do you want?"

"Well, I've been struggling since the age of twelve. Everyone has to look after themselves now. As Mussolini said, '*Chi mi ama, mi segue.*'"

I started setting the table for lunch. When Father returned, drying himself off with a towel, I asked, "Can I go to Antoinette's this afternoon for the measurements?"

"What measurements? Didn't you hear me? Here everyone has to look after themselves. You're staying at the factory with your mother."

"I'm not even fourteen," I said. "I want to go back to school."

His tone was calm. "What's the point of going to high school if you can't go to university?"

University seemed a long time away. "But I want to! You want me to stay at the factory and cut threads for the rest of my life?"

"The rest of your life?" my father laughed. "Don't you ever want to get married? You know, it costs here to get married. You don't just go to church, sign papers and you're married. Look at Alfonso's wedding—the hall, the flowers, the cars, the photographers. Ehh! There's no end. Everything we do here costs money. Where do you think I'll get it?"

I looked at my mother for help, but she was suddenly taken up with cooking, and never looked my way.

My father kept talking as if the decision had been taken and the discussion was over. "In five or six years, you'll be married, having children, and staying home. School will have been a waste. Instead, think of putting aside a few thousand dollars for your future."

I couldn't believe what I was hearing. And neither my mother nor Luigi, who had just joined us, seemed to react. She kept stirring and tasting the pasta, while my brother fidgeted on his seat, eating some bread. I threw the cutlery down on the table and walked to the living room, crying.

"Hard-headed bull," my father said in his joking voice.

After a while my mother called me, "Come eat your pasta before it gets cold."

"Eat it yourself," I shouted. I sank my head into the sofa armrest, and there I spent the rest of that Sunday afternoon.

35. BACK TO SCHOOL, FALL 1961

SUMMER WAS FINALLY COMING TO an end. We could feel it in the crisp breeze as my mother and I walked along St. Hubert Street during our lunch break from the factory.

"What nice air. If it could only stay like this for the rest of the year," said my mother, trying to engage me in conversation. I didn't answer. She was right about the air, but I wasn't about to agree with her. I now spoke to both my parents as little as possible.

I had just walked out on her at Maison Diana after she had bargained a discount on a fall coat she had tried, and then at the cash, she had insisted on not paying the tax. "*Mais voyons donc, madame,*" the saleslady had said in a disgusted tone, pulling the coat from my mother's hands as I left the store, my face flushed in embarrassment.

Mother followed me, muttering—"Tell her to keep it"—not the least bit bothered by the abrupt treatment. She also took my sulking in stride and, once outside the store, she tried to appease me. "Don't worry about the saleslady. Don't you know that they're all *zingare*? They're used to the haggling. They expect it."

I gazed at the store window and caught a glimpse of my mother pushing a strand of hair away from her face. She turned her head and said, "I'm so ugly. I look like a scarecrow."

My mother was not yet forty, but she acted and dressed like a middle-aged woman already. She was thin, with frail, sloping shoulders and no bust to speak of. In proportion to her top, though, her hips were considerable. Finding ready-made clothes for her was next to impossible. They were either too big at the top or too small at the hips.

"What do you want me to do?" she would plead whenever I became impatient with her shopping. "You know I'm built crooked."

And whenever we found something that fit, she always seemed to find it too colourful, too low-cut or—as with the fall coat—too expensive. Then, she would expect me to translate and bargain for her, which I usually did, sometimes arguing with her first, when her demands were unreasonable. But she always relied on me to finish a sale. This time I let her do her own bargaining in her broken French.

What irked me the most about my mother was that, thin and delicate as she was, with the right clothes and a little care, she might look as pretty as the American mothers on TV. But she purposely chose her clothes to make herself disappear—to look so inconspicuous that she'd never even make it as a scarecrow. It didn't help that she kept her sparse, thin hair pinned back with plain black bobby pins around her head. She was very conscious of the bald spots on the top of her crown. Most of the village women of my mother's age who used to carry heavy loads over tightly braided hair suffered from the same hair loss. Her only hints of vanity were her efforts to cover up these smooth, irregularly shaped patches by keeping her hair pinned flat. She was particularly concerned that the *bossa*, the French forelady at the factory, might notice the premature bald spots when she looked down at my mother's head, bowed over the over-lock machine. Her tiny head and face, made to appear even smaller by the severe hairstyle and the absence of make-up, made her look rather like a naked sparrow that hadn't yet grown its feathers.

As we reached the corner at Saint-Zotique, we crossed the street and turned back, as if on cue. This was as far as we could walk and still return to the factory on time. My eyes followed the window display of school clothes on the mannequins—plaid skirts, navy blue pullovers, grey flannel pants. These all made me think of the pictures in my first English reader, in which two wide-eyed, freckle-faced children run excitedly, red hair flying in the wind, to their first day of school. This time of year always filled me with the expectation of something new starting, rather than anything dying, but this particular season promised me little.

I walked slowly. I was in no rush to get back to the factory, though I could sense, from my mother's quickening steps, that she was afraid to be late for the bell that would have us all scattering to our posts like a flock of pigeons. It had already been four years since we crossed the ocean and yet we were still scrambling for crumbs.

Our co-passengers and their families were all faring much better than us. Lucia and Pasquale had bought a big bungalow in Laval. Full-page ads for Alfonso's housing projects were plastered all over the Italian community papers, while Nicodemo's pictures as Nico Demon, the wrestler, appeared regularly in the French tabloids. However, the Ville Verte project was still in limbo, while Father made monthly payments to repay the bank loan.

As we reached the factory, my mother made a last effort at conversation, trying hard to cheer me up. "Don't think that you're going to cut threads all the time. I'm sure they will let you work on the over-lock machine soon."

I punched my time card and joined the fat Syrian ladies. We all sat silently, and snipped at loose threads for the rest of the afternoon. I dreaded getting home, where the question of school still lay hanging, suspended in the humid air of our apartment. I was afraid to cause any more outbursts, but the longer I kept quiet, the more I was giving the impression that I had given in to my father.

When the factory bell rang, everyone in unison proceeded

to brush off the fine nylon dust that infiltrated our hair and clothes and covered our faces, legs, and arms.

On our way home, walking toward the bus, Mother broke the ice. "Your father is not himself these days. He hasn't been feeling well either. He needs to go see a doctor. Don't be so hard-headed with him."

"He's the hard-headed one. I only want to go back to school. It's not as if I'm asking to go out dancing on Saturday nights."

"That's all we need," sighed my mother. "What exactly did they tell you when you called for the card?"

"What card?"

"The social insurance card."

"I couldn't get one because I wasn't fourteen yet."

"If you're too young to get a card, then you must be too young to leave school," she said.

I hadn't thought of that.

"Look, don't make it seem as if you went around asking, or he'll get upset again. Maybe if he hears from someone else that you should stay in school, he'll give in. Don't let him think that you're stubborn, though."

"And what about when I turn fourteen?" I asked.

"Think about today," she answered, "and God will think about tomorrow."

At the 92 bus stop, a messy queue of people, mostly other Italian women, inched their way aboard. I was ready to say, "What good is God to us, if we have to worry about each day?" But Mother was pushing her way up into the full bus already. I had heard Mother's answer about God countless times before. I had also heard it from other village women. It had never meant anything to me; it was a stock answer they repeated to each other. Though I was crowded in the midst of all those working women in the bus, a small crack of space seemed to be opening up for me, and I felt as if I could start breathing again. I saw a subtly different take on the blind faith in destiny that had irritated me most about the women from the village. If we take control of each day as it comes, whichever way we can, then we don't really need to rely on God for miracles. Maybe, I thought, the women have always known this, and they've only paid Him lip service out of generosity, to make Him feel good.

Two days later, Johanne, my friend Antoinette's neighbour, called. She worked as a secretary at my school and spoke Italian very well. She asked to speak to my father, wanting to know why he had not sent in a form confirming my attendance at school. He didn't know of any such forms, he told her. And in any case, I would not be attending school anymore.

She replied that, by law, I was required to be in school till the age of sixteen—we added the two extra years for good measure. The school, she explained, could alert the police if a family refused to send an underage student back to school.

My father was impressed that the school secretary spoke such good Italian, and he was very polite with her. He said that he would respect the law, and I would return to school.

"You're going to school, but watch your step, and come straight home every day," he told me.

I knew that he still thought of me as too obstinate and unreasonable, but I didn't care. I could already taste the pleasure of going to the Syrian boss to inform him that I would stop working at the factory to go back to school. I felt confident that the small deception we had devised would buy me an extra year, maybe two. What would my father and the world be like after that? Already he was not the man I had known as a child, nor was I the same child that he had left behind long ago.

36. NOVEMBER 1961

MY MOTHER CALLS NOVEMBER the month of the dead. The month begins with *tutti i santi* or All Saints' Day, followed on the second by *tutti i morti*, the Feast of the Dead. The fourth is the Day of the Fallen Soldiers, and then nature takes over with its inexorable course towards the obliteration of summer. She still sets rows of photographs of dead relatives on her dresser and lights as many candles as possible, as though wanting to lighten up the gloomy period that follows.

On a bleak, late November afternoon in 1961, a group of people gathered on the outskirts of Mulirena, on the road across a ravine—the spot where people came to see others off, or waited impatiently for someone to arrive. The bare details of this scene were described to me when I returned to the village a few years later. I imagined the mood as if I had been there.

It was a sombre gathering. The older ladies, still dressed in the remnants of the *pacchiana* costume, let their long, heavy, black skirts down to the ground, black shawls covering their heads. The weight of the heavy winter shawls made their heads tilt to one side, giving them the appearance of *addolorate*—women destined for sorrow and mourning.

The younger ladies, dressed in ordinary clothes, were also in black. The men wore black ties and black armbands. The village band—carrying tubas, trumpets, and clarinets under their arms—was clearly not in a festive mood. This group was waiting for someone to arrive.

Across the ocean, the vapid songs of Ricky Nelson, Frankie Avalon, and Fabian ruled the hit parade. Elvis was still away in Germany doing his military service, and a younger set of teen singers had taken over his territory.

Things had completely turned around that summer between my father and me. Even though I'd gotten my way about school, we hardly ever spoke to one other.

On the day after Labour Day, I had started my first year of high school at Saint Pius X, the newest and largest of the English Catholic High Schools in Montreal. Boys were taught by the Christian Brothers and girls by the Sisters of Saint Anne; we were segregated into two separate buildings, connected by the administration offices.

"If I hear reports that you are hanging around with boys, it will be the end of school for you," my father threatened me. As if I needed this admonition! I used to turn scarlet when I so much as saw a boy from the other side of the building. I had been placed in 1A, the class with the highest marks, yet I still mumbled self-consciously in highly-accented English when answering questions from my teacher. My Italian girlfriends had all changed their names from Maria to Mary, Antoinetta to Tonie, Giuseppina to Josie, but I still gave my name as Caterina.

After the first few weeks in class, I was puzzled when Sister Mary Rose returned my first composition assignment with a question mark.

"Sister, I didn't get a mark ... like the others," I said shyly.

"I don't believe you wrote it," she said.

The topic of the composition had been "The Autobiography of a Car," and I had written about an old American Chevy used by a teenager and his friends. A humourous story had just flowed naturally, without much effort, and I had had fun writing it. But I just looked at the teacher and my unmarked composition, not knowing what to answer.

"You don't talk like that, so how can you write like that?" she asked.

I was mortified. "I can write better than I can speak," I told her. "I need time to think about words."

She looked at me with a frown, not quite sure what to make of me. I knew that she could not understand the kind of battles that had been fought in the language department of my brain, leaving behind casualties. Calabrese dialect had resisted Italian, and before Italian had had a chance to take the upper hand, it had been invaded by French, and then by English. Unfortunately, no one language had won complete control, and no matter what I spoke, words did not flow easily off my tongue. They often failed me, left me stranded in mid-sentence, flushed and embarrassed. So I spoke up as little as possible.

My brother was growing impatient with school and had finally convinced my father that he didn't want to pursue an academic education. In the summer, he enrolled in a private hairdressing course with a friend. My father was still trying to convince me that I would be better off working at the factory.

By the middle of November, though, things were looking up. My hair was being styled almost every day by my brother, who used me as his mannequin. I was the first girl in class to sport a teased-up hairdo—a bouffant, he called it. Sister Mary Rose joked that she wanted her hair styled just like me and Jackie Kennedy. I had joined the Sodality of Mary. I had also auditioned for the glee club, and had been given a singing part in the musical *Porgy and Bess*. My brother reaffirmed his suggestion that I study music seriously and take voice lessons so we could put on shows together. He had a stage scene he called "Staircase to the Stars" all worked up already. I'd come down a long lit up staircase singing "Summertime," a tune he had been practicing since I got the part, while he played the trumpet below the stairs, on the sideline.

"Why do you want to stay behind the scenes?" I asked him.

"The trumpet is loud enough. It doesn't have to be seen," he answered. He kept on practising while I memorized the lyrics from his music sheet.

On the first parents' night, in mid-November, Sister Mary Rose praised my efforts to my mother, and to show that she finally believed me, had my first composition printed in the school newspaper, *The Sartorian*. Tenth Avenue had sparkled in the vibrant colours and soft warmth of Indian summer, but that too was coming to its end.

About a week after that parents' night, my aunts Rosina and Maria, and their husbands Giuseppe and Giuseppe—both called Peppe for short—along with my cousins Pat, Luigi, Joe, and Sal, came to visit. My father's name, Giuseppe, had instead been shortened to Joe. At such gatherings, there were always two Peppes, two Joes, and two Luigis. When called, their names had to be qualified by the wife or mother's name.

On this Saturday evening, my relatives came with an unusual surprise. My paternal grandfather had sent, via a *paesano,* a recording of his voice with a message to all of us. An Italian radio station had sponsored a project to have parents' voices sent to their immigrant children. Everyone was so anxious to hear the recording that my mother hardly had time to make and serve coffee before my older cousin Sal set up his portable record player on the kitchen table. We all gathered around the machine, almost expecting to be transported to my grandparents' black, smoke-filled kitchen, where we used to sit around the fireplace as they cooked over a tripod. As soon as my grandfather uttered the first word, my aunts, who were very emotional, started crying. As for my brother, my younger cousins, and me, we could not help but snicker at my grandfather's grandiose manner of speaking. It was his style to talk as if giving a political speech. Addressing his family on a recording machine, he sounded like a pompous Roman orator, sending us all his *saluti* and good wishes. Then he addressed my father, his only surviving son.

"My dear son, I am speaking to you from our small and poor Italy. Always remember that once we were great and that we will be great again. Destiny has been cruel to us and to our country. Italy fell because we were betrayed. The past is like a wound in my heart. How can I forget the pain of seeing your return?"

At the mention of this incident, my aunts became almost hysterical. My aunt Maria said, "Oh, I can still see you, as if it were today. What a sight, what a sight!"

I couldn't understand the reference to my father's return and the pain it elicited.

My father also broke down as my grandfather went on. "But times are changing here too, and those black days are over. I hope that I will live to see you come back to Mulirena in luxury and glory."

"What luxury, what glory?" answered my father, wiping his tears. "Do they know that, here, we can't work almost half of the year because of the weather?"

"Joe, don't complain. At least here, when you work, you get paid at the end of the week. Did you forget the summer that we worked in Cassino—like beasts!—and they never paid us a lira?" asked Aunt Rosina's Peppe.

"Things have changed there too, now. It's not the same anymore," said the other Uncle Peppe. "Even Don Raffaele drives a Fiat now. Christ rode on a donkey but our priest now drives a Fiat. How do you like that?"

"A Fiat Topolino!" exclaimed the older Uncle Peppe. "You call that a car? Compared to a Chrysler or a Pontiac, it's a tin toy. Don't kid yourselves. Nothing has changed there."

"For things to change they need to burn the city hall again—with everyone in it," Aunt Maria's Peppe said. "And the government in Rome too. It's always the same crooks who run everything there, from the church to the government. We forget too fast." He had had communist leanings back in Italy, and had been refused a visa to the States because of it.

"You can say whatever you want, Pe', but in Mulirena, with a few *lire* a day, you feel like a king," my father said. "Here, it's never enough. I'm going back, one way or another, I'm going back."

"You're talking nonsense," replied my mother. "With two children growing up here, where are you going?"

"The children will be old enough to fend for themselves, like I did. They won't die of hunger anymore."

Aunt Rosina's Peppe said, "You tell them what Mussolini used to tell us: '*Chi mi ama, mi seque.*'"

"Eh! If you knew how many times I've told them that," Father said.

"Eh, you and Mussolini! Is it possible we always end up talking about Mussolini?" asked my aunt Maria, and everyone laughed.

There was nothing unusual about the bantering. It was always like this when we got together. My mother had warned my uncles not to mention the Ville Verte project or make fun of my father for his gullibility in investing in it so readily. She hadn't believed in it from the beginning, and didn't think it would ever fly again, but had stopped pestering Father about trying to get his money back.

When everyone had left and Father had gone to bed, I asked my mother: "Why was his return remembered with pain? Weren't they happy to see Father?"

"Well, there are two returns that your grandfather may have meant. Once after the war, and the other after your uncle died in Milano," Mother said sighing.

I had heard about Father returning from Milan after his younger brother died in a construction accident under his supervision. He didn't have the courage to give the news to his mother so he had one of his friends do it for him. My grandmother never recovered from that death and wore black for the rest of her life. I didn't know of his other return.

"I certainly was happy to see your father come back from the war—no matter what condition he was in," Mother said. "We hadn't heard from him in months and were afraid he might be dead. But you know how your grandfather is. He likes to think big. It was always, 'Mussolini here, Mussolini there.' He thought that they were going to conquer the world. Instead, your father and so many others returned hiding, in the middle of the night, like thieves. But what else could they do, those poor men?"

That evening I couldn't fall asleep. I remembered a group picture of soldiers in uniform, in which my father was smiling broadly, his face darkly tanned, and much slimmer than I had ever known him. I had heard that he had fought in Yugoslavia.

Was it there, I wonder, that he would decide to run back home? How would he make the long journey back? I see trainloads of people, pushing their way for a spot on the trains, sacks of belongings over their shoulders. Soldiers could get lost in the hordes of refugees fleeing the larger northern cities for the rural villages of the south. Where and how did he get a large peasant scarf and dress? He must have slept in many farmhouses and barns, for my mother told me that when my father showed up in the middle of the night at my grandparents' house—to change clothes before showing himself to her—he was dressed like a woman, and covered from head to toe in lice.

I had finally fallen asleep, when suddenly I heard my mother's scream. "Cateri, Luigi! Wake up! Your father is not breathing well!"

We ran into the bedroom. My father was unresponsive to our calls, but breathed heavily. The three of us shook him by the shoulders. We called and called, but he would not wake up. The bedroom was filled with the sound of his laborious breathing. He just kept gasping for air, as if his heart was trying to escape his chest. Soon, our Italian neighbours who had heard noises came up and called an ambulance.

Within a few minutes, ambulance attendants rushed in with an oxygen mask. First, they opened the window, then, they sent everyone out of the room and closed the door. My mother, moaning in fear, rocked herself on the edge of a kitchen chair, her arms crossed over the chest, as she listened to the groaning and the pumping of the attendants in the closed room.

A few minutes later, one came out to tell us that our father had died of a heart attack. Next, I saw the attendant inject my mother with a tranquilizer to keep her from screaming and crying.

The next week was a blur of people kissing and shaking hands.

"Only forty-two," they all repeated. "He was so young ... just when he could have enjoyed his family."

Without any hesitation, my mother decided to spend whatever money they had saved for an expensive casket, a large flower arrangement, and a plane ticket to send my father's body back to Mulirena.

The gathering of people who had waited patiently on the road became animated as they spotted a black vehicle across the ravine, emerging from Amato. My grandfather raised his hands in the air. "My son, my son is here." And they all moved to meet the car.

The hearse moved slowly, turned at the bend, and came into full view, the ornate, Canadian oak casket secured on its roof, and a huge white dove, made of white chrysanthemums, perched on top, as if reaching for the sky. From there, they formed a procession. The band in front, playing a slow march, was followed by the casket, then the men and the women in black. As the cortege proceeded up the narrow streets toward the church, others joined in, until most of the villagers had come out to see the sad, triumphant return home of Giuseppe Anastasia.

Once the mourning period was over, the prospect of our returning to Italy was raised. My mother's brother, Zio Pietro, wanted us to go back so that he could look after us. All our Montreal relatives were from my father's side of the family.

"What is a woman alone going to do in a strange country?"

my uncle wrote. After initial uncertainty, my mother made the decision all by herself. "No, we are staying here. At least here I have the job at the factory. We won't have to depend on anyone else to look after us."

I was a little disappointed, as I had secretly hoped to go back to Italy. Mother must have been terrified. But, for once, she didn't let herself be bullied by her own fears, and I looked at her differently. With her sparse hair pinned tightly back against her tiny head, she still reminded me of a little sparrow, but one not to be taken for granted, ever vigilant and tenacious. I had to relent about school, though.

"How can she be so stubborn?" my aunts pressured my mother when I insisted on completing my first year of high school. With no money from life insurance and a loan to repay, the only money we had was my mother's meagre salary from the factory. My teachers all came to my rescue and we reached a compromise. I would stay in school one more year to obtain the ninth grade leaving certificate, and then take a trade course—perhaps hairdressing, like my brother.

On my return to school after the funeral, Sister Mary Rose came to me one day when I seemed distant and absent-minded. "Don't worry too much, Caterina. I know you'll be fine."

There were other compromises. I wore a black blouse under the navy tunic and I wasn't permitted to wear lipstick or have my hair styled for a year. I was allowed to stay in the Sodality of Mary, but I had to give up the glee club and my singing role for good.

When Luigi resumed practicing "Summertime," Mother snapped at him, "How can you play music after your father has just died?"

"I'm doing it for him. We have to stop crying and do what he couldn't do," he answered.

I hadn't cried much throughout the ordeal, though the numbness really hurt. I felt especially sad for my mother and father who had had so little time together in spite of their love for one other and their struggle to be reunited. As for me, I wasn't as much as worried as blanked out. I saw life ahead of me as a series of boxes that I knew held nothing to make me want to run and open them up. I tried to write about how I felt, but the words didn't flow any easier than my tears. One evening, though, I played with a few words that I had jotted down, and formed my first poem in the shape of a tombstone:

> *November, month of the dead*
> *leaves, soldiers, dreams,*
> *thirst, emptiness, yearning*
> *after the summer sun.*

PART VI
OCTOBER 13-17, 1980

37. THANKSGIVING

MY LIFE IS ABOUT TO TAKE a new turn. I tiptoe into the bedroom to snuggle with Sean. Change, or the anticipation of any type of change, always makes me feel happy. I review the conversation I had with Sean the night before, to make sure it was real and not part of my jumbled dreams. His proposal could not have come at a better moment.

Marriage will finally lift me from that makeshift space in which I have been living. I had only kidded myself into believing that, somehow, our almost clandestine living arrangement would free me from the constraints of my rigid upbringing. Instead, it has weighted me down and I have yet to experience the carefree existence I had anticipated.

A fifteen-pound turkey, sitting in the sink, waits to be stuffed and roasted. I'll be preparing everything from scratch, from the zucchini and apple soup to the sausage stuffing and the pumpkin pie.

Thanksgiving is not an Italian tradition. I'm the only one in my family who has mastered the art of roasting a succulent turkey. I've also learned that it's all the side dishes, the trimmings and sauces, which accompany the bland meat that makes the meal special and festive.

Sean is still sound asleep and won't budge for hours. I have the entire morning to myself before I put the turkey into the oven, the perfect time to collect my thoughts. Not only Lucia's story, but part of my own since the landing has remained suspended in the blurred images and dreamlike memories of the past.

There are still too many circles floating around me, all bits of one life! How to make sense of it all in a linear form? There are still some huge gaps in Lucia's story between our ocean crossing and now. I feel certain that Angie will help me put the pieces together. In unravelling that story, I might even face up to mine. My early years in Montreal are tinged with a sadness that I've tried to keep under cover, but have subsequently tightened around me like a second skin. I now feel the urge to shed them once and for all by putting them down on paper. But will my writing be able to avoid the themes that the journalist deems too ethnic, too stereotypical?

"The bricklayer father, the submissive mother, the criminal son, the copious food, let us not propagate our own stereotypes," the journalist had pronounced in one of his essays. I had written in response:

Dear Antoine,
Your last essay left me a little confused. How can one write about an Italian living in present-day Canada and skip over some of those subjects you claim are negative stereotypes, like our food? Are we not local, regional beings before claiming fellowship to the universal? Should we be selective about describing the characteristics that make us who we are?

Dear Rina,
Well said, but you may have misunderstood me. I'm by no means a proponent of assimilation, but by using the same tired clichés—Italians as buffoons, criminals, suffering mammas—we play into the hands of the mainstream media who are conditioned to expect the same thing from so called "ethnic" writers—their label, not mine. They thus can more easily

dismiss works from the margins as superficial and inconsequential. The trick is to uphold our distinct colours, even our stink, while contributing to the universal fabric, without being bleached out by the whitening powder of assimilation. There's a fine line between specificity and stereotyping that only a true artist can thread.

The more I think about the standards set by the journalist, the more cautious and insecure I become.

At Thanksgiving dinner, my brother beams with pleasure at both the news about Sean's impending entry into the political arena and our plans on getting married, but the wedding plans receive the most attention. Mother seems guarded about the announcement. "You're having a civil wedding?" she asks.

"No, in a church," I say.

"Protestant?" she hazards.

"At Our Lady of the Consolata," Sean says. "I'll convert to Catholicism, if necessary."

Then we discuss the reception and the guest list. I insist it should include only the closest relatives and a few friends. But even that means close to a hundred guests.

"Can't we cut out the cousins?" Sean asks.

"How can you not invite first cousins? Some are like brothers and sisters," Mother answers, as I had expected. "If we invite one, we have to invite them all."

"We'll help out with the expenses. We'll leave the cousins out for the engagement party but you'll have to include them for the wedding," Luigi adds.

"Do we really need an engagement party?" I ask.

"Just a dinner at a restaurant with uncles and aunts, and J.P. of course," my brother suggests. "I only have one sister getting married. I'll pay for it."

To my surprise Sean doesn't object. "Sure," he says, "But be sure to schedule it after the ball and before Christmas."

"Mid-November," my brother says. He will look after the details and he'll also speak to the priest, whom he knows well, about what Sean needs to do to get married in a Catholic church. He already has a list of musician's friends lined up for the wedding ceremony.

"*Torta de cucuzza,*" Luigi says, digging into the pumpkin pie and tapping the top of his head, and we all laugh. It is both a novelty and an oddity for my mother to eat pumpkin as a dessert, and *cucuzza* is a slang term in our dialect for a hard head.

Alfonso and Angie arrive as I'm getting ready to serve coffee. Before stepping in, Alfonso hands me a wad of money, and whispers, "Angie's got enough spending money for the week. This is something for the rest of her expenses."

"No, no," I answer. "Don't worry about it."

"Okay. We'll arrange everything at the end," he says.

Alfonso doesn't sit down for coffee, but shakes hands with mother and Luigi, and I introduce him to Sean.

"*Complimenti,*" he says to me after Mother mentions our impending marriage. He looks at Sean and adds, "Give my regards to Jean Pierre."

"Sure," Sean says.

"Will he be in town for the ball?" Alfonso asks.

"That's correct," Sean nods.

"We'll see each other then," Alfonso says and leaves.

Mother asks, "Alfonso and Sean know each other?"

"He knows J.P.," I say.

"Alfonso knows how to make the right connections," she replies.

I lead Angie into the den, afraid my mother might say something disparaging about her uncle.

Angie looks around the room. "You have a lot of freaking books in here. Have you read them all?"

"Not yet," I answer. "Come and have dessert with us." She reluctantly follows me back into the kitchen where she sits quietly, looking disgusted at the piece of pumpkin pie in front of her.

"Whom does she look like?" Mother says. "She doesn't look at all like her mother's family."

I throw an irritated look at my mother for speaking about Angie in the third person, in front of her. Angie tucks a strand of hair behind her ear.

"Angie looks like herself," I say.

"Be good in school," my mother now turns to Angie. "Your grandmother already has enough on her mind." A pause and then Mother continues: "Your mother was like a daughter to me. It seems like yesterday she arrived with us."

38. THE HAIR STRAIGHTENING LESSON

ON THE RADIO'S MORNING CALL-IN program, the topic is space exploration. "We should take care of our homeless before throwing money into exploring empty air," a woman says in a thick North European accent.

The evening news carries earth-based photos of Saturn, released by Voyager 1. The space probe has been cruising toward Saturn since it swept by Jupiter twenty months earlier, startling scientists with one discovery after another. The photos show a subtle face of glowing yellow surrounded by bright rings. Both Jupiter and Saturn appear as multilayered globes. "We're involved in a very exciting adventure. Everything's new on Saturn," the scientists insist gleefully.

I can't wait to see what the photographs will reveal. Maybe it is all empty air, but I disagree with the last caller. Whatever the rings might contain, whatever the cost, they are certainly worth exploring. It seems like a logical progression that one day people will be travelling through space, just as the first settlers navigated across the oceans. Where would we all be, my family as well as the lady with the accent, if Christopher Columbus' voyage had been deterred by costs?

Sean is in the kitchen, having his milk and cereal, reading the morning paper. He's never at his best in the morning.

"Why did you sleep in the living room?" he asks.

"I wanted to read and write, and didn't want to keep you awake."

"What are you writing?"
"Old stuff," I say.
"Still?"

On Thanksgiving evening, after the family had gone home and the kitchen was cleaned up, I had stayed up late trying to write a beginning paragraph to introduce my new project—a book of linked short stories about the early years in Montreal that would bridge the past to the present, but nothing pleased me. I had found the concept of different stories with a common theme in *Lives of Girls and Women* by Alice Munro really interesting. *The Betrothed* also has an unwieldy number of individual stories, but Lucia and Renzo's love story ties them all into one. My love story about Lucia and Totu had fizzled out after their failed attempt at elopement, like the second-rate village firework display on the Feast of San Francesco.

What had seemed like such a promising writing project in the morning felt like a delusional pipe dream late at night. Tired from the cooking and the banal conversations around the engagement, my imagination felt dry and I only managed to juggle papers from one pile to another.

The last time I wrote to the journalist was after one of his tirades against both the Canadian literary establishment and the Association of Italian Canadian Writers. He stated that there could not be a literature without a tradition. Canadian literature is still in its infancy and too provincial, he wrote, and as far as Italian Canadian writing went, he ended with the question: Is there yet an Italian Canadian literature in this country? I wrote:

> *Dear Antoine,*
>
> *Doesn't tradition need time to flourish? It's like blaming a young man for his youth. Why not give local writers credit and encouragement for what they have achieved so far and acknowledge that we're also*

> *influenced by our Canadian experiences and literature?*
> Rina

> *Dear Rina,*
> *Forget about copying the Canadian literary model. They may have perfected the short story, but they can't look beyond their kitchen windows. Canadian literature is about burnt toast. We have a richer European literary tradition to back us up: Foscoli, Leopardi, Pirandello, and the contemporaries, Svevo, Calvino, etc. Look them up and study them before writing your next line.*

With my hidden identity it was easy to garner some audacity, and vent my pent-up frustration. I responded:

> *Dear Antoine,*
> *Get off your Italian marble pedestal for once. You're an intellectual snob!*
> Rina

To my surprise, he answered the week after:

> *Dear Rina,*
> *My ultimate aim is to raise the quality of writing to reflect our tradition without falling into the traps imposed on us by the establishment and their containment strategy, which is multiculturalism. How many books can our basements hold? We get grants for publishing "minoritarian" literature but then no one reviews or buys our books. Our differences of opinion are not only philosophical but strategic as well.*

I stopped writing to the journalist once I realized that his rants sounded like a broken record, and his responses were almost always politically motivated.

"Don't wait for me for dinner. I'm going to the library to work on my paper," Sean says, without looking up from his reading.

"I kind of had hoped that, before dinner, we'd go order that bedroom set we saw at the Danish House."

Sean puts down the newspaper and says, "This isn't exactly the best time for me to be looking at furniture. I have the paper on Jung to finish by the end of the month, the fundraiser ball to organize, and an election campaign to get started. Be realistic."

"I want a new bed for when we get married."

"Fine, but what's there to look at?" he says as he closes the door. "We saw the furniture already. You know I don't have that kind of dough, yet. If you buy it now, you'll have to pay for it with your own money."

"Yes, of course," I say.

I have enough money to buy the furniture outright, but for how long will we still be thinking in terms of "yours" and "mine" instead of "ours"?

I knock lightly on Angie's door. "Wake up, Angie. We can't be late."

In the shower, I close my eyes and let the water release the tension that has begun to take hold of me again. "Jung as in Yin and Yang," I say to myself and think of the Taijitu design I saw in one of Sean's books. The two black-and-white mirrored shapes resemble intertwined lovers lying on a bed. Would Sean start reaching out for me again once we got married, instead of both of us curling on our sides, facing away from one another, our backs rarely touching? He has been closed in his own world for quite a while. In our first years together, he spoke freely about his thoughts and dreams, and expressed aloud whatever crossed his mind. Maybe a new job, marriage, and a new bedroom set will jumpstart our new life together.

I finish shampooing my hair and linger, eyes closed, letting the warm water run down my face. I'll have to ask my mother what to do with the old set. Can she bear dumping it after all the years of loving care? She had discouraged me from using the bed, had considered it bad luck—because it had seen death.

My father had struggled on it, gasping for air, in the middle of the night.

"I wasn't born lucky," Mother would say later, when talking about her life.

The old bedroom furniture has had its day, but everything falls into place in its own time, I tell myself. The right time for a new bed is now that Sean and I are getting married for real.

While I set some bread, milk, and cereal for Angie, Sean collects his books from the kitchen table and leaves. "I didn't know he lived here," Angie says.

"I had mentioned it to your uncle. He didn't tell you?"

"He never talks to me. Probably thinks I'm retarded or something."

"Well, Sean and I will be getting married very soon."

On the drive to school, we're quiet for a long stretch, until Angie says, "Students talk about you at school ... if you have a boyfriend.... They wonder how long it takes you to get ready in the morning. Your hair always looks so perfect."

"It's because I care about how I look. You should too. It's part of being a hairstylist."

"I don't know if I want to.... I mean it's a lot of frigging work."

"We'll have to trim your hair in class, one of these days," I say. Angie's curly hair looks as if she hasn't combed it since the night before. It has the wiry texture that lends itself to being shaped into an afro, but the back is too long and the crown hair is a shapeless mass.

"I like it long," Angie says, passing her hands over the hair on her neck, as if to protect it.

I let Angie off in front of the school garage. "Don't be late for class," I insist.

"Don't worry, Miss."

I smile thinking that in spite of all the dire predictions, Angie will prove everyone wrong. A hair makeover and some new clothes should help Angie shed some of her awkwardness.

Classes have resumed normally. The corridors at WLHS seem unusually quiet. I report the tire slashing to the principal. Mr. Champagne sighs and shakes his head. "I was afraid that the chaos of last Friday would incite students to vandalism."

"Maybe it wasn't a student," I say.

"That would be too preposterous to think about. I've called a meeting to address all this," he says.

The daily bulletin announces a meeting for students after recess, followed by one for the staff. I figure that the meetings will take care of at least two periods. Some teachers complain about too many class disruptions, but at times like these, ill prepared as I am, I pray for them.

At the office, I try to line up another volunteer for a permanent demonstration, but Susan can't make it. Since the stink bomb incident, the office staff has been inundated with extra work, revising the teachers' supervision schedules and preparing for the meeting. Then she invites me to a Halloween party at a country place she has rented for the winter.

"I'd love to go," I reply. "But I have a fundraising event that evening—a ball—to go to with my fiancé."

"Fiancé? I didn't know you and Sean were engaged."

"Well, we're planning on getting married soon. But don't say anything, yet."

This is the earliest I have gotten to school in a long time. I'll have time to look over some notes on hair relaxing, the next topic on the program. Unlike the academic teachers, who have a different class every forty-five minutes, I have the same small group of students for five hours a day—a long time to keep the students interested and occupied. Thankfully, because of the meeting, I only need to plan for three hours today.

In class, I pore over the thick program of study provided by the Ministère de l'Éducation, but am not inspired by it. I give up on the lesson plan. Students don't look forward to theory lessons, and are generally not very curious about the why and how hair is affected by the various procedures. "Why are we studying chemistry?" they'd ask. All they want to do is style hair.

Angie walks into class early with Linda and Gina and, as the other students drift in, they all give Angie a high five, except Franca and Mary, who sit quietly. After reading the bulletin to the class, I ask the students to continue the same exercise as Friday.

"Miss, when are we going to practice on real people?" Gina whines, as the rest of the class get their hairdressing implements and mannequins ready. "I'm getting tired of these dummies."

"Stop talking about Franca like that," Angie says. Everyone laughs—except Franca, of course.

"I wouldn't talk, if I were you," Franca snaps back.

"I can talk all I want," Angie retorts.

"Just because you live with the teacher?" Franca replies.

"That's enough from you two," I say. I have a brainwave. "Angie, how about we straighten your hair?"

I had been itching to do something to Angie's hair since she first arrived in my classroom.

Angie raises both hands to her mass of unruly hair, "No fucking way. What if I don't like it, and who is doing it?"

"I'll do it as a demonstration, Angie, but please ... watch your language."

"Oh, shit, I'm in real trouble now!" Angie says.

"Language again ... please!" I say, gathering products for the demonstration.

"I only said 'shit'."

"Angie! Enough already!"

"Go for it, Angie" Linda says.

I ask Fotini to wash Angie's hair.

"You're jealous, aren't you, puke-face?" Angie sticks out

her tongue at Franca as she sits on the hydraulic chair in the centre of the semicircle.

"Stop bugging me, you retard," Franca says, getting up and looking like she's about to punch Angie.

"Okay, girls! Let's stop the nonsense and get back to business," I say, separating the two. "I can't believe you're acting like first graders." I try keeping a good-natured tone, but am flustered at the change in Angie since the morning.

"Straightening Angie's hair is not exactly what I'll be doing. The right term to use is hair relaxing."

"You should have given her some Valium to relax her before bringing her to school," Franca mumbles.

"I heard that, shit-face," Angie tries to get up again. Standing behind her chair, I push Angie down by the shoulders with force.

"Hair straightening is one of the most aggressive hair treatments," I say in a strained tone, while the class laughs.

I keep the theoretical lesson simple. I draw diagrams of three thin tubes on the board: the first, sharply curved; the second, less so; and, the third, a straight line. "These are hair follicles, as they look like inside the dermis," I say. "How curly or straight hair grows out of the skin depends on the shape of the follicles." I point to the sharply curved tube, and draw a tight, zigzagged line next to it. "This is Angie's hair follicle," I say. "As the hair is pushed out of the curved tube, it grows out frizzy. It's genetic. We can't change the shape of our hair follicles. In hair relaxing, all we can hope to achieve is to loosen the tightness of the waves as much as we can, and maybe get something like this." I draw a wavy line next to the second diagram. "Of course, the more resistant the hair is, and the tighter the natural wave, the less relaxing we will achieve."

Angie has inherited her parents' curly hair. Whereas her mother's hair is soft and fine and used to fall gently on her shoulders, Angie's hair is coarse and has a wiry feel—probably from her father's family.

"The curly hair gene is dominant over the straight one," I explain.

This statement usually triggers a flurry of questions and comments from the students, but this group is the most lethargic I've had in years. I skip all the chemical information about the different types of products available and show them the lotion we will be using—the same lotion used to perm hair. While straightening is the reverse of permanent waving, the same principle applies. "In the case of a permanent, straight hair takes the shape of the rod; in chemical relaxing, curly hair is forced into a straighter shape by combing it with a fine comb."

I explain to the class that hair straightening had been most popular in the early 1960s, when women ironed their hair and slept with giant rollers. Then, during the anti-fashion, back-to-nature, make-love-not-war movements of the last decade, the procedure lost favour, and women actually curled their hair to a frizz to achieve the wash-and-wear look.

"Judging by the new tendencies in fashion, though, it won't be long before women will want to smoothen out the frizzies again—like Angie here…"

"This was your idea," Angie shoots back.

This is one of the hairdressing procedures I like the least. It's messy and the products used smell like rotten eggs. I section Angie's hair into four parts and start to apply lotion on the nape.

"As you force comb the hair, the product breaks the hair bonds; the hair becomes soft and limp and takes on a new shape. You comb and comb until you feel that it's the straightest it can be. Then you neutralize it like a perm."

Angie's hair feels like steel wool. And to think that her mother's hair had been the envy of all the girls in Mulirena! I remember Lucia using a wet comb to part it into waves over her forehead before going out for the evening *passeggiate*.

I have everyone take turns combing and smoothing the hair down. "Angie's hair is in good condition to start off with, and it can stand the trauma. But remember to analyze the hair carefully before starting, just like for a permanent. There is a risk of dissolving the hair at the roots as it is being combed."

"Can you get sued for that?" Franca asks.

"For sure," I reply.

I accompany Angie to the sink, rinse her hair, and then comb the neutralizing lotion through it. I rinse the hair one last time again and then it's ready to be cut and blow-dried.

"Wow! It looks less bushy," Gina says.

Angie runs her hands over her hair. "It feels like I have nothing left."

"Maybe it's not as straight as you'd like it," I say. "But it's the best we can do without hurting your hair."

"I never wanted it straight to begin with," Angie says

I'm happy to have gotten through the lesson, unprepared as I was, and hope that by the time I'm finished styling Angie's hair, she'll cheer up.

"Your hair needs to be re-shaped," I say, lifting the wet hair with an afro comb.

"It will look much better after a haircut."

"No way!" Angie yells. "I don't want to cut my hair. I told you already. It's taken me forever to grow it." Angie gets up from the chair and I know there's no way to convince her to cut her hair this time.

Without proper styling, Angie's hair will look just as out of shape as it had before—only less full. I'm disappointed as I watch Angie's unhappy face at the result. This procedure needs to be repeated every couple of months. Her hair will keep on growing wiry and bushy, just as it has been programmed by the genes she has inherited from her parents. I leave the class with a niggling feeling that maybe I acted too impulsively, leaving Angie with a hair battle she's unprepared to take on.

39. BAR À GO-GO

IN THE AUDITORIUM, WE HEAR a vague report about the police investigation of the stink-bomb incident from Sergeant Prevost, and then we are introduced to two new aides in charge of security, Dave and Stefan. They both look as if they spend a lot of time at the gym. The two would make good bouncers in a nightclub or a good wrestling tag team.

Mr. Champagne goes on to present a new set of rules concerning dress codes, entry and exit, as well as attendance and vandalism, and hands the microphone to the Sergeant.

"We are monitoring a very serious situation," he says. "There are bad crowds circulating around the school." He goes on to tell students that the authorities know of a group of youths—not WLHS students, but outsiders—who push drugs and participate in other illicit activities around the neighbourhood. Drug dens have been discovered in close proximity to the school. Students are warned to stay away from any outsiders who try to enter the building.

A new improved supervision schedule is part of the principal's plan of action in combating this problem, and students will need to carry their school ID cards at all times. The student audience grumbles and boos, until the end-of-period bell rings and they're dismissed. The secretary distributes the new schedules to the staff and we are reminded that the dress code and no-smoking rule applies to us as well as to the students.

Bruce asks a question, "Did any other teacher besides Cathy

find their car tires slashed on Friday afternoon?" No one else has.

"These incidents are a direct result of the examples you're setting for students. Please stick to the new rules," Mr. Champagne replies and leaves while teachers grumble and boo just as the students had done a minute before.

Steve takes over the meeting and asks teachers to count our supervision minutes with a fine-toothed comb, and make sure that the total doesn't go over the number of minutes stipulated in our contract.

Someone asks, about the safety issue for teachers supervising the entrances, "Students are slashing our tires. Who the hell do we call in case of a confrontation?"

"They've covered their asses by scheduling two teachers at a time," Steve replies. "I'll bring the safety issue to the attention of the union, but for my intervention to carry more weight, you should all file a complaint right away."

On that note, the meeting is called to an end. Some file out, others line up in front to speak to Steve. Bruce catches my attention and waits for me outside the auditorium. "Did you get home all right on Friday?" he says.

"I'm fine. Thanks for bringing up the tire."

"Didn't do much good. Did you notice? They have us two guarding the southeast exit on Day Four, Period Five."

I had noticed.

"Are you lodging a grievance?" he asks.

"I'm not complaining if you're not," I reply.

"Is that a come-on?" he asks, elbowing me with a grin.

I laugh, but can't come back with a witty remark.

We walk together towards the stairs in awkward silence and then we go our separate ways. I wonder whether Costa and George, from Miss Park Ex, have already heard about the two security guards.

In the cafeteria I join some of my students who are sitting together talking about the meeting.

"Miss, have you heard that there's a ring that deals with white slavery?" Franca asks.

"No I haven't," I say, amused. "You might be exaggerating, Franca."

"No, Miss. The same people who are pushing drugs are also forcing girls to have sex with older men," she says.

"That's not white slavery," Linda says. "That's pimping."

"Whatever. But I've heard people talking about white slavery too," Franca says.

I feel drained by the day's activities, and all the conjectures. I go to my classroom to be alone and wait for Angie. I had told her to meet me in class at the end of the school day.

After the last period bell, I wait for thirty minutes, but Angie doesn't show up. I drive slowly around the school neighbourhood looking for her. I honk at Fotini and Mary, who are walking together, and ask them if they have seen Angie.

"I saw her walking with Linda and Gina. They probably went to the Club," they say.

They'd have to take a bus at Park Avenue. I hope to catch up to them. I can't stop Linda and Gina from taking dancing lessons at the Bar à Go-Go, but I have to forbid Angie from going there—of all places! I speed towards the bus stop.

I know Charlie Matteo, the bouncer at the Club. He'd gone to Pius X High School at the same time I had. His name often appears in the French language tabloids, *Allô Police* and *Montreal Matin*. Quite a number of boys from my old high school have also made news in these papers, usually after an arrest.

Charlie turned out to be one of those. At school, older than the rest of the class by a couple of years, he had never fit into regular school life. These boys generally didn't continue beyond high school, or they quit without graduating.

I occasionally run into these old acquaintances, and I've attended a number of their funerals, dead under circumstances not clearly explained, though the papers generally attribute it to a "settling of accounts."

It has been heartbreaking seeing the rest of their families, hardworking people leading simple lives, in shock and dumbfounded by what had happened. They had either lost control of their son's actions, been too busy working to notice any changes, or they simply chose to deny what they might have suspected—that their son's new-found wealth could not possibly be the fruit of running a café, or some excuse of a small business that had no chance of being that lucrative.

Nicodemo, or Nico Demon, is something else. The many newspaper reports on Jack Russo and his underlings have painted a picture of ties to criminal families in the old world and of the intermarriages between them. If diagrams of family trees and all their interconnections could tell a bigger story it would be that centuries of illegality have rendered its members immune to any sense of guilt or of social or civic responsibility. The honoured Don is a myth perpetrated by Hollywood movies.

As I drive towards Park Avenue, I spot the three girls and a young man I've seen hanging around the class. I stop the car on the curb ahead of them.

"Eh, Miss, are you coming with us to Charlie's?" Linda asks.

Angie doesn't say anything, but looks annoyed at seeing me.

"I don't think so. Angie you're coming home with me. You were supposed to meet me in class, remember?"

"I waited for you outside, but you weren't there," Angie says.

"Really? You didn't look very hard," I reply.

"Miss, come to the club with us," Linda says, approaching the car window. "Charlie is a lot of fun. We already told him you're a cool teacher."

"Sorry, girls, Angie really needs to come home with me."

"You go ahead. I don't even feel like going anymore," Angie says, her voice gruff.

The young man next to her moves nervously but doesn't say anything.

Angie gets in and I drive away. After a few minutes of silence, I reprimand Angie for hassling Franca.

"That stuck-up bitch!" Angie says.

"You can't misbehave in class or at school, in any way. You remember Mr. Champagne's conditions."

"I can't even say what I think?" Angie whines.

"You can't start arguments and pick on people."

"I wish you had minded your business this morning and left my hair alone," Angie says.

"Why?" I said. "Your hair will look good once I trim it."

"No fucking way. You're never gonna touch it again!"

"Okay," I say, after a while. "But there are school and class rules you can't break and get away with because you live with me. Be reasonable. You do anything foolish and Mr. Champagne will send you back to the other school board."

"They can't send me back. I got kicked out of there already."

"No, they didn't kick you out. They referred you to a special program at the hospital, which is where you'll have to go if this doesn't work out. They'll keep you there until you're sixteen, and then they'll kick you out. Do you see the importance of following all the school rules?"

"Why only me? The place is a zoo, anyway."

"Worry only about yourself, Angie, not the others. I'm especially upset, though, at you taking off with Linda and Gina without telling me."

"I can't go out with my friends?"

"Not to a strip club! What would your mother say if she knew?"

"My mother doesn't know a strip club from beans. She never gives a shit what I do."

"Who's the guy?"

"It's Eddie. He was in my English class, but he just got kicked out of school,"

"What for?"

"Who knows? Drugs ... prostitution ... chewing gum in class. I don't ask questions."

"Stay away from him as long as you're in my care, and you're not allowed to go to Charlie's either. Do you understand?" I raise my voice.

"Don't scream at me. You're not my mother."

"You're not to go to that nightclub," I lower my voice as we near my apartment.

"Fuck. You Calabresi are all the same," Angie snorts with disgust.

40. BRUCE

BRUCE AND I ARE STATIONED at the southeast door exit of the school. The doors are locked on the outside, but for fire-safety reasons the doors must open from the inside. Our task is to make sure that students don't let anyone in during the lunch break, but hardly anyone passes by that corner of the building. "What a waste of time," I say.

"It beats supervising the stinking locker rooms," Bruce says, leaning against the closed door.

I notice how tall Bruce is next to me. His frame fills the space. I can hardly see his eyes, though. He wears black-rimmed glasses, and his dark, shaggy hair skims his forehead. He keeps an unlit pipe in his mouth. With his cords and a loose, plaid flannel shirt, he exudes comfort and ease—like the Hush Puppies shoes he wears. I wonder whether he owns a suit. I have never seen him in one.

"You always this laid back?" I ask.

"No point in getting uptight." He keeps taking his pipe out of his mouth as though he were smoking it.

"That's a good attitude," I say.

I ask if he knows Eddie, the young nervous man I saw walking with Angie a few days earlier. He has called Angie at home a couple of times, and she told me he called to help her with her homework.

"Oh yes, I call him the snake. He's a slippery one, that one. A smooth operator, a wheeler-dealer, real smart, though, a

Park Ex inner-city kid." Eddie is one of the first casualties of the principal's policy to kick troublemakers out of the school as soon as they turned sixteen. But Bruce told me not to worry about Eddie calling Angie. He had been in the same English class as Angie and it was Bruce who had asked him to help Angie with her English work.

"He's a rarity in this school, one of the few English kids," he says. "He stutters, but writes unusually well for his age. I think Angie may have a crush on him."

"Of course! She had to fall for a troublemaker," I say, raising my hands and shaking my head.

"Angie is subdued these days," he says. "It must be her new hairstyle. You did a job on her."

"It still looks awful. She won't let me cut it into shape," I explain.

"Do you think I need a makeover?" he asks, touching his own wavy hair.

"Your bangs could use a trim," I say, smiling.

"Only if you do it."

I giggle. I remember the late sixties when I worked as a hairstylist. Mothers used to drag their long-haired teenage sons to the salon because they refused to go to their barbers for a full-fledged haircut. Bruce still maintains the scruffy look of those rebellious but gentle-mannered young men.

"Where you born in Montreal, Bruce?" I ask.

"No. I'm from the Abitibi region, Val D'Or."

"Where's that?"

"It's up north, way up north, past La Vérendrye Park."

"I'm sorry, but I don't know where that is either."

"I bet you've been to Europe a number of times."

"Three or four times," I answer, not quite understanding the connection he is trying to make.

"But you don't know where Abitibi is."

"I've never had a reason to go there."

"Shame on you, Cathy!" Bruce says. "You should get to

know your own country. I crossed it with two buddies the year I graduated from teacher's college—from shining sea to bone-chilling sea. It was a great experience."

"It's such a big country," I say. "Where do you start?"

"Maybe your own province?" he offers.

He's right, I think. I have lived in Montreal most of my life, and yet I know so little about the rest of the province—let alone the country.

"What was it like growing up in a place like Val D'Or?" I ask.

"Not many opportunities anymore up there for us Anglos. Left early to go to college ... only went home in the summer to work in the mines."

"I like the name Val d'Or," I say. "It sounds romantic—valley of gold—like the gold can be picked off the ground, or from the trees. Is it really a valley, with mountains all around it?"

"No, actually it's very flat. You might say the mountains are all hidden underground. That's where the gold lies."

"Extracting gold from rocks—how do they do it? It sounds as hard as extracting blood from a stone," I ask.

"Actually, comparing gold to blood is not a stretch. The gold runs in yellow veins in the walls of the mines. When they find it—even minute traces—they blast the rocks off the wall, bring them up to mill, mix them with water, and then crush them until it all turns to muck. Somehow the liquid yellow gold gets separated from the dirty slush."

"Interesting, and not at all how I had imagined it."

"Angie tells me that her bedroom is surrounded by wall-to-wall books—not what I had imagined either."

"I've always been an avid reader, and ... I also like to write."

"Your hairdressing experience must have given you lots of stories to draw from. Hairstylists make the cheapest psychiatrists, they say."

"That's true." I confess my compulsion as a teen to set my memories down on paper before they dissolved into oblivion. "I'm trying to write a book of linked short stories."

He strokes his chin with one hand, and holds his pipe in the other. "You're wasting your time," he says after a few seconds. I'm taken aback by the remark, until he continues, "I mean, it sounds as if you have a lot of material. Write a novel instead."

"Oh, I couldn't possibly write a novel. It seems a little too ambitious for me." I feel my face flush as I speak.

"Bullshit," he replies. "If you're good at spinning yarns, you can write a novel." Bruce moves closer, shaking his pipe at me as he speaks. "Here's what I tell my students: just pretend you're telling a story to someone from Mars, who knows nothing of the world you're writing about."

"I guess that could work if you're starting from scratch. I already have a lot of different stories, and I would need material to connect them," I say joining my two hands together. "I don't know if I can be that creative."

"Harvest your dreams. That's also something I tell my students. They're a real gold mine of material. Good writing is about unlocking our dreams and fears and presenting them to the world. Remember the nightmares as well as the happy dreams ... a very scary proposition at times. It's the creepy stuff that adds the spice."

I look at him pensively as he continues. "It's a challenging job, writing a novel. You have your work cut out for you. Give yourself at least five years."

"Wow! That seems like a long time. I wouldn't know where to start ... or where to finish for that matter."

"Well, endings are tricky, but not as difficult as beginnings. I'd say, start from where you are now—the middle—and radiate toward the beginning and the end." He fills his pipe with tobacco as he speaks.

I'm sorry to hear the end-of-period bell ring. "See you next Wednesday," I say.

"I'll see you around before that." He nudges me on the arm. "I'm going out for a smoke, but watch this first." He opens the door, and steps out. He lights his pipe, inhales deeply, and then lets out perfectly formed smoke rings. He winks at me as I watch the Os float up into the air.

41. MODERN FURNITURE

A QUEEN-SIZE MATTRESS AND a dozen other boxes of different sizes fill the hallway, the kitchen, and the living room. Sean is on the phone in an animated conversation.

"What the hell?" Angie says, as we enter the apartment.

I gather from the telephone conversation that J.P. is coming into the city on the weekend as he had previously planned.

"Thanks for warning me," Sean says when he hangs up with J.P.

"I told you I'd be ordering it."

"Why this weekend? You knew about J.P. coming in."

"I'm going to do my homework," Angie says and shuts herself into her room. She spends most of her time in the den listening to the radio and working on her English and French assignments. Her uncle will be picking her up before dinner.

J.P. had called to announce that he would stay in town the rest of the week to finalize arrangements for the Halloween fundraising ball that is taking place the following Friday evening. I'm expected to attend. It has been a while since I have gone to a party with Sean, let alone a ball. At other times, I would have been in a frenzy to find the perfect outfit, but with all the goings-on of the past weeks, I had blotted out the event altogether. What preoccupies me most is having to put up with J.P. and Angie in the same house for a week. Sean thinks Angie should stay at my brother's.

"I can't do that," I answer.

"Then Angie will have to sleep on the sofa when he comes in on Sunday. I can't ask J.P. to give up his room."

"When did the den become J.P.'s room?" I say, raising my voice.

Sean moves to the bedroom. "No need to have a temper tantrum. Calm down."

"I'll calm down when I feel like it. I can't understand why he can't sleep in the living room or in a hotel for a few days. He has an expense account. How will it seem to Angie's family to have another man sleeping in the house?"

"I don't give a damn about what her family thinks. This is one of your problems, not mine. I don't conduct myself in relation to how other people think...."

"Except for public opinion polls," I yell, and walk nervously back from the bedroom to the kitchen, kicking the boxes of furniture and mouthing, "Fuck, fuck, fuck."

"Cut the crap. You're overreacting." Sean takes a beer from the fridge. "I'm sure we can work this out. But it's going to be a messy weekend. You could have waited before ordering new furniture. What was the big rush?"

"I was really fed up with the shabbiness of this place," I say.

"Have you thought that maybe the furniture may not be the problem?" Sean asks, and takes a long sip of beer.

"Tell me what the problem is, and we'll try to fix things." I sit down and motion for him to sit too. "You're the intellectual."

He remains standing. "Please, not now ... if a new bedroom set makes you happy, I'm fine with it. Just get it organized before the weekend. I have more important things on my mind."

"Yes, of course, synchronicity and integration," I say. Then in a whisper, I add, "The fact that we haven't made love in over a month is irrelevant to you."

"You're the one who sleeps on the sofa at night, writing in your journal or whatever. You wouldn't understand what's on my mind, anyway."

"Try me some time. I might surprise you." We're quiet for a few seconds and I reflect on how the initial good feeling of the marriage proposal lasted less than a few days.

"Where will you put the old set?" Sean says

"I'll call Gaetano to come with his truck. Maybe he'll find some way of fitting the old furniture into my brother's basement."

"You better call him soon or the apartment will get pretty crowded."

Gaetano comes promptly after dinner and, even without Sean's help, quickly carts the furniture away.

"Where do we sleep tonight?" Sean says as he walks back into the empty bedroom.

I open one of the boxes in the kitchen. The new furniture needs to be assembled.

"We'll just put the mattress on the floor for tonight. Luigi will give us a hand next week to assemble the rest of the furniture."

"It's going to be a fucking big job," Sean says. "There must be thousands of pieces. I thought it would have come all set up."

"So did I," I reply. "But it's modern furniture. It comes like this."

"You could have called the Salvation Army and given the old furniture away, instead of hoarding it." He shakes his head and says, "You can't ever let go, can you?"

PART VII
OCTOBER 18-24, 1980

42. THE ETHNIC WIFE

THE FRONT PAGE OF THE Saturday morning *Montreal Star* is filled with a photograph of a slain man lying in a pool of blood on a sidewalk. The headline reads: "Jack Russo's nephew gunned down while leaving his Saint-Michel home." The police don't have any leads, but say that the gunman must have been an expert marksman. The killing surprises the police. Pietro Russo, aged thirty, is not known to be active in the underworld.

In a second page article, the usual "expert" on organized crime includes an "underworld organizational chart," which shows that Jack Russo heads a division that includes all of Quebec, and parts of Eastern Ontario, with tentacles that extend to Sicily and as far as South America. The division is said to have connections to the feared Mafia chieftain, Francesco Botti, of New York City. The expert further claims that Jack Russo is still the "real boss" of the Montreal Mafia, but in the last months, events suggest that his control is being threatened by a younger and ruthless Sicilian clan with more influence in the world of illegal drug trafficking.

"Lots of action going on," Sean says. "The war between the Sicilians and the Calabrians seems to be intensifying."

"I couldn't care less," I say.

What irritates me most is another article in *The Montreal Star* with the title: "Italian Montrealers Mum on Mob." The reporter tries to interview passers-by on Boulevard Saint-Laurent as they leave a popular Italian grocery store, and is surprised to be met by blank stares.

"What does he expect these people tell him?" I ask as I throw the article at Sean.

Not only is it idiotic of the reporter to think that average Italian Montrealers know what is going on within a criminal organization with tentacles in the global drug trade, but it's an outright insult to imply that their shrugs of "no-comments" is associated to a code of *omerta,* as if being Italian in Little Italy automatically makes one a member of a secret organization.

"It's naïve of him, to say the least," Sean says. "It's strange, though, that a family member is hit. Doesn't it make you wonder what was said about that *paesana* of yours?"

"Not at all. This guy must have been involved somewhat in his uncle's activities. Lucia most certainly is not a mobster."

"*Bonjour, Maman,*" J.P. says when he arrives late Saturday afternoon, and plants a kiss on my cheek.

I cringe, as I always do when he calls me that, but say nothing. J.P. called me "*Maman*" the first time he met me, and then Sean took to saying, "Yes, Mommy," whenever I made a suggestion around the house. I couldn't hide my irritation from Sean and he finally stopped.

The cool October weather prompted me to prepare a hearty vegetable soup and pork roast for dinner, along with scalloped potatoes. Sean complains when I go all out to entertain other guests, but insists on only the best for J.P. This time, I bought an inexpensive pork roast that requires little fussing. I don't want to be fretting in the kitchen for J.P. while he and Sean drink scotch and discuss some esoteric philosophical topic to which I cannot contribute.

When J.P. arrives, the kitchen is infused with the homey odours of the garlic-studded meat, and the applesauce simmering on the stove. I like cooking and I revel in experimenting with different recipes, and in serving delicious food to friends and relatives. But as much as I become vexed when the media makes it sound as if all Italians were mobsters, I'm just as irritated at being defined only by my housekeeping abilities, as J.P. does every time he calls me "*Maman.*"

My mind is packed full of the ideas I have read about. I never forget a face, an incident, or a concept that I find interesting. But when I'm nervous, as I always am when J.P. is around, I mumble. I'm becoming more and more aware that I have been deprived of a very crucial skill—that of remembering words. Is it because of my intermittent schooling or because of having to function in different languages? Or is it a physiological condition with a medical name of its own? Whatever the reason, I know that for me the one great casualty of my immigrant journey has been the poor mastery of verbal expression in any of the three languages I speak.

Sean has already poured two scotches by the time J.P. has arranged his things in the den, and they sit in the living room. I can't hear their conversation since I have started slicing the roast with the electric knife. J.P.'s background is in political science, more particularly in international relations, but he dabbles in writing poetry, which he shares with Sean whenever they meet. They seem to be discussing one of his poems now. Writing poetry is a mystery to me, and I'm afraid to even attempt it.

Sean and J.P. continue their discussion while devouring the scalloped potatoes and meat, disagreeing over a line in the poem. Their conversation seems obscure to me, but because they are talking about writing, I listen attentively. The topic is hermeneutic circularity and its contradictions: to understand the whole, Sean explains, there must be a connection between the individual words, and to understand the parts, one must comprehend the whole. It sounds like a riddle, and to better understand it, I try to visualize the concept as a geometric shape.

As I take J.P.'s plate, he says, absent-mindedly, "*Merci, Maman.*"

I look directly at his face and say, "I wish you wouldn't call me *Maman, Mama,* or Mommy. I'm not your mother or anyone else's, yet."

J.P. pulls his chair back. "But I don't mean it as a derogatory term," he answers. "You're just so ... very motherly."

"How am I motherly?" I ask, and put my hands on my hips.

"Physically, I mean. Look at your childbearing hips, your moon face, all the traits of the earth mother figure—a Jungian archetype. Isn't that right, Sean?"

Sean has started putting dishes into the dishwater and doesn't answer.

"What does having a round face have to do with Jung's archetypes? I haven't read that anywhere."

"Have you been reading my notes?" Sean asks.

"No, I've been reading your books. I can read, you know."

"Why this sudden interest in reading my books?" Sean asks.

"I'm intrigued by Jung's mandalas and what you were talking about before ... circularity ... about understanding the parts to understand the whole. I'd like to understand how it applies to writing a novel."

They both look at me blankly.

I finally splutter, "It's because I'm trying to write a novel, and ... well, it's funny, but for years I've had a tendency to draw shapes, especially circles, just like mandalas."

Sean and J.P. are quiet for a while, and then look at one other. J.P. says, "I would think that many people doodle with shapes, and with writing novels. It can be ... therapeutic."

"Yes, schizophrenics, neurotics have been known to experience these spontaneous images of mandalas," Sean says with an amused laugh, then adds, "Sorry, Cat, I didn't mean to imply..."

"Let's have a toast for mandalas—the archetypes of wholeness," J.P. says, raising his wine glass to Sean.

Sean returns to his seat and clinks his wine glass with J.P.'s. "On a more serious note," he says, "the focus of my paper is, in fact, the significance of the fundamental conformity in mandalas, in spite of time and place. Whether we call it synchronicity, or the Chinese I Ching, anything that happens is related to everything else that happens at the same time."

"Isn't that a little scary?" I say.

"What do you mean, Cat?" Sean asks.

"It means that if our lives are controlled by what happens to others, we're not in control of our own destinies."

"That's a good point, Cat. Some people think of destiny as magical, as some invisible force, but the beauty of the Chinese I Ching is that it reveals our story, and gives us some advice about how to co-author it."

I'm quiet for an instant, trying to absorb what Sean has said. "When I was little, I always wondered what my mother meant by destiny…"

J.P. interrupts, "Speaking of mothers, there's something I wanted to ask you, if I may."

"Yes?" I say, annoyed he has interrupted the discussion, and at the way he swishes his wine around in his glass before he takes a drink from it.

"The girl who lives here…? Aren't you worried, what with everything that is happening?"

"I'm not worried in the least."

"Well, you must have read the papers this morning. It seems to be open season on mobsters. They're settling accounts and are getting nasty. Family members are being hit."

"Angie is not a mobster, she's a helpless teenager," I say.

"Oh, stop sounding so naïve, Cathy. This girl may mean trouble for Sean. Already, her family has been connected to Jack Russo. You know that Sean will be in the public eye soon. If the papers make any more connections, they'll have me and Sean connected to Jack Russo too … through you."

"Through me? That's too funny for words. Why me? I have

nothing to do with Jack Russo."

"Well, your name for one—Anastasia. There's a Tony Anastasia in the nightclub business who is a close associate of Jack Russo. Do you know him?"

"I know of him. People have often asked me if we're related, but I have no idea who he is. I never met the man. Anastasia is a common name in Calabria, like Menard in Quebec."

"Names have resonances in the media, which may trigger investigations," J.P. says gravely.

"Don't forget the infamous Albert Anastasia of Chicago," I say. "Next thing you know, they'll have me connected to Al Capone."

"Don't laugh. Media people never miss a chance to connect politicians with criminal elements. You saw the papers this morning. There's a turf war going on."

"The papers covered the hit of the nephew of a known criminal. What does that have to do with me?" I ask loudly. "But you can stop visiting us if you think it might taint your reputation."

"No need to get defensive," Sean says. "J.P. wants to make sure that our names don't ever come up in connection with Angie's family."

"I find what you're saying extremely insulting ... after the years you've known my family," I say to J.P.

"It's not your family, per se, that would be questioned, but your relationship with this girl's family."

Then I remember. "You already know her uncle, Alfonso. He told me he's going to the fundraising event next week. So what's the big deal?"

"Yes, I've met him at other fundraising events, together with many other people," J.P. answers.

"You know, I remember a time when Di Principe and Jack Russo were pretty close, in fact involved in a project together that went bust," I say.

"Alex cut those ties ages ago, long before he became involved in federal politics. I suggest you see if there's any way the girl can return to her home before the ball next week. We will be getting a lot of media coverage and we want to be sure it's positive."

"I can't believe you're asking me this," I say, looking at Sean.

"Blame it on the media," Sean replies, shrugging his shoulders.

"Alfonso may be linked to Jack Russo, and his niece is living with us; I worked for Di Principe, who has been appointed a senator ... interesting connections for the media to make."

"I see; you're afraid of synchronicities ... meaningful coincidences," I say.

"I believe Sean was against the idea of you playing mommy with this girl..." J.P. shoots back.

"So you go around discussing our personal matters with him?" I ask Sean as I get up.

"There was nothing personal about that discussion," Sean says. "Take it easy. Don't get all worked up."

"Look," J.P. says. "I don't want to cause a family quarrel here. I don't want this girl to cast a negative light on Sean, and on my relationship to both of you. I'd appreciate it if you considered our position, what with an election coming up. Is she returning to her family this week?"

"She's returning to her family when and if her mother gets better. Angie is my friend and she's staying here. I'm not her mommy, only her friend. And I'd appreciate it if you called me by my name once in a while."

"Okay, but which name? You have a few: Caterina, Cathy, Catarí, and I've noticed Cat lately."

"That's because I've developed nine lives ... the better to deal with bigots like you," I retort sharply.

"That's an insult I won't even dignify with a comment. I've had nothing but respect for you and your family. And everyone in our group was in agreement last week with Sean's decision to get married to a serious, discreet, and hardworking ethnic woman like you."

I don't respond for a while. I look at Sean, but his face is a blank page I can't read. "I see. Now I understand." I get up, coolly, and leave the table. "You discussed our marriage with a committee before proposing to me."

"I talked it over with some friends. What's wrong with that?" Sean says, shrugging his shoulders.

"I'm going to my mother's for the evening," I answer. Suddenly I need to get out of the house. Having to listen to J.P., in my own kitchen, pontificate about what I can or cannot do is humiliating enough. I don't want to argue with Sean in his presence. I call my mother with the pretense of wanting to help her organize the furniture Gaetano has delivered.

"No, it's late. Save yourself the trek in the dark," she says.

I go out anyway and walk around the block. I take the car and circle the block one more time, and then think of spending the evening at some friend's house. But then I'd have to explain the reason for my state of mind.

I debate looking for a motel, while driving around and around the block, my anger rising with each circuit, as I mull over J.P.'s comments. I swerve toward Jean-Talon Street and stop at a Harvey's. I order a large coffee and sit by a darkened window, staring blankly out. A sad, drawn-out face is reflected back in the glass. Who is this person? What is the connection between the person that she was and who she has become? I reflect calmly over the events of the last few weeks and try to weigh if I've been amiss in my relationship with Sean. Maybe in my concern over Angie I was neglectful of his needs, ignoring his efforts to forge a political career for himself—a career that I had encouraged him to pursue long before Angie came into our lives. But the question that I have never asked and perturbs me now is: what is the role he envisions for me as his life partner?

It becomes clearer and clearer to me that Sean's proposal is part of a strategy to help him win over ethnic voters. In exchange for the honour of being married to him, I'd have to maintain the image of the long-suffering, dutiful, submissive Italian woman—*Maman* to J.P. and the token ethnic woman. Worse still, the token ethnic wife. My story has already been written for me. My anger rises again. I get back in the car and circle the block over and over again until I yell out loud, "I can't go around in circles forever!"

I return to the apartment. Sean and J.P. have moved to the living room, sipping their scotches, clearly surprised at seeing me back.

"That was a short visit," Sean says. "What happened?"

I don't respond. "Angie will be back here Sunday evening and I expect the den cleared by tomorrow morning," I nod at J.P.

"J.P. and I have work to do," Sean says. "Be reasonable."

"You can go work with him at a hotel. My house is not the headquarters of the Liberal party. In fact, I expect you both out of this house and out of my life by morning!"

The two men get up and look at each other as if thunderstruck. J.P. haughtily walks to the den, muttering something I don't understand and shuts the door; Sean moves to the bedroom and also slams the door. I throw myself on the sofa. I finally cry, but my cries are more like wails, trapped and muffled by cushions, sounds that no one will hear.

43. THE CANADIAN BRIGAND

MY WEDDING INVITATION LIST IS ready. My brother hands it to me at Sunday lunch. He has also reserved the restaurant Da Paesano on Cotes des Neiges Road for the engagement party for November 15th, and all my aunts and uncles have been invited. I mumble that he shouldn't have been so quick. "I'm lucky I got this date on a Saturday. You know this restaurant gets filled up every weekend, and with Christmas parties coming up, it was getting difficult to find a free date."

"I know ... I know," I say.

Early in the morning, I had pretended to be asleep as Sean and J.P. moved about packing their papers and personal effects, whispering to each other. They left without even having breakfast. Sean left a note on the table: "We're going to a hotel. We can't work in this hostile environment. I'll speak to you in a few days after you've calmed down."

I tried preparing a speech on how to tell my mother and brother that I had called the engagement off, but found myself at a loss about how or what to tell them. I can't formulate in words my mother would understand the reason for throwing Sean out. I tell them I'll only have time to look at the list after the fundraising ball at the end of the month. I'm hoping that between now and then, another more concrete reason will come up to explain the break-up.

On my way home, after lunch, I stop at the hospital to pick up Angie. Comare Rosaria is sitting alone next to the still-comatose Lucia. Angie, Alfonso, and Pietro are in the waiting room, huddled around another visitor. The two men listen attentively to what Filomena—the talkative distant relative of Pasquale—is recounting. They nod at me as I sit next to Angie, but I say nothing, not wanting to interrupt the chatty woman.

"Who knows what's going through his head; maybe he's gone completely crazy," Filomena is saying.

"Crazy or not," Alfonso says, his voice a pitch higher than usual, "I'll call my lawyer in the morning, and he'll inform the police. He won't get away with anything just because he's in his own *paese*."

"Is there some news about your father?" I venture to ask Angie.

"The idiot's been arrested in Italy," Angie says in a monotone voice.

"What a *stronzo*," Alfonso says, shaking his head, as the others laugh.

"Not only arrested, but his picture is even in the paper there, in the *Gazzetta Del Sud*," Filomena says. She then recounts how Pasquale appeared unannounced at the home of his brother's son, Alfredo. His nephew received him with open arms, until Pasquale started inquiring about deeds to the family home and farmlands.

"Pasquale insists that the family house in town is legally his, because he's the eldest son," Filomena says. "He's not completely wrong. He did send his mother the money to completely rebuild the house after the war."

"But that was in 1950," Alfonso says. "The law has changed since then."

"The world has changed since then, except, of course, for Pasquale," Pietro says.

Filomena heard this news through a telephone call from Alfredo's wife, who told her to inform Alfonso of Pasquale's whereabouts and doings.

"The woman is furious," Filomena shrieks. "Especially when she heard Pasquale suggest that they draw an account of what they owed in back rent and what they had spent on the house in taxes so they could settle the difference. They kicked him out, and that's when he went crazy and made the news."

Under house arrest, Pasquale then appeared in Mulirena with a lawyer to check on his wife's family property there. He had also contributed a large sum of money for that property when they first married, so that Alfonso could convert the old farmhouse into a processing plant for his oil exporting business. The farmer, Micu, who used to work for Don Cesare, lives alone in the farmhouse. It seems the old farmer took Pasquale in.

"Pasquale is hard-headed," Filomena concludes, talking directly to me. "He doesn't understand Italian law. It's a crazy law ... not like here. You lose the rights to a house if you don't live in it."

"He's lucky Micu let him in the house. Imagine those two old men living together. One is drunk from morning to night; the other is crazy," Pietro says.

"He told them he wants to settle back in his own town. They named him *Il brigante Canadese,* and everyone is making fun of him there now," Filomena adds.

Driving home, I ask Angie, who has been quiet all along, how she feels about these new developments.

"I don't know. I feel sorry for him ... now that everyone is making fun of him. Why would he go to the village, of all places? He knew he'd be found. Maybe he didn't go there to hide after all."

"Why do you say that?"

"He talked about that house all the time, I figured it was his. He always said: 'My house in the *paese.'* Sometimes I even told him: 'Why don't you go get lost there, so I won't have to see you?' I don't know. Something tells me that things are going to get bad for him there."

"You really feel sorry for your father, don't you?" I ask.

Angie stares ahead, her expression blank, as if she hasn't heard the question, but then she replies, "I've felt sorry for him since the night they argued."

"What night was that?" I ask.

"The night my mother was beaten up," Angie says absentmindedly.

"What?" I exclaim. I brake and pull the car over on the curb. "You never said you heard them argue. What happened?"

"My uncle, my father, and my mother argued all evening ... about land, houses, farms.... Those three always argued. I didn't pay any attention to it."

"Your uncle argued about land? Why didn't you say anything to the police?"

"Because it's none of their business," Angie says angrily. "Anyway, I went out and don't know what happened next. Really, I don't."

"Why do you say you feel sorry for your father then?"

"I don't know, but he seemed so alone. My mother left him, and everyone seemed to gang up on him ... like now. What a family!"

I have nothing to offer her as a response, and I remain quiet for the rest of the drive. At the apartment, Angie shuts herself in the den, and I leave her alone, hoping the girl will have a good cry. I want to do the same, but I don't even have a spot to do it in private. I won't lie on the new mattress in my bedroom. The love and trust I had searched for so long, and thought I had found, feels violated. The new bed will never be the love nest for Sean and me that the old one had been for my parents.

Pasquale's image—unshaven bony face, protruding teeth, and dark, wiry hair—appears in this month's *Arte&Cultura*, the local Italian community paper edited by the journalist, Antoine.

"It's not a nice story. I don't know how you're going to tell her daughter," Mother says when she calls me to tell me about the article. I decide not to say anything to Angie until I have a chance to read it myself.

That morning, on my way to school, I stop at the Italian bar next to the travel agency to pick up a copy of the thin paper. The photo gives him the look of a caged monkey.

The article is a full reprint of the one that appeared in *La Gazzetta Del Sud*.

CALABRIAN BRIGAND RETURNS HOME FROM CANADA
CLAIMS PATRIARCHAL HOME AND HONOUR
October 19, 1980

A Canadian man, Pasquale Tonnelli, 55, wanted for questioning for his wife's near-death beating in Canada, was arrested in Serra San Pietro, in the province of Catanzaro, for disturbing the peace. Mr. Tonnelli is trying to set back the clock on Italian civil law, by proclaiming his right to his ancestral home and his right to plead to a crime of honour committed in Montreal, Canada, on October 1 of this year.

Pasquale Tonnelli returned to Serra San Pietro after a 37-year absence, to settle his ownership rights to the Tonnelli family home. A family argument ensued when his 30-year-old nephew, Alfredo Tonnelli, who has lived in the home since 1965, locked him out of the house. The older Tonnelli tried to obtain the assistance of the local authorities who refused to get involved in the family squabble.

A distraught Tonnelli arrived at City Hall accusing civil servants of corruption and inefficiency, and threatened arson. He was quickly arrested for disturbing the peace, released after one day, but then detained again for questioning with regards to the attempted murder charges laid against him by his wife's family in Canada. Pasquale Tonnelli is the main suspect in the coma-inducing beating of his wife, Lucia Abiusi.

Tonnelli has secured the services of lawyer Filippo Rizzi. Mr.

Rizzi states that his client, who has retained his Italian citizenship, has the right to be tried in the Italian courts.

In an interview with *La Gazetta del Sud* reporter, Gianni Macri, Mr. Rizzi read the following statement on behalf of his client:

"Mr. Pasquale Tonnelli claims that both his wife and her family have betrayed him for years, in business as well as in personal matters. The alleged crime against his wife was a momentary act of passion to defend his honour, provoked by the revelation that my client may not be the biological father of his daughter. As we know, in our country, legislative provisions that allow for partial or complete defense for honour killings are still part of the penal code. Mr. Tonnelli confesses to striking his wife and leaving the premises, but he was too distraught by the shock of what he had heard, and the scuffle that ensued, to remember if his wife had fallen on the floor in a coma as it was reported. He now wants to set the record straight on all the dealings that his own brother and brother-in-law, Alfonso Abiusi, manipulated over a span of 20 years for their own gain, both in Italy and in Canada. He claims he also has incriminating information about some prominent members of the Italian community in Montreal, the details of which he says he'll provide in an affidavit at the opportune time."

To the same reporter, Pasquale Tonnelli stated: "My wife and her family have cuckolded me for years. I couldn't take it anymore. I lost my head when I heard that my daughter is not biologically my daughter."

When asked why he locked his uncle out of the house, Alfredo Tonnelli said: "He can't buy back the years of work we have put into the land and the house while he has been absent in Canada. He can come back as a visitor for a week or two, but the house now belongs to us."

Pasquale Tonnelli is being detained under house arrest, awaiting procedural coordination between Canadian and Italian law-enforcement agents.

"What's with the Italian paper?" Angie asks, as I return to the car.

"Your father's picture is in the story that appeared in Italy."

"You're not serious. What the hell?" Angie exclaims when I hand her the folded newspaper. I had thought of not telling Angie, but she would have heard it from others at school.

"Your father is desperate to say anything to excuse what he did. Don't believe what's written."

"Look at him. He looks like a chimpanzee," Angie shrieks.

"Obviously, he's very troubled, and said some crazy things."

"You know I can't read the frigging Italian. What does it say?" Angie asks after scanning the article.

I can't bring myself to mention the last part of the interview.

"Angie, your father is very angry at your mother, so he said some nasty things about her ... that he hit her ... slapped her because he thought ... she had been unfaithful to him."

"With whom?" Angie says.

"I'm sorry to be telling you this while driving to school. Maybe you want to take the day off, and we'll talk about all this tonight?"

"There's nothing to talk about. I'm fucked."

"Look, I can drive you back home. I'll explain your absence to Mr. Champagne."

"I'll walk home, but I'll go see my mother first, since I'm right here ... not that she'll tell me anything."

Angie takes her knapsack from the back of the car. "I don't understand what ticked my father off now. They lived like strangers for years. They even slept in separate bedrooms."

"Don't think about it, Angie. Go and see your mother and then try to catch up on your English assignments."

"Yeah, I'm really worried about my English assignments." Angie walks off with the newspaper in her hands. I meant to add that her homework might take her mind off what was happening, like writing does for me. I notice a pained look on her face I have never seen before.

44. SUPERVISION DUTY

I JOIN BRUCE FOR OUR SUPERVISION duty, and I quickly tell him the latest developments, and how surprised I am at Angie's reaction. Up to now, she has taken her family's problems in stride.

"People have different strategies for coping, but she should be in school and talking things over, rather than alone at home," Bruce says. "But don't worry, I'll arrange for some counselling in the next couple of days."

"I don't know how receptive Angie will be to counselling. The girl distrusts everyone. She even refuses my help with her homework."

"Don't push her on her work," Bruce says, and tells me that Angie has until the end of the week to hand in her composition assignment.

Bruce has been doing some investigating of his own. Through his contacts with youth counsellors, he found out that Angie's friend Eddie is suspected of being a drug pusher for a gang of young punks, who might even be associated with a larger biker gang.

I raise my hands in exasperation. "He's been calling quite often lately."

"I'd keep my guard up about Eddie if I were you. I don't trust the little snake," Bruce says.

"I didn't need this latest news," I say sounding discouraged. "There are too many complications piling up."

"Complications are good for writing," he says.

"I haven't done much of that lately. I have too many other things on my mind."

"I hear you're also planning a wedding," he says.

So Angie had mentioned Sean to Bruce. "My personal life is pretty mixed up too," I say.

"If you want to talk to someone about it, I'm here for you."

"I'll take you up on it one of these days," I say, smiling.

I haven't yet spoken to anyone about my breakup with Sean. My emotions are becoming more and more conflicted the longer I keep everything all bottled up inside. I cannot accept that Sean proposed to me out of political expediency, yet I'm beginning to rationalize the pros and cons of a breakup. Sean and I were together even before he became interested in politics. Don't we all have some sort of self-interest in any relationship? This dithering has only made me feel powerless, with a wearisome inertia settling inside my head. I'd love to talk to someone about it, but I don't know how to approach the subject with Bruce during supervision in a school corridor. I resume talking about Angie until the end of the period bell.

I walk to the office to check my mail. I'm worried about Angie being at home alone. Then I wonder if Angie knows more than she cares to reveal. "With whom?" Angie asked of Pasquale's insinuation of his wife's infidelities, and she looked puzzled. I shouldn't be too surprised by Pasquale's revelation, though Angie's abrupt mannerisms, and her unruly hair, had me convinced that she belonged to his kin. I can't, though, help but do some calculating of my own, which involves recalling Angie's birth date, April 1965, and backtracking nine months. It brought me back to the summer of 1964 and the deceptions I had witnessed on my first trip back to Italy. But then in my mail slot I found a note from Mr. Champagne asking me to see him at the office, and I put those thoughts aside.

45. RÈGLEMENT DE COMPTES

WLHS HAS MADE THE NEWS on the *Journal de Montreal*. Mr. Champagne hands me a copy with Pasquale's picture, and the headline, *Crime d'honneur et règlement de comptes*.

The article runs an interview with Antoine who has firsthand startling evidence of a possible link between Alfonso Abiusi and corruption in the construction industry. Antoine paraphrases, in French, the content of an Italian letter he has received personally from Pasquale Tonnelli:

> "Alfonso Abiusi and Jack Vaccaro's construction company got its first big money in the 1950s in a fraudulent scheme to sell plots of land in Laval for a residential development that never materialized. Vaccaro planned that swindle from the very beginning with the help of mobster Jack Russo and Alex Di Principe—none other than the Liberal Party Member of Parliament, recently appointed Senator. That deal was only the start of a partnership that has continued undetected over the years. Russo has total control of a ring of construction companies who together colluded to bid for major infrastructure projects related to the Montreal Olympics. He received a cut from every project and his personal bodyguard, wrestler Nick Demon, was the in-between man that collected money from the contractors and brought it to Russo.
>
> All this has been carried out with the involvement of corrupt city officials who received a cut for their complicity. The names

of the officials will be handed to the authorities if and when they request it.

On the evening of October 1st, Alfonso Abiusi called Pasquale Tonnelli and his wife, Lucia, to a meeting. Abiusi had demanded that Pasquale and his wife sign some papers to protect his home and company in Laval in case of an investigation. They both refused and an argument ensued between Alfonso and his sister. She threatened to give away information to Abiusi's wife about his past in the village and information to the authorities about his business dealings with Russo. Alfonso then turned on both his sister and Tonnelli, accused his sister of infidelity with various men, and then threw the bombshell about their daughter that made Tonnelli slap his wife and flee. Tonnelli reiterates what he had first claimed: the slap could not have put his wife into a coma."

Antoine goes on to claim that the infidelity is just a smokescreen. At the end, the article also mentions that the daughter in question, a troubled youth, has been admitted to Wilfrid Laurier High School despite the fact that she doesn't qualify for English schooling according to the Quebec language laws since neither of her parents attended school in Quebec. The article asks: "Has the Mafia also infiltrated the English school system to interfere with its language laws?"

"Frank brought me this," Mr. Champagne says tersely. "It implies our school is connected to the Mafia."

"That's ridiculous," I mumble and can't resist a laugh.

"This is no laughing matter," the principal says.

"I'm sorry. This is beyond reason. I don't understand what made the journalist do this."

"You know the reporter?"

"I know the man who was interviewed. This guy always looks to stir up trouble, and papers always look for the sensational. I think it's all blown out of proportion, Mr. Champagne."

"It's not important what you think, Cathy. But since the

mother's beating, Jack Russo's nephew has been killed. How do we know it's not all related? And now these revelations! It's scary! What if Angie is a target?"

"Angie, a target? Can't be!"

"And what about our image? True or not, what comes out of the story is that we've eased on the rules set by the government for a Mafia-connected student, as if we're in cahoots with this family. Frank was right all along. We should never have taken Angie back."

I don't respond. Mr. Champagne continues. "We're in a fine mess! I'd suggest that Angie stay home, until all this dies down."

"She stayed home today, but she needs counselling. I'll have to call Social Services and see what we should do to help her," I say.

"No need to do that just yet, Cathy." Mr. Champagne sounds irritated by my suggestion. "You've caused enough harm already. Let her stay home for another day, and then we'll speak again. Just make sure she doesn't get into any trouble. I hear some of your students—Angie's friends—have been seen at a strip club, owned by this wrestler mentioned here. You should have monitored the situation."

"How could I?" I try to hold back my anger but my voice is shaky and I'm close to tears. "I have no control over what my students do after school hours."

"Angie is under your care. You should control who she hangs around with. How are you two related again?"

"We're not related. Her mother is a friend." I try not to raise my voice, but I remember having explained my relationship with Angie to Mr. Champagne before.

"I see," the principal says, shuffling some papers on his desk. "By the way, the department head votes are in." Mr. Champagne tells me, informally, before distributing the notice, that Mike will be appointed department head of Tech. Voc.

The department headship was the last thing on my mind, yet the negative news coming as it does causes my held-back tears to erupt in an embarrassing display of emotion. I hear but hardly pay any attention to his explanation of the vote breakdown, as I try to wipe the flood of tears with my shirt sleeve. "Ultimately, I based my decision on Mike's decision-making and leadership abilities...."

He stops when he looks up and sees me crying. "I'm sorry," he says. "I didn't think this was all that important to you. You even brought in your application a day late."

I collect myself. "That's fine, Mr. Champagne. Thank you for your consideration."

As I turn to leave, I ask that Angie be allowed to come back to school for the Halloween party.

"Sure, it's only a half day, anyway. Is her mother getting any better?"

"She's the same," I say and leave the office.

"Sorry," Susan whispers as I pass by her desk.

I shrug my shoulders as I pick up a tissue from her desk and wipe my face. Being a department head had never seemed important to me until Bruce had urged me to apply, and now, I wish I hadn't bothered.

Susan hands me a map to her country place, and a mimeographed invitation to her Halloween party.

"Thank you," I say, "but I can't come. I have a previous commitment."

"Too bad," Susan says lowering her voice. "I even convinced Bruce to come with me."

"Oh?" I say.

"I don't know if he'd call it a date, but we're driving together and he might stay over if it gets late," Susan says, a happy lilt to her voice. I start crying again as I walk away realizing that I'm still pretending to be together with Sean.

Once in class, I ask the students to move the chairs in a semicircle for a demonstration on hair colouring, and then I call the apartment and speak to Angie. I ask her about her hospital visit and if any of her family has spoken about the article I had shown her in the morning. Angie replies flatly: "What are they supposed to say?" Her voice sounds cold and confrontational, and I worry again about her being alone in the house.

The noise level in the class is unacceptable. The students haven't seen the article on the *Journal de Montreal* yet, but they have a copy of *Allô Police* with front page coverage of Jack Russo's nephew's funeral, showing pictures of the hoard of people lined up outside the Notre Dame de la Defense Church and the dozens of flower-laden limousines that followed the funeral cortege. The article names Notre Dame de la Defense a Mafia church, because all of the Mafia-related funerals have been held there. The church and the fresco of Mussolini on its ceiling always get mentioned at every funeral of a known criminal. That the church has been witness to the great story of immigration in the community, and is where thousands of humble honest Italian immigrants have been married, christened, and laid to rest is of no consequence.

Students are preoccupied with the upcoming Costume Day and Halloween party.

"Are you dressing up, Miss?" Gina asks.

"Will you all be quiet and get ready for work?" I answer impatiently.

"Where's your school spirit?" Gina responds.

I don't reply. I disappear into the stockroom to look for the colour chart and products I need for the demonstration. I shut the door behind me and sit on a stool, eyes shut, unable to go on with the lesson. The allegations have brought up memories of past betrayals that had never been spoken about after Father's death. I think of him and his unrealized dreams, and of my lingering resentments toward him. Everything is unravelling around me and I don't know what to do. Nothing is what it seems. I have invested years in my relationship with Sean and, in my family's eyes, my reputation. It has all been for nothing. I feel trapped. I don't want to face the class or anyone else; but

I can't hide in the stockroom for the rest of the period. I take a few deep breadths and return to address the class. To their great bewilderment, I dismiss them early for the day.

Risking a reprimand from the principal, I also leave school early to check on Angie, but I find the apartment empty. The den is messier than usual. The piles of manuscripts that I had sorted and arranged on the weekend have been disturbed. Someone has rummaged through the old notebooks on the bottom shelf. The pages are not in the same order as I had left them. The story I have kept hidden at the very bottom of the pile is missing or possibly misplaced. I had thought that Angie would never have shown any interest in any type of reading, let alone deciphering my scribbles.

I sit on the den's sofa bed, stunned and confused at the disorder in the room, when I gaze at an even more incongruous item on the floor—a copy of *Le Journal de Montreal* folded to the article I just read at Mr. Champagne's office. I spring up and run out the door.

It's finally time to visit my *paesano,* the journalist, the editor and publisher, the travel agent, the PQ supporter, the know-it-all Roman pope as I've sometimes thought of him, *le Grand Antoine*, née Antonio Scalise, Totu for short in the village.

I have my own score to settle with him.

PART VIII
TOTU, 1964-1967

46. THE ITALIAN TOUR, 1964

IN THE SIXTIES, CHARTERED FLIGHTS and youth fares made air travel to Europe affordable. Mother longed to visit my father's grave and I happily agreed to pay for the trip.

After my father's death, we had moved from Tenth Avenue to a cheaper and smaller apartment in central-east Montreal. As feared, Aménagement Ville Verte went bankrupt and we had monthly loan payments to honour on my mother's salary. Di Principe promised that once all was settled we might get some money back, but Mother didn't count on it. After completing ninth grade, I attended a hairdressing school in the seediest part of town, Saint-Laurent and Sainte-Catherine. I had not been allowed to visit my girlfriend in Sainte-Michel, but I travelled unenthusiastically each day through areas with strip clubs, X-rated movie theatres, and dubious rooming houses to get to the school.

I desperately wanted to keep a grasp on the sense of wonder and joy that I associated with my happy childhood in Mulirena. After working as an assistant hairdresser for a year, I saved enough money on tips for two plane tickets to Rome and train tickets to Calabria.

Rome's Stazione Termini was as bustling and as crowded as I remembered it, with the south-bound train jammed with *ferie* travellers, short-tempered from the excessive heat and lack of empty seats. The train sped swiftly through the sun-drenched cities and towns. It passed the same pastel-coloured apartment buildings with peeling stucco and lines of laundry flying in the air that were imprinted in my memory. I looked for small boys in short pants and sandals, kicking soccer balls and waving at the speeding train, but I could hardly see through the windows. We stood, sardine-like, in the train corridor, unable to move for fear of losing the few inches of space we had secured. At each stop, people swore at those of us who were blocking the cabin entrances, while vendors pushed stuffed *panini* and bottles of mineral water up through the windows.

Once we passed Naples, the train thinned out, and we found seats in a cabin. The conversation I overheard between two women from Milan on their way to a beach resort near Naples stunned me.

"They have ruined Italy," one of them said, pointing to a family, clearly southerners returning to their homes for the summer, sitting on their suitcases outside the cabin's doors. "We give them bathtubs and bidets and they use them to grow tomatoes."

My mother and I kept quiet until the two women got off at the next station.

The more we sped south, the more the landscape became unfamiliar to me. Had the mountains always been so arid and barren, the trees so craggy and sparse? After a six-hour train ride, we reached Lamezia Terme station, where Zio Pietro was waiting for us.

"Why didn't Luigi come too?" was the first thing he asked. Then he maneuvered his little Fiat 500 up and up the steep mountain roads, honking at every turn.

"In these roads you never know whether you'll hit a donkey, a herd of goats, or a motor scooter," he laughed.

I wondered what inspired the village founders to settle in these out-of-the-way mountains. As we rose higher and higher, a smattering of other villages became visible below us, and before we knew it, we had reached the town of Amato, and Mulirena appeared across the ravine.

Once in the village, I noticed the cobblestone streets had been resurfaced in dark asphalt. The town piazza and the streets looked a lot narrower and greyer than I remembered, and the flies were a real nuisance. It's funny how I had never once remembered the abundance of flies in all my reminiscences.

We entered my grandmother's house through what had once been the family's grocery store. It was here that I used to come every day after school to meet my mother, who helped bake the bread they sold at the store. The shelves were now empty, but the heavy wooden counter with the old-fashioned scales had been left behind. My uncle had moved to the city of Catanzaro to open a bigger, more modern store. But the smell of the burlap bags and flour seemed to have seeped into the old cement cracks, and I could almost taste the fragrant, freshly-baked bread and the provolone cheese that my mother used to have ready for me as a snack. The empty store was the coolest spot in the house and my grandmother still sat there in the afternoons to do her crocheting and to hold court with the neighbourhood ladies. As soon as they saw the car and the suitcases, they all rushed to greet us.

We hadn't slept properly for over twenty-four hours, but we were unable to lie down. People kept trickling in and out. Comare Rosaria came in with a basket of fruit. Her husband had died and her daughter, Lucia, was in town. Her son, Alfonso, was expected to come for a few days to sell his home and prepare for his mother to fly to Montreal in the fall. Lucia had been coming for a month every summer, but kept to herself. Comare Rosaria apologetically told us that Lucia spent most of her afternoons in the country and never visited anyone. She wanted to eventually refinish the farmhouse, so that she'd have a place to come to if she ever returned to Mulirena now that the house in the village was being sold.

Maybe it was the fatigue, or the jet lag, but from the moment I set foot in the store on Thursday afternoon until the following Monday morning, I moved around as if I were in a stupor, and in strange and alien surroundings.

On Sunday we attended a wedding and had a chance to visit with most of the *paesani* I hadn't seen yet. It was a simple ceremony and reception. A gramophone played some dancing music and a few young men asked me to dance. They were very polite and proper. Even Totu, on a holiday from Rome, tall, elegant, and speaking a flawless Italian, had danced and chatted with me. He asked me many questions about Montreal, and was fascinated by the fact that French was spoken there, a language he had studied, and said he hoped to take a trip to the city someday. He knew a lot more about Canada and Quebec than anyone else I had met in Italy.

I secretly hoped I'd see more of him during my stay, but he was going back to Rome the following week, and told me he'd give me a tour of that city whenever I passed through. I noticed good-looking men eyeing me as I walked through the village, but Totu was the one who intrigued me the most. When I was a child, he had seemed so much older than me, but now the age difference hardly showed. All I could think of was meeting Totu somewhere in a Roman café to explore the wonders of Rome with him all over again. Years earlier, he had played guide to my family and me when we travelled to Rome to get our visas.

At the wedding, I also spoke to a couple visiting from Brooklyn. They were planning a bus tour of Italy's major cities, starting in Naples, and invited me to join them. The trip would be the perfect opportunity for me to do some sightseeing, and meet up with Totu in Rome, unencumbered by my mother's presence. My grandmother and uncle balked at my plans. They told me that one of the young men I had danced with was interested in sending his brother to the house, the first step in arranging a match.

"I don't like these set-ups," I told my mother that evening. "I'm going to Rome on Friday."

"Don't be so stubborn. We've just arrived. There will be other opportunities to go sightseeing," Mother pleaded with me. Grandmother maintained that the interested party came from a good family, was one of the most level-headed young men in town, and was probably the best opportunity I would ever get.

I didn't dislike the young man. In fact I found him handsome and gentle looking, but the prospect of his brother and my uncle mapping out my life and my future while I sat on the sidelines scared me.

"Do what you want, but we're only thinking of your welfare," my uncle said, disappointed, "But after this, I'm not going to speak up for you with anyone in town." I told them I wasn't interested and prepared a suitcase for my sightseeing trip on the weekend.

Two days before I was to leave for Rome, the town was hit by a torrential rainstorm. Comare Rosaria came to my grandmother's store, worried about her daughter, who had gone to the country with a young relative with no umbrellas. "She'll get sick with pneumonia," she said.

Two older neighbourhood children, armed with umbrellas, volunteered to assist Lucia. They came back a few hours later breathless and agitated by what they had witnessed. They had walked as far as the farmhouse and found Old Micu with a hunting rifle sitting mute on the kitchen floor.

"She and her brother will never set foot in this farmhouse again," he hollered at them when they asked about Lucia. He sounded clearly inebriated. Frightened, the boys ran away. They hadn't bumped into Lucia on the way up, so they feared that something terrible might have happened. They decided to check the nearby farmhouse in Don Cesare's property through a shortcut. There they found Totu also sitting on the floor but with a bloodied leg raised on a chair and bandaged with a woman's scarf. He had been hit by a stray bullet. Old Micu had been hunting on the grounds before the rain started, he told them, and shot him by accident. One of the kids stayed behind with Totu while the other ran to alert Don Cesare so he could drive as close as possible to the farmhouse and get Totu to a hospital. On the way, they came upon Lucia running, drenched and visibly in distress, yet she didn't seem to appreciate their offer of an umbrella.

Totu lost a lot of blood, but was expected to recover. The whole town was abuzz with conjecture about the shooting. Micu had had a bone to pick with both Totu and his father from way back, so it was plausible that in a drunken stupor he tried to shoot him and pass it off as an accident. Yet the story told by Totu didn't line up, grandmother and her women friends affirmed. The young relative that had accompanied Lucia was not with her when the kids caught up with her. If Lucia had come directly from her farmhouse, they would have met her on the way there. Why did Micu say that Lucia and Alfonso would never set foot at the farmhouse that belonged to them? The peasant and his wife had complained for years that Alfonso had never compensated them fairly for their work on the farm. Did Totu catch the shot meant for Lucia or Alfonso? What was he doing at Lucia's farm? Neither Totu nor his uncle laid any charges against Micu, an unusual lack of action for both of them.

Displeased by the turn of events, I kept my word and left with the Americans. The tour by bus was a seven-day, sight-seeing marathon. The dizzying viewing of so much art in such a short period of time made me immune to its beauty. In Rome, I searched for a public phone and called my uncle's home and asked for news about Totu. He was out of danger and back in the village with a cast. Had I been able to meet him in Rome, I had planned on skipping the tour to Florence and catching up with the group a few days later in Naples. In the haste to find a phone between stops, my wallet went missing, with my travel documents and traveller's cheques, and I had to borrow money from the Americans. Back in Mulirena, I was mortified to ask Zio to call authorities so I could get my papers in order before returning to Montreal.

Alfonso had been in town while I was away, settled his business without seeing anyone, and left right away. The shooting incident remained the main topic of conversation in my grandmother's store.

The town was full of the visitors who worked in the cities during the rest of the year. They looked so full of themselves in their fine clothes and speaking in proper Italian, but the conversation of the two Milan women on the train made me realize that an imaginary border, somewhere around Naples, still separated Italy into two very distinctive worlds that even the Italian Economic Miracle had not managed to erase.

I didn't see much of Totu, as the crutches clearly made his movements around the hilly village difficult. He spent time organizing a group of young communists, antagonizing half of the town as well as his uncle.

I tried to weigh all possible explanations for Totu's shot leg, but I didn't speculate aloud for fear I'd reveal my newly-found, and ever-intensifying infatuation with him. I also had my own problems of the stolen documents to worry about. If we hadn't flown charter, I would have tried to return home earlier.

47. OF MEN AND HIS WORLDS

THE YEAR 1967 WAS THE most exciting time to be living in Montreal. To mark Canada's centennial, the city hosted a world fair, Expo 67, and opened its doors to visitors from all over the world. The Fair provided the illusion of travel, and a vision of the world containing different worlds. Tickets to the fair sites and newly built amusement park, La Ronde, were sold as passports. We could skip and jump from pavilion to pavilion—from Canada, to Russia, to France, to Ethiopia, and back to Canada—as often as we wanted.

Along the waterfront, at Cité-du-Havre, they built Habitat 67, a unique apartment building structure. It resembled a Mediterranean village perched atop a mountain. The logo for Expo 67, called Man and His World, was a circle of men with outstretched hands.

With British Vidal Sassoon setting up a shop in downtown Montreal, hairstyling became as sleek and trendy as a Mary Quant tunic. On my return from the Italian tour, I found my first job as a full-fledged hairstylist at a small neighbourhood salon in Little Italy. This job gave me the opportunity to speak and practice my Italian, as well as listen to the stories that my clients told about their lives, about their voyage from Italy, and about their first years in Montreal. In many ways their stories were like mine, but somehow, in each there was something that made them different. I often thought of Lucia and our days on the ship, though the memories became hazier and hazier. When I tried to incorporate some of my clients' accounts into my stories, I felt guilty. I was afraid this would seem like lying or, worse still, like abusing their confidence in me.

It was during those hours of undisturbed reflection that I started thinking of life as broken up into bits and pieces of what and who we become as time passes. It seemed that, at every stage, I could look back at who I had been before, and see someone different.

It was during this time that my name changed to Cathy, though I don't recall a specific moment when this occurred. My non-Italian clients often mispronounced my name as Catterrina, so my boss took to introducing me as Cathy. They in turn started asking for me by that name. I had entertained the idea of changing my name to the shorter Rina, but that seemed confusing after everyone had already started calling me Cathy. I had also changed the way I looked. I spent a lot of time playing with make-up and different hairstyles. Wigs had become fashionable and I had fun changing my hair colour and length according to my moods.

How was it, I often wondered while I sat alone in the salon, that, of all the things I had wanted to be, I had become destined to spend my days styling other people's hair and being known, of all things, as Cathy, the hairdresser?

By the time Expo 67 opened, my brother and I had succeeded in setting up our own beauty salon in the city's west end. Our clientele was made up mainly of well-to-do matrons from Westmount, Snowdon, and Hampstead; of nurses and office workers from the area's two hospitals; and, of the cocktail waitresses from the Crazy Horse Saloon on Côte-des-Neiges Road.

To maintain my Italian language, I enrolled in evening courses in Italian literature. I listened attentively to the stories of my new clients. Many of them were first-generation Jewish immigrants from northern Europe and survivors of Nazi persecution.

When I washed their hair, I often spotted stamped numbers on their arms, which made my own arm hairs stand on end. Not all of them liked talking about their war experiences, and they lived in wealthier neighbourhoods than ours, but I felt we had something in common because we had all made a trip across the ocean.

The wave of immigrants from Italy had stopped. Italy was enjoying an economic boom, and many Italians we knew in Montreal started making trips back home, with the intention of remaining there permanently. The majority of those who tried to resettle in Italy came back in less than a year. They said they were unable to find their bearings in Italy anymore—their home country had changed and become more alien to them than Canada.

"Montreal is such an exciting cosmopolitan city," said my *paesano*, Totu, when he visited. "It seems less like America, and more like Europe."

He showed up at our apartment one evening to pay his respects to my mother. It had been three years since our trip to Italy, but no other man that I met or had courted me since could measure up to him or intrigue me more. His surprise visit exhilarated me. He had been staying with friends, and said he'd fallen in love with the city. He'd decided to prolong his stay, and even hoped to look for work. He was really impressed by how well my brother and I were doing with our new business. Before he left our house, I pulled out my Italian books, and spoke to him about the Italian literature courses I was taking.

"So you know three languages? I'm amazed," he said.

I flushed with pleasure, and added, "Yes, I can write better than I can speak, though, in all three languages." Then I told him how much I liked writing.

"Oh, do you write poetry?" he asked.

"No, I'm not much good at poetry. I like to write stories, stories about the past, about Mulirena," I replied.

"Why Mulirena? Four houses and four cats; what's there to write about?"

I had always remembered him by the languid look of his dark eyes. Being finally so close to him, I knew I could easily lose myself in those eyes. I wished I could spend more time talking to him about all the things I wanted to write about, though I found it difficult to explain exactly why I wanted so badly to do so. So I just mumbled, "I want to preserve my memories."

Then I was mortified to hear him reply, "The only thing worth preserving is *giardiniera*, and even then, if kept too long, it becomes soft and rancid." Maybe he noticed that his remark had put me ill at ease, and he added, "My English is not very good, but I'd like to read one of your stories." He had studied English and could read it, he explained, but he spoke better French. That is why he liked Montreal so much.

I left him with Mother to run to my room and find a piece I had written about my fourth-grade teacher, Signor Gavano. I quickly tore it out of my notebook and gave it to him. As he left, I invited him to attend Italian Day at Expo, which was coming up soon and during which I would be working as a hostess at the Italian pavilion.

At Expo 67, each nation had its own day set aside for celebrating its ethnic character. All at once, it seemed chic to show off one's heritage, and every nation tried to outdo the others in pageantry and folkloric displays. I had been recruited by the Italian Consulate to work as a volunteer at the Italian pavilion for the day. When I saw Totu and two friends walk toward me, my heart skipped a beat. He introduced me to Franco, whom I recognized as the editor of one of the local Italian newspapers, and Chantale, a tall Quebecois woman with stringy hair, no make-up, and gold-rimmed glasses.

"I still can't get over how much you've changed; you're a real *signorina*," Totu said. He invited me for coffee at the Italian bar while his two friends checked out the pavilion.

He said he had made some connections in the Italian community, and Franco had offered him a position as a writer for his paper. I asked him if he had read my story.

"I looked it over," he said casually. "It's full of interesting anecdotes.... You have a natural ability to write, and are very observant—a good trait for a writer."

I sipped nervously at my empty espresso cup.

"Maybe you should write a memoir," he added. "After all your family has gone through. It could be therapeutic."

Who would want to read my memoir? I thought. I didn't think my life had been that interesting. "I don't want to write about my life, but about the experiences that I have gone through and that are similar to others'. Do you know what I mean?" He seemed to be straining to understand me, so I raised my voice. "I want to write about others too. I want others to see themselves in what I see."

"Ah! A little universalist," he said, smiling and amused. "If that's what you want, use your imagination then. Invent!" He spoke at length about the writing process while I soaked in everything he said with adoring eyes.

He reached his hand across the table, as if to stroke mine, then hugged me and kissed me on the cheek, just as Franco and Chantale returned. He moved to leave, but not before making plans to go sightseeing the following Sunday.

"Ciao, Totu, See you soon," I waved cheerfully

"*Totù, quel genre de nom est Totù? Allons-y, mon Grand Antoine*," Chantale said, as she slipped her arm in his.

"*Allons-y*," he said, smiling. He looked back at me sheepishly.

I smiled back and shrugged. I didn't really think a man like Totu would be interested in a type like Chantale—a serious bespectacled woman who smoked non-stop—or in a married woman like Lucia—with a baby and no cultural interests—when there were so many available young women in Montreal.

Throughout the week, I reworked my story on the sea

voyage and titled it "The Voyage." I fretted about whether to keep all the details of Lucia cavorting with Armando and Nicodemo, but I couldn't bring myself to cut them out and I even made up some of the dialogue. The story would not be the same without those parts.

I dared hope *le Grand Antoine* would agree.

48. THE ROLLER COASTER RIDE

I HAD NEVER ENJOYED ROLLER coaster rides until I spent an afternoon at La Ronde with Totu. It was a perfect Indian-summer day in late September. We had walked in old Montreal in the morning, and then left the car and rode the metro to Île-Notre-Dame. He held my hand as we walked. He squeezed it and said, "Let's go for a ride."

I had always been afraid of the height, the speed, the force of the wind on my face that took my breath away. But he dared me to go with him on the scariest ride in the park, and without batting an eye, I followed him.

Île-Sainte-Hélène's flaming colours sparkled below us as the train ascended the steep rails to the top of the man-made steel mountain, and then dropped. It was like free falling into flight while holding hands with someone special. After the first drop, I looked forward to the next, and then the next, and I thought I could follow Totu to the highest precipice without fear.

We ate smoked meat sandwiches and Belgian waffles filled with ice cream. He talked non-stop about his love for Rome, his work in the Communist youth movement, and his decision to leave Italy when, at the same time, his dreams of social equality and of a career in journalism began to fade away. Montreal, he said, made him feel alive. He seemed genuinely amused by my hairdressing stories of fussy matrons wearing wigs and hairpieces, and laughed out loud when I told him some stories about fake-breasted waitresses from the Crazy Horse Saloon.

Walking next to him, I marvelled at how magical his unexpected reappearance into my life had been, and my imagination soared, thinking of all the things we could do together. He'd tutor me in my writing, discuss Italian literature with me, and open up a world of words to help me untwist my tongue so that I could claim the language I had never quite mastered.

It was late afternoon when we finally left La Ronde, and we drove to the lookout on Mount Royal, to see a panorama of Montreal by night. As the sun set, the city lights lit up slowly, casting shadows at the blazing mountain around us. It was too beautiful an evening not to take a walk on the treed path. We walked and walked and found ourselves in a cemetery.

There we found a clearing and sat on the grass, our legs lightly touching. When he brushed his lips against my cheeks, I felt myself sink into the circle of his arm. I closed my eyes and, for a time, I completely forgot where I was. When I reopened my eyes, dusk had already set. "We have to go," Totu said. "I have an appointment to meet a friend in less than an hour." I walked as if in a daze, disoriented and embarrassed. I couldn't recognize any of the reference points we had passed earlier.

"There are no tall cypresses here to indicate the entrance, as in Italian cemeteries," he said. "Who would have thought I'd be lost in a Montreal cemetery with you?"

As we walked, looking for the path back to the paved road, I wanted to remind him of the night I had sat alone in the twilight, across from another cemetery, while he and Lucia disappeared into a ravine, attempting to elope. Of the ominous vroom-vroom of Alfonso on his motorcycle, who saw me and discovered the tryst and caught up to them. About the shattering of water jugs on rocks and, finally, the dreadful emptiness I'd felt when I picked up the pottery shards, knowing my water jug would never be made whole again. But I kept that all to myself, figuring that what I remembered, he'd want to forget, and that it wouldn't matter anymore now that we had found each other. All the past hurts, the drought, the yearnings were coming to an end, and all would be healed.

When we finally made it back, I rushed to drop Totu off on the corner of Jean-Talon and Côte-des-Neiges. As he got out of the car, I pulled out my sea voyage story, and timidly gave it to him. He seemed surprised and, in a rush, folded it, then stuffed it into his jacket pocket. He told me he'd call me soon and thanked me for having been such a "good little guide."

"It's what I do best," I said, and he squeezed my knee as he left the car.

I was disappointed that we would not spend the evening together. I drove away with a heavy heart.

But instead of driving back east, I circled around the first side street, and parked strategically, in full view of the traffic-heavy intersection and Totu waiting at the bus stop. I figured he'd be meeting Chantale. When a blue Impala honked and then stopped, my jaw dropped. I saw Lucia open the passenger seat door and Totu jump in.

I felt fresh resentment for the willowy woman with the heart-shaped painted lips and head of feathery curly hair that framed her tiny face like an aura, who was, once again, cheating on her husband and getting in my way.

For days, for weeks, for months, I waited by the phone for the call he had promised me. I reviewed each moment of our day and wondered what I might have done or said to offend him or put him off. Had I been too cheerful, too quiet, too yielding to his touch? Maybe I had become too Canadian for his taste, or maybe I had remained too Calabrian. If love was more than he had to offer, why couldn't he just call me—as a friend—to talk about my writing? When I gathered enough confidence to call him, and ask about my manuscript, he apologized profusely and told me he had lost it. I recalled the folded bulky envelope protruding from his jacket pocket, and I had been afraid it would fall out. Maybe he dropped it in Lucia's car. Could she make out her name in the writing if she found it? Maybe they too went to the mountain and laid on the flaming ground. Could the manuscript be buried in a bed of autumn leaves? It was my only copy and it had meant so much to me, but he must have thought it pretty unimportant if he misplaced it so easily and I and didn't even think to offer an explanation.

Then, at the end of October, all my hopes were crushed when I heard that he had entered into a civil marriage with Chantale, and that he would be settling in Montreal with her.

Oddly enough, when I tried writing about our day together, I felt as humiliated by having been led too easily down the treed path by Totu, as I felt guilty about having deceived Lucia on two counts: by desiring Totu for myself, and by what I had revealed in my story about her. Lucia had trusted me with her indiscretions and I had betrayed her just to show off to Totu, who deserved neither of our affections. The childhood guilt of having been so inept at helping Lucia in her elopement plans resurfaced again, even if I knew how irrational that guilt really was. I couldn't help but imagine Lucia's heartbreak when she heard about his marriage. I had only desired him for a while, but he had been her first—and maybe only—love.

I wrote a prose poem in a trance, and I couldn't decide whether to write it for myself or Lucia. So I wrote it for both of us. I felt bound to her by the same pain I knew she was suffering. When I was done, I threw everything in a box, and put it out of sight.

PART IX
OCTOBER 24-27, 1980

49. A SETTLING OF ACCOUNTS

THE JOURNALIST GREETS ME EFFUSIVELY. "What a nice surprise, Caterina. I can still call you Caterina, right? Or do you prefer Cathy now that you have an English fiancé?"

"It doesn't matter what you call me, Totu. Or do you prefer I call you *le Grand Antoine*?"

"Ahh, the beauty of Canada and our multiple identities! But no one calls me Totu anymore. Call me Antonio; Antoine sounds odd coming from you, and," he scratches his head, "*Le Grand Antoine* ... you remember that?"

"I don't forget anything," I say. I point to the *Journal de Montreal* on his desk. "Why are you doing this? Is the letter even real?"

"Caterina! I'm offended by that question. Of course the letter is real. I actually spoke to Pasquale by phone before he sent me the letter. Pasquale went to my uncle and asked him to reach me."

"So, Don Cesare has gotten into the action ... again. I should have known."

"It's too good a story to let die. It just landed in my lap," he says, a mischievous smile on his face.

"But this is not just a story. These are your *paesani*, your friends."

"*Paesani*, yes, but not necessarily friends. I'm a journalist after all. What could I do?"

"You could have handed Pasquale's letter to the police

without splashing it all over the *Journal* with your personal spin, which may or may not be correct. Why the interview?"

"Because truth is not only stranger than fiction, in this case, it's stronger, Caterina. If I had plotted the story, I couldn't have come up with a better scenario. Pasquale's decision to fly back to Italy is the perfect resolution to this sordid tale. A lot of truth will come out of this, and I'll be vindicated."

"So, that's what you're really after—vengeance—family vengeance at that, after all these years! Getting back at Alfonso for all his past offences toward you? Is that what this is about? Blabbing all over the city and claiming to be interested in the truth! Your timing makes me wonder whether this has anything to do with your political agenda and PQ friends."

"I don't think in terms of friends or enemies when I investigate the news, only ideologies. What I do have is a deep hatred for those incompetent crooks in our community who claim to represent me, but only look after their own wallets, and for those who walk all over others. Or, maybe you want to speak on behalf of your fiancé's Liberal friends? I understand he might be running in a by-election."

"I don't give a damn about my fiancé's friends. But I'm afraid of people getting hurt by your insinuations. Reputations can easily be ruined by gossip. You, of all people, should know that. Some innocent people may be hurt, especially Angie. You remember Lucia and ... Angie, don't you?"

"What a silly question," Antonio answers, moving back behind his desk. He adds gravely, "People have already been hurt. I can't change that."

"It has taken you a long time to finally act. And what do you do? Use people's tragedies for your own political motives, for your fifteen minutes of journalistic glory ... snitch on people who can't defend themselves, like Angie."

"That thing about Angie being an illegal student ... someone else picked up on that, I swear." Antonio places his hand on his chest.

"You have to accept your share of blame," I say. "You're playing with this story, at Angie's expense."

"I don't know what you mean by blame, but when did you become so outspoken, Caterinella? You were always so quiet...." His voice trails off, as if he were sorry to have brought up the subject.

"Yes, maybe too quiet and ... agreeable," I answer.

Antonio looks down at his desk for a few seconds before speaking. "Caterina," he says slowly, as though searching for words. "Is there something you want to get off your chest, something of a more personal nature?"

"Yes. There's some unfinished business between us." I look directly into his eyes.

"I know, Caterina. I never got back to you about your writing. I'm sorry, but I was overwhelmed by ... circumstances. Now that you're an adult, I can admit that ... that the day at La Ronde ... it felt very awkward. I didn't know how to handle it ... and by nature, I avoid anything I can't handle."

"I was hurt that you assumed *I* wouldn't know how to handle it. You gave me so little credit. You treated me like a child."

"You were a child," he says gravely. He pulls out a manila envelope from his desk. "I believe this is yours," he says, and hands it to me. "Now, you tell me who is playing with the truth."

I open the envelope gingerly, puzzled. It's the missing stories from the pile of notebooks in my den, including the prose poem that had caused me so much pain to write. "How did you get these?"

"Lucia's daughter brought them to me ... to confront me."

"I wrote these a long time ago. They weren't meant to be read by anyone. Angie had no right to give them to you."

He raises his voice. "Angie is a very confused young lady. She's trying to figure out who her father is, and do you blame her with all that has been going on? She seems to think your stories may hold the clue as to who her real father is, and I'm one of the suspects."

"Well, aren't you?" I feel like asking but I hold my tongue. He continues. "Caterina, being a writer is not child's play. It's serious business. Don't you understand the heavy responsibility in putting things down on paper, especially when writing fiction? People read whatever they want to read into it."

"I understand that," I manage to say.

"You really don't know anything about Lucia's life here in Montreal ... the people around her...." he says.

I nod my head. "I would really like to know more about it—"

He cuts me short. "Angie tells me you're still writing. You haven't given up, have you? What are you writing about now?" he says, sounding annoyed.

I hesitate, but then blurt out. "The past, the present ... my own immigrant journey."

"Ah, the immigrant experience! You too?"

"I've decided to write a novel around all that I remember and all that is going on."

"A novel? You don't kid around. I thought you were writing a memoir."

"In 1967 you told me to go out and use my imagination, to invent, remember? But then you completely ignored me. I was very hurt by your silence."

"I've already apologized for that. But you have slandered me by your writing. Angie wishes so badly to find a father figure after Pasquale's statements, that she'll believe anything she reads. You have put me in a very awkward position with her."

"Well, certain facts point to you." I point to his foot. "No one believed your story of the hunting accident. Why won't you admit that you and Lucia were together in 1964, nine months before Angie was born? It's all very plausible."

His face becomes stern. "That's a nasty thing to bring up. Plausible doesn't make it real. Being seen with Lucia doesn't make me Angie's father, just like being seen with Aurora, years ago in Mulirena, didn't make me her lover either. You should know better, Caterina. You're on the wrong track here."

"Well, then," I say, "more reason to research the story. This time I'm not going to stop writing. It's too important to me."

"And so is finding the truth important to me."

"I understand," I say thoughtfully. "If you're concerned about the truth, instead of pulling in different directions, why don't we help each other?"

"I don't understand."

"Of all people, you may be the key I've been looking for. I'm having a hard time getting started, and remembering things ... filling the gaps. Sure, one can invent, but I still want the invention to be grounded on truth, to write something that is worth telling. Something that pays due respect to places and people."

He shakes his head. "Caterina, I still don't understand what you want from me. It's hard enough to write about one's memories; imagine trying to synchronize them with someone else's. I don't even want to think about it. You're treading on black ice—it's more slippery than it seems. Why do you think I hold the key to your writing puzzle?"

"You also hold the key for its ending. I want to find a fitting ending."

"That's a tall order, Caterina. What's a fitting ending? You're worried about the ending when you can't even get started? I don't think you realize the absurdity of tying it all together in this day and age."

"This isn't only about the writing. There are real people involved ... who have been living in limbo for years ... in fact are still in a coma. Maybe, finding the right ending will make it seem worthwhile having lived the story."

I point to the manila envelope on his desk. "We can work together if you ... we can come to grips with the roles we each played in the past."

He gets up and starts moving around the room, visibly agitated. "I don't follow you, Caterina. You say you want to write a novel and not a memoir, and now you talk of our own roles? There's something skewed about your argument,

Caterina, and I still don't understand your motive."

I raise my hands and speak angrily: "My motive is to get to the truth whether I write a novel or memoir. I also question your intentions for using Pasquale's story, and broadcasting it to everyone. Is it personal or purely for political reasons to help your PQ friends?"

Antonio sits back behind his desk, and puts on his glasses. "Well, since you brought politics up, let me ask you some questions, Caterina. If you're so keen on filling gaps, why are you so upset about me revealing what Pasquale has to say about Di Principe if not to protect your fiancé's boss? You know there's going to be an inquiry coming up sooner or later, and Di Principe and his Liberal cronies will be revealed for the scumbags that they are."

I make a move toward the door, open it, and then stop. I say calmly, "I don't care about my fiancé's friends; say what you want about them. I'm worried about Lucia and Angie, and … mostly, I'm afraid of unfairly representing the past, and I'd like the present to be worthy of the past … maybe to make up for it."

"Of course, the past, how could I forget? You came with a head full of romantic ideas. Yes, now I remember vaguely the story of the voyage—the love story of Renzo and Lucia overcoming all. But that was not your fault. You were ten, eleven years old then? Manzoni was inculcated in you and in everyone else in Italy at the time. But you're a grown woman now. We're living in a different world."

"I thought you hadn't even read that story, that you had lost the manuscript," I say.

"I had looked at it quickly, before … misplacing it," he says dismissively.

"You could have mentioned it, in all these years."

He gets up again, next to me, put his two hands together, and shakes then up and down impatiently. "Caterina, Caterina, what can I say now? Write if you must, but forget about capturing an idyllic past or preserving old memories, or about tying it all neatly together. It's as old-fashioned an idea as ... yesterday's hairstyles, for lack of a better example."

"Styles keep reappearing, in slightly different forms, but it's the same old stuff coming up—*gira e rigira*...."

"Okay, bad metaphor to have used on a hairstylist."

I get up to leave and take the prose poem from the manila envelope. "This was something I had to get off my chest at the time, and now, it needs closure, to be complete, to close the circle, so we can all go on with our lives. It's the last thing I wrote, after our day at La Ronde."

"Ah, la Ronde! Yes, 1967, Montreal—a special time and place. What promises..."

I push the manuscript into his hands. "Then respond to this once and for all. Tell me the rest of this story. The reasons for leading me on, for leading Lucia on, the reasons why people deceive one another, but especially themselves.... I want to understand why people do the things they do."

He pauses for a while before he answers, "I still don't understand what you want from me, but I'll reread this, if you promise there won't be any more ill feelings between us."

"There won't be as long as you acknowledge this. Tell me your own version, so I can understand."

He smiles and pats me on the cheek. "You're an ace, Caterina. Come back in a couple of days. Don't misunderstand all I've said. I'm happy to see you again."

Lost in a Cemetery

> We left the lookout on Mount Royal to explore the city forest, all fiery-red leaves shining like small fires in the moonlight, crackling under our feet. His voice mellow as we walked and talked until we stopped in a clearing and he embraced me. He kissed my face, and then his tongue moved up and down, past my opened

blouse to my neck and my breasts, before returning to my lips, and to the inside of my mouth, until I completely forgot where I was. I found myself falling on the leaves, the world opening up to moist lips, tongue on tongue, warm hands on legs. I closed my eyes as he rose up and up, and then my body fell down next to him, and we lay quiet, as though asleep on a bed of leaves. It took us forever to retrace our steps to the lookout, picking leaves off each other's clothes, getting lost in the mountain cemetery, in a maze of tombstones, while Saint Joseph's Oratory loomed like a fat, disapproving chaperone ahead of us. "I'll call you," he said to me ... to her. For many days, weeks, months, we waited for the sign that he would return us to life. We continued as if nothing had disrupted the monotony of our daily existence, but at times, the weight of the silence pressed so heavily on our fractured hearts and souls that we feared we might crack into a thousand bits and pieces. Sunlight dissolved into blankness as another Indian summer slid past us, leaving nothing ahead but another November and another death.

50. THE HAIRDRESSING LESSON

I WORKED FRANTICALLY OVER THE weekend to draft an outline of a novel to show Antonio, by incorporating the stories I had written recently while identifying the gaps in both the old stories and the new ones. At Sunday lunch with my family, I took the time to look through last month's issues of *Arte&Cultura* and found the advertisement for the launch of Antonio's last book at the Casa D'Italia. Was this the event Lucia attended a week before her beating? I'd have to ask Antonio. The thought of finally working with him both excites and intimidates me. But, I feel as if I must tread lightly, as he offered his help only halfheartedly.

On Monday morning, in class, I read the bulletin on the upcoming Halloween dance, while the school technician installs the TV set and VCR I had ordered to show a film on colour harmony. The students gather their chairs, sit in a semicircle around the TV, and chatter about their planned costumes while I fidget with the VCR. The film provided by the tint company, L'Oreal, will serve as an introduction to my lessons on hair colouring.

I distribute a diagram of a colour wheel—a circle with two intersecting triangles, which forms six smaller ones—and ask the students for a few minutes attention before I turn on the film.

"No notes today," they groan.

"Come on, girls," I say. "This is fun. Whether you're painting a house, a canvas, or hair, you must understand the principle of colour harmony." I then let the blonde and perky colourist in the film take over, as she holds the same diagram of a colour wheel I distributed.

She tells the students that all colours on earth are a combination of three primary colours—red, blue, and yellow—and points to the three major points of the triangle. When these colors mix, they produce the secondary colours: green, orange and purple—all very useful in hair colouring.

All hair, no matter how dark, has subtle shades of red, yellow, or gold pigmentation, which gives it its own distinctive shade or highlight, but the more red, gold, or yellow in the hair, the harder it is to produce the light cool blondes favoured by fake blondes everywhere.

"This is where the secondary colours kick in," she says as she moves her hands from the primary colours to their corresponding opposites. "They are used to neutralize the brassy reds, the oranges, and the yellow highlights."

I've watched this film for years, and for the first time I realize how dramatic the principle really is. A gooey slate-green concoction will remove any hint of warmth that nature imparts on hair. How ghastly, I think, when the rule is applied to other facets of life!

I stare blankly at the colour wheel on the screen. With it, a thought emerges that has nothing to do with hair colouring, and I can't wait to sit down and put it on paper.

I take a blank colour wheel and I write "Cathy," "Lucia" and "Angie" in bold letters next to the points of the triangle. I must make these three women the primary characters in my novel, the connecting glue that will hold it all together.

I muse about which names will ring truest—Caterina or Cathy, Angelina or Angie? Is changing one's birth name a selling out or a betrayal of one's truest identity? I consider the question for a whilet. What is one's identity if not the agglomeration of all the lives one has lived throughout the years? The name Caterina sounds right for the past, when there was no doubt about who she was. But then, she has been taken on a long journey, not fully of her own volition, and Cathy is who she has become. Is it fair to deny those years and that process of transformation? I don't quite know the answer. The same applies for Angelina/Angie. Lucia has always remained Lucia, in and out of her coma. That is the way it happened, and there is no use forcing the issue.

I see how, though different, the three women have something in common. In some way or other, they've been deceived and hurt by the men closest to them. In wanting so badly to find their true counterparts, to feel whole and complete, they have allowed themselves, passively, to be neutralized, subdued, silenced, and even neutered.

After class, I'm emboldened to drive to Antonio's office. I show him my outline but hold on to the colour wheel.

"You've been busy," he says while perusing my notes. "This will end up with more layers than a Calabrese lasagna." He smiles and I'm not sure whether he's mocking me or he's pleasantly amused.

"I've put these ideas down, but the material needs to be organized...."

"Who said, 'I have no plans, only material?'" he smiles, Then he adds, "Jokes aside, there are lots of compelling ideas here, but if you want me to read it, start on a word processor. Your handwriting is illegible."

"Did you read the prose poem?" I ask.

"Sorry?" he says as if he didn't hear me. I repeat the question. "Not yet. It's been crazy these past days, with interviews and all," he says.

I change subject, "Tell me the truth, had you been seeing Lucia before the night she got hit?"

"I hadn't seen her for years, until she came to my office in the spring." He put my notes down, ready to fill me in.

He tells me that Lucia had shown up at his office with her daughter to inquire about flights to Italy and then brought up

Angie's problems at school. She had wanted to go to Mulirena with Angie that summer. She hoped the trip would be good for Angie who had been expelled from school. She was especially concerned about her daughter and felt guilty that she had neglected her.

Lucia was finally getting medical help for a debilitating depression she had suffered for years. She seemed to have woken up and wanted to make necessary changes in her life.

"And did you see her after that?"

"A week later," he says in a low voice.

Before booking her for a trip to Italy, he'd felt it his duty to let her in on some stories he had heard, but, not wanting to discuss it in front of Angie, he'd invited Lucia for coffee and had a long chat with her then. She then cancelled her plans to go to Italy, called me about Angie, and moved out of her home.

"Did you see her again?"

"One last time. Maybe that turned out to have been a mistake."

She showed up at a cultural event that he was hosting, a fundraising banquet for his paper, at the Casa D'Italia, and the launch of his latest book.

Finally my student's comment about the dance and Lucia made sense to me.

"I was surprised to see her. She came in all dressed up, with a new short haircut that made her look half her age. Maybe that, and the stories I had already told her incited the argument between her brother and husband."

"What stories?"

"I told her about the farmhouse and 1964. I thought she'd have known all the details by now, but I was surprised that she had been left in the dark"

"Can you tell me those details?"

He is quiet for a moment, as if unsure to go on. "We go back a long time, Caterina. Remember Piazza Don Carlo and the lazy afternoons there? You used to sit on your doorstep by yourself and play there for hours, so serious, so intense."

"Yes, remember when Professor Nucci called it *Piazza d'Amore?*"

He takes my hand and holds it for a while. "I always thought it was such a boring place, that nothing ever happened there, until you dig deeper ... and look under the surface, as I did last summer. I dicovered it was anything but...."

Antonio pulls his chair next to mine and for the next hour recounts what he had learned from his uncle on his last visit to Mulirena, the summer before. He had gone to bury his father and finally make peace with him as well as with his uncle, the man that had been like a second father to him. Don Cesare had rehashed events from the past.

Some of the revelations stun me; others, confuse me. I also wonder whether they are all true or simply Totu's attempts to justify his actions as a young man. He takes great delight in the retelling, and I also can't help but feel that he has told me these stories too readily, maybe to divert attention from my request to respond to my prose poem and my unasked questions about his relationship with Lucia just before her assault.

"Thank you for sharing all this with me," I say. "Do you think Lucia had hopes of a reconciliation with you?"

"I can't speak for Lucia," he says.

I try to rephrase my question, "What would you do if Lucia came out of her coma?"

"The prognosis for someone in her condition is not very good," he says sadly.

My questions may be premature, and I don't press him anymore, but in spite of his prognosis I leave with a sense of hopefulness that a happy ending may still be possible.

Back in my classroom, I reconstruct the complex web of stories I heard so I won't forget any details.

The secondary characters, Aurora and her parents, Micu and Paola, and Lucia's husband, Pasquale, had played important roles in the village tale, yet had been given such little space in my own writing. With Antonio's latest revelations, the pieces of the puzzle are slowly fitting in. Still, I'm amazed that events that happened in a remote village years before continue to impinge on the present lives of some of the characters, motivating their actions and reactions and precipitating some of their downfalls.

What might Pasquale and Micu be up to, at this minute, huddled together in the farmhouse in Mulirena? Are they talking about how futile their lives have been?

51. PASQUALE AND MICU

SIX HOURS DIFFERENCE BETWEEN TIME zones means that it is already bedtime in Mulirena while people in Montreal rush home from work through Halloween-decorated streets. Just as thoughts of ghoulish party accoutrements swirl around the commuters' heads, the wheel of memory turns relentlessly for Pasquale and Micu, causing them to think about their plight after years of passivity as secondary characters.

Shut inside a humid farmhouse, the two men have taken to drinking and commiserating their shared misfortunes. Life had not been fair to either of them, they agreed. Wasn't it strange how the same people had meddled in the stories of both their lives? They had been born in different towns, lived on different continents most of their lives, and yet found themselves together at the end of their roads, sitting under the same crooked umbrella, trying to keep warm and dry as constant drips of rain leaked from the roof over the fireplace. They had eaten cold roasted chestnuts for dinner, washed down with Micu's heavy homemade wine. The host had been too lazy or too drunk to cook and Pasquale was still unaccustomed to the chore of preparing a meal in someone else's house, and in a ramshackle farmhouse at that.

How long could he last, living like this? Even with all of his experience in construction, Pasquale had to admit that insulating the stone hovel before the winter, to the Canadian standards to which he was now accustomed, posed an impossible challenge. Maybe he was getting old and soft, or maybe it was his arthritis acting up, but never, in Canada, did he remember the humidity seeping into his bones as it did when he moved away from this fireplace to go pee or go to bed at night.

Yet, this is what he had dreamed of most of his life in Canada—coming back home to the mountains. He imagined his acquaintances back in Montreal in their comfy, heated dens, their wine cellar, stocked with all the cheeses, salami, and meats that money could buy. He cursed his brothers for having swindled him of his house in Serra San Pietro, and his wife and her family for having cheated him out of a life in Montreal. He had no friends, no family, and now, no home.

Micu drank his vinegary wine from morning to night, oblivious to any bodily discomfort and to his own fetid smell. He didn't know any better. He'd never travelled beyond the confines of the province, except during his military service. He had spent the last twenty-odd years in this farmhouse, keeping warm in front of this same fireplace, and he had never seen fit to repair the leaky roof. Tiled roofs leak all the time. You move one tile, you disturb a dozen others. Better let them be.

The only bond between the two men was the rancour they felt toward those who had played tricks on them, especially Alfonso. Pasquale figured that finally he had nothing to lose. It was time to settle scores, if for no other reason than to show the world that he was not the imbecile life had made him out to be. He came to this farmhouse on a hunch that Micu, the senile drunkard, might talk about Alfonso and the past.

Pasquale knew of the ancient quarrels between Lucia's family and their relative, Don Cesare, over politics, the use of water, and the right of passage over the same farmland and house in which he now slept with Micu. Alfonso never hid his scorn and jealousy for Don Cesare's widowed brother-in-law, Gennaro, who looked after the land as if it were his own. In gatherings, especially amongst men, Alfonso often liked to tell of how he let the peasant Micu discover that his wife was having an affair not with Don Cesare as everyone thought, but with the soft-spoken Gennaro that no one had suspected. Alfonso told of the tryst in the old *casale* by the river with relish over and over again to his friends in Montreal, especially punctuating that the quiet but sneaky Gennaro was the father of the holier-than-thou snob of a journalist that poked fun at the community leaders who formed Alfonso's entourage in Montreal. Not only did Totu's father, Gennaro, have an affair with the peasant Micu's wife, but Totu himself seduced that same peasant's daughter, Aurora, who most likely was his half sister. So much for his moral integrity!

"I heard you had wanted to shoot both Totu and his father years ago. Why didn't you?" Pasquale asks.

Micu opens his eyes. "What good would it have done me and my family? Alfonso made me a partner in his export business, so instead I left Don Cesare and Gennaro to fend for themselves."

Pasquale becomes agitated. "He made you a partner? The import/export business was my idea. I was his only partner. When I first set foot in Montreal, there was nothing worth buying in the food stores. The bread was like a white sponge, the cheese was yellow, and they had baloney for salami. What shit! And the oil made from corn looked like piss. You couldn't find an Italian *grossetteria* if your life depended on it."

"*Ma*, what's a *grossetteria*?" Micu asks, slightly more awake now.

"A store, where you buy food," Pasquale replies.

"Ah, *alimentari*. You talk funny. I don't understand half of what you say."

"That's because I also speak English and French. How many languages do you speak?"

"Eh, how many languages do I need on this farm?"

Pasquale continues, raising his voice, "I could have started a cheese company right there in Canada with all the money I sent Alfonso while he still lived here. Instead he let the Montreal

Sicilians beat me to it. He and my brothers sucked me dry, but if you can't trust your own brothers, who can you trust?"

"Not your own wife, that's for sure," Micu says.

"Nor yours," Pasquale answers. "How many of your children were Gennaro's?"

"On that, I can put my hand in the fire," Micu says. "The children all look like me."

"I also thought my daughter looked like me until Alfonso planted a doubt in my mind," Pasquale retorts. "A doubt is worse than knowing for sure, and to think I moved my wife to the country in Laval so she'd be away from her old boyfriend in Montreal."

"I did the same with my wife—moved her here."

"But my house is a palace compared to this shack."

"It's a shack because Alfonso never sent me enough money to finish rebuilding it properly, and I thought he was such a big shot there."

Pasquale gets up, wrapping the blanket around his shoulders, "Sure, sure, he became a big shot because of me. I introduced him to all the important people: How could I know that he would marry one of the Vaccaro daughters, become best friends with Jack, and take over the project that I had been working on?"

"So he also double-crossed you? *Complimenti.*"

But why had Alfonso—that sly fox—let Micu become the rightful owner, with legal papers and deeds, not only of the farmhouse but also of the extensive land that Pasquale had thought would eventually belong to him and his wife? Pasquale wants to know.

"The farm was my dowry. You had no right to give it away," Lucia had yelled at Alfonso on the night they had all ripped at each other. "I'll tell your wife why you did it."

Since Lucia had gotten into her head to move in with her mother in Montreal, Pasquale was obsessed by the thought that she might leave him for good. His friend, Nicodemo, had warned him that Lucia had visited her old boyfriend at his office and then attended a fundraising dinner for him. Was the old flame being rekindled?

When Alfonso called him to a meeting, Pasquale had hoped it was to talk some sense into his sister, but Alfonso had other motives, and all Lucia harped about was the old farmhouse. Alfonso's temper then flared up and all hell broke loose.

Why did Alfonso turn so violently against his own sister after she brought up the old farmhouse? If Pasquale could sift the past with Micu, some stubborn granule of truth might give something or someone away. Pasquale had enough evidence to destroy Alfonso's business in Canada; he'd only feel fully revenged if he could also hurt Alfonso in his personal life.

"Then why did you shoot at Totu years after all the talk about your daughter?" Pasquale asks Micu.

"I saw a man with Lucia and I thought it was Alfonso. The shot was meant to scare Alfonso off the property. Totu simply happened to be at the wrong place at the wrong time. You know, you too were born a *cornuto*," Micu answers.

"I was born a *disgraziato*," Pasqule says. "That has been my destiny." He reflects for a while. "I don't understand ... the property belonged to my wife."

Micu was falling asleep. He slurs, "Old stories. I'm going to bed."

"Tell me. I like old stories." Pasquale insists. He wants to keep Micu awake. "I have stories about Alfonso to bust your head. Do you know what he did in Montreal during the Olympics?"

"No. They had the Olympics in Montreal?"

"You're so ignorant! Well, Alfonso and his friends boasted for months about how they drove their trucks loaded with material into the Olympic sites and drove right out to unload at their other residential projects. I have the names of the city workers who collected bribes. And you know who is also involved in all this?"

"How the fuck would I know?"

"Never mind. Wait till I tell the journalist."

"And are you not involved in all this?"

"They kept me out of it. Alfonso always treated me like a *cafone*, and to top it all, at the end, he called me a *cornuto*."

"You should be used to that name by now."

"All along I thought it was always about the journalist. But this time, Alfonso kept on talking about one of my friends who wanted my wife to go live with him ... so he could also have her sign some papers for his properties ... said she owed it to him since he was the father of her daughter, my daughter! They talked as if I wasn't even there."

"So that's why you hit your wife in the head?"

"No, I only slapped her once and ran away."

"So who did it?"

"Can't say for sure, but I'll give some information when I contact the journalist in Montreal."

"Why? Is he not the one I shot in the leg? Your wife made you a *cornuto* twice and you laugh at me? At least I got something from Alfonso," Micu says.

"It doesn't matter anymore. The journalist is the only person I know that will use the evidence I send him." Pasquale takes his arm out from under the blanket, pours himself and Micu another glass of warm wine, and sits down. "Now tell me, Micu, why did Alfonso give you this dump of a farmhouse on a silver platter?"

Micu, wrapping his worn-out coat around his shoulders, says, "This house may look like a dump to you, but at least it's mine. I'm not such a *cornuto* after all. You can go back to Montreal and tell everyone how I got it."

52. VENETIAN MASKS

ALL THE NATIONAL PAPERS AND TV news have reported the allegations about the soon-to be-appointed Senator, Alex Di Principe. It seems the party men have huddled together in support of the man who as a Member of Parliament has worked relentlessly to raise funds and boost the fortunes of the federal Liberal Party in Quebec, and helped beat the separatists in the referendum. The Liberals form a majority government, and they have nothing politically to fear for the moment, except possibly losing the upcoming by-election.

"We have chosen to ignore the rumours completely," a spokesperson declared. "No one takes a third-rate journalist with an overactive imagination seriously." However, the federal Opposition party won't let the revelations go unnoticed, and jumps on the chance to grill the Liberals about the questionable reputation of their main "bag man" in Quebec. In the House of Commons, during question period, a member from Calgary asked for an inquiry about Di Principe's past association with known criminal elements. Photographs of Di Principe in the company of Jack Russo and other mob figures who are rumoured to be at war with each other, and are alleged to have manipulated the construction trade for years, have made the rounds in newspapers across the country. An editorial in *La Presse* reiterates its call for a Commission to investigate corruption in the construction industry and powerful construction union, especially regarding the cost overruns of the beleaguered

Olympic stadium, still without a roof, whose expense is still borne by the citizens of Montreal. Other editorials call for Di Principe to explain his close ties to those individuals suspected to be involved in high-level collusion in the awarding of city contracts.

One Toronto editorialist writes, "This will set back the Italian community in Canada by a generation." I'm incensed. Is the labour and contributions to this country by thousands and thousands of honest working Italians over a generation completely erased by the wrongdoings of a handful of mobsters and other greedy characters? Many dishonest officials and bureaucrats of other backgrounds have been caught red-handed in corruption. How come their actions are not seen to reflect on their cultural groups?

Unexpectedly, Sean shows up at the apartment on Thursday late afternoon. My insides are still in knots whenever I think of our last conversation. I have waited for him to make the next move and here he is, carrying two large clothing bags, our costumes for the ball, as if nothing has happened. Mine is a long, hooped dress in brocade and a tight-fitting bodice with adjustable strings; his: tights, a long tail coat and frilly shirt. Both come with wigs and Venetian masks. Angie is in the kitchen and I don't want to say anything to Sean in front of her.

"What are you supposed to be?" Angie says.

"Cathy's is actually a Marie Antoinette costume, but with a mask she can pass for a Venetian lady, Desdemona, and if I wear the black mask, I can be Othello."

"Who are they?" Angie asks.

"A Venetian woman and her husband. The woman was killed by her husband out of jealousy," he says.

"Her too?" Angie answers and leaves the room.

I wait till she closes the door behind her. I turn on the volume on the TV. "You can't expect me to go through with this farce," I say.

"I'm sorry if J.P.'s comments insulted you the other night," Sean says in a whisper. "But you're not going to end our relationship for that. J.P. and I had drunk half a bottle of Scotch, besides the wine. He spoke out of line, but he did it for my own good."

"The revelation hit me in the face, and I've been walking around like a zombie for a week."

"What revelation?"

"You're using me, Sean. All of my plans, my dreams to start a new life with you ... with a new bed ... feel desecrated. I had dreamed of a love nest, but I now feel deceived."

"The drama is coming out now. Italian opera all over again. *Vesti la giubba*," he starts singing. "Sometimes you have a way with words," he laughs. "Love nest ... desecrated bed ... who holds on to these notions anymore?"

He stops talking when Di Principe appears on the screen. He is being interviewed on the six o'clock news. Di Principe also laughs off the allegations against him. "Anyone who knows the geography of Italy will see that the Veneto region I come from is very, very far from Sicily and Calabria."

"What the hell is that supposed to mean?" I ask, furious.

"The idiot!" Sean says, walking nervously around the room. "He should have kept his mouth shut. It would all have been forgotten by next week."

"I'm not going to forget," I say. "And you still think I'm going to attend this party to celebrate his appointment, after all that has happened, and dressed as a Venetian on top of that? Maybe J.P. can wear my dress and be your date. With the wig and the mask no one will notice."

"What a stupid thing to say," Sean says, then begs me to reconsider. "The ball is just as important for me as it is for Di Principe. Your family is planning an engagement party, and you want to throw it all away for a comment? Please come to the ball and then we can work this out between ourselves later on."

Angie comes out of her room. Sean continues, "This ball is more important than you think. The *crème de la crème* of the Italian community will be there: politicians, radio and television personalities, business people, and representatives of various associations. We all need to put up a united front, especially because of the mudslinging and defamation going on. The Italian community is also being targeted."

"Di Principe and his cronies don't represent all of the community, only their greedy selves. Don't you understand that? I can represent myself, thank you very much. This ball has lost all its luster," I say.

I ask Angie to come to the apartment locker with me, and we return a few minutes later with two heavy boxes that we plunk down on the coffee table.

"I'm afraid to ask," Sean says.

I shrug and ask Angie to look through the clothes for a costume for the school party. She sits, uninterested, on the sofa. I pull out a silk tie-dyed shirt and a long, gauze skirt to go with it.

"You could be a flower child," I say.

"I don't have to wear a costume," Angie replies, her arms crossed. "And if I did, the last thing I'd want to be is a flower girl."

"I mean a flower child—the make-love-not-war kind—a hippie," I reply. I hold the peasant skirt, with its bright shades of pinks, mauves, and blues, against my body.

Sean dumps some clothes in his knapsack to return to the hotel. "I remember that skirt," he says. "I liked it on you. Why did you stop wearing it?"

"Because now it looks like a costume."

"I see," Sean says. "So it was only a passing fad."

I look at him as if to say, "Yes, what did you think it was?" He had spent that period immersed in Beatles' music about love and peace, and here he is now, working for jerks like Di Principe and in cahoots with a bigger jerk, that carpetbagger, J.P.

Sean moves around nervously as he is about to leave. "I've rented a limousine and can come pick you up at six. Let me know by three if you'll come."

I keep rummaging through the box and don't answer.

Angie is quietly watching us. She pipes up: "I want to go to a party, after school ... with Linda and Gina ... at Charlie's."

"Of course not," I say. "Why would you even bother asking? Your uncle won't allow it."

"He doesn't have to know," Angie says. "I can tell him the school party is at night and I sleep here for the weekend."

"No way, Angie," I say. "You go to the school party in the afternoon, and then you come home as usual."

"It's the first time I have ever asked you for a favour," Angie says, getting up. "My grandmother said I can stay here for the weekend if you let me."

I slip a caftan on over my clothes, and walk out to the hallway mirror to look at myself. "Angie, you're being unreasonable. I can't lie to your family about something like that. How long would it take your uncle to find out you had been at Charlie's? You know he knows people there."

"What is he going to do when he finds out? Shoot me? Don't tell me you never lied to your mother about things like that. Were you always such a goody-goody?"

I find a white turban with a heavy rhinestone broach, and put it on. At one time, inspired by the Great Gatsby movie, I had worn it over wavy hair, with the broach over one ear. "Angie, I'm sorry," I say. "With everything that's been going on, I can't let you go out with your friends without your family knowing about it. Who knows where I'll be. There's even another Halloween party up north I've been invited to."

"What are you talking about?" Sean says.

"Susan, the secretary, is having a party up north,"

"You're not thinking of driving up north, for a juvenile Halloween party, rather than go to the Ritz with me, are you?" Sean says, raising his voice.

"I didn't say I'll go, just that I was invited," I scream back.

"Oh my God, what's with the two of you?" Angie yells and kicks the leg of the table.

Sean jots down a phone number on a piece of paper. "Call me in the afternoon, one way or the other," he shouts, and storms out.

Angie sulkily turns to go to her room. "Thanks a lot for your help. I'll tell my uncle to pick me up at school then, after the dance."

"You do that now. Call the house and let me speak to your uncle or grandmother."

Angie calls from the kitchen phone and carries on a short conversation in French, and then hangs up.

"He wasn't home and my grandmother is already in bed. So I told my aunt."

Angie goes back to her room and slams the door.

"I'll call him myself tomorrow," I say. I call Angie back, and hold up the white turban.

"What now?" Angie asks, annoyed.

"Look at this turban. It looks great with the caftan."

Angie makes a face. "Then you wear it."

"Let's just see what it looks like on you," I say, putting the turban on Angie's head. I adjust the broach over Angie's forehead. "I need to reshape your eyebrows."

Angie pulls back. "Get off me. Leave my eyebrows alone."

"You have big, beautiful eyes, but they get lost under those bushy eyebrows."

Angie frowns. "If I start plucking them, they'll get bushier."

"That's an old wives' tale. It only takes a few seconds a day."

"Yeah, that's why it takes you forever to get ready in the morning."

"Well, I've already told you I care about the way I look. What's wrong with that?"

"Well, maybe I care about the way I look too," Angie tries to imitate my voice. "Maybe I just don't want to look like you."

I take off the caftan and put it into a plastic bag from the kitchen, together with the turban.

Angie follows me around, talking. "What I mean is, I don't want to be like you. I mean, you think you're perfect. All I ever heard from my grandmother was how perfect Caterina is. Well, I've lived with you for a month, now. You're not so perfect. Your life is not so perfect, and you're a little liar."

"Well, the caftan is the best I can come up with. Use it if you like." I walk back to the living room, and start preparing the sofa for the night. I can't bring myself to sleep on the mattress on the bedroom floor

"You're just like her, you know," Angie continues, standing next to me.

"Like who?"

"My mother. She just hid in her room, in her own little world. No guts!"

I had never noticed how tall and lanky Angie seemed next to me. The girl is practically breathing down my neck as she speaks, and I feel a sudden urge to be rid of her constant, brooding presence. I impatiently throw a pillow on the sofa.

"Look," I say. "I've had it now. I'm just trying to help you find a costume. You could show a bit of appreciation, you know.... And there's no way I'll cover for you on Friday night."

"Of course not," Angie says mockingly. "That wouldn't be the proper thing to do for a queen like you—Cathy, the queen of fucking everything!"

"Why have you turned so nasty towards me?"

"Well, I used to think you were really hip, living with someone like Sean. But you're just like all of the other Calabrese women—a big liar. And you have been trying to change me since I moved in with you."

"I've been trying to help you."

"Oh, you're just a busybody, that's all. Nothing is ever good enough for you. How many times have you moved the furniture around since I've been here? And your bedroom—are you ever going to set it up for good? Are you really ever going to get married to your fiancé?"

I don't answer.

Angie continues, "The funny thing is, you're so ashamed to let people know you've been sleeping with him, when you're not even sleeping with him, or ... should I say ... he's not sleeping with you?"

"I don't think that's any of your business," I say, raising my voice. "What right do you have to pass judgment on me? What do you know about life?"

"Well, I know that your fiancé is out of the house every chance he gets. He spends more time with his snobby friend than you."

"Angie, just go to bed. And please stay out of my personal life, will you?"

I retreat to the bathroom to prepare for another uncomfortable night on the sofa. When I come out, Angie has gone to her room. I hear her making noises. It sounds like she's moving books. Is she doing homework, or snooping into my things again? Have I been a fool to let this girl into my apartment and let her disrupt my life?

The exchange has left me unsettled. I let my mind withdraw into the village tales I heard from Antonio.

53. THE MISSING PIECES

HER NAME WAS AURORA; they called her the little *zingara*. It was the villagers' custom to nickname people according to their family's histories or some idiosyncratic habit. Aurora's mother, Paola, was known as the bigger gypsy.

Paola had the body of a goddess and who could blame her for finding warmth in Gennaro's arms. Her husband, Micu, only responded to the feel of the olive presses in his rough hands and drank himself into a stupor whenever he wasn't working. For years it was assumed that she served Don Cesare in more ways than one, but Alfonso's constant scrutiny revealed that it was with the quiet widower Gennaro that she shared her leisure hours.

Totu was only two years old when his mother died and his father Gennaro moved to Mulirena to work for Don Cesare. Aurora was born a year later, very likely, but not certainly, his half-sister. Aurora and Totu were both protégés of the childless Donna Rachele, Don Cesare's wife. As a former teacher, Donna Rachele delighted in teaching the two children good manners and proper Italian, yet they never thought of her as their mother, more like a governess—two semi-orphans hungering for the love of absent parents.

As children, Aurora and Totu would cross the enclosed courtyard in the back of Don Cesare's house to go play with Lucia. The three were inseparable and Lucia and Totu grew into childhood sweethearts. Lucia's older brother, Alfonso, resented both Totu's and Aurora's constant presence in his home, and picked fights with the threesome at the smallest provocation.

Because of her blue eyes, Aurora would always play the part of angels at school. At sixteen, she was given the role of Our Lady of Lourdes. This is when Alfonso started planting stories that Totu had seduced the girl.

Aurora had become such a fixture at the Abiusi's home that neither Lucia nor her mother, Comare Rosaria, took notice of her comings and goings. Had they been more vigilant, they would have noticed that as the "little gypsy" developed into a little woman, Alfonso enticed her into spending long summer afternoons in the abandoned stall underneath their home, even as he scorned the girl and later forbade his sister from being seen with her.

Aurora had always confided in Totu until she started spending time with Alfonso at the stall. Alfonso forced himself on Aurora when she was fifteen, then continued to seek her until she became pregnant. Aurora led a double life she herself could not understand. She responded to the courtship of another young man, Saverio, as if nothing had happened; she kept quiet about Alfonso's first sexual attack, and then followed him into the stall whenever he asked. The only person who saw what was happening to Aurora was the teacher from Piemonte, Signor Gavano, who had noted a change in her behaviour. She opened up to him only when she became pregnant.

The kind teacher spoke to Alfonso, and tried talking Aurora into telling the truth to her parents. Alfonso denied any responsibility, accusing Aurora of having become a slut for Totu and other men. In a moment of utter helplessness, she saw no other way out than by ending her own life. Everyone around her remained silent after Don Cesare convinced her old boyfriend, Saverio, to marry her. The young man accepted on condition that Alfonso's role would never be mentioned. He had his own honour to think about too. As long as the gossip going around Totu remained unconfirmed, and chucked off to jealousy, there was still a chance for Aurora to build some kind of life with Saverio. No one knew how many months Aurora had been pregnant and so it was conceivable that Saverio was the responsible party since he had been on a short leave a few months before the incident. He knew differently, but he'd rather be blamed for his amorous ardour than for settling to marry someone spoiled by Alfonso. Don Cesare shipped Totu to Rome, not only out of fear for his safety after the rumours about Totu and Aurora, but also to keep him away from Lucia and her family. In turn, Totu became resentful of his family, the village and its petty politics, and fled from all, including Lucia.

This part of the story resurfaced much later:

Aurora had kept up a correspondence with Signor Gavano throughout the summer after her hospital stay, while he was on school break in Piemonte. The letters and Signor Gavano's comments corroborated Alfonso's role in her pregnancy. After Aurora left for Argentina, her mother showed Don Cesare the letters and they both, being as astute as they were, formed a strategy for revenge.

They had tried in vain to threaten Alfonso with claiming acquired rights to the farm, to pay Aurora's father, Micu, the money owed him, but with little success. Alfonso had laughed them off, since not enough years had expired for such a law to come into effect. Then they heard that Alfonso was planning a trip to Mulirena to sell his home. When Micu saw a man going into the farmhouse with Lucia from a distance, he shot him in the leg, as a warning that he meant business, and thinking that it was Alfonso. The scare worked. When Alfonso arrived a week later, he was cornered by Don Cesare and blackmailed with Aurora's letters. Don Cesare asked for nothing less than that Aurora and her parents be given the deed to the farmhouse and land, and Don Cesare full right to the water that passed by the land. Alfonso protested, but in the end, he didn't want his wife's family to hear of his spotted past. His sister didn't seem to care for anything or anyone, and he figured that once their mother moved to Montreal, there was nothing to draw her back to the village. Lands were abandoned by everyone else as they emigrated. Alfonso convinced Comare Rosaria to sign the house over to Aurora and her parents, but to keep the conditions quiet. What sweet revenge for Micu's wife, Paola, to finally get the land from the man who had jilted her daughter and had revealed her affair with Gennaro. Don Cesare finally got the right to the water he so desperately needed. He kept these details hidden even from Totu who had become distanced from him. But when Totu's father got ill, he felt his duty to write and convince Totu to go home and make peace with both of them.

His letter ended with these words: "Making peace doesn't mean condoning the past; only understanding it in its context of time and place, and accepting the finality of its passing."

PART X
OCTOBER 31, 1980

54. COSTUME DAY

STEVE, HOLSTERS HANGING FROM HIS hips and an oversized cowboy hat on his head, aims a toy gun at me as I step up the loading dock at school. I stop and watch him try to grab a passing female student by the bum with his free hand. "Stop!" he shouts at the student, "You're under arrest for indecent exposure." The girl, dressed as a baby wearing an oversized diaper, giggles and scoots away.

"Where's your costume, beautiful?" Steve asks, as he jumps back beside me and hugs me.

"It's in the bag," I answer, lifting two plastic bags and trying to squeeze out of the bear hug.

Mike passes us and hisses, "How do they expect us to teach in this zoo today?"

"Lighten up, Mike," Steve replies. "Costume Day only comes once a year."

"Yeah, maybe we should have a teaching day at least once a year too."

Halloween celebrations start early in the morning at WLHS. It's a yearly tradition, in which students and teachers are expected to follow a regular day's schedule, while disguised as their alter egos. Admittance to the students' dance in the afternoon requires a costume; and a prize is awarded for the most creative outfit.

This morning, I packed the caftan and turban, in the event that Angie changes her mind about dressing up. I also brought the Marie Antoinette costume Sean chose for the ball for me.

"Why did you go see Antonio, the journalist, on Wednesday afternoon?" I asked Angie while driving to school.

"Do you always have to follow me like a shadow?" she said.

"I wanted to ask him about my father since he wrote about him. That's all."

"How did you know to go to him?"

"I visited him once with my mom. She went there for help when I was kicked out of school and she wanted to go to Italy in the summer. Then she changed her mind about the trip."

So Antonio had told me the truth. "Have you seen him since Wednesday?" I ask.

"No, but he told me to go see him if ever I have a problem, or if I want to talk anything over with him."

"How come you never talk anything over with me?"

Angie sneers. "Because you don't have the guts to stand up to people. Like my mother, you sulk but do nothing. So what's the point?"

The comment grated on me. How could she possibly compare me with her mother, who had spent most of her adult life as an automaton, sneaking occasional stolen moments of happiness? I'm trying to be in full control of my life and not make hasty decisions based on emotions. Overnight I thought long and hard about Sean's suggestion to let things cool down before walking out. There's a lot at stake in making the right decision right now. Should I at least wait until after the ball, and in the meantime weigh all the pros and cons of staying versus leaving?

Bringing Angie to Antonio's office was not in character with Lucia's past passive but secretive behaviour, and it surprised me. She had taken a big step, leaving her home and then being seen at a banquet all primped up. Had Antonio told her that his latest live-in companion had left him? Antonio may have had a bigger role in Lucia's sudden re-awakening than he is ready to admit.

I asked Angie whether she had finished her composition for Bruce's class.

"I finished it. I finished it," she grumbled, "even though I hate writing compositions."

"How come?"

"Because whatever I write sounds fake."

Once in school, Angie and I are both drawn into the dress-up games played by the rest of the school. All day long, my classroom's many mirrors will attract students like magnets. I'm usually a good sport and will let them adjust their wigs, and even help them with their make-up. But this year, teachers have received strict instructions to stick to regular class schedules, and homeroom teachers are to approve the costumes before letting students out of class.

The students buzz around the room, creating their alter egos: a hobo, a Barbie doll, and a blonde movie star. Angie comes out of the stockroom sporting a studded black-leather jacket over black leotards that don't belong to her.

"Angie, you make a great biker," Linda says. She's wearing a nun's habit, cut strategically low on the bosom.

"I'm a naughty nun. Gina is going to be a priest," Linda says.

"You won't be allowed in at the dance with that outfit," I warn her.

"I rented it for tonight's party at Charlie's. It cost a fortune, so I'm wearing it!"

Gina works on spiking Angie's hair. For the finishing touch, she applies a heavy coat of black lipstick on Angie's large lips, making her look even more menacing.

"That's sooo you, Angie!" Gina exclaims. "Doesn't she look like Alice Cooper?"

"She looks like a bum. I don't think she'll be allowed into the dance either," Franca says, wrapping a white veil around her head.

"And you look like a wimp," Angie retorts. "What are you supposed to be anyway, a virgin?"

"A genie, don't you watch *I Dream of Jeannie?*" Franca pulls a bottle from her purse.

Someone wearing a witch's hat and a black cape comes in. A man's voice booms: "The Wicked Witch of the West is here. Let me look at you goblins." It's Mr. Champagne.

"I hate to be a poor sport," he says, pointing to Linda. "You'll have to change your costume."

"Why, Sir?" Linda pleads.

"It's in very, very bad taste. This is a Catholic school, girls. Remove it or cover it up. Remember, it's a regular school day."

As the principal leaves, Linda grumbles. "Yeah, right, a regular day! What planet is he from? I'm not changing. I'm going out to Jarry Park."

I remind Linda that if she leaves, I'd have to mark her absent.

"Sure, Miss," Linda says, and she and Gina leave.

Angie runs out to join them in the corridor. They whisper together for a few minutes and then Angie returns to class.

I'm pleased to see Linda and Gina leave. It's going to be a long, difficult day, trying to keep the students quiet and occupied, and it will be much easier keeping Angie in check without her two friends around. The administration staff can deal with the students skipping classes if they wish.

I try in vain to give a semblance of a lesson on hair colouring. No one volunteers for a demonstration with their costumes and make-up on, and the theory lesson falls on uninterested ears. When the lunch bell finally rings, I rest my head on the desk, exhausted by the nerve-wracking morning. After a few minutes, I collect myself to look over the material I had shown Antonio. I study the colour wheel I had improvised with the names of my novel characters. In the play of circles and triangles, I see a mandala.

"'Formation, Transformation, Eternal Mind's eternal recreation.' And that is the self, the wholeness of the personality, which if all goes well, is harmonious, but which cannot tolerate self-deceptions." Jung's words come back to me.

Self-deception! Maybe I have been wavering too long, listening to the voice in my head that is whispering fears, doubts, and all the rational justifications about why I should re-consider my relationship with Sean, making expediency the moving principle that guides my life. I cannot accompany Sean to a masked ball pretending I'm Desdemona and he the wronged Othello. I call Sean's office, leave a message, and return to my writing.

Franca disrupts my thoughts and brings me back to the present. She's the only student who shows up after lunch, but that's because she needs to adjust her costume.

"Nobody can tell I'm a genie," she says, removing the long veil wrapped around her head.

"Would you rather be Marie Antoinette?" I offer her my costume and mask.

"Wow!" Franca is thrilled and changes costumes.

I look at myself in the mirror. I see a tired face; my hair badly in need of a shampoo. I have been assigned a thirty-minute supervision. "Can I borrow your veil for the rest of the day?" I ask.

"Sure, Miss, but why did you give me your costume?"

"It's not for me. I'd be too uncomfortable in it. Make sure you bring it back on Monday."

"Sure, Miss. See you at the dance."

I slip the caftan over my clothes, put on the turban and then pin Franca's veil on it to cover my face, except for the eyes. There is something to be said about the anonymity of a veil.

For the sake of students wanting to go trick-or-treating at night, the Halloween dance in the cafeteria is held—to the seniors' disapproval—in the early afternoon. It's open to all levels, but senior students snub it as being too babyish, and leave school instead. They know the administration can't check attendance at the dance.

Except for the dizzying strobe lights, the cafeteria is pitch black and, when I enter, I have to stand still until my eyes become accustomed to the dark. Rock music, played by a professional DJ, blares, and I wonder how long I can stand it. It also feels unbearably warm. I walk around the room watching the students dance feverishly, but can hardly recognize anyone, except for Franca whose blonde wig can be seen prancing above everyone's heads.

Supervisors have been asked to look for signs of drinking and drug use. Students continuously stream in and out of the cafeteria, venturing along the train tracks to sneak a drink or smoke pot. I look for Angie, but know she won't stand out in the dark in her black leather jacket. Other teachers, dressed in their regular clothes, walk by without recognizing me, and I feel a sense of freedom. The only person who acknowledges me is Bruce. He smiles and says something, but I can't hear him. At the end of our shift he is waiting for me outside the cafeteria.

"I need fresh air," I say.

"Let's go outside. But you might be cold without a coat."

"Are you kidding? I'm wearing three layers of clothes. I'm surprised you recognized me."

"It's the eyes."

It's still light outside, though the sky is a monotonous expanse of murky grey. Bruce lights his pipe and we walk toward the train tracks. There's a huge hole in the wire fence, through which students cross the tracks to get to Jarry Park. Bruce holds the edges of the broken fence so I can pass through safely. "Watch your robe," he says.

I lift the hem of the caftan and move carefully. Bruce's small, courteous gesture makes me feel warm toward him, but also sad at the absence of a man's tenderness in my life. It has been a while since a man has watched out for me, or has seemed to care about my well-being.

The veil pinned on my turban has remained in place over my face. No one seems to notice me, and the park is full of the costumed students who have left the party.

"I haven't seen Angie since this morning," I say. "Have you?"

"I saw her at lunch with a nun and a priest. They made quite a trio."

"Was the nun showing some cleavage?" I ask.

"I didn't want to bring it up, but yes, the nun was ... well-endowed," he says. "In fact, I think she was one of those nuns who sees to it that other nuns get none."

I laugh.

"Eh, I made you laugh. That's good."

"But I need to see her. I have no idea what she's up to—Angie I mean, not the nun."

"She seemed a little high from all the attention, in her studded leather jacket, but she was fine."

I walk around nervously, looking around. Someone in a white mask is staring at me.

"What's the matter?" Bruce asks, holding me by the shoulders.

I feel steadied by Bruce's hands. "I'm worried about Angie," I say and move on.

"More than worried, you're incredibly sad."

Tomorrow will be the first of November, the first day of the month of the dead.

"I'm sorry. I can't help it," I say weakly.

"That veil can't be doing you any good. Come on, there you go..." he says, lifting the veil from my face, draping it over my head.

I just smile and he squeezes my shoulders.

"Don't you have a party to go to?" I ask.

"Yes, of course, Susan's. Aren't you going?"

"I don't feel up to the drive. I'm tired."

"Come with us. I'll drive," he says, holding my gaze. "I'll pick you up right here in about forty-five minutes."

"I might be intruding," I say.

"Of course not."

"Okay. I'll wait for you at the entrance. Maybe I'll have seen Angie by then."

"Good, let's go back to the zoo and get our stuff."

The sky is turning darker by the minute, and I can't shrug off the nagging feeling that Angie may be getting into trouble.

Despite Mr. Champagne's orders to carry on as usual, Halloween is turning out to be as disruptive and chaotic as any other WLHS Costume Days. Along with the school's two thousand students, my concerns over costumes, parties, and friends have taken priority over school regulations and rules of conduct. I never took the time to call Alfonso's house to check about him picking up Angie at school, as I had intended. After the walk in the park, I became fully engrossed in preparing for Susan's party.

She waves at me from the front seat of Bruce's car, "What a great costume, Cathy!"

"I hope I'm not the only one dressing up," I say.

"Everyone has to. It's a masquerade party," Susan replies, and I notice she has changed from the clown costume she wore during the day into a very sexy nurse's costume.

I feel oddly out of place. If only things were as they should have been between Sean and me, I'd be driving with him to the ball. I think of him and J.P., elegant in their costumes, and smiling their fake politician's smiles. I feel like recoiling into my shell, like a snail, and disappearing.

Susan passes me back an open bottle of wine and I take a swig. She offers some to Bruce but he says he'll wait until the drive's over.

The wine relaxes me. I close my eyes for the length of the drive.

55. DECEPTIONS AND FLOATING DEVICES

"YOU HAVE TO TAKE A SHOT to get in," Susan says, pouting a little, as each guest arrives. It seems that in the absence of Bruce's attention, Susan is turning her flirtations to others. Soon the cottage is filled with the loud throbbing of music, the buzzing of voices, bottles being opened, and liquor being poured. The dining room table is pushed against the wall to clear a dancing area. The reflections in the large picture window show a bunch of overgrown kids in funny hats, moving their arms and legs to the beat of the Bee Gees.

"Let's dance," Steve says, and pulls me up from the sofa. We move awkwardly.

Bruce appears out of nowhere to rescue me. "I need air," I say, fanning my face with my hands.

"Let's walk out to the lake," Bruce says. As we exit, I look back and see Susan dancing with Steve, but she is looking our way.

We walk beyond the patio; Bruce offers me the last sip of whiskey from his glass. I make a face after drinking it, and tiptoe on the squelchy dead foliage that lines the banks of the lake.

"Care for a swim?" Bruce asks.

"It looks pretty cold out there."

"It's a shallow lake."

We stand and look at the water. A full moon shines off and on through heavy clouds. It lights up a bright yellow and brown object in the centre of the lake.

"What's that floating in the water?" I ask.

"Just a loose a pedal boat carrying a load of dead branches and leaves."

I cross my arms tightly, and Bruce gives me his coat.

"Thanks," I answer, looking up at him and wanting to tell him how grateful I am for his concern. Instead, I say, "This must be a pretty spot in the summer."

"Except for the fucking black flies. The little bastards will eat you alive. I've lived in the bush all my life. I know."

I look around the lake and then back at Susan's cottage. The surrounding chalets are silent, their lights off—the maples, birches, and evergreens indistinguishable one from the other in the menacing shadows of the night. Susan's picture window is all lit up, moist and hazy from the heat of the dancing bodies inside. Some people have come outside, and are dancing and drinking on the patio. The whole house is vibrating with light and music. Their frenzy overwhelms me—so much effort and energy for such little joy.

"You're very quiet," Bruce asks

"I'm feeling down. All of the business with Angie and school, it's taking a toll."

"It must be more than that. What are you thinking of?"

"I don't know.... This lake freezing over soon ... with the boat, the mud, the weeds all preserved till the spring, and then...." My voice trails off. My whole life, I think, I have been trekking and trekking for miles, looking for clear water, only to be stuck in stagnant, backwater pools.

"Then let's get the *pedalo* to shore," Bruce says running into the lake.

I have never drank so much hard liquor before and my limbs feel weightless. I follow him into the water, as if floating on air, but stop at ankle depth to hold my costume up.

Bruce turns back, lifts me up in his arms.

"I can't swim," I scream, thinking he'll throw me into the water.

Instead he sits me on the pedal boat and pulls it to shore.

Back on my feet, I'm shivering but exhilarated by the unexpected adventure. Bruce is dripping wet from the waist down; my shoes and the hem of my caftan are also soaked.

"Let's go back in," I say.

"No, it's too loud in there. I have a blanket in my car. There's a bar just off the highway. We can talk."

"What will the others say?"

"Ah, they won't miss us. Look at them. They're too busy dancing their worries away." He runs towards the car.

I look inside and catch a glimpse of Susan's face peering out the door. Should I go back to the chalet and speak to her before leaving? She will certainly feel stranded by our sudden departure. But Bruce has already returned with a blanket, wrapping it around both of us and enveloping me in a bear hug to warm up. He smells good. I can hear his heart beat. The clear-minded shoulds or should-nots will have to wait, I think. I take Bruce's hands, and we hop and trip through the mud towards the car.

Bruce drives along the country road quietly.

"It's getting late," I say. "I'm all wet. Maybe going to a bar is a bad idea. Let's just go home."

Bruce stops the car in the bar's parking lot. We're overlooking the silent black lake, the vibrant white moon, and far in the distance, the tiny flickering light of Susan's cottage. Bruce brushes his face against mine, and then unpins the veil still draped over my head. "We can talk right here," he says.

"Where do I start?"

"Tell me about you and Sean."

"I find it hard to talk about it."

"You know that the longer things remain lodged deep inside, the harder it is to get them out," he says. "They might petrify."

I blurt out the story of my last encounter with Sean and J.P. "I feel trapped.... I've decided to leave, but I'm still afraid to face the consequences."

"You can't do anything tonight, so don't fret about it" Bruce starts the car again, "Why don't we go to my place for a drink?"

"I can't have another drink." My head is spinning as the car moves.

"I have something to show you. It's about Angie ... a composition."

"Is it that bad?"

"Don't be alarmed, but I find the content ... troubling, to say the least."

"What did she write about?"

"She kept to the theme of the composition, all right– Halloween terrors, dreams, fantasies." My head is aching. I can't quite grasp everything he's saying. "But she's embellished it with sex and graphic violence and I am not sure how to read it ... whether I should take it seriously, or dismiss it as an adolescent's overactive imagination."

"Violence and sex? Didn't you say her friend, Eddie, helped her?"

"Yeah, but the writing's too sleek for either one of them and the symbolism is too crafty."

I suddenly fear that this may have something to do with the day that Angie had been left home by herself, and then brought Antonio my notebooks. It's all too much to try to explain to Bruce.

We drive quietly to Bruce's apartment, which is on a side street not far from WLHS. The apartment is sparsely furnished—a well-worn sofa and chair, low bookshelves made from wooden boards and bricks, and a number of empty wine bottles serving as candle holders. The place smells of the pipe tobacco Bruce smokes. The apartment is orderly and neat, and has a warm, homey feeling.

"Sit down. What can I get you to drink?"

"Oh, I've drank more than enough," I say

"Ahh, we have to celebrate Halloween. I have a bottle of Italian sparkling wine someone gave me that you might like."

He comes back from the kitchenette with a bottle of Asti Spumante. He uncorks it, pours the wine into tall glasses.

"Happy Halloween," he says.

I slip the turban off my head and giggle. "I can't believe I've kept this on all day.

"Oh, I think it's been longer than that," Bruce says.

We sip our drinks, and then Bruce gets up from the sofa to look through his record collection.

He puts on a Buffy Ste-Marie record, then pulls out a copybook from a pile on the desk, and opens it to Angie's assignment. "Read on and tell me what you think,"

COMPOSITION FOR MR. BRUCE MCLAUGHIN
ON HALLOWEEN TERRORS
by Angie Tonnelli

Lost in a Cemetery

I'm walking happily towards my grandmother's house with my pet on a leash, a little black sheep that is the envy of all my friends. She has short curly hair that I style every day. I call her Curly. I take good care of my pet and take her to dancing classes and dress her in the girly clothes that I have in my closet and refuse to wear. I'd want to look like Curly, but only if I were a sheep.

We walk slowly with jugs under our arms to fetch water for Grandma, admiring the fall foliage. A tall man with soft eyes says hi and he takes Curly by the hand. "Let's go for a walk," he says. I follow them and watch.

He takes her to the lookout on the mountain to explore the forest. He hugs her and kisses her face, her neck, and her breasts. They stop in a clearing. He embraces her and his lips touch hers. He kisses her face, and then his tongue moves up and down, past her opened blouse to her neck and her breasts, before returning to her lips, and to the inside of her mouth, until she completely lets go and falls on the leaves.

"Let's go," I yell. I hear wolves closing in on us, sharpening their teeth against the tall trees all around us. In the distance I hear my grandmother singing a lullaby and we run towards the farmhouse. Then Curly starts doing a dance number, showing off her small round breasts. Out of nowhere, a wolf with black teeth throws himself at the sheep.

"You look like a slut," he says. "You should be ashamed of yourself." I run out back where it's dark and quiet, until the vroom vroom of a car breaks the silence and fills the air with a crescendo of doom.

The car swerves close to the farmhouse, and drops a man off. I turn my face away in fear. The man has a small forehead with the hair growing in a point and a large hooked nose. He looks like a hawk and carries a bat.

From the back door a hunter swoops in with a rifle and scares the wolf off. "I'll smash your head like this," the hawk yells, then smashes my water jug against the jutting rocks. The cold water splatters all over me and I jump up from the jolt.

The hunter holds Curly up by the legs, while the hawk hits her water jug with the bat until the jug smashes into pieces and blood splurts out all over Curly. The hawk speeds off and the cemetery turns dead quiet again, until the hunter takes off his coat and turns into a wolf. I scream and wake up next to the tall man, and we look for the way back but we walk and walk in circles and can't find our way. We're lost in a cemetery.

I scream and scream in terror until my grandmother wakes me.

The weird part of this night terror is that cemeteries are still my favourite places to visit.

Bruce keeps his eyes on me as I read the composition. I wish now I had kept my costume veil over my face, to hide the sense of astonishment, fear, and anger I feel as I read. Is Angie trying to reveal something more sinister than what we had suspected about Lucia's beating or did she plagiarize my writing and use it for her own twisted version of *Little Red Riding Hood* because it was there for the taking? The most bizarre element in all this is the use of my prose poem that she had brought to Antonio. Did she confess anything more to him? He has ways of making people confide in him. He never mentioned anything to me. I put the notebook down, and shake my head.

"What do you think? Should we read something in between the lines?" Bruce asks.

"I don't know. I just don't know."

I'm as distraught reading my words used by someone else as I am devastated by the mention of the lullaby—a plaintive song my mother used to sing, about a wolf and a sheep, a Calabrian version of the story, *Little Red Riding Hood*. Did Angie hear it from her grandmother or from Antonio?

"Maybe she has more resources and imagination than we give her credit for," I say. "Or maybe she has a good teaching coach. This Eddie—he must be really good. I'd like to meet him; maybe he can help me with my writing too," I add bitterly.

"She never asked for your help?" Bruce asks.

"I told you I never even saw her writing it."

"Should I show it to the police? Besides the violence, the sex scene is inappropriate for a high school composition and it smacks of sexual abuse of a minor."

"I don't know ... vivid imagination, or maybe, a dream?"

"Dreams aren't that coherent. Is the hawk recognizable to you?"

"No," I lie.

In fact the hawk is the most unsettling metaphor of the story for me, because it is indeed the most recognizable. I used the same image in my voyage story. It's how Armando, the ship's steward, referred to Nicodemo. Antonio never returned that manuscript I gave him, and he admitted to browsing through it. Did he help Angie in her composition and plant the hawk? If yes, how reliable is the composition and her recollection? It's all so bizarre! It could also be that reading my stories caused Angie to have nightmares. Can anyone make accusations based on a dream—a night terror at that?

"You did ask her to make something up—to be creative—didn't you? For now, I'd judge the composition on its merit as fiction," I say.

"I still have an eerie feeling about this, though, as if she's trying to say something that she doesn't want to admit to herself or others."

"Before using this to point fingers, we should try to find out who really helped her write this; whoever did might have his own agenda."

"I don't follow you," Bruce says.

I sip my wine, and hope its warmth will quickly move through my body and relax the tension that has kept me on edge all evening. Angie's story has turned the tension to pain. The lullaby is all about a mother's grief in seeing her little sheep being eaten alive by a bad wolf. Mothers sang it to both lull their babies to sleep and to warn them about the evil out there in the world. That the evil could be found in one's own home is the ugliest terror of all.

"I don't know what to think. I'm just tired, but for sure she must have cheated on her assignment."

"Let's discuss this on Monday at school, when we're both sober," he says.

I'm happy to change the subject of conversation with Bruce, but an awkward silence follows. I'm terrible at small talk.

"Tell me about the gold mines you worked at," I say to break the silence.

"What do you want to know?" He seems surprised by my sudden question.

"What do they do with the empty mines once the gold is extracted from them?'

"They grow mushrooms in them," he says, his face almost touching mine.

"Are you serious?" I smile.

"You find it amusing?"

"I find it funny. I can picture a bunch of men with headlights, tapping at walls in the dark looking for yellow veins, but picking mushrooms?"

"I'm serious," he says in a low voice. "Mushrooms don't need light. They grow in dark, damp places, just like mould."

"Too bad they can't grow gold the same way," I say.

"There are still plenty of unexplored gold mines in the north. Canada is a big country."

Bruce removes his glasses and I notice for the first time that his eyes, which in daylight had appeared light hazel with specks of green, have turned a shade of blue-green. He brushes his lips on mine, and I feel the impulse to hug him.

"Time to get rid of this," he says. I get up so he can help me slip off the caftan over my head.

We instinctively walk to his bed. We lie quietly, side by side, for a few minutes, his arms around my shoulder. I feel like wrapping my legs around his, but I wait for him to make the next move. He's still in a talking mood. "I'm discovering a new person every day I speak to you," Bruce says, pulling me closer to him. You're always so quiet. Why don't you talk more about the things that matter to you?"

"I can't seem to string the right words together to do justice to the things I want to say. What comes out of my mouth never sounds anything like the images I carry in my head. The two never match."

"Tons of muck gets unearthed for a few ounces of gold. It's hard work. It's fucking hard work for everybody. But if you have the images, at least you have something worth digging for. Sooner or later they'll find their way to the surface, don't worry."

"Do you write?" I ask.

"I try.... I wrote some poetry in college, but I dried out after a few not so successful attempts. Words are not enough, you know. The terrain I come from is pretty barren."

"I thought it was full of gold."

"Ah, maybe I'm jaded and weary, or just fucking lazy. Writing is just ... too ... fucking ... hard." He seems to drift into sleep.

After a few minutes he adds, half-slurring, as if he were talking in his sleep. "I have to give it to you. You've got a lot of guts wanting to be a writer."

"Oh, I wouldn't consider myself a writer. All I want to do..."

"Whatever your aim," he interrupts. "I hope you realize what you're getting yourself into. You've begun another journey."

"But I feel as if I haven't reached any destination yet."

"Writers are the eternal nomads. They are exiles from another planet. You may be destined to be a traveller all your life."

He turns to kiss me, but I raise my head off the pillow and look at the alarm clock next to his bed. It's close to three a.m. It's November first already—All Saint's Day.

"Bruce I can't stay here the night. I need to go home. I'm sorry. I have too much on my mind. I should have called the house earlier, to check that Angie had been picked up at school, that she's okay. Maybe some other time...."

"Another rain check? I was kind of afraid you'd say that," he says, slowly climbing out of bed.

56. LOOKING FOR ANGIE

THE LIGHTS INSIDE MY APARTMENT are all on. As Bruce turns the corner onto Cartier Street, I also notice my brother's car in the driveway. "What's Luigi doing here?" I ask. "It's three in the morning."

"I'll wait at the corner for a while. Wave if you want me to come in," Bruce says.

The door opens before I have a chance to put my key in the lock. Sean is standing on the porch, glaring at me. My mother is shifting nervously behind him.

"Isn't Angelina with you?" my mother asks immediately.

"No, why would she be with me? Can someone please tell me what's going on?" Luigi is sitting on the sofa, his face drawn.

"Where's Angelina?" Mother asks in a shrill voice. "She hasn't come home yet. Alfonso has been calling every fifteen minutes."

"How am I supposed to know? I left Angie at school. Alfonso was supposed to pick her up."

"And where have you been?" Mother asks.

"I went to the country for a school party. I had left Sean a message." I point at Sean, standing quietly.

"Oh, I'm not the one who got alarmed," he answers.

Luigi explains why they're all there. He and Mother had let themselves into the apartment with their spare key after a series of phone calls from Alfonso and Comare Rosaria. Alfonso had gone to the apartment to pick up Angie as usual, and found no one there. Neither he nor his wife had received a call from Angie the night before, but he wasn't alarmed. Knowing that we were all attending the ball, he figured that he would pick up Angie on his way home from the ball.

At the Ritz, Sean explained my absence by saying I had a bad case of the flu. He told Alfonso that I had most likely decided to spend the evening at my mother's and that Angie was at an after-school party with friends. This is when the phone calls between Comare Rosaria and Mother started. Mother, alarmed, called another friend with a daughter in the school. This friend told her that she had noticed my car still parked in the school garage, but had not seen me at the school dance. When, after midnight, I didn't respond to calls at the apartment, Mother and Luigi drove there in case I had fallen asleep and not heard the phone. Alfonso had had the same thought and asked Sean to accompany him to the apartment after the ball. It was past two in the morning and everyone was panicking when neither I, nor Angie, were found at home. Sean reassured them that, being Halloween night, we may have both decided at the last minute to attend a party somewhere, but they couldn't explain my car in the garage. Alfonso then made some phone calls and drove home with his wife.

I tried to explain to everyone that, as far as I was concerned, Angie had spoken to Alfonso's wife the evening before. "Maybe Angie played a trick on you," Sean says. "You should have been more alert."

"I guess she did!" I shout. "The little bitch lied to me."

"Call Alfonso to tell him you're home," Mother says.

"You call him. I can't believe I have to tell everyone where I've been." I throw my stuff on the floor.

"If it wasn't for the other one, I wouldn't worry," Mother says, as she dials, then hands me the phone. "He wants to speak to you."

Alfonso insists that no one had called the house the evening before, and, even if there was a misunderstanding, where was the girl, now, at three in the morning?

"Have you tried calling the Bar à Go-Go?" I ask hesitantly. "She may have gone there with her friends."

"Of course!" Alfonso says. "I know your students go there. It's the first place I called. But no one saw her there. I even called the police."

"I'll try calling her friends. I'm sure they know where she is." After I hang up, I exclaim, "Oh my God! Has he called the goon squad too? It's Halloween and parties are still going on. We go out one night and they have the police after us."

"I don't know why you're so angry," Luigi says. "He called the police for his niece, not you. Do you think he cares where you go at night?"

"And what did the police say?" I ask.

"They won't do anything unless a teenager is missing for twenty-four hours."

"She's not missing. She's with her friends at some party. All he would have had to do was speak to her friends, if he'd known who they were."

I search for Linda's and Gina's phone numbers in my school papers. I speak to someone at Linda's house, who sounds very hung over and irritated by the call, and who tells me that Linda won't be home for the night. Then I call Gina's house, and this time apologize profusely for the late call. I'm told that Gina is sleeping over at Linda's house. I don't tell them that their daughter has lied to them too. "Well, everyone is useless. I'll go and look for her myself," I say, looking for my coat in the hallway wardrobe.

"Are you crazy?" Mother shouts. "Where do you start looking for someone at this time of night?"

"I know where she wanted to go. She may still be there. If not, one of her friends might be there and will tell me where I can find her."

"Why don't you just phone the place and ask if she is there?" Luigi says.

"They won't tell me the truth on the phone. Those girls are very sneaky," I say angrily. "You two go home and stop worrying."

"How can we not worry with all that has happened lately?" Mother replies. "Look at all the enemies Pasquale has made. They can't take it out on him, so they take it out on his daughter." She raises her two hands and shrieks, in a panic, "*Madonna mia*, why did we have to get mixed up with these people again?"

"There's a full moon tonight," I yell back. "You're all going mad."

"There are some people you just don't fool around with," Mother says.

"The girl wanted to go to a party tonight, and she tricked all of us. I'll find her in no time at all." Then I remember I don't have my car and ask Luigi for a lift to school so I can go to Charlie's club.

"You're not going to that place alone," he says.

In the car, Mother calms down. "I don't understand. Why didn't you go with your boyfriend tonight?"

"It was a big fancy event. I didn't feel comfortable going," I yell.

"Okay, okay. Don't get all upset now," Mother says. "As long as you're all right. If only we could find the other one now."

"Don't worry. I'll find her."

The *Danseuses Nues* sign at the Bar à Go-Go is well lit, but from the outside, the club shows no sign of life. The windows are covered with blown-up pictures of half-clad dancers in suggestive poses.

"Nice place for a teenager," Luigi says, "but it looks closed."

"It's too early to be closed. They had announced a special Halloween party," I say. "Wait for me here."

"I'll come in with you," Luigi says.

Mother also gets out of the car.

"Wait for us in the car," I say crossly to her.

"I'm not going to stay in the car all alone, around this place," Mother says.

"They won't let you in," I say.

"Why not?" Mother asks. I don't have an answer for her, and look at my brother.

"You're not of age, Ma," Luigi says, laughing.

"This is crazy," I say, realizing how ridiculous the whole situation has become. The thought of taking my mother to a strip club at four in the morning seems surreal.

Luigi tries opening the door, but it's locked.

I ring the bell. In a few moments, a doorman opens the door and looks us over suspiciously. I explain I need to speak to two of his dancers.

"Linda and Gina who?" he asks in a gruff voice.

"Linda Albino and Gina Di Marco. They take dancing lessons here." I can hear loud music and hooting coming from inside. "I'd like to ask them a few questions."

"They're not dancers. What kind of questions?" He's not ready to let us in.

"Can I speak to Charlie Matteo?"

"You know Charlie?" he asks.

"Yes, I do. I went to school with him." I say. He closes the door again.

Luigi looks at me. "Is that the same Charlie that drove a car to school? He must have been involved in funny business even then."

"I know. He was so good looking. All the girls went after him," I say.

"*Madonna mia!* Who are we dealing with?" Mother asks.

"Who did you expect to find here, the parish priest?" I ask. "I told you to stay in the car."

The door opens and Charlie shows up, the surly doorman behind him. "Sorry, but the club is only open to regular members at this time," Charlie says. As he speaks, he keeps his eyes on me, as if trying to place me. "Do I know you?" he asks.

"Maybe. I'm Cathy Anastasia. I'm Linda and Gina's teacher. This is my brother, Luigi, and my mother, Teresa."

"Oh yes, they've spoken about you. Are you related to Tony Anastasia?" he says.

"Not at all," I answer impatiently. "We're looking for Angie Tonnelli, one of my students. Do you know her? She usually hangs around with Linda and Gina."

"No, never seen her. Her uncle Alfonso Abiusi has already called. We told him we haven't seen her at all."

"I'd like to speak to one of her friends. Maybe they know where we can look for her."

"I think Linda left already, but Gina is still here. She's in the dressing room," he adds hesitantly. "She wasn't feeling well. I think she's had one drink too many. You know how it is. I'll call her, and tell her to come out."

"I would rather go inside and speak to her there," I insist. I want to make sure Angie isn't hiding inside the club.

"Sure, come in. But you need to go through the bar and around the stage to get to the dressing room." Charlie looks at Mother with an amused grin. "It's a strip club, you know."

"It's okay," I say. "She might as well see once and for all what a nightclub looks like."

Charlie smiles, shrugs, and nods at the doorman to let us through. Then he turns to Luigi. "Your face looks familiar to me."

"I went to Pius X. You did too, right?"

"Now I remember you. You used to play the horn."

"I still do," Luigi says.

"Come in and have a drink." He walks with us through a narrow corridor that is covered with wall-to-wall photos of Nick Demon in his wrestling trunks posing with well-known personalities.

I look at my mother, but she just looks puzzled. I can't help but think of a Calabrian saying as I look at her expression,

Cumu nu ciucciu intra i suani—like a donkey in a music hall. The music gets louder and louder as the corridor opens onto a darkened, smoke-filled room. A bar runs along the length of the room on one side. Charlie offers us a drink, but Mother and I decline. He pours Luigi a brandy. The blaring music makes it impossible to carry on a conversation, but the eyes of all those present are fixed on the cavorting dancers at various stages of undress. Charlie leads me and my mother to the dressing room, while Luigi stays at the bar.

The club patrons are mostly men, but there are a few women in costumes and masks sitting around the tables next to the stage and the runway. I try to focus on the people in the audience, looking for a sign of Angie in a black leather jacket. Some men sit on stools in front of the mirrored bar, hooting and whistling at the stage on the opposite side; others stare intently but vacantly at the reflections of gyrating bodies in the mirror behind the shelves of liquor bottles. Amidst dry-ice smoke and dizzying strobe lights, a parade of nude girls shake their tinseled breasts, spread their legs, bend forward and backward to offer the audience a full view of their most intimate body parts. Some completely nude dancers with lacy garter belts stand on individual tables, shaking their bodies right above the faces and upraised hands of the overheated patrons, who slip money into the girls' garter belts for the sole thrill of touching their exposed flesh.

I turn back to look at my mother, who just follows impassively.

Inside the dressing room, a half-dozen women chat as they sit in front of mirrors, adjusting their make-up, their corsets, hats, and capes. The ones in full regalia wait behind the closed door for a cue to go onstage. Other nude girls rush in, carrying their shed clothing in their hands, put on robes, and sit down to rest on a cot in the corner.

Charlie yells. "Gina, someone's here to see you."

Gina's eyes look glazed over and she doesn't seem particularly surprised to see me. She's still wearing the priest costume and has a distant and spaced expression as she gets up from the cot to greet us.

"Hi, Gina," I say. "I've come to give Angie a lift home. Where is she?"

"She came and then left right away, Miss." She speaks in a drawl. She's obviously quite drunk.

"Charlie said he never saw her here."

"She was wearing a mask."

"Gina, are you sure? I need to find her and drive her home."

"I swear to you, Miss. She came in, walked to the bar, and then said she had to leave. Everything got screwed up today. Linda never even waited for me."

Gina doesn't sound coherent. I can't trust what she says.

A tall statuesque woman in tall boots, a mask and cape, and holding a whip, looks at Mother, and says, "*C'est ta maman, Gina?*" But Gina doesn't respond.

Mother whispers to me, "A woman like that ... why doesn't she find a job somewhere else?"

"It's for the money. They make more money here," I say impatiently, looking intently at each dancer's face. But there's no sign of Angie in the room.

Some of the girls look suspiciously at us. "*Mais qu'est-ce qu'elles font icitte?*" the dancer with the whip asks Gina, who looks at her blankly.

"Angie? Angie?" Mother screams at the top of her voice.

"*Il n'y a pas d'Angie icitte. Allez-vous chez vous,*" the dancer sounds annoyed.

"*Vous, allez chez vous ... travailler,*" Mother yells back.

"*Va ffa nculu,*" the dancer says as she struts out of the room snapping her whip.

"She's even Italian?" Mother says, astonished, and crosses herself.

"You should have stayed in the car. This is no place for you. Stay here while I walk around," I tell her outside the dressing room.

I walk slowly to the other end of the bar, looking intently at the faces of the patrons, but Angie is not there. I return to the dressing room. Gina stares at me blankly. "Gina, are you okay? How are you going to get home? How come you didn't go home with Linda?"

"That bitch left without me. I bet she went to see George. I'll take a cab."

"Let's go. I'll give you a lift," I say, and the three of us leave. We walk past the bar, nod, thank Charlie, and exit the club with Luigi.

"I don't know how they can stand working in all that smoke and noise," Luigi says. "Now what?"

"Angie came to the club, but for some reason left right away."

"*O Dio mio*. Where could she be?" Mother asks plaintively.

"I don't know," I say, then turn to Luigi and whisper, "If you drive me to the school, I'll pick up my car and take this girl home. She's in no shape to go home by herself."

Luigi shakes his head in disbelief and speaks in dialect. "What is a fifteen-year-old girl doing in a place like this?" Then he turns to Mother, "So now you can say you've been in a club. What did you think?"

"They can keep them, for all I care. All that smoke, just to look at a woman's ass? In my time, a man had to get married to see it."

"Now all you have to do is pay six dollars for a drink," Luigi says.

"Do you know where Angie went after she left the club? Maybe she went with Linda?" I ask Gina. She looks pale, as though she is going to vomit.

"No, Angie left as soon as she came in. I think she went looking for Eddie, in TMR. Linda spent the evening with a guy I've never seen, and then she left with him. I got stuck in the dressing room all night, helping the girls."

"Do you know Eddie? Does he live in TMR? Where can I find him?"

"He was going there to trick-or-treat, he told us at the park. Maybe he's back at school."

"Gina, it's four in the morning. Nobody's at school, except the night janitor."

"Try George's office."

"Who's George?"

"The night janitor. The two hang together at the office."

"The office? What office?" I ask impatiently.

"I'll show you. Angie and Linda and Eddie and George...," Gina mumbles vaguely.

Luigi looks at me and makes a face, as if asking if Gina is all right. I just shrug my shoulders.

"So, what are you going to do now?" Mother asks.

"I can't do anything else. Just drive us to school," I say.

"She'll probably wake up drunk in some other club, like this girl," Mother says. "What have we come to?"

"Not everyone lives like us, Ma," Luigi says.

"I'd go hide in a mountain if you two lived that way," Mother answers.

"Yes, there is a full moon tonight," Luigi says, looking up at the sky.

I'm feeling dizzy; I hold on to the car's door.

At this time of the morning, somewhere, maybe back in my own apartment, Sean is gloating about my failure as a guardian of the girl he never wanted in the house. Antonio may be busy firing scathing editorials and accusations against people he's hated for years. Bruce is alone in his bed; and a few short miles from here, Lucia dreams, blissfully unaware of what her desire to start a new life has unfurled. Her brother is scheming; her husband is hiding; her lover, if indeed she had one, remains somewhat of a mystery; and her friend and rival from a lifetime ago has lost her only daughter, whom she was asked to take under her wings and protect. Images from Angie's composition suddenly come alive and fill me with dread.

57. THE OFFICE

"What's the matter, not feeling well?" Luigi asks once I'm in the car.

"I'm scared," I say, holding back tears.

Luigi taps my hand. "You're tired and you've worked yourself up, and there's a full moon. Look up!" His words and touch reassure me.

"But Mother is right. How did we end up this low? Is this where you'd think we'd be twenty-five years ago?" I say.

"A quarter century already!" Luigi says as he drives away. "We didn't do so badly."

"We had much bigger expectations, though. Remember the stairs to the stars? I was supposed to become a famous singer and you were going to be a big trumpet player. We've just dragged Mother to a strip club where a stripper told her to fuck off. It's so unreal."

"In a few years, we'll laugh about tonight and tell stories about it."

"No, it's too humiliating … to have travelled so far and stooped so low," I say.

"Look," Luigi says, "Don't exaggerate now. We still have a full life ahead of us. We've done what we could with the means we've had so far. We neither left a paradise, nor came to one. If we're disappointed, it's because we all had dreams of grandeur. It's an Italian trait, you know, to dream big. Let's admit it to ourselves."

"Well, there's been no big dreaming around Angie, I'm sorry to say—a real cop-out. We failed her. It's so humiliating. I blame myself. I let her slip through my fingers."

"You're too hard on yourself. She'll show up soon enough. You'll see."

"And the corruption ... the lies, the greed, this place ... it's so depressing."

"These types of places have always existed and always will. Remember there are more of us shmucks who go to work every day, who pay our taxes, who build good families, who sleep well at night, than there is of them. They make more smoke than us, that's all, but they're only a handful."

Luigi lets me and Gina out in front of WLHS, but he waits until George, the night janitor and short-order cook, has opened the door.

"We're here to get my car," I say, and then motion to my brother to go ahead.

"Did Linda come to see you?" Gina asks.

"No, I haven't seen anyone," George answers and seems in a foul mood.

"Do you know Eddie?" I ask.

"Eddie who?"

"You know little Eddie ... Eddie Marshall," Gina says.

"I told you, I haven't seen anyone all night long," George says. He glares at me. "Next time you keep your car overnight, you need to ask permission, or I'll have it towed." He walks away, in the direction of the auditorium.

"He's not very friendly. Do you know him well?" I ask Gina.

"He used to work at Miss Park Ex too," Gina says.

"I know. But is he always this unfriendly?"

We walk past the dark cafeteria. A couple of night janitors, whom I don't recognize, look us over suspiciously as if resentful of our intrusion. A thorough cleanup and floor-washing has cleared away all signs of the partying students. The only tell-tell sign of student life is the graffiti on the walls, which Mr. Champagne tries so hard to wipe out. Suddenly it occurs to me that once painted over, the students' scribbles, their love notes, their four-letter words are never completely erased; they become layers of hidden words, screaming to rise above the surface.

We walk past the hairdressing classroom without stopping, past the loading dock and the receiving area. Instead of taking the stairs up to the garage, Gina walks straight into the empty space used for the storage of used furniture, where the swimming pool was to have been. "I'll go check George's office," Gina says dazedly. "See if Eddie is there."

I follow her, past piles of old desks, portable blackboards, boxes and boxes of old books, and the car parts that have spilled over from the nearby automotive classes. In all of my years at WLHS, I have never bothered to cross this dark, cluttered space.

Gina walks to the far corner and, sure enough, there's a cubicle with glass windows, similar to the cubicles next to the labs on the upper floors. This "office" must have been intended to serve the instructors who would have a view of the swimming pool area. The windows are covered with faded construction paper. The door is unlocked, but there's no one there.

A second door leads into another room that contains a table, a couple of chairs, and a futon. Posters of metal-rock bands are plastered all over the walls. Used Styrofoam cups, plastic plates, and cardboard pizza boxes from Miss Park Ex litter the floor.

"We missed them," Gina says. "Everyone's gone already."

"Who comes here?" I ask.

"Lots of kids do, and they bring their friends. It's George's office."

"What goes on here?"

"You can buy stuff here. I even heard that some girls do tricks here for ten dollars a pop."

"Are you serious, Gina? Are you making all this up?" I shake her by the shoulders.

"I've just heard about it from Eddie. I've never seen it."

"But when do they come here?" I ask, as we walk back toward the stairs.

"George only works at night. Eddie hung around during the day before he was expelled. At night, people come through the door next to the delivery garage. But I heard that, even during the day, Eddie used to let some girls bring guys into the office. They lock the two doors and no one can see what's going on."

"Let's go home," I say wearily.

We walk to the car and drive out of the empty garage. "Why did you think Angie might be here with Eddie?" I ask Gina, while driving.

"Angie likes him, and he sometimes stays here overnight with George, so I thought she might have followed him here. Some of the kids said they were going to party at the office after everyone else left."

I still can't believe what I've heard from Gina. I tell her, "It's impossible for this stuff to be going on during the day when there are supervisors going around. You're making it up."

"I'm not making anything up," Gina says shrilly. "Mr. Master knows all about it. Linda and I saw him there once. Believe me."

Gina lives only two blocks east of the school. I let her off without arguing with her, but I decide not to go home yet. I want to speak to Costa at Miss Park Ex. He told me once that he knows everything that goes on at school, but it's too early for the restaurant to be open.

I stop the car on a side street to collect my thoughts. I believe that Gina has told me the truth. The booze or whatever she was on loosened her tongue. Besides the club and the school, I don't know where else to look for Angie. The girl had wanted to go to Charlie's party so badly, I had been sure I'd find her there. What could have made Angie change her mind? The clue has to be Eddie. He might have sidetracked her from staying at the club, just as Bruce had talked me into leaving Susan's party. I put my head back, close my eyes, and try to piece together all

I've heard, but I'm so tired that I doze off and it all plays out like a crazy surreal dream.

When I open my eyes at the sound of traffic, I realize I've been dozing for almost two hours. It takes me a few seconds to orientate myself and decide to drive to Miss Park Ex.

"Eh, what brings you here so early?" Costa asks.

"I've been up all night. I need a coffee badly."

"An all-nighter, Miss? Celebrating Halloween, eh?"

"Kind of. Did you have a lot of action here last night?"

"We were swamped with orders, Miss. Halloween is a big deal, and this year it fell on a Friday night. But I'm not complaining. Business is good."

I order toast and coffee, and then ask, "Did you deliver pizzas to WLHS late at night?"

"Not that I know of," he says. "Why?"

"I saw some empty pizza boxes there, in George's office," I say.

"They could have been pick-ups. Lots of students came by last night. George has an office there?"

"What do you know about it?'

"All I know is that he works there at night, as a janitor. When did they promote him?"

"I'm looking for someone who may have stopped by here last night. Angie Tonnelli. Does her name ring a bell?"

"Miss, I'm no good with names. I might know her to see her. Do you know how many students come by here every day?"

"She would have been dressed in a black leather jacket, with metal studs and spiked hair."

"That's most of WLHS students, these days," Costa replies as he butters the toast.

"She hangs around Eddie. You know Eddie, right? He's a friend of hers."

"Eddie Pinto, the Portuguese?"

"I think this guy is English ... Marshall, I think."

"Oh, little Eddie. I know him, but he doesn't hang around here."

"I thought he was a friend of George—your cook."

"We kicked George out last week. My father doesn't like him—doesn't like the crowd he hangs around with. George only worked here part-time—when he felt like it. Not very dependable, that guy ... was up all night. And there were always people looking for him, even when he wasn't here. My father didn't like it."

Costa comes closer to me and whispers, "Miss, now that George doesn't work here, I can say what I think. He and Eddie make a good tag team. I like to mind my own business, but I'd tell this girl not to hang around Eddie ... very bad influence."

"What kind of business is Eddie into?"

"This is just from what I hear, Miss. Everyone in Park Ex knows he's a scalper. And he ... for a little guy, let's say he gets around. He's a real con artist. I heard he can forge signatures and gives students parents' and even teachers' notes. He and George are into everything," Costa now whispers, "Whether it's true or not, I don't know. But I heard that if you want a joint, a quickie, or even an advance copy of a provincial exam, they can get it." He talks loudly again. "I don't know how he does it so openly, but one of these days, George is going to get burned. He'll learn his lesson, too, believe me. He doesn't know how good he had it here."

"I need to find Eddie," I say, "only because Angie may be with him. I need to find her."

"I can't help you there. I haven't seen either Eddie or George."

"Costa, what do you know about what goes on at school ... at night, in George's office?"

"Miss, I told you. Me, I mind my own business ... whatever goes on there at night, it's none of my business."

"Okay. I have to make some calls," I say, then walk to the public phone at the entrance. I call the house, and wake up Sean. He says he hasn't heard from anyone since we left the apartment.

Then I call Bruce and tell him about Angie's disappearance.

"You had a premonition," he says. "Can I meet you somewhere? I want to help."

"You can help me find Eddie. She might be with him."

"Could her running away have anything to do with the composition?"

"How could it?" I answer, but the feeling of fear is back. "There could be another person involved in her mother's beating. Remember the hawk? He might want to keep her quiet. I still have a responsibility to mention it to the police. We can't take any chances."

"But there are no real names mentioned in the composition. What would they have to go by?"

"Hints. The police work from hints all the time. Maybe they'll even recognize the name. It could be someone's nickname."

"The police won't do anything for twenty-four hours. Give me a few more hours. We may have a lot more to tell them, about Eddie and the office in the basement... about George...."

"What office in the basement?"

"All of our supervision has been a total waste of time. We blamed the outsiders, but the rot is inside the place."

"What are you talking about, Cathy?"

"I know it doesn't make sense. I'm so exhausted."

"Wait for me. I'll look for Eddie's number and call him. Are you okay, Cathy?"

"I'm all right. Just check with Eddie. I'll call you back in a few minutes."

I eat my toast and listen to Costa's chatter, but can't get him to say anything more revealing.

I wait ten minutes and then call Bruce again.

"I spoke to Eddie's mom. She hasn't seen him in days, but she told me he works at the market on weekends selling grapes. The market won't be open for another hour."

"Why don't we meet at the market?"

"Good idea. See you in front of Shamrock Fish market in an hour."

The coffee and Bruce's offer to help has perked me up. I take a notebook from my tote bag. I jot down notes about everything I've observed and heard throughout the night. Together with Bruce I might be able to solve the puzzle.

Only a few outside stalls at the market are open at this time of year, most displaying pumpkins and bushels of pickling vegetables. The tomato-canning season is over, but wine making is at its peak, so boxes and boxes of plump green grapes and tiny black ones are being unloaded from trucks onto the sidewalk of the vegetable store next to the Shamrock Fish Market. Bruce is already there and talking to the thin and fidgety Eddie, who moves nervously on the spot as he rubs his hands together to keep warm. He is wearing a black leather jacket with studs, the same one worn by Angie.

"Where did you get that jacket?" I say before even saying hello.

"Hi … hi, Miss," Eddie stutters.

Bruce adds, "Cathy, don't worry. Eddie and Angie exchanged clothes and he saw her last night trick-or-treating in TMR."

"But she hasn't come home. Did you see her earlier yesterday?"

"I sa-sa-saw her at Jarry Park in the afternoon. Tha-that's when we exchanged costumes. Di-di-di-didn't you see her there in the Ja-Jason mask?"

I try to think of all the masks I had noticed, and then I remember someone in a white plastic mask staring at me by the train tracks. Had that been Angie?

"Wasn't she supposed to go to the club for the party?"

"I don-don't know if sh-sh-she … went."

Eddie keeps stuttering and tells me that after exchanging costumes at the park, he told Angie he'd meet her at the school later since he had to see some friends first. A supervisor didn't let him in so he went back to the park for while. When he returned, Angie was sitting on the overpass in front of the school entrance all by herself with her eyes closed as if mediating, but he didn't feel like climbing those stairs and he left her there. He spotted her in her mask again later in TMR with a group of teens he didn't know—they looked like street kids—but when he tried to cross the street to call her, she disappeared into the crowd. Maybe it was just someone else with the same mask. It was hard to tell in the dark.

"Sh-sh-she kept on dis-disa-appearing on me ... like a gh-gh- ghost."

"Why did you go to TMR?" I ask.

"I ... I ... used to do that as kid. Th-they have the b-b-best ca-ca-candy there. A lot of ki-kids from Park Ex ... go ... there. A lot of stre-treet kids meet there on Ha-Ha-Halloween to ... get ca-ca-candy be ... before par ... partying. I go ... go there every year. I to-to-told her I'd go there."

"Eddie, what time did you think you saw her in TMR?" Bruce asks.

"You ... you're ... ki-kidding me, sir. I don't ca-ca-carry a wa-wa-watch, sir. May ... be ... eight or ni-nine?"

"Where did you go after TMR? Did you go to the Bar à Go-Go?"

"No ... no sir ... I don't ever go ... go there. They're not my frie-friends. I went par ... partying with so-so-some other friends."

"Do you have any idea where Angie could have gone?" I ask

"Sh-sh-she'll be back when it suits her, and ... when you see her, te-te-tell her I want my ma-ma-mask back." He takes off the jacket and gives it to me. Holding it against my body feels eerie.

"I want to ask you something else, Eddie. Did you help Angie with an English composition on Halloween?"

"Yeah, wa-wa-wasn't that a cool story? I ... I told Angie she sh-sh-should have dre ... dressed up like Little Red Riding Hood, b-b-but she didn't find that funny."

"Who wrote it, though, you or her?"

"We ... we ... wrote it together the day she stayed home

from school. Her spelling is shit. But fuck, her i-i-ideas are scary. She's re-re-really fucked up, you know."

"Something else. Did you remember something about a hawk in her story?"

"A what?"

"A hawk, you know, a big bird."

"I re-re-remembered a sh-sh-sheep and a wolf. The ... the wolf ate the sh-sh-sheep and ... *bon jour la visite.*"

"Did she ever tell you what happened the night her mother was hit?" I ask, keeping my eyes on Eddie to watch for his reaction.

"I don-don't know, hon-honest, Miss. She wa-wa-wasn't even at home," he answers, putting his hand on his chest as if swearing in court. "Do ... do you make wine? We ha-have the best prices on Zi-zin-fandel grapes."

"Listen, Eddie, if you come across anyone who saw Angie last night, please give me a call." Bruce jots down his phone number on a piece of paper, and hands it to Eddie. We leave.

"We're not getting much more out of him," Bruce says. I piece together for Bruce what Gina had told me and the two stories match. Angie went to the club alone but didn't stay there. She had wanted so badly to go to that party. What made her run away so fast?

"If we can trust what Eddie said, what I want to know is, where would a group of street kids go to party on Halloween night?"

"I wouldn't know where else to look," I say.

Bruce takes me by the shoulders. "You're in no shape to keep on looking. Go home to sleep for a few hours."

"Okay," I say, "but I have one more place to stop before going home."

PART XI
NOVEMBER 1, 1980

58. THE FALL OUT

"PASQUALE KILLED HIMSELF EARLY THIS morning." Before I have time to ask him about Angie, Antonio tells me the news. "I just got a call from my uncle in Mulirena," he says. I can't process the information and don't react to it immediately.

"I don't have all the details yet," Antonio says, "but they found him hanging from a tree in his hometown, gone there to visit his mother's grave. Before leaving Mulirena, he stopped at my uncle's with another letter for me—I'll tell you about that later. Pasquale's nephew found him, in the orchard of his own backyard ... hanging like Judas."

I break down in tears, and I can't stop sobbing.

"Why are you crying for Pasquale?" he asks. "You hardly knew him."

"I'm crying for Angie," I say. "She ran away. I've been looking for her all night. Her father's dead and she's not here to mourn him ... and it's my fault entirely."

"Ran where? A strange kid, you have to admit. Morose and secretive. Why blame yourself?"

"I gave my word to her mother and grandmother that I'd look after her, but I got too involved with my own problems to help her with hers. I worried about how I looked, about the party, about Bruce ... and I ignored her calls for help!"

"Now you've lost me. Who's Bruce?"

"He's a guy from school—a nice Canadian guy. He's helping me look for her." Antonio looks puzzled. I continue, "I was distracted yesterday, and I paid no attention to Angie, and she fooled me, and went trick-or-treating in TMR instead of coming home, and she's still out there ... I don't know where." I look through my purse for a tissue, don't find one, and give up. Antonio still looks confused. I realize I'm not making any sense to him.

"I don't follow you, but I understand that you got distracted. She caught you off-guard and tricked you. It's Halloween! She's smarter than we think. She won't get lost, believe me, and ... in TMR?"

"She even watched me ignore her. She was right there in front of my nose and I didn't see her! And now this—her father kills himself—and she's not even here to cry for him, or ... maybe laugh. I don't know what I'm saying, but nothing makes sense. I should have stayed home with her." I collapse into a chair and wipe my nose on my sleeve.

"The worst part is," I continue, "even if I find Angie, what do we have to offer her? A dead father, a comatose mother. Her school is rotten to the core. She can hardly read or write and she has a crush on a petty criminal." I start sobbing loudly again, "What chances does she have of rising above all that?" I lower my head into my hands.

"Maybe you aimed too high for her," he says gravely. "It wasn't realistic."

"But to fall so low ... it's really depressing," my voice becomes shrill. "I've been going around in circles searching for her: in a strip club, in a school basement hidey-hole, in a greasy spoon, at the market." My sobs become uncontrollable.

Antonio hands me a tissue and waits for me to wipe my nose and eyes.

"I don't know where else to look, Antonio. And I hate giving up and going home. I came to see if maybe you had heard from her."

"No, the last time I saw her was a couple of days ago."

"So, she came to see you again after she brought you my

papers, my writing?" I get up and begin pacing.

He takes a few instants to reply, "Look, after she threw your writing at me and very brusquely asked me if I was her father, I calmed her down and tried to get her to talk about what was troubling her. First she defended her father to me ... she didn't think he was the guilty party."

Antonio stops to reflect, then shakes his head. "It's a really sordid story, no matter how we look at it, but what do you know? It turns out that the most honourable man is Pasquale. What Pasquale wrote matches with everything my uncle told me about Aurora and Alfonso. He clears my name of past accusations, once and for all."

"Who cares about that anymore, Antonio? That's ancient history. Let's focus on Angie. What did she tell you?"

"She admitted that Lucia had also had a heated argument with her brother. I felt guilty that maybe I had provoked the argument ... unintentionally, of course, because of what I had told Lucia. Try to understand the irony here. It is ancient history and it's this same history that has doomed these people. That's why I brought it up. An old worthless farmhouse caused the incident and all that has followed. Pasquale's testimony of events corroborates what Angie had hinted at when she came to see me, so I believe him."

"Angie wasn't there. How could she know what happened beyond the usual family squabbles?"

"She didn't say much more that first day. I told her to come back anytime she wanted to talk. She returned a few days after. She showed me a composition she had written with a friend."

"What was in the composition?"

"Enough to raise my suspicions further. Angie, like most teenagers, hates snitching on people, or maybe she was afraid, but her story didn't add up. When I asked her how long she had been away at the park, she said about half an hour, that she went returned home after the stool pigeon waiting outside the house had left."

"So there was someone else?"

"Precisely. I surmised that she knew more than she cared to tell. She was either traumatized by what she saw or knew, or she was plain scared to talk, considering some of the friends her uncle hangs around with."

"Did Angie or anyone else identify the person waiting outside?"

"I don't yet know what's in the rest of Pasquale's letter, but I'm a journalist, so I quizzed Angie that day. The car was a black Mustang. It's what that hawk, Nico, or Nick, Demon drives."

"The hawk?" I get up from my chair.

"Yes. Don't you remember calling him that in your own story about the voyage?"

"So you suggested the hawk for Angie's composition, didn't you?" I say.

"Caterina, the metaphor came naturally ... was called for by the story."

As I had thought, Antonio had helped Angie plant the hawk into her composition and he condoned the use of my prose poem, without any concern for my feelings, or for Angie's well-being. He used both of us as in a game, for his own reasons. What a perverse, devious tactic on his part to get revenge for past wrongs. And yet he has always professed to have left the past behind.

He continues pensively. "When Lucia came to see me, it looked as if she had finally woken up and wanted to make a new start. I can't really understand the dynamics of her relationship with the hawk ... don't know how consensual the relationship was. Some women—vulnerable, lonely women—are drawn to dark characters ... or are too passive to say no to them, but Lucia told me she wanted a new life; she wanted out of her marriage and to be done with the past. Maybe he was stalking her."

"Why didn't you tell the police? You told the papers everything else."

"I was trying to gather as much information as possible. Pasquale's letters will certainly corroborate everything. I sure hope Angie's disappearance has nothing to do with the arguments her parents had with Alfonso that night, or with Nicodemo."

At that thought I panic. "I wish you had taken Angie's call for help seriously," I yell. "You just used her and sent her off ... like you brushed off her mother. Why didn't you help them when you had the chance to do so, instead of just thinking of building up a case against your enemies?"

"I take offence at your tone," he says, standing up. "What could I have done differently?"

"You've triggered a lot of this. Lucia may have still held some hope for you, especially now that you're single again. Didn't you have any feelings for Angie and her mother? I wish you had done more for them when you had the chance, Antonio. Just think ... Angie could be your daughter, too, you know."

"That's nonsense," he says. "She wasn't ... isn't. Even her brother thought otherwise."

"But we don't know for sure. Unless Lucia wakes up, we may never find out. You have to take some of the blame."

He looks squarely at me, speaking in a low voice. "Caterina, I don't know where you've been all night, or what you've been up to, but now you're clearly hallucinating. You're blaming me for what's happened?"

"Just think of all the years during which Lucia was totally ignored and neglected—by you. You have to take some blame for what Lucia became after you abandoned her."

"I am not responsible for other people's choices."

"Yes, but I find it curious that all at once you're interested in helping her daughter with her homework. Why? Why didn't you speak to me about what Angie told you? We were supposed to be collaborating. I could have tried to get her some counselling at school ... help her unburden herself of what she saw, if what you say is correct."

"I didn't expect her to run away. She didn't look as if she cared about anything really."

"Angie ran away because of situations you helped create. She probably couldn't make sense of her life—or of her mother's life." I shout, "You ruined both their lives!"

He raises his voice. "You have no right to blame me for whatever happened between Lucia and me. You know there were circumstances I couldn't control—of a political, philosophical, ethical nature…"

"Sure, you let those circumstances control you a little too easily, I thought. You cared more about appearances than about love. Even when I was little, when I travelled with her on the ship and read about the other Lucia, I remember wondering why you did nothing to stop her from marrying Pasquale. You gave up too quickly, Antonio." I sit down in my chair and continue, "You took to your bed with a fever, like a Don Abbondio. No one dares to strive for ideals anymore."

Antonio walks around the desk and places his hands on my shoulders. He shakes me. "Caterina, please, calm down. You're an intelligent girl, but you've totally lost your mind. Don't bring Manzoni into this discussion. Get him out of your head once and for all! This is 1980! Let's not pretend we can do the impossible—fix things that we ourselves have shattered beyond any hope of repair. You know there was nothing I could do. Marrying Lucia was just never in the cards."

"Lucia may have been silenced forever. And for what? A chance to dance again with you … *le Grand Antoine*, the Great Antonio … and her daughter has disappeared, maybe fearing for her life."

Antonio speaks quietly, "I agree. Angie and Lucia are tragic figures—one has no past to support her, the other no future to look forward to. There is nothing anyone can do for them, least of all me."

"So, you have no intentions of ever owning up to your responsibilities to Lucia, or to Angie?"

"Our chance was over years ago," he says. "It's part of the past."

"But why did you lead her on, time and time again? You continually gave her false hope."

"How would you know that?"

"You saw Lucia many times after she was married, in 1967 for example. It's in my poem."

"You made that up. It was part of your fiction writing fantasy."

"No, I didn't make that up. I saw you get in a car with her that day, after we came back from the park, after you threw me on the grass and made out with me."

"You were confused. You couldn't even find your way back. You imagined it all."

"And what about the summer of 1964 and the shot in the leg? Did I also imagine that? It coincides with Angie's conception. Why do you think Angie came to you? She read my stories, and probably wanted to see you up close, but instead of reaching out to her, you exploited the situation for your own motives. In 1964, Lucia spent the whole summer at her farmhouse and you spent every afternoon in the country. I have a good memory."

"Memory! Is there anything more fickle than memory? I'm certainly questioning yours."

"Well, you remembered the hawk from a story I gave you in 1967, yet you never bothered to comment to me on it. And why didn't you ever get back to me about my prose poem? Instead, you manipulated Angie into incorporating it into her composition."

"Maybe it's because I never took your writing seriously..."

"You're such a snob, and you're full of hot air!"

"And you're full of naïve and romantic ideas about writing, and you can't face reality. A real writer stands back from what is thrown at her by circumstances and looks at things rationally, while you have turned hysterical."

"Well, you have finally expressed what you think of my

writing. And to think I wasted so much time looking for your approval. You're a phony, Totu! A pompous, stuffy, anal-retentive fart, a coward and a fraud. All your essays on social justice, your work in the Communist party, your own writing—it's all nothing but a pose. You won't ever own up to your responsibilities."

I get up to leave. Antonio takes me by the wrist. "You know I've been a victim in all of this too."

"Yes, you have a limp to show for it, but Lucia is in a coma and Angie has disappeared."

"Why do you blame me?"

"I blame you for your indifference. It can be as numbing as any blow to the head."

I walk out of the door, then turn back after I hear him say, "Goodbye, *Rina*."

I stare at him for an instant, "Yes, goodbye Rina," I respond and run out.

59. ANGIE'S HALLOWEEN PARTY

IN THE LATE AFTERNOON OF Friday, October 31, as the sun's last rays faded into the dimming shadowy sky, Angie, wearing a Jason Voorhees mask, climbed the overpass that connects Saint-Roch Street with Jarry Park—not to cross safely from one side to the other, but to find a secluded spot to sit. No one else bothered to use the overpass; she was alone and she liked it that way.

Her head had been spinning since she had first donned the heavy leather jacket that morning. Wearing it, she'd had to play up to the hard, cold-hearted defiance that the jacket with the metal studs required. And just as she was getting used to it, she switched with Eddie into the Friday the 13th horror movie costume.

Angie realized how much she hated following rules of any kind. She sat cross-legged, high on the overpass landing, looking down at the tracks, the park, and the students parading back and forth through the hole in the chain-link fence below.

She wouldn't be meeting her uncle after school as she had told Cathy. She had just pretended to talk to her aunt on the phone. Lying to Cathy had been easy enough. The woman had been too preoccupied with admiring herself and her jewelled turban in the mirror to care.

But the day was not turning out as she had expected. She had wanted badly to go to the club with Gina, Linda, and especially Eddie, but Eddie had backed off. "Those people are not friends of my friends," he told them at lunch. Sporting a Jason mask and wearing a heavy flannel shirt over his usual Sex Pistols T-shirt, he had generously shared his joint with them. He wanted to hang around the park and school until the dance was over.

"That bitch Cathy!" Angie said. "She wouldn't cover for me tonight."

"What's the big deal?" Gina said. "Italian girls lie to their families all the time. I bet when she was our age, she must have done it hundreds of times herself."

"You ... you can ha ... have my mask," Eddie told Angie. "Your un ....un ... ncle will ne ... ne ... ever know you were at the club."

The mask was the smartest idea ever. She could look straight into anyone's face and remain invisible.

Linda and Gina went to the club early, but Angie wanted to hang out with Eddie. He was the first boy who had ever shown any interest in her. Though they didn't talk much when together, she could tell that he knew much more than he led on, including people that hung around Bar à Go-Go. Then Eddie went to talk to some students, and she lost sight of him. Disappointed, she returned to school, but there was no sign of him anywhere at the dance either.

She then stood alone in a dark corner of the cafeteria waiting for something to happen. Nothing had. The only event of interest had been watching Cathy in her glittering caftan walk around the cafeteria like the Queen of Sheba. Something must have been up if she ditched the Marie Antoinette costume. Bruce followed her around like a little dog. Neither one of them had recognized Angie in her mask as she walked aimlessly along the tracks smoking her joint through a hole in the mask. She passed right by them as Bruce held Cathy by the shoulders and seemed to want to kiss her right there. She watched them and they never even noticed. Cathy could pull the wool over other people's eyes, but Angie saw right through her.

Angie first began looking into Cathy's notebooks to make fun of the teacher with her friends.

"Do you think she fooled around before shacking up with her English boyfriend?" Linda had asked her once.

"She keeps diaries. I'll find out," she told her.

Angie couldn't spell for beans, but with her new glasses, she could read well enough to understand the drift of a sentence. She brought one of the juiciest stories to school and shared it with Eddie. He helped her better decipher the scribbled handwriting. Halfway through the pile, a light went off in Angie's head.

"I bet she's been writing about my family too," she told Eddie.

"Let's find out." He was as curious as she was.

"She's a fucking liar," she said to Eddie. "I can't tell if what she writes is true or make-believe."

Then Cathy showed her the story about her father published in the paper. Angie ran straight home and called Eddie. Together they raided the notes, looking for clues about Angie's mother, her father, or whoever her father was supposed to be. She went crazy trying to dig into the writing as well as into her own head to put pieces of the puzzle together. Who was this journalist who wrote about her father in the papers, and who seemed to know so much about her family? She had never seen her mother get as excited as she did when they had gone to see him at his office.

"Come see me if ever you have a problem," the journalist had said. Then he had gone ahead and splattered her father's story all over the papers. Was he her friend or enemy?

According to the notes, Nicodemo, who became Nick Demon, had been a close friend of the family, but if he had ever been at her house, she had never paid any attention to the man. Now with all the news in the papers, Eddie kept on asking questions about him.

The Lucia who was married by proxy to an older man had to be her mother, but had her mother ever been as pretty and vivacious as the Lucia of the notebooks? Her mother slept all day long and kept the windows shut on summer days to keep sunlight out of the house. In their home in Laval, you could never tell whether it was summer or winter outside. Her mother never took her skating, swimming, or to dance classes like the French mothers at school, and all Angie did at home was watch TV by herself. On Friday nights, her father drove her to her grandmother's house to keep her company, and that's how she spent her weekends.

Of all the people around her, Angie liked her grandmother best. They both liked watching TV together, especially *The Price is Right* and figure-skating competitions. Angie wished she could dance and move as lightly as those slim skaters who seemed to be made out of air, instead of skin, bones, and fat like she was. Angie moved like a lump of cement. In high school, her father had refused to allow her to take ballet lessons. He said that he didn't want to pay to make a ballerina out of his daughter, so that she could go dancing every Saturday night in clubs.

Her father still spoke as if he had just gotten off the boat, and when her mother did go to school on parents' night, Angie was ashamed of Lucia's broken French. Could this same person—who walked around like a zombie, who was in a time warp most of the time, who seemed to care about no one, not even herself—have been a carefree young woman once, sneaking out to see her boyfriend and standing up to her brother?

Angie had envied Cathy when she had first gone to live with her in her apartment, which wasn't furnished with ornately carved furniture or with sofas covered up in plastic, like the other *paesani*. But she and her Canadian boyfriend were no different from her own mother and father. They hardly spoke to one other and slept in separate beds. Didn't she think it was weird that her boyfriend spent more time with his male friend than with her?

The only thing she still envied was the fact that Cathy could write things down. With her new glasses, Angie could read but she still couldn't spell. Bruce kept insisting that spelling didn't matter, that she should write her thoughts down any way she could. Write about what you dream at night, he had said. Write the things you're passionate about, the things that scare you the most. Where would she start?

But the week before Halloween, she had found a way out. While alone in the apartment, and with Eddie's help, she took the story that she had laughed at and turned it into a composition for Mr. McLaughin on Halloween Fears and Terrors. Eddie had helped her change it around, so that it was not the usual kid's stuff about ghosts and haunted houses, but a grownup story about Little Red Riding Hood and a big bad wolf. That would shake Bruce and the other people up at the school, make them take notice. Then, in the afternoon, Angie went to see the journalist on her own. She showed him Cathy's stories to see how he'd react. She wanted to ask him, "Who are you? Are you my real father? Are you Cathy's lover?" Instead he kept quizzing her about the night of October 2nd, the night her mother fell into a coma, as if he knew something about it.

"Come to see me if you need help," he told her. While still home from school, she decided to go back to the journalist and show him her composition for Bruce's class, and again check out his reaction. Not only did he correct the story, but after asking all kinds of questions, had helped her make it even scarier and more realistic.

On Halloween day, after watching the Fairy Queen holding on to Prince Charming along the tracks, Angie ran to puke behind the school. All the smoking on an empty stomach had made her feel nauseous. She leaned against the wall with her eyes closed until she felt better. She sat on the ground for another while, but then noticed her vomit and some dog shit next to her, and she sprang back to her feet in disgust. She looked up at the overpass and figured it would be a good place to get away from all of the garbage below.

The overhead lights in Jarry Park lit up just as the sky turned dark, and Angie could see the goings-on in the street below, as clear as day. The neighbourhood kids on Saint-Roch Street, all dressed up and masked, were scurrying excitedly from their houses, maybe toward the Town of Mount Royal, swinging their orange plastic bags and UNICEF boxes. Eddie had said he still went trick-or-treating in TMR. Maybe she'd meet him there later on.

Angie could hardly keep her eyes open. The cement landing felt cold on her bum. She decided to get up before she fell asleep. Some of the teachers supervising the dance were out having a smoke. There was Frank, with his usual big grin, chatting away with some of the older girls from the school. Frank was such a pervert. He'd told Linda she had bedroom eyes after he walked into the girls' gym changing room. Everyone around her was such a hypocrite, especially Cathy.

Angie saw Cathy emerge from the school's entrance. She looked as though she were searching for someone. Was Cathy looking for her? Then she saw Cathy run toward a car—Bruce's car. What was up with those two? Imagine, telling her not to lie to her family, and then driving away with Bruce. Who did she think she was fooling with that stupid veil hiding her face?

There was so much confusion in Angie's head, so many deceptions and lies around her. She didn't have the heart to pretend to be as lighthearted as Gina and Linda on this Halloween night. They were the only friends she had, but all they thought about was dancing half-naked at the club.

What would her mother be thinking right now, in her comatose sleep? Bruce had told Angie to talk to her, that she might hear everything being said around her. Imagine hearing everything but being unable to answer. And her father in Italy, his family home had been taken away from him, and he had nowhere to go. And her grandmother? Poor woman. She had no one but Angie to watch TV with her.

Angie huddled against the overpass's protective wire fence. One would have to climb over it in order to fly off into the air. She wished she could simply roll herself into a ball and let herself slip off the edge, and dissipate into the sky like a shooting star.

Instead she slowly made her way down the overpass, walked to Park Avenue, waited for a bus, and entered the Bar à Go-Go, all by herself.

She ran away in terror when she recognized the hawk from the photos on the wall.

60. GIROTONDO

I'M SURPRISED TO FIND SEAN is still in the apartment. In all my wanderings through the night and day, I never thought to call him for help. Nor does it seem he has worried much about me. *We're not even good roommates anymore*, I think.

"Call your mother," he says, "She's worried sick about you."

Except for my mother's insistent calls, no one has called with any news about Angie. I don't want to speak to anyone. I ask Sean to call my brother and tell him I'm home but have no news. I'll call them later, after I've had a short rest.

"Why aren't you back at the hotel?" I ask Sean.

"I've been paying half the rent. This is also my apartment. I have no intention to move before the elections. I'm sure we can work things out after, one way or the other, but please let's keep cool heads till then."

I'm too tired to answer or to care, but I call Bruce. "Please tell the police about the composition."

In the bedroom, the boxes of new furniture are still unopened. Some are serving as night tables next to the mattress on the floor. Others hold Sean's clothes and books. All I want to do is crash on a bed and sleep, but I can't bring myself to do it on the mattress in the bedroom, and Sean has taken over the living room.

We'd have a marriage built out of cardboard boxes, I think. I retire to the den, close the door and open up the sofa bed. The sheets smell of Angie.

I toss and turn but can't find a comfortable position to sleep. I find myself walking through a maze of cardboard boxes—huge boxes towering over me. Some are gift-wrapped and I'm anxious to see what's in them, but I have nothing to open them with. I tear at them with all of my strength, and hundreds of pieces of wood, bolts, and screws rain down all over me. I'm floating in a sea of mismatched furniture pieces. I hold on to the biggest piece of wood for dear life.

It's unbearably hot, and the smell is nauseating. A sickening feeling overtakes me just thinking of the hundreds of furniture pieces that need assembly. And how will I face the world after failing so miserably with Angie? Will I find her in time for her father's funeral? Will there be a funeral, and who would show up for it? Poor man, I cry as I fall back to sleep. Imagine dying so unloved and unmissed!

I see Angie playing ring around the rosie on a street that is all done up in Halloween decorations. A profusion of orange chrysanthemums covers the rock gardens of each mansion. While I watch the children play, a man makes love to me on a grassy field. "Your insides are as soft as silk," he says to me, in a voice that is as smooth as liquid gold.

When I turn my head to look at the view, I see arms and legs sprouting from the leaf-covered grass. I get up to read the inscriptions on the tombstones to look for names I recognize. Along the way, the man picks a bouquet from the flowers scattered around the tombstones, and hands it to me. I hide the flowers in my purse. They are made of plastic and I'm embarrassed to show them. Is that all I ever get? The manicured lawns of the mansions have been turned into cemeteries for children to play in. White ghosts flutter from trees; skeletons rattle in the wind, a large grey parrot with bright red tail feathers screeches in a cage swinging from a portico. I watch Angie turn round and round with the kids at a dizzying pace. All I can see of her is her made-up face, without eyes, nose, or mouth—a fluorescent, lifeless mask—turned toward the sky.

"*Giro giro tondo, com'e' bello il mondo,*" the children sing, over and over. "*Ring around the rosie....*"

This is my song, I think, and I am happy to have finally found her. I join the kids and swing round and round with them. I raise my eyes and an unsmiling woman waves at me from her balcony. She points at the balcony next to hers, and I catch sight of my father sitting on a chair, teetering on its front legs, and leaning against the railing for support.

"Why did you leave me?" I yell at him. He smiles and puts his hands to one ear, as if to say he can't hear. I scream louder. "Why did you have to die before I could sing in the play?" He throws his arm down at me, as if giving up.

"It was only a play. It's kid's stuff. Will you ever let it be?" he says.

The balcony railing lets go and everything dissolves into the sky before I have a chance to reply. I'm alone in the night, in front of a strange house lit up with fluorescent orange lights. Sounds of fireworks in the distance, the ring of a telephone.

I wonder where I am, and wish I could get up and go home ... if only I knew where home was.

"I've made some calls," Bruce says on the phone. "Sergeant Provost, the one that spoke at our school meeting, is ready to help us look for Angie. We must give him as many leads as possible. Can you meet us at the police station?"

"I think I know where Angie went after TMR," I say

"Really? Have you spoken to someone else?"

"No, but the answer is in the writing. Remember the last sentence of her composition? 'The weird thing is, cemeteries are still my favourite places.' Let's check the cemetery."

With Sergent Provost and his men we search the grounds of the Cotes des Neiges Cemetery until we find a group of teens slumped asleep by tombstones, with crowns of chrysanthemums on their heads and flower petals scattered all around them. I spot Angie from far away by her spiked hair, pouty lips and her face as pale as the white mask beside her. As we get close, I notice a bloody wrist, and I panic.

"Angie," I yell and shake her shoulders. She opens her eyes and recognizes me.

"I want to go to the police," she says weakly. "I want to tell them everything I know."

"The police are right here," I say and point her to Provost.

"We'll have to go to the station for that, but not before looking after that wrist," says Provost.

Angie's sobbing revelations at the clinic while waiting to have her wrist bandaged, and then her more detailed version to the police, are shocking but not altogether surprising to me. I had witnessed an act of uncontrolled violence toward Lucia in the remote past that had provoked frightful dreams, and had left its mark on my psyche, but nothing compared to what Angie must have suffered in the last month.

On the evening of October 2nd, Angie was in the basement, watching *The Price is Right* as she did every night with her grandmother. Her mother, father, and uncle argued loudly in the upstairs kitchen as they often did. Her grandmother was away at her son Pietro's home.

Angie couldn't take the yelling anymore. She left halfway through *The Price is Right*, the TV still on, to take a walk to the park, just around the corner of the house. She saw a man sitting in a big car on the curb. He looked scary and suspicious. When she reached the park, she sat on a swing and watched the goings on at the front of the house. After a few minutes, her father left and the man in the car went in. After half an hour or so she saw the man leave alone. She walked back home, through the back door and straight to the basement. The news was on, but the upstairs was unusually quiet. She went upstairs to get something to eat, and that's when she saw her mother; her face and head were bloodied and she was lying unconscious on the floor. Her uncle sat quietly by the kitchen table. He had called the police who soon arrived. The other man was no longer there. Her uncle didn't mention him to the police and neither did she.

Everyone blamed her father for the assault and she believed them at first. When questioned by the police, she declared categorically that she had been away the whole evening and had seen nothing.

One day at the hospital, she heard her grandmother and uncle discuss the phone call that Lucia had made to her that evening to ask about their lands. Her uncle ordered her not to say anything about the call, that the police already knew what they needed to know. After the visit to the journalist, when he quizzed her about the people she had seen and the time of her leaving and returning to the house, she turned suspicious.

Angie asked her grandmother if she remembered the time of her mother's call. Her grandmother didn't remember but she said that *The Price is Right* had just finished, and the news was on. This information, as well as other revelations from her father in Italy, alerted Angie that things did not add up. If her mother had called her grandmother at the start of the news, and her father left the house before the end of *The Price is Right,* then Lucia had to have been beaten later by someone else, and the only men Angie saw enter and leave the house were her uncle and his friend whom she recognized as Nick Demon, the wrestler, when she went to the club and ran away in fear.

I hug Angie when she comes out of the officer's office, "You'll be fine," I tell her. "You're strong."

The officer explains their plan to place Angie in a teen home where she'll receive the support she needs until her family situation stabilizes. I offer all of my help.

"I'll stay close to you," I tell Angie.

From there we drive to the hospital to see her mother.

61. THE LULLABYE

COMARE ROSARIA SITS BY THE bed on the edge of her chair, eyes closed with a rosary in her hands, moaning quietly. I stand there for a while before she notices me, but she doesn't say anything, rocking herself as if in a trance. Angie is slumped on the bed, crying, one arm across her comatose mother, her wrist bandaged.

I catch snippets of phrases from Comare Rosaria: "*Tutti i nudari venanu a ru piettene*—all the knots come to the comb ... Pasquale was a piece of bread ... went to Italy for grace and found justice...."

She has heard about Pasquale's death and so has Angie.

Comare Rosaria is venting out her pain, like women did at funerals in the old villages, lamenting while narrating details of the life of their loved departed one, her voice alternating between shrill cries and whispered moans. The old woman, for whom time has stood still, speaks in archaic expressions of an archaic dialect, full of proverbs, sayings, metaphors. She seems to be saying that sooner or later your deeds will catch up to you. Pasquale was a good man. Like a medieval vassal that bows to his feudal lord begging for grace, Pasquale went to his hometown thinking he'd find a home and understanding, only to find punishment.

I can hardly stand on my feet. I get close to the bed and tap Angie on the arm to let her know I'm here.

Comare Rosaria looks up at me and grasps my hands. She

keeps on repeating, "...All the knots come to the comb..." and moans, "*O higlia mia, chi te capitau a ttie.*"

I close my eyes and I'm transported to another time and place, listening to a lullaby:

O ninna ninna, o ninnarella
U lupu se mangiau la piacurella
O piacurella mia cumu facisti
Quandu intra vucca de lu lupu ghisti?

Oh, lullabye, oh little lullabye
The wolf swallowed the sheep
Oh, my sweet sheep, what did you do
When into the mouth of the wolf you had to go?

PART XII
NOVEMBER 2, 1980

62. A NEW BEGINNING

It is the day of the dead, the day after All Saints' Day. I wake up early on the sofa bed in my den. The room, its blinds opened, is awash with sunlight. For the past month, characters from my early years have stubbornly re-entered my life to disrupt an already tenuous tranquility. Twenty-four hours earlier, on Halloween night, a whirlwind of events took me unaware, playing tricks on me, and I went through the night and following day without any sleep and with little food, searching for Angie. Angie had been with me only for a short time, yet it was as though she had been part of me forever. The girl, and her mother, had turned into ghosts. Exhausted and sleep deprived, I blamed my journalist friend, Antonio, for the tragedy. This morning I do not feel so adamant. Can one man alone be blamed for the years of neglect and indifference that brought these women to this end?

Antonio provided the authorities with enough leads to feed the daily newspapers' hunger for news of the crime and corruption that plague all levels of society. To me, he had said that the Lucia and Angie were tragic characters, one without a past to support her; the other deprived of the future she had wished for herself. But he was wrong about Angie. We all have a past, and how we confront it will determine our future. Angie will not live by deception, will not be silenced, and she will survive despite the hand life has dealt her. Her mother's prognosis is not as auspicious. I see that the morning paper has already covered the news of Angie's courageous statements to authorities, on what she witnessed the night her mother was savagely struck. Speculation regarding the motives and ancient passions that led to the deed—jealousy, personal revenge, greed—will also keep the journalists' word processors hot for days, until the next newsworthy story.

Fears and nightmares haunted me last night, until I woke up and looked out at the moon. Its eternal cycle has remained undisturbed by the turmoil of this past month, I thought, and I returned to bed in peace with myself. I have woken up rested. I make a pot of coffee, sit back on the sofa bed and, serenely, plan my day.

Sean, my ex-fiancé, will be sound asleep until noon, on a mattress in what used to be our bedroom, surrounded by unassembled furniture still in boxes. I will not disrupt his plans. He can stay in the apartment till it suits him. On Monday, I will call the Danish House to return the furniture I bought a few days before, but have had neither the time nor the heart to put together. The prints, lamps, accessories, and dishes that Sean and I bought together, I don't want. Sean can take whatever he likes, or leave it all behind with the rest of the furniture for some other gypsy-minded couple to call their own.

I will have to come back for the old trunk that contains the embroidered linens from my mother's trousseau, as well as other keepsakes that travelled with my family almost fifty years earlier when we crossed the ocean to settle in Canada. Lucia, a teenager then, almost the same age as Angie is now, had travelled with us. Her story is contained in the notebooks I now pack together with a few clothes and my school textbooks before I turn and walk away. A diagram of an unfinished mandala lies on the kitchen table. I put that in my purse.

Then I stare at the wall-to-wall shelves of books in the den, and I realize that I cannot leave those behind. They are my most valuable possessions. In case Sean gets the notion that part of the library is his, I decide to pack the books into my car before he gets up. Before even washing up and changing, I start sorting books into the order I would like to take them. First, I choose all the literature books. It feels good to handle the old, worn-out tomes—*From Shakespeare to Shaw, Blake's Poems and Prophesies, Tom Jones, The Stories of Anton Tchekov*—with handwritten notes in the margins. I resolve to someday take the time to read and study the poetry, the classic novels, and short stories contained within them. I use a plastic laundry basket to carry the books to the car, and then pile them onto the floor of the back seat.

Next I choose and carry the writings of Saint Augustine, Thomas Aquinas, Socrates, Hegel, Sartre, Thoreau, de Beauvoir, Marx, and Churchill, and stack them on the seats. The basket feels heavier and heavier with each trip down the stairs to the car, but I am determined to take as many of the books as possible with me. One day I might regret not having them. The books on music and art I will give to my brother, for his own inspiration.

After the back seat of the car is stuffed to capacity, I pack the trunk. Except for Sean's books, the shelves are now bare. I am amused that I have made over twenty trips up and down the stairs still wearing my housecoat.

Finally, I take my copy of *I Promessi Sposi* and, before placing it carefully into my tote bag along with my notebooks, I open it to the last page and read:

> *Man, as long as he is in this world, is like an invalid lying on a more-or-less-uncomfortable bed, who sees other beds around him which look outwardly smooth, level, and better made, and imagines he would be very happy on them. But if he succeeds in changing, scarcely is he lying on the new bed than he begins, as his weight sinks in, to feel a piece of flax pricking into him here and a lump pressing into him there; so that, in fact, he is more or less back where he started.*

I remember that I first read this book as a child. I have to reread it again, to look at it with new eyes. On the final trip, I quietly move the standing mirror from the bedroom into the kitchen. It is lighter than I thought and I consider taking it to the car as well. The mirror will be a trusty reminder of who I am from day to day—someone different from the person I was the day before, or who I will become the day after. My stories, too, need rewriting.

My hands are dirty and feel grimy from handling the old, dusty books. I shower, wash and dry my hair, and put basic toiletries into my tote bag. I stuff some underwear and a few of my favourite clothes in a garbage bag for the upcoming days. The rest I leave behind together with the mirror. I am afraid it will crack.

It is almost one o'clock and Sean is still sleeping. Life is going on as if nothing has happened. My mother, brother, and sister-in-law will still be sitting for their Sunday lunch. When I join them, they will be discussing the events of the last few days, the funeral mass they will be attending, and the engagement and wedding not taking place as planned.

"As long as you're well..." my mother will say.

"Cheer up. You have your full life ahead of you, and lots of stories to write," Luigi will say.

If I leave now, I will be in time for coffee—though my mother will insist that I eat a plate of leftover pasta.

I think of scribbling a note for Sean, then change my mind. I will have to call him later and speak to him.

"I've left the apartment for good, not only because I feel deceived by you, but because I don't love you enough to want to work out the differences between us. Our marriage would be as much a marriage of convenience for me as it would be for you. I don't know where I'll spend the night, but it won't be here, nor will it be at my mother's. I'll have to find a place of my own, as I hope you'll find the life that is meant for you."

But what I wanted most of all was to write this ending:

"I find Angie at the hospital next to Lucia's bed, caressing her mother's brow. Lucia wakes up and smiles. The three of us walk out to meet an elegant, tall man with dreamy eyes who takes Lucia by the arm. Angie waves at me and follows them toward their new home."

The image evaporates as I drive away in my yellow Pinto, in silent unrest, my head filled with unread and unwritten books.

The yearly autumn show of brilliant colours is at its peak, and the tree-lined street is more luminous than ever. I realize I will have to complete the mandala, if only to salvage what is left of this sunny Sunday afternoon.

EPILOGUE. ROME, JUNE 2016

SOMEONE ONCE TOLD ME it would take at least five years to write a novel; mine has taken fifty plus. Not that I have spent the best part of half a century isolated from the world, weaving the proverbial web of tales. This novel has grown in spurts and has been shaped by the innumerable starts and finishes of life, with long pauses in between.

Why did I take this long to complete this novel? The most plausible excuse is that life does get in the way of artistic pursuits—work, marriage, children, an aging mother, deaths—layer upon layer of life to manage and comprehend. But ultimately, I must admit that it has been my stubborn nature, my need to finish what I set out to do, at whatever cost, that kept me from bringing this story to a close. Above all, I was determined to find a fitting ending that would justify the arduous journeys of my characters. But time and time again, as I managed to patch up one fractured circle, another snapped open beyond repair. "*Lavoru e pazzi,*" my mother would have said, so finally, with her death, followed by other painful deaths, I had to concede that what we lose, we lose for good. No passage comes without loss.

Well over thirty years after the events that made me confront who I was and where I came from, I immersed myself again in the memories of the past. First, I put order to the village tales of my childhood and contained them in a short novel. Next, I returned to the place where it all started, searching for comfort and reconnection with the spirit of loved ones I have since lost.

After a prolonged absence, I found Mulirena both unchanged and foreign. I walked the familiar streets and alleys. I recognized only a few old people. They stared at me blankly for a while until they captured my name and family's affiliation. Otherwise, no one took notice of me, except for a smiling young girl, sitting on the parapet above the Funtanella, eating fries from a McDonald's bag. She asked me, in perfect Italian, if I needed assistance. I gave her my family's name and asked for hers.

"They call me the *marocchina*," she answered.

Her parents, immigrants from Morocco, run a small convenience store in town. The village has a website; all the young people have Facebook pages, and everyone carries a cell phone. Young men, however, are still complaining about not being able to earn a living in the village, while farmers import field hands from Morocco.

The Italian TV talk shows carry never-ending debates on the problems of illegal refugees and their integration, while videos of migrants in capsized vessels, arms waving frantically in the distance waiting to be rescued, play in the background.

We've reached the new millennium, landed on the moon, circled Saturn, found water on Mars, yet people are still risking their lives in overcrowded boats in their desperate search for a safe harbour and a chance at a job.

The story of immigration never ends.

On my return trip, I vacationed in Rome for a few days, at a hotel booked online, curiously named Ping Pong Hotel. Isn't it magical how, in writing, the most incongruous places and events coalesce in our imagination and suddenly help us find the links that make perfect sense to us? It is on this trip that I finally found the closure to the story I set out to write in 1980, but couldn't finish because the perfect ending evaded me.

At Stazione Termini, I took the two-tiered bus that loops around the city and permits tourists to get off and on at will.

I secured the best spot in front of the upper deck to take an eyeful of the Eternal City. I circled the whole city once and then started the loop again and got off at St. Peter's Square.

It occurred to me as I approached the Basilica, from Via della Riconciliazione, that St. Peter's Square is a misnomer. It isn't a square at all, but an enormous circular gathering place—a broken circle with a wide opening—that allows in and spurts out millions of people each year, of as many colours, languages, nationalities, and creeds as there are people on earth. I felt good being part of that huge circular hug, and lucky that I understood several of the languages I heard. The mish-mash of people and tongues produced a sense of familiarity, and I felt at ease, as though this was where I belonged. The North Africans faces, the Asian ones, the Slavs, the Latinos, didn't look foreign to me at all. After all, I have had the fortune of living in Canada for so long.

Have I come full circle?

If I have, it is not how I had envisioned the outcome. Maybe the closing of the circle is an unrealizable chimera for our days, or, maybe, its importance has been highly overrated.

Questions will always remain. Lucia remains lost to us, the sacrificial lamb of our nomadic adventures; the only act of defiance left is to plug the void with written words. Here was the ending I was looking for.

And a new beginning....

—Caterina Anastasia

ACKNOWLEDGEMENTS

As this novel is closely connected to my first book, *The Girls of Piazza D'Amore,* both drafts having being conceived and written during my studies at Concordia University, I owe my gratitude to the same writing instructors, and other friends I acknowledged at the publication of the first novel. I would like to single out again my thesis supervisor at Concordia University, Terry Byrnes.

In the long stretch of time it took to bring this second novel to light, many colleagues and friends—too many to mention—offered advice and encouragement. I thank you all. But this novel would not have found its rightful home without the enthusiastic reception of Luciana Ricciutelli of Inanna Publications, who believed in the book and has helped me polish it with great patience and skill.

I would not have been able to keep up the dream without the emotional support and love of my family. My late husband, Robert, encouraged all my endeavours. My brother Vincenzo, Vince to many of us, was my biggest fan and my strongest tie to that other life we left behind as children, and that inspired parts of this book. My memories were also his. I thank my nieces Felica, Nina, their spouses and children for having kept our family traditions alive. To my sons and their life partners, David and Melissa, Anthony and Valerie, thank you for just being here and now. Robbie and Kate, you are the future. Thank you for bringing joy and laughter to my life.

Photo: Anthony J. Branco

Connie Guzzo-McParland has a BA in Italian Literature and a Master's degree in Creative Writing from Concordia University. Upon graduation from the Master's program, she received the David McKeen Award for creative writing for her thesis-novel, *Girotondo*. In 2005, an excerpt from this novel, "On the Way to Halifax," translated into Italian, won second prize at the ninth edition of the Premio Letterario Cosseria in Cosseria, Italy. Her novel, *The Girls of Piazza d'Amore,* published in 2013, was shortlisted for the Concordia First Novel Award by the Quebec Writer's Federation. Since 2010 she is Co-director and President of Guernica Editions. She lives in Montreal